PROTECTIVE ORDER

RITA HERRON

BURIED SECRETS

CAROL ERICSON

MILLS & BOON

First Published in Great Britain 2020
by Mills & Boon, an imprint of HarperCollins*Publishers*
1 London Bridge Street, London, SE1 9GF

Protective Order © 2020 Rita B. Herron
Buried Secrets © 2020 Carol Ericson

ISBN: 978-0-263-28046-3

0920

MIX
Paper from
responsible sources
FSC™ C007454

Printed and bound in Spain
by CPI, Barcelona

PROTECTIVE ORDER

RITA HERRON

To all those counselors who work as victims' advocates for abused women. God bless you.

Prologue

He'd kill her if he found her.

But Reese Taggart couldn't go back. Not to being smothered and held captive by his anger and his erratic mood swings. Not to pleasing him when that was impossible.

Not to a life without friends and a house where she had to follow his rules or be punished.

She tugged the ball cap over her head and struggled to stay in the shadows as she climbed in her car and pulled away from the gas station. A big burly man wearing a hoodie was watching her from the gas pump.

Tension gathered in her belly. Had Robert paid the man to find her?

Shivering, she pressed the accelerator and sped onto the highway. Nerves on edge, she looked over her shoulder to see if the man had followed.

Finally, when she veered onto the entrance ramp to the freeway, and she didn't see him, she breathed a sigh of relief.

Although a feeling of despair mingled with fear as night fell. She'd left her apartment. Had packed everything she owned in her car and was on the run. She had no idea how to rebuild her life, but her first priority was to escape him.

The protective order she'd filed hadn't mattered to him. He'd ignored it. Had broken in and threatened her. Had promised to make her pay if she ever tried to leave.

Then he'd tied her up and left her naked and alone. His ugly gray eyes had pierced her as he'd told her she needed to think about how to be a good wife.

They weren't married. She'd turned down his proposal. Had made several attempts to break it off with him.

He'd refused to accept that it was over.

When she'd managed to free herself, she'd spent the night in a cheap motel somewhere on the highway, terrified and debating where to go. The police had said they couldn't help her unless he hurt her.

She didn't want to die.

This morning, she'd made a decision. Move to Raleigh where her sister lived. The two of them needed each other. And Tess deserved to know why Reese had cut off communication with her the last few months.

A gust of wind slammed against her vehicle, the windows rattling with the force. A storm was brewing. She had fifteen miles to go.

Her phone dinged with another text. Him again. He'd started calling and texting the minute he'd discovered she was gone.

You'll be sorry for leaving me.

The only thing she was sorry for was ever believing he was a nice man. For signing up for that stupid online dating site.

Her friends said it would be easy. Safe. They were all doing it.

All she had to do was create a profile. Post some pictures. Swipe if she liked someone.

Meet in a public place. Like a coffee shop.

And she had.

He'd been so charming in the beginning. Almost shy. Quiet. Like a gentle giant, he'd complimented her and wined and dined her. She'd lost her mother the year before and had still been grieving. He'd offered a shoulder to cry on. Had understood the reason she'd dropped out of college to work for a while.

He'd promised to take care of her.

She hadn't known that meant isolating her from friends and family and trying to control her.

Finally, she reached the exit for Raleigh. She considered giving her sister a heads-up she was on her way, but figured she needed to explain in person. Perspiration beaded on her neck as she took the exit ramp and veered onto the side street leading to her sister's little house. Tess was an artist and worked at a coffee bar near the downtown area.

But she chose to live outside the city limits for the privacy. She said the countryside inspired her creativity.

The ten miles to her house seemed like an eternity, but Reese grew more relaxed as she approached. She'd missed her sister these last few months. Needed her now.

But as she rounded the corner, she spotted smoke in the air. Thick plumes drifted up into the clouds and swirled in a blinding haze of gray.

She punched the accelerator and sped the next mile. Just as she'd feared, her sister's house was on fire.

Terror pulsed through her as she screeched to a stop. She punched in 9-1-1 and asked for help, then threw the car door open and hit the ground running. Flames had caught the roof and seemed to be coming from the back room. Tess's studio.

The chemicals she used to paint and clean her brushes were there. Oh, God…

The wind howled as she ran toward the house. Maybe her sister wasn't here. Although her little Toyota was in the drive.

Reese pushed the front door open and screamed, "Tess!"

She called her name over and over as she raced through the small bungalow. Tess wasn't in the living room or kitchen.

Smoke billowed everywhere. Wood crackled and popped from the back rooms. She coughed and covered her mouth with her scarf but refused to turn back.

Heat scalded her as she inched down the hallway. The guest room was empty but filled with smoke. Tess's bedroom…so much smoke she could barely see inside.

She ducked into the room anyway. But Tess wasn't in there.

Terror clawed at her. The studio.

Flames were starting to lick the edge of the doorway.

"Tess!" She blinked and peered inside. Flames crept up the wall. Her sister's canvases were on fire, the beautiful colors of paint dripping like blood. Smoke and fire consumed the shelves of art supplies.

Then she saw her sister. On the floor. Not moving.

Screaming her name again, she raced toward her. Fire ate at the window curtains. A piece of burning wood splintered from the shelf and pelted her. Flames licked at her shirt, but she threw the splintered wood aside and beat at the flames. She knelt and shook her sister. Tess was unconscious.

Please, dear God, let her be alive.

Fear driving her, she grabbed her sister's arms and began to drag her from the room. Sweat poured down her face and neck. Something shattered. The floor was growing hot, the fire spreading. She had to hurry.

She yanked and pulled with all her might, hauling her sister through the living room to the front door. A siren wailed in the distance. Lights twirled and glittered across the dark sky.

She pulled Tess onto the porch then down the steps and dragged her across the grass to a nearby tree. Then she dropped to the ground and shook her.

"Tess, honey, hang in there!" She felt for a pulse, but

nothing. Seconds ticked by. A fire engine roared into the driveway. Firefighters jumped from the fire engine and sprang into action.

She shouted for help. "My sister. She's not breathing!"

One of the firemen ran over, his face etched in worry as he stooped down and pressed two fingers to her sister's neck.

A second later, he shook his head.

"No..." She refused to give up. She shoved him aside and started chest compressions. Understanding on his face, he murmured that he'd take over.

She stared in shock as he worked to try to save her sister. But as he performed CPR, she spotted ligature marks around Tess's neck. Saw the imprint of someone's fingers. A man's.

Her hand flew to her own throat. Robert had choked her once. Had left marks like those.

His threats taunted her. *You'll be sorry.*

An ambulance careened up. Medics hopped out and raced to help. Firefighters rolled out hoses, dousing the flames with water. The roof collapsed.

The medic traded a look with the firefighter. "It's been too long," he murmured.

The medic checked Tess's pulse. Her heart. Then his look turned to sympathy. "I'm sorry."

Reese shook her head in denial. Tears leaked from her eyes and dripped down her chin. She dragged her sister into her arms and held her, rocking her and crying as the truth seeped into her consciousness.

Robert had been here. He'd killed her sister to punish her.

Tess, the only person she had left in the world. Her best friend. Her little sister. Gone.

Dead at twenty-six.

And it was all her fault.

Chapter One

Three years later

Firefighter and arson investigator, Griffin, *Griff*, Maverick gritted his teeth. Wildfires were springing up all over the mountains. Some were accidental while others had been set by careless hikers—or, as he suspected in this case, teenagers.

He had to put a stop to it. If only he could catch the little culprits. But so far, they'd evaded the police.

At least there were no casualties at this point. But there was always the chance, especially with March winds roaring through, that one would spread and not only destroy property and the beautiful forests along the Appalachian Trail, but that someone would be injured or die in one of the blazes.

He'd nearly lost a member of his own team today when a tree had cracked and splintered down on top of Barney, trapping him in the midst of a brush fire. His leg had been broken in two places, and he'd had to be airlifted to the hospital. Just in time, too, before the flames had caught his clothing.

The scent of smoke and charred wood clung to Griff's clothes as he loped inside the bar to join his three brothers for their weekly burger and beer night. Now that Jacob and Fletch were married, occasionally they had to skip a week, but they were all committed to keeping up the tradition and the brotherhood bond. The Maverick men stuck together.

They'd also joined forces to find the person who'd set the hospital fire in Whistler five years ago and killed their father.

Fletch, Jacob and Liam were already seated with a bucket of fries and a pitcher of beer. Recently Fletch, who worked search and rescue with FEMA, had found evidence of a possible suspect living off the grid in the mountains.

Finally.

"You look like hell," Fletch said as Griff slid onto the bar stool.

He felt like, it, too. "No time to go home and change."

"Still no idea who's responsible for these wildfires?" Liam, FBI, asked.

"I wish I did." Griff accepted the mug of beer Liam offered. "Third one in two weeks."

"Happens every year," Jacob, sheriff of Whistler, commented.

Liam dug a fry into the ketchup then popped it in his mouth. "I've been looking for similar instances across North Carolina, but so far no unsolved ones."

"I spoke to the principal at the high school," Jacob interjected. "Asked both the school counselor and principal to alert us if they hear any chatter. Counselor wants to protect the students' privacy, but I emphasized that it's only a matter of time before someone loses his or her life and that will constitute murder. She said the school plans to hold an assembly this week. Maybe you can speak at the school, Griff."

He grimaced. The last thing he wanted to do was talk to a bunch of unruly, rebellious teenagers. He'd been one himself.

Of course, that made him qualified, he guessed.

"I could come along and watch the kids' reactions to see if anyone gets nervous," Jacob suggested.

Griff shrugged. "It's worth a shot." He took a swig of his beer. "Where are you on that forensics Fletch found in the cave in the mountains?"

Liam shifted. "Like I said before, the prints match Barry Inman's."

Inman had come unhinged after his wife died in the ER at the hospital. He'd filed a lawsuit, but it had been thrown out the day before the fire. He'd threatened revenge.

Liam plucked another fry from the bucket. "I spoke to his brother, but he hasn't talked to him in years. Said he disappeared after the fire and none of the family has heard from him."

"How about the wife's family?" Griff asked.

"According to the wife's mother, Barry completely lost it after his wife's death. Apparently, he'd been laid off from work and they were having financial problems before she got sick. Mother didn't believe the hospital was negligent and urged him to drop the case, but she claimed he was crazed and obsessed with the idea of making the establishment pay."

"He could be our perp," Jacob commented.

Liam nodded. "When we find him, we'll bring him in for questioning."

"I've been staking out the area where he'd holed up in my spare time and conducting routine searches for him," Fletch admitted.

Anxiety tightened Griff's shoulders. The fire five years ago had taken multiple lives and destroyed families. Cora Reeves's baby had been kidnapped in the chaos, although recently Jacob had found the missing little girl and reunited her with her mother. Then he'd married Cora and made the child his stepdaughter.

"We'll keep working it," Liam said, and they all murmured agreement.

They spent the next hour catching up on sports and other work news. Just as he was finishing his burger, Griff's phone buzzed. Jacob's phone rang, as well.

They answered at the same time.

"9-1-1 report. Fire in progress," his captain told Griff over the phone. "Texting you the address now." Griff stood as the message appeared on his screen. The address—Joy Norris's apartment above the nail salon she owned. Damn. He hoped Joy wasn't there. He'd dated her a few times, but learned she'd lied about her divorce being final. Griff didn't tolerate lies, so he'd broken it off.

"Be right there."

"I'm on my way," Jacob said, tossing some cash on the table.

Griff added a twenty to the pile, and he and Jacob headed to the exit.

Not knowing how long they'd be at the scene, they drove separately. Jacob flipped on his siren and led the way. A mile from the salon, Griff spotted the smoke. The other storefronts nearby looked safe—for now. But the blaze had to be contained.

Jacob's tires squealed as he veered onto the curb. Griff pulled in behind him, then jumped out and met the crew from his firehouse by the truck. He quickly yanked on his gear.

Jacob caught his arm before he went inside. Déjà vu of the blaze where they'd lost their father struck him. One look at Jacob, and he realized his brother was reliving that horrible day, too.

"Careful, bro." Jacob's eyes darkened. "You're gonna be an uncle."

"I'm always careful." Then Jacob's words registered, and

he gave his brother a hug. "Congrats, man. You'll be a great father just like Dad was." He was already a great stepfather.

Emotions clogged Griff's throat, but he swallowed them back and headed into the burning building.

REESE TAGGART HAD been living a lie for the past three years. Hiding out from life. Hiding out from her real identity.

Hiding out from *him*.

Darkness surrounded her. Her sister had been the one who'd seen the colors. Tess had used soft, muted shades of blue and green and vibrant reds and oranges in her landscapes.

When she died, the colors faded for Reese. Now the world was nothing but an ugly brown like the brittle ashes of her sister's house when it had burned to the ground.

She pounded the punching bag, giving it a sharp right hook, then swung around, lifted her leg and kicked it with all her force. Perspiration beaded on her neck as she went another round, releasing her rage and frustration on the bag as if it was the demon who'd forced her to give up her life and go on the run.

The police had said they'd protect her. They'd looked for her sister's killer. Issued an APB and BOLO and utilized every other kind of official method of tracking down Robert Bouldercrest possible. But he had virtually disappeared.

No credit cards had shown up, no driver's license in another state, no banking information, no posts on social media.

Just like her, he'd changed his name and started over somewhere else.

Had he already found another obsession? Or was he still looking for her?

She slammed her foot into the bag again, then spun her body into a one-eighty turn and gave it a hard-left jab.

"Looking good there, Ginny."

Virginia Bagwell—Ginny—was the name she'd assumed. This gym rat wanted to get personal. Just like Ian Phelps, her instructor at the shooting range, did.

Not going to happen. She'd never trust another man again.

Ian was a former cop and still had friends on the force. She'd actually considered asking him for help once. But too many bad memories had surfaced. Cops who hadn't believed Robert was the monster she claimed him to be. Cops who hinted that she'd asked for what had happened to her.

Besides, Ian had friends who might become curious about her and unearth her real identity. She couldn't let that happen.

No one would find out the truth, not until Robert was behind bars.

Or dead.

She preferred the latter. In fact, she'd been training for it.

The gym rat sauntered over to her, mopping his sweaty face with a towel. "How about we grab a drink when you're finished?" His killer smile and toned body had charmed the pants off half the women who belonged to this gym. She'd watched them croon over him, choose machines beside him to nab his attention. Even request personal training sessions.

Once he conquered them, he dropped them like hot potatoes.

But he was persistent, and if she ignored him, he'd simply go for the chase. That was the kind of guy he was.

"Can't. Got a date," she lied.

"I didn't know you were seeing anyone."

"Yeah. Long time now."

She turned her back to him and punched the bag again, knowing her knuckles would probably be bruised and bloody when she finished. Even the gloves didn't protect her when she unleashed her rage. But she wanted to be strong. Had to be.

If Robert came after her again, she'd be ready.

"Joy!" Griff twisted the doorknob and the door swung open. Heat blasted him, the fire already eating the floor and crawling along the worn carpet. "Joy!"

Flames danced in the kitchen and living area. He maneuvered through the hallway, dodging the flames as he searched the apartment. Living room empty. No one in the bathroom.

"Joy!" He darted through the doorway which was surrounded by flames and spotted Joy on the floor by the bed. Fire engulfed the curtains and crawled around the windowsill.

His heart hammered as he dove through a fiery patch and bent to scoop her up in his arms. She was so still and lifeless that he didn't think she was breathing. Flames nipped at his heels as he carried her through the house, down the steps and outside.

The building crashed and exploded as he rushed to escape. It was chaos outside. More police had arrived. Neighbors, business owners and curiosity seekers had gathered to watch. Sirens and lights twirled against the night sky. Fire hissed and wood crackled. The windows blew, glass shattering and spraying.

One of the medics met him, and Griff eased Joy's body onto the stretcher. Her hair had started to singe. Smoke and soot stained her clothes and limbs.

At least he'd rescued her before the fire had gotten her.

The medic checked Joy's pulse. Then her heart.

His own hammered as the medic murmured that she was gone.

Jacob jogged over to them, his face worried. "Griff?"

He spoke through gritted teeth, "She was already dead when I went inside."

Jacob grimaced. "No one else in there?"

"It's clear."

"How did the fire start?" Jacob asked. "Did you smell gas or an accelerant?"

"Don't know yet," Griff said. "I'll have to wait until it dies out and cools down before I can go in. But if someone had set the salon on fire, the chemicals and acetone in that salon would have been a natural accelerant." He hesitated. "Although why would someone want to burn down the nail salon?"

Jacob shrugged. "We'll look into that. Maybe she was in financial trouble and wanted the insurance money."

Griff mulled over that possibility. He didn't remember Joy having financial problems, but small businesses were a tough go. Hers could be suffering.

"Does she have family to notify?" Jacob asked.

"No, just the ex."

A pinched look marred Jacob's face as he examined Joy's body more closely. "Look at that." Jacob pointed out bruises on Joy's neck.

Griff's blood went cold. "Dammit, this was no accident. She was murdered." And the fire had been set to cover it up.

Two hours later

GINNY CHECKED OVER her shoulder as she unlocked the door to her Asheville apartment. She'd driven a different route home from the gym today and kept alert. Varying her routine had become a necessity for survival.

Stalkers studied behavior patterns. Robert had certainly learned hers. Even after she'd tried to break it off with him, he'd watched her from the shadows. He'd known where she shopped, ate, the trails she liked to jog, her friends, even the drugstore she frequented. She'd even caught him combing through her trash.

She'd never considered he'd hurt Tess, but she'd learned her lesson. Since her sister died, she hadn't allowed herself to get close to anyone.

She couldn't live with another person's death on her conscience.

She twisted the main lock on the door as she entered the foyer, then the two dead bolts. Still, she kept one hand on the .22 in her pocket as she searched the rooms. Satisfied no one was inside, she stowed her pistol in the drawer by the sofa, then poured herself a whiskey and carried it to the table.

She opened her laptop and once again searched the internet and social media, hoping to find a picture of Robert somewhere. He'd hunted her like a dog that last month.

It was time he learned what it felt like to be hunted.

An hour later, her muscles ached from fatigue, and she flipped on the TV to watch the evening news just as she did each night. The weather report aired, then national news, then a special breaking story.

A fire in Whistler, NC.

She clutched her glass with a white-knuckled grip as the reporter interviewed Sheriff Jacob Maverick. He stood in front of a burning building, flames lighting up the sky. The street was chaotic, emergency lights twirling.

"Sheriff, can you tell us what happened here tonight?" the reporter asked.

Beads of sweat trickled down the side of the sheriff's face. "We're on the scene of a fire at Joy's Nail Salon.

"Although our local fire station responded immediately, the chemicals inside the salon caused the blaze to spread quickly. At this point, workers are trying to contain the blaze and keep it from spreading to neighboring businesses."

The camera panned to an ambulance, a doctor standing with the medics and a tall broad-shouldered fireman.

"What about the owner?" the reporter asked. "Was she inside the salon when it caught fire? Were there injuries? Casualties?"

The sheriff shifted. "Unfortunately, the owner of the shop, Joy Norris, was dead when we arrived."

A photograph of the woman flashed on the screen. "If anyone has information regarding her death or the fire tonight, please contact my office."

The number for Whistler's sheriff's department appeared, but the numbers blurred in Ginny's mind as her gaze latched on to the woman.

Joy Norris had shoulder-length auburn hair. Green eyes. A heart shaped face. And ivory skin.

Ginny's chest constricted. She was Robert's type. And a dead ringer for Ginny herself.

Chapter Two

The next morning, Ginny mentally reviewed the news report on the Whistler fire as she drove toward the small mountain town.

Joy Norris's death had been ruled a homicide. The sheriff hadn't revealed details, but she was dead before the fire started. They hadn't reported cause of death though, which raised her suspicions.

She thumped her fingers on her thigh. Was she trying to make a connection where there wasn't one?

Determined to find out if her suspicions had merit, she followed the winding mountain road to Griffin Maverick's cabin. She'd decided to approach the arson investigator instead of the sheriff. Although he was the sheriff's brother, at least he wasn't law enforcement.

Winter was still hanging on, the wind roaring, the trees bare of leaves. As she parked in front of the rustic log cabin, she took a second to admire its sprawling front porch. It looked post card picturesque, much like the little town that was nestled amongst the Appalachian Mountains.

The wind rolled off the mountain, creating a chill in the air. Yet the sound of the river thrashing over rocks drifting from the property in back added a calmness to the breathtaking natural beauty.

She rubbed her hands up and down her arms as she climbed the porch steps, then knocked. After a minute, when she didn't hear sounds inside, she rang the doorbell, mentally bracing herself. She'd planned her cover story on the drive. A way to finagle information without revealing her identity or her past or having to rely on the sheriff.

She'd put all her faith in the law before, but they'd let her down from day one. Two years ago, she'd chased a similar lead/story and confided in a detective working the case in Charlotte. But he'd only paid her lip service. Then he'd accepted a bribe from Robert to find out where she was.

She'd barely escaped alive and had been forced to change her name again. Thank God for the underground society who helped women like her.

Like her. She'd thought she was strong and independent. Had never dreamed she'd be in this situation. Had had the ridiculous misbelief that domestic violence and stalking only happened to weak women.

She was wrong.

Crazies came in all sizes and styles, some of them cunning and handsome and so manipulative they knew exactly how to get in the mind of their victims and find their weaknesses. They preyed on women, women who were oblivious to the fact they were being targeted.

Her downfall had been trusting others.

No more.

She took a deep breath, fluffed her layered bob, which was now a soft black instead of auburn, and adjusted the dark blue blazer she'd picked up at the thrift store.

Finally, she heard a noise inside. Footsteps.

She peered through the window and spotted Griffin Maverick shuffling toward the front door. His hair looked mussed, and he ran a hand over his eyes as if he'd just woken up.

She should have called. But she'd suspected he might deny her an interview. And if Robert had set the fire the night before, she wanted to know.

He swung the door open, blinking at the morning sunlight with a frown. Dear heavens, he was a handsome man. Tall, built like a linebacker, a broad face, shadow of a beard, dark hair, deep brown eyes with flecks of gold.

"I'm sorry," she sputtered, thrown by her reaction to him. Of course, any red-blooded female would be shaken by his raw masculinity. But she didn't allow herself to fantasize that there might be a good man beneath the package.

Not anymore.

"Sorry?" he said his voice gruff. "What, are you lost or something?"

She shook her head, willing her voice to be steady and not reveal the fact that she was about to feed him a big fat lie.

Protecting herself and getting revenge were all that mattered. If she had to use this man to do that, then let the lies begin.

GRIFF STARED AT the woman in confusion. Strange, beautiful females didn't just show up at his door early in the morning, not out here.

Hell, he'd been up half the night working the crime scene and felt as scruffy as he must look.

She lifted a dainty chin. "My name is Virginia— Ginny—Bagwell," she said in a voice that sounded almost angelic. Or hell, maybe he was still asleep and dreaming. In deep REM.

"I'm an investigative journalist," she continued. "I'm writing a special series on arson, specifically arsonists and their motives, and would like to interview you for my piece."

Griff narrowed his eyes. "I'm sorry, but I've been up half the night working. Why don't you contact my firehouse and talk to the captain? He has people who handle media coverage." Griff hated the press. Being in the spotlight. Last night he'd left Jacob to handle the reporter at the salon so he could concentrate on his job.

"Please," Ginny said with a soft smile that probably disarmed most men. Or had them falling at her pretty feet. And he bet they were pretty and girly although you wouldn't know it from the plain black flat shoes she wore. They were as nondescript as the black sedan she was driving.

"I did my research," she went on. "I know how well respected you are, that you're a leader among your team. I saw the story about the fire last night. You worked it."

Griff shifted. "So did other members at my station."

She clamped her teeth over her bottom lip, a lip so plump and ripe that for a moment Griff's body stirred with desire.

Good grief. What was wrong with him?

Sleep deprivation. That was all.

She fidgeted with the button on her jacket. "I'm sorry for bothering you. You obviously were up late. Maybe I could buy you a cup of coffee later? Or breakfast? How about it, Mr. Maverick?"

She was persistent.

"Who did you say you work for? A paper? Magazine?" Griff asked.

A second of hesitation, then she breathed out. "I'm not with anyone at the moment. I'm trying to get an in at a TV network, and the only way to do that is to come up with a good story."

"You can get information on arsonists' motives on the internet," he said, sensing she was trouble.

"I don't want simple rote facts," she said. "I want the real story from someone who's worked fires, who knows arson, who's been in the head of a fire starter and understands his actions."

He leaned against the doorframe. "Understanding means I sympathize with the arsonist, and I don't. But I do recognize their motives. Human nature makes us want to know why people do the things they do, especially actions that hurt others. And knowing those motives can lead to finding the culprits."

"That's exactly what I'm talking about," she said. "Please meet me for coffee later."

She extended a business card with her name and phone number in black and white. "I'm going to book a room at the local inn. Just let me know when you're ready to talk."

Their fingers brushed as he accepted the card, and the sleeve of her jacket rode up slightly. Just enough to reveal a scar on the underside of her wrist. Puckered red skin. Raw looking.

A burn scar.

His pulse jumped. Ginny Bagwell might be researching a story, but she was holding something back. This was personal to her.

She'd come to him because she'd researched him.

That roused his curiosity.

"All right, I'll call you after I get some sleep," he said, hoping a couple hours of z's would make her look less sexy when he talked to her.

Either way, he'd find out what she was up to.

GINNY STRUGGLED TO calm her raging nerves as she drove through the small town of Whistler. Nestled in the mountains only a couple of hours from Asheville, it looked like a quaint little village with its gift shops, handmade quilt store and signs for boiled peanuts and homemade fudge. The area catered to campers, hikers, white-water rafting, canoeing and skiing in the winter.

She'd read everything she could find on the town the night before. Five years ago, a terrible fire had destroyed the local hospital, caused several casualties and cost the Maverick brothers their father's life.

Griff knew what it was like to lose a loved one. Her

heart went out to him. Yet that fact could give them common ground.

Reminding herself to stay alert in case Robert was in Whistler, she scanned the streets as she drove and the parking lot of the Whistler Inn when she pulled into the drive. Set against the backdrop of the sharp ridges and hills beyond, it looked almost ethereal. Not that she could relax and enjoy it while she stayed here.

Not with her sister's killer still on the loose.

She retrieved her overnight bag from the trunk of her rental car and started up the cobblestone walkway to the front door of the inn. The hair on the back of her neck prickled, and she turned and scanned the street again.

Robert couldn't know she was here. Could he?

No. She'd been careful. Rented a car using her fake ID so it couldn't be traced back to Reese Taggart. Her hair was a different color now and shorter. Thanks to colored contacts, her green eyes were blue.

Reminding herself that she was here to find him, and that she'd trained for the moment, she slipped inside the inn. The woman behind the guest-services desk smiled and offered her the room she called The Sunflower Room. Ginny expected it to be painted bright yellow, but it was white with muted shades of green and coral, and fresh sunflowers in a vase on the desk.

The room was so bright and cheery that it looked at odds with the reason she'd come. But it reminded her of a happier time when she and her sister had dreamed about their futures together.

Tess had lost her future because of her.

Tears blurred her eyes. Some days she made it through without succumbing to the overwhelming anguish. Other days, the grief came out of nowhere and hit her so hard it stole her breath.

It was the little things that triggered the memories and

made her choke up with emotions and regret. Tess's favorite ice cream was mint chocolate chip. On her birthday, Ginny ordered a cone of it to honor Tess, but halfway through she'd started bawling like a baby. Another time she'd heard her sister's favorite song in a coffee shop, and she'd had to leave.

She swiped at the tears and forced herself to focus on her mission. Hopefully Griffin Maverick would call her.

If not, she'd find another way to see if the death of the woman in the nail-salon fire was connected to Robert.

She settled her suitcase on the luggage rack, then set her laptop on the desk. Her muscles ached from tension and tossing and turning all night. The dead woman's face taunted her in her sleep. Joy looked so much like she had three years ago that Ginny felt like she was looking in the mirror.

If she'd never gotten involved with Robert, Tess would still be alive.

And if she'd stopped Robert a long time ago, he couldn't have hurt anyone else, like Joy.

She grabbed a bottle of water from the gift basket on the corner table, uncapped it and took a long drink as she sank into the chair and booted up her computer.

This trip to Whistler might not turn up anything on Robert. Joy Norris's murder might be unrelated to Tess's.

But that picture, Joy's looks… She had to know for sure if she was another victim of Robert's.

She spent the next hour combing the internet for pictures or any mention of Robert Bouldercrest. She checked local news reports and social media, trolling through random photographs people had posted.

But she found nothing.

Determined to explore every avenue, she decided to search online dating sites again. She'd met Robert on a site called Meet Your Mate and went there first in case he stuck to a pattern.

She created a new profile under the name June Embers and found a stock photo to use. She answered the questions in a similar vein as she had when she'd created her first profile.

If Robert had been attracted to quiet, shy journalism student Reese Taggart who lived alone and had just lost her mother, he might fall for bookstore owner June who'd grown up in foster care and wanted to get married and make a family of her own. She posted the profile, then added it to several other dating and singles sites.

Robert liked playing the savior, the knight riding in to save the lonely damsel. Like June.

And he *had* been chivalrous. Affectionate. Romantic.

Until he'd turned into a monster.

THREE HOURS LATER, Griff rolled from bed, still foggy from sleep. He felt as if he was in a phantasmagoric state, where real images and imagined ones blurred together. Had he been so exhausted he'd dreamed that beautiful woman had shown up at his door this morning?

His phone dinged with a text as he stumbled into the kitchen. Jacob.

One p.m. Meet at ME's office for results of Joy Norris's autopsy.

Griff sent a return text: See you there.

He started past the breakfast island to make coffee when he spotted the business card Ginny had left. So, he hadn't imagined her.

He filled the coffee carafe with water and poured it into the coffee maker, inserted a filter filled with his favorite ground beans, then punched the start button. While the rich, dark coffee brewed, he picked up the card, turned it over between his fingers and studied it. Simple office stationery. Classic design.

The name Virginia (Ginny) Bagwell was scrawled in italics with the title investigative journalist printed below her name along with a phone number and address in Asheville.

He tapped the card between his fingers, his curiosity piqued. How had she gotten that scar? Why was this story important enough to travel to Whistler and knock on his door?

His pulse jumped as a random thought struck him. Could she possibly know something about the fire from five years ago?

The scar…could she have been at the hospital that day?

Chapter Three

The scent of chicory filled the air, and Griff poured himself a cup of coffee, carried it to his computer then sat down and retrieved the file he, Jacob, Liam and Fletch had compiled over the past five years. He plugged in the name Virginia (Ginny) Bagwell and ran a search to see if her name was listed as one of the victims in the Whistler Hospital fire, or if she'd lived in town at the time.

Nothing popped.

Even more curious than before, he snagged his cell phone and pressed the number on the business card. He had a couple of hours before meeting the ME and Jacob.

She answered on the third ring. "Hi. I didn't know if you'd call, Mr. Maverick."

He hadn't known if he would either.

"It's Griff. I can do a late breakfast at eleven at Mitzi's Café in the town square." The young woman had just opened, and he'd heard the food was good. She was not only attractive, but she made a mean stack of hotcakes with fresh blueberries and cream. He did have a sweet tooth.

"I'll be there."

He hung up, then headed to the shower. While she probed him for information about arsonists, he'd find out what she was hiding.

GINNY CHECKED TO make sure her auburn roots weren't bleeding through before walking to the café. Outside, the sun was battling its way through dark clouds that hinted at rain, and the wind tossed debris through the air.

She checked over her shoulder a dozen times, keeping a lookout as she crossed the street and bypassed the mercantile and arts-and-crafts store.

Hunching her shoulders against the wind, she hurried past a dark gray SUV, averting her face until she reached the awning of The Brew, the coffee shop on the corner. She ducked beneath it, slipping into the shadows, then pulled her binoculars and aimed them at the vehicle.

Was Robert inside?

She hovered there for several seconds, watching. Finally, the man opened the door and stepped from the SUV.

Not Robert. This man was heavyset, bearded, with graying hair.

Relief surged through her, and she rushed down the sidewalk to the café.

Mitzi's looked like a throwback to the Wild West with its saloon door and red-checked tablecloths. Country music wafted through the speakers, and the sound of voices, laughter and dishes clanging filled the dining area.

She stopped at the hostess stand and told the young girl she was meeting someone, then asked for the booth in the rear. She always faced the door, never put her back to an entry point. She also scanned the room for a rear exit in case she needed to make a hasty escape.

Once seated, she ordered coffee and checked her phone, searching for updates on the story about the fire. Nothing new.

Footsteps sounded, and she looked up and saw Griff approaching. His big body seemed to take up all the space, stirring a myriad of emotions inside her. Fear, because he was big and muscled and strong. Desire, because he was handsome as sin.

Just the kind of men she avoided. She glanced at the scar on her wrist as a reminder. *Play with fire and you get burned.*

Sometimes you didn't survive.

She had to survive long enough to get revenge for Tess.

GRIFF NARROWED HIS EYES as he claimed the chair across from Ginny. He'd seen her outside on the street. Watched her checking over her shoulder as if she thought someone was following her. Saw her duck beneath the awning, pull out her binoculars and surveil the man in that gray SUV.

What in the hell was she doing?

Was she really here for basic information on arson or was she chasing another story?

She offered him a smile that instantly made his gut tighten. "Thank you for coming."

"Had to eat," he said gruffly.

She nodded and sipped her coffee. The waitress sauntered over and he ordered coffee and the stack of hotcakes with blueberries and whipped cream. She asked for the same except she chose strawberries for her topping.

She wasted no time but jumped in with basic questions about causes of fire.

"Many are accidental," he said, playing along. "Faulty wiring. Someone left a candle burning or dropped a cigarette or left the stove on."

"How about those recent wildfires?"

Their food arrived, and his stomach was growling so he dug in. "Could be campers or hikers not properly extinguishing their campfire. The March winds can whip up embers and spark flames even after the fire has been thought to have been snuffed out."

"Is that what you think is happening?"

He shrugged. "Honestly I think some teens are the cause, but we haven't found a suspect, or suspects." He waved his hand. "This is off the record. Do you understand?"

"I do," she said quietly. "You found an accelerant?"

He nodded. "A couple of packs of matches. Empty beer cans. Evidence of lighter fluid."

"That does sound intentional. Is there a pattern with the timing?"

"Not really. Although two of them started at dusk. Just enough time for kids to get out of school, head to the woods and drink a few beers before their folks got home from work."

He finished off his meal, then sat back and studied her while he sipped his coffee.

"Tell me about pyromaniacs," she said. "They're obsessed with fire, aren't they?"

"True. Some have impulse disorders. They love the thrill of watching the flames burn. But that's more rare."

She licked whipped cream from her lips. "A large percentage of arsonists set fires to cover a crime, don't they?"

Now he sensed they were getting to the heart of the matter. "As a matter of fact, yes. Fire can destroy valuable evidence and make recovering forensics difficult." He paused. "But a fire doesn't totally destroy a body. Specialists can still uncover important forensics and evidence by examining the remains."

"Is that what happened last night at the nail salon? Do you think someone killed Joy Norris then set the salon on fire to cover his tracks?"

He folded his arms. "I can't divulge information in an ongoing investigation."

"But that's what you suspect?" she pressed.

"Is that why you're here?" He narrowed his eyes. "Do you know something about that fire last night or Joy's murder?"

Her eyes widened slightly. "I explained that I'm writing a piece on arson—"

"I'm not buying it," he said. He'd been lied to before by Joy and didn't like it.

She shifted and traced a finger around the rim of her coffee mug. "All right. I'll share if you do."

A frown creased his mouth. "We're still investigating. I'm supposed to meet with the ME and sheriff after breakfast to learn the results of the autopsy." He snagged the bill and gave her a pointed look. "Now your turn."

Her gaze met his for a tension-filled minute. He thought she might answer, but then she yanked her gaze from his as if he'd burned her.

Suddenly a commotion sounded from up front. Loud footsteps. Then a man's voice bellowing.

Griff turned to see what the problem was, his heart hammering when Joy's ex-husband Wayne stalked toward him, hands balled into fists. Griff went still, his jaw clenched as the man grabbed him by the collar of his shirt.

"What the hell did you do to my wife?" Wayne snarled. "First you screw her when we're still married. Then what? She broke it off, so you got mad and killed her?"

GINNY GRIPPED THE chair edge as the man's accusations rang in her head. Griff had slept with this man's wife while she was married to him?

Disappointment filled her. She'd almost confided the truth, at least part of it, to Griff. Had thought that maybe he was a good guy. He saved lives.

But he'd slept with another man's wife.

His body stiffened, and he curled his fingers around the shorter man's hands and pulled free. "Listen to me, Wayne, I did not hurt Joy," he said bluntly. "The minute I learned your divorce wasn't final, I broke it off."

"I don't believe you," the man hissed. "I think you still

wanted her, but she told you the two of us were getting back together and you got mad."

"If you two were reconciling, then good for you," Griff said, his tone edged with doubt. "Although maybe you're the one who hurt her. Maybe she told you there was no way she'd come back to you, and you snapped."

Ginny fidgeted. If Joy's husband was jealous enough to hurt her, or even kill her, she might be wrong about Robert being in Whistler.

She didn't know whether to be relieved or disappointed. As much as Robert terrified her, she was desperate to get rid of him forever.

"Now, I suggest you go somewhere and cool off," Griff said in a deep voice. "I have a meeting to attend."

He didn't bother to say goodbye to her. He pushed past Joy's husband, strode to the counter to pay the bill, then stormed out the door.

Joy's husband turned and glared at her. "You may think he's some hero, but he's not."

Venom spewed from the man's eyes and tone. Venom that told her he was dangerous. Venom that reminded her of another man who'd shed his charming outer skin to become a snake when she'd crossed him.

Had Joy's husband killed her and set that fire as payback for sleeping with Griff?

Humiliation washed over Griff as he left Mitzi's Café. He hadn't been proud that he'd slept with a married woman, but he hadn't known at the time or it would never have happened. He'd been angry with Joy for lying to him, not for dumping him, but he sure as hell would never have hurt her.

His father had drilled his personal motto into his sons' heads—Respect and Protect, Especially Women and Children. Griff had become a firefighter to honor his father's death.

Wayne Norris, on the other hand, was less than honorable.

He'd driven Joy away with his bullying and drinking. She'd insisted to Griff that she'd never go back to him.

Which meant Wayne was lying about a reconciliation. Maybe about more…

The bastard could have publicly made accusations against Griff to waylay suspicion from himself.

He climbed in his truck and drove to the ME's office, still steaming. His phone buzzed as he parked. The head of the forensics lab.

"Maverick, I have some results," Lieutenant Miller said. "The only accelerant in the building was the acetone and chemicals at the salon."

So, the arsonist was smart. He'd known he hadn't needed additional fuel.

"But tests prove that it wasn't just small amounts spilled here and there. Someone poured acetone throughout the seating area and around the doors and walls."

"He wanted it to spread and spread quickly," Griff surmised.

"Exactly." Lieutenant Miller paused. "Oh, and we also found traces of acetone upstairs in the woman's apartment. Large amounts."

Definitely intentional. "So, there were multiple points of origin?"

"Yes. This guy didn't want to take any chances the fire would die out before it destroyed the whole place."

Griff twisted his mouth in thought. "I'll relay that to the sheriff. I'm sure he'll want to look into Joy's financials and her ex's in case of an insurance payout." If Wayne hadn't killed Joy out of spite, he could have done it for money.

Jacob pulled into the parking lot in his police-issued SUV and parked beside Griff.

"Any forensics that might belong to our perp?" Griff asked.

"We're still sorting through," Lieutenant Miller answered. "The fire destroyed most of the place. Add the water and smoke damage to the fact that this business catered to multiple customers daily, and it's a big fat mess."

He agreed to keep Griff updated, and Griff climbed from his vehicle. Jacob did the same, and they walked up the sidewalk together. He filled Jacob in on the forensics report as they entered the building.

"Will definitely look into the ex," Jacob said.

"I just had a run-in with him at Mitzi's Café." Griff explained about the confrontation.

"Sorry about that. I had to inform him of her death last night. But I wanted to wait until the autopsy before I brought him in for questioning."

Griff understood. Jacob would want to be armed with evidence and the ME's report.

"He's a ticking time bomb," Griff said. "Who knows what he's capable of."

"I'll dig up everything I can find on him."

They walked down the hall, then Jacob knocked on the ME's door. Dr. Hammerhead opened it, his thick brows marred into a frown. "Come on in. I'm just about to finish."

The scent of formaldehyde and other chemicals blended with the acrid odor of death. Griff said a silent thank-you to the heavens that Joy's body hadn't been burned. It didn't matter how long he was on the job, he'd never get used to the scent of charred flesh and tissue.

The doctor led them over to the exam table where Joy lay half draped in a cloth. Bins and instruments the ME used lined a sterile stainless steel tray next to the body.

Griff's stomach knotted at the sight of the Y incision on her chest. Her pale skin looked stark white beneath the bright fluorescent light.

Emotions churned through him. Joy might have lied to him, but she hadn't deserved this. She had her whole life ahead of her.

Last night, when he'd carried her from that burning apartment, her skin had looked bluish.

This morning bruises marred her arms. Another one darkened her shoulder.

"I did a full tox screen, and she had alcohol in her system, but no drugs." Dr. Hammerhead lifted one of her eyelids at a time, and Griff swallowed hard.

"Petechial hemorrhaging." He lowered the sheet and gestured toward bruises on Joy's neck. "Official cause of death is asphyxiation due to strangulation."

Just as he and Jacob had surmised. Griff zeroed in on the fingerprints emblazoned on Joy's neck. Large fingerprints.

Wayne's? Or had Joy been involved with another man?

GINNY COULDN'T STAND the wait. She had to know if Joy Norris was strangled. If she'd died at the hands of her husband, Ginny could leave Whistler.

Go back to hiding out.

She was so tired of hiding.

She'd let that jerk ruin her life. Control it for the last three years.

It had to end.

She texted Griff: What did the ME say about Joy Norris's death?

When he didn't respond, she darted outside the cafe. She'd go to the morgue and confront him.

Her senses remained honed as she hurried to cross the street. But just as she stepped off the curb, a car flew around the corner. She jumped back a step, but suddenly someone pushed her from behind.

She lunged forward, hands flailing to stay on her feet, but she plunged into the street, hitting the asphalt on her hands and knees.

Tires screeched and brakes squealed. Then she looked up and saw a car barreling straight toward her.

HE KNEW WHERE Reese was. Had known the moment she'd entered town.

She thought she was so smart. Dying her hair. Changing her name. Skulking in the shadows.

He'd done the same.

But he'd kept tabs on her. Had left her alone for a while and entertained himself with another. Had intended to lull her into a false sense of safety.

She'd come to Whistler to find him. His plan had worked. She must have seen the story about Joy. Joy, who looked so much like Reese that he hadn't been able to help himself.

Joy was gone now though. And he would have Reese again. Nothing would stop him this time.

But he'd have some fun first. He'd toy with her just to watch her squirm and suffer.

He disappeared into the woods by the park, then paused behind a tree to watch the chaos as she rolled sideways on the street to avoid being hit by the car.

Laughter bubbled in his throat. She'd been working out. She looked as if she'd developed muscles beneath the sleeves of that boring suit jacket.

Of course, she'd look better in something more feminine.

His body hardened at the image that played through his head. Reese in a black satin teddy. Red lace panties.

A teddy and panties that wouldn't stay on her long.

Chapter Four

Ginny froze as the car careened toward her. A second later, the screeching of the tires and someone screaming nearby jolted her back into motion, and she rolled sideways. The car swerved to avoid her and jumped the curb, brakes squealing.

Chaos erupted around her. Someone reached down to help her up. A man ordered people to back away from her. Ginny tried to push herself up to stand, but she was shaking all over. Her hands were scraped, bloody and raw. Her knee throbbed where she landed on the pavement.

"Come on, sweetie." A middle-aged woman and her teenage son took her arm and helped her over the curb. Ginny's legs felt weak, her mind racing. Voices rumbled around her. A small crowd had gathered.

The driver of the car, a young woman, leaped from inside and ran toward her. "Oh, my god, are you okay? I... thought you were at the crossing."

She had been. But...someone had pushed her before the traffic light changed. A dizzy spell assaulted her, and she rubbed her temple.

"Someone call 9-1-1," an older man said.

"No." Ginny shook her head and blinked to clear her vision. "I'm fine. No need."

She looked up into the panicked eyes of the driver. She

looked shell shocked and terrified. "I hit the brakes when I saw you falling," she said, her voice bordering on hysteria.

"It wasn't your fault," Ginny murmured. "I tripped and fell right in front of you."

"But I could have killed you." The other woman burst into tears, and an elderly woman patted her back to comfort her.

Ginny threw up her hand to stop the chatter. "I'm really fine. It was just an accident, but I'm not hurt." And she sure as hell didn't want to deal with the police.

She rubbed the young driver's arms to calm her. "Look at me, sweetie. You stopped in time. I'm fine now. Really. I was at fault, not you."

Tears blurred the other woman's eyes, and she accepted a handkerchief from a gentleman in a navy suit.

"Please, everyone, go back to your business," Ginny said. "I'm going to my car and clean up now. I'll be fine."

Without waiting for a response, she forced herself to walk toward her car. She'd cross at the other end of the sidewalk. Right now, she wanted to escape the concerned bystanders. They stood talking and whispering for a minute, and Ginny scanned the street across from where she'd fallen. Her ankle throbbed, and she tasted blood. Must have bitten her lip in the fall. Her hands stung and her knee was aching. But she kept walking until she found the next crosswalk. It was practically deserted, and the sign blinked for walkers to cross. She glanced around her, behind her, to the sides and across the street before she stepped into the crosswalk.

Wind ruffled her hair and sent a chill through her. Or maybe she was chilled from the fall. Except she hadn't simply tripped and fallen.

She pressed the key fob to unlock her car, then slid inside and locked the door. Trembling all over, she dropped her forehead against the steering wheel and dragged in huge gulping breaths. Tears burned her eyes, fear pulsing through her.

She'd felt those hands shove her into the street. Felt someone watching her all day.

And right before she'd fallen, she'd detected the strong scent of a man's cologne. Earthy and musky.

The same scent Robert had worn.

GRIFF AND JACOB drew in deep breaths of fresh air as they stepped outside.

"I'll never get used to the smells in that morgue," Jacob muttered.

Griff raked a hand through his hair. "Me neither."

They paused on the steps, and Jacob turned to Griff. "You said Joy's ex accused you of hurting her because she broke it off. What really happened, Griff?"

He'd been too ashamed that he'd slept with a married woman at the time to confide in his brothers when he discovered Joy's betrayal. "When we met, she told me she was divorced. We dated a few times, nothing serious though. At least not on my part."

"Was she serious?" Jacob asked.

Griff shrugged. "She hinted she wanted a future. But it was an act. One night on the phone, I heard her talking to one of her friends. She said the divorce wasn't final, but she was going to teach Wayne a lesson because he'd cheated on her. She used me to do that."

"That sucks," Jacob said.

"But you're thinking I had motive?"

"Someone else would say that."

Griff's pulse jumped. "Was I mad? Yes. So, I broke it off with her. That was over three months ago."

"Do you have an alibi for last night?"

Anger shot through Griff. "You don't seriously think I'd hurt a woman, do you?"

"Of course not," Jacob said. "But you know I have to eliminate persons of interest and that means anyone involved with Joy or who had a personal beef with her. It's just routine."

The tension in Griff's chest eased slightly. He understood, but he didn't like it. "I was putting out those wildfires all afternoon and evening, up until the time we met for burgers and beer."

Jacob shifted. "I need to bring Wayne in for questioning and find out if he has an alibi."

"Anger at Joy over leaving him could be motive." An idea occurred to Griff. "Or if Joy used me, maybe she used some other man as well."

Jacob's brows shot up. "You're right. I'll speak to her friends and coworkers, find out if she had any other love interests or enemies."

GINNY HAD TO pull herself together. She'd come here looking for Robert.

Maybe she'd found him. Or rather, he'd found her.

The cloying scent of his cologne made her nauseated, stirring memories of him touching her. Hovering over her. Refusing to let her go.

Never again.

Renewing her resolve to make him pay, she lifted her head, inhaled and reached inside the console between the front seats. She removed a pack of sanitizing wipes and cleaned the bloody scrapes on her palms, wiping away streaks of blood and pavement debris.

She glanced at her face in the mirror and checked her appearance. A mess of tangled hair, and tear-streaked cheeks stared back. She dabbed at her face with another wipe, then pulled her compact from her purse and added a thin layer of powder to cover her dark circles and pale skin.

She started the engine and veered onto the street. Using

the car's GPS, she followed the directions to the morgue. Maybe she could meet Griff outside and persuade him to talk.

Traffic was slow as she maneuvered through town, checking the side streets and alleys at every turn, and peering at pedestrians and bystanders as she passed the park. A black sedan caught her eye, and she squinted to see through the windows, but the dark tinted glass made it impossible to distinguish the person inside.

Rain clouds gathered above, threatening a spring storm as she approached the morgue. She slowed as the facility came into view. Griff stood hunched in his jacket on the front steps with his brother the sheriff. She swung her car into the parking lot across the street, hoping they didn't see her, and waited for the men to part ways.

They looked serious, deep in conversation, almost tense with one another. What had they learned from the ME? Had they recovered Joy's computer or phone?

She wished she could search the woman's apartment, but that had burned down in the fire. The sheriff shifted, then patted Griff on the shoulder, turned and walked to his squad car. Griff remained still for a moment, staring at the street, his brows furrowed.

Maybe he was more upset about her death than he'd admitted. If he was in love with Joy, and he discovered Robert had killed her, Griff might blame *her* if he knew the truth about her relationship with him.

All the more reason to keep quiet about her reason for being here until she knew for certain Robert was responsible for Joy's death.

The wind ruffled Griff's thick hair, giving him a rakish look that reminded her men were dangerous. Good looks didn't matter and could be deceiving. What did she know about Griff Maverick anyway? Just that he was a fireman and ran into burning buildings on the job.

He could be a totally different person in his personal life. Just like Robert had been.

Robert's polished clothes, bulging wallet and slick smile had worked well for him as an investor. He'd certainly sold himself to her. Took her on expensive dates, to lavish dinners, showered her with romantic gifts.

Then he'd thought he owned her.

When she'd finally balked at his possessiveness, his true colors had surfaced.

Griff shaded his eyes with one hand and scanned the street, and she ducked low in the seat. Had he noticed her?

She held her breath for a minute, then raised her head just enough to glance through the window. He was gone.

Pulse hammering, she gripped the steering wheel and scanned the sidewalk. Where was he? Not in the road, not crossing to her.

A shadow of movement caught her eye, and she spotted him several hundred feet away.

His hands were jammed in the pockets of his leather bomber jacket, his posture tense. When he reached a black pickup truck, he climbed in, started the engine and backed from the parking space.

Ginny started her car and veered from the parking lot, then drove slowly, remaining a car length behind, hoping he wouldn't spot her on his tail.

GRIFF's MIND REPLAYED his relationship with Joy as he headed back toward his place. She'd been sweet at first, had been friendly at the town council business meeting. She'd just moved to Whistler and was excited about opening her salon. Said she was divorced and starting fresh.

She'd seemed intelligent, independent and was easy on the eyes. He'd taken her to dinner one night and they'd had a few drinks, then she'd asked him back to her apartment. Coming off several days of work, and at the time frustrated with no leads in the hospital fire as he faced the impending anniversary of his father's death, he'd been feeling down and…lonely. Having a pretty woman come on to him had been flattering, and he'd climbed in her bed.

They'd gotten together a couple more times, but soon he'd sensed she wasn't the woman she pretended to be. Then he'd discovered she was still married, and he'd called it quits immediately.

He didn't fool around with married women. And he didn't tolerate lies.

She was both married and a liar.

He swung onto the road leading toward the town square. Maybe he'd ask around town for word about Joy's love life. Perhaps she'd used someone else as she had him, and that man hadn't taken it well. He could always check the bar she frequented.

He glanced in his rearview mirror and frowned. Two cars back, he spotted Ginny Bagwell's little black sedan. Was she following him?

Curious, he made a sharp right turn and sped up, checking the mirror again. She turned and accelerated. If she was following him, she was a damn amateur. Irritated that she thought he wouldn't notice, he drove a couple more miles, then made another turn. She was close behind.

Why the hell was she so determined to talk to him? If she wanted information about Joy's murder, she should go straight to Jacob instead of him.

That baffled him. So did the fact that she'd asked specifically about Joy's death.

Deciding he'd had enough deception to last a lifetime, he swung into a parking spot in front of town hall. She parked two cars down.

Griff slid from his truck and stalked toward her. When he reached the sedan, he rapped on the window. She hit the automatic button to lower it, then looked up at him with a doe-like expression.

"Griff, funny we meet again," she said feigning surprise as if this was a coincidence.

"It's not funny at all," he growled. "I made you way back there." He folded his arms and glared down at her. "Now, why in the hell are you following me?"

She lifted her chin. "I told you I want a story. I texted you and asked about Joy Norris's COD, but you didn't answer. Was she strangled?"

The sense that she was hiding something intensified. "Why don't you go to the sheriff? Why ask me?"

"Was she strangled?" A hint of desperation laced her tone that roused his curiosity even more.

"Yes," Griff said. "How did you know?"

Her face paled, but she squared her shoulders. "I didn't. It was just a guess."

Griff studied her. Something about her was off…

He leaned against the window, his gaze meeting hers with a warning look. "Listen to me. If you know something about Joy's murder, you'd better come clean. Right now, all we have is her ex. If he's innocent, we've got nothing."

She jerked her gaze from his and stared at her hands which were clenching the steering wheel in a white-knuckled grip. "I… I'm here researching a story," she said again. "I didn't even know Joy."

Maybe so. But she was holding back something.

"If you're scared or something else is going on, I'll go with you to talk to my brother," he offered.

She clamped her teeth over her bottom lip and shook her head. "I have to go. Sorry for disturbing you."

"Just tell me—"

"I won't bother you again. I'll get the information on my own." The window slid up, then she started the engine, backed from the space and drove away.

Just what the hell was she planning? A single woman asking questions about a murder could be dangerous. Didn't she know that?

Chapter Five

Ginny silently chided herself as she drove away. She couldn't allow another man to intimidate her. But Griff Maverick had done just that.

She would just have to do what she'd said. Investigate on her own. Find another way to determine if Joy had been dating Robert.

After deciding to start by chatting up Mitzi at the café, she drove to the quaint little spot, parked and scanned the property before she went inside. Just because she didn't see Robert didn't mean he wasn't lurking around.

Watching her. Trying to unnerve her.

He'd done that before when she'd first left him. When his more subtle pleas and promises to win her back had failed, he'd started stalking her. Showing up in random places. Outside the coffee shop she liked to go to in the mornings. At the library when she'd decided to study and go back to college. At the restaurant where she'd worked part-time to pay for the room she'd rented in the rear.

Sometimes he'd simply sit and watch. Other times he'd leave her notes, reminding her that she was his. Twice she'd gone back to the apartment and realized he'd been inside.

He'd left a gift for her on the bed. Flowers. Perfume. A silk teddy he wanted her to wear.

That same cloying cologne he wore had lingered in the air, suffocating and nauseating.

She inhaled to ward off her nerves and entered the café. The scent of coffee and apple pie wafted toward her. Mitzi stood behind the counter pouring coffee into two mugs for an elderly man and woman. The couple carried the mugs to a corner table and huddled together as if they were newlyweds.

Ginny's heart gave a pang. At one time she'd dreamed of love and happily-ever-after. Then Tess had been taken from her. Tess who would never have a chance to love or be loved or hold her own baby in her arms. Tess whose art brightened the world. A world now void of color without her in it.

Ginny slid onto the bar stool and forced a friendly smile toward Mitzi. The young woman's blond hair accentuated her narrow face and was twisted into a claw clip on top of her head. She was probably midtwenties, looked friendly and easygoing as she managed the various orders tossed at her.

"What can I get you?" Mitzi asked as she handed off a cappuccino to the waitress to deliver to another table.

"Just plain coffee," Ginny said. Her stomach couldn't handle anything richer today, not after the scent of that cologne.

Mitzi arched a brow in question as she slid a steaming mug toward her. "You're the woman who was here with Griff earlier, aren't you?"

Ginny drizzled honey into her coffee. "Yes, I'm an investigative journalist researching a story on arsonists. I heard about the fire at the nail salon and was hoping he could add some insight."

Mitzi rearranged the condiments on the bar. "Then you're not from around here?"

"No, and I don't intend to stay," Ginny said, deciding to let the woman know she wasn't a threat in case Mitzi was interested in Griff. "I'll be leaving as soon as I finish my story." She stirred her coffee. "By the way, did you know the owner of the salon?"

Mitzi's lips pinched into a frown, and she propped her elbows on the bar. At this time of the day, the place was virtually empty. Still, Mitzi spoke in a conspiratorial whisper. "We met, but I didn't think much of her. I heard she'd used Griff and that she went through men like some women change their shoes."

"Really?" Ginny absorbed that tidbit. "Do you recall seeing her with anyone specific?"

Mitzi twisted her mouth in thought. "A couple of times she came in with this really handsome fellow. Said he was an investment banker who helped her secure the loan for her salon."

"What did he look like?" Ginny asked.

"Late thirties, brown hair, neatly trimmed, well dressed. He seemed really flirty with her, so I wondered if there was more to their relationship than business."

"Do you recall his name?"

Mitzi shook her head "No, don't think she ever mentioned it."

"Was there anyone else?"

"I don't really remember, but I've only been here a few months. I had the impression Joy liked the nightlife though. Dancing and clubs and bars, you know that sort of thing."

"I do know." Ginny shivered. Robert had similar interests. And he preferred expensive restaurants.

None of it had been her scene though.

The bells over the door jingled as a group of women entered, and Mitzi waved at them.

"I gotta talk to those ladies. They want to plan a private women's luncheon here, and I can use all the business I can get."

Ginny offered her a smile. Under different circumstances, she and Mitzi might be friends.

"If you think of anything else, call me." Ginny pushed a business card into Mitzi's hand.

"Sure thing. Good luck with your story."

Ginny's phone dinged as Mitzi maneuvered around the corner of the bar to greet the women.

She pulled her cell from her pocket and checked the text. She had a message from the dating site Meet Your Mate. Rather, June Embers had a message.

A man named Karl Cross requested a date. She checked the man's profile in search of a photograph, but the one that was posted was taken from a distance and in shadows so she couldn't distinguish the man's face.

He looked to be about Robert's height. He was also dressed in a tailored suit, said he liked nice restaurants, fine wine and strong women.

All the things Robert had first said. All were true, too, except the part about the strong women. He wanted meek and docile. One he could control. Who'd do what he said, pleasure him and bow down to his every wish and order.

Her gut instinct told her that Karl Cross could be Robert. The only way to know was to meet him in person.

Nerves bunched in her stomach as she responded that she'd meet him at the bar called Whistler's Nightcap at seven.

GRIFF GRIMACED AS he walked to the sheriff's office. He hadn't handled the encounter with Ginny very well. But he didn't intend to allow another woman to use him—or fall for her lies.

Still, he felt bad for coming on so strong. She'd looked frightened, and he'd been raised better. His father would have given him a good talking to for his terse tone.

Why *had* he been so angry?

Because she's pretty and tempting and you want to trust her, but you don't.

Thunder rumbled, dark storm clouds gathering, rain on its way. He glanced back to where Ginny was parked. But she was gone.

Maybe she'd give up the story and leave town. Unless his instincts were right, and she was here for more than a story.

The wind battered the thin windowpanes as he entered Jacob's office. "I need to see Jacob," he told the receptionist.

"He's interrogating Wayne Norris at the moment."

"I'll wait in his office." Griff bypassed the deputy who was on the phone, then strode through the double doors and down the hall to his brother's office. Jacob's desk was a mess, but Griff noticed a grainy photo on the side of his computer. He leaned closer to see what it was, and realized it was a sonogram of Jacob and Cora's unborn baby.

A smile tugged at his lips. The Maverick family was growing. Odd that he hadn't pictured any of them married and now the longing for someone to fill his lonely nights with niggled at him.

Ginny's face teased at his mind.

Do not go there.

While he waited for Jacob, he seated himself and decided to dig deeper into Ginny. The fact that she was still here roused his curiosity even more.

He should have googled her before now but figured she'd be gone in a day and forgotten. But he plugged her name in and found two Virginia Bagwells. One was seventy-five and owned a pet store for cats in Maine. The other was deceased.

Next he entered the words *journalist* and *investigative reporter* and spent the next half hour researching various publications and articles but found no byline for a Virginia or Ginny Bagwell.

She said she was trying to break in to a TV network, so he researched those as well, but if she'd had any experience in the media, he couldn't find it.

Footsteps sounded behind him, and he glanced up and saw Jacob in the doorway.

"What are you doing?" Jacob asked.

Griff stood. "Ginny followed me from the morgue," he said. "I think she may know something about Joy's murder."

"Really?"

"Something's definitely off about her. She claims to be researching a story on arsonists and saw the news on TV, but she's been asking questions about Joy, how she died, if she was strangled."

Jacob's brows shot up. "She specifically asked about strangulation?"

Griff nodded. "Since you haven't released that detail, it made me wonder if the murder was what brought her to Whistler."

Jacob gestured toward the computer. "So, you were researching her?"

"I was, but so far she's a mystery. I can't find anything about a Ginny or Virginia Bagwell. It also struck me as odd that she came to me, and not you."

Jacob worked his mouth from side to side in thought. "Could be she's just a nosy journalist or that she's hiding something. Either way, it's worth looking into. I'll have Liam see what he can dig up." Jacob folded his arms. "Meanwhile maybe you should keep an eye on her."

Griff's stomach tightened. "I guess I could do that." He would just have to remain objective. "How'd it go with Wayne? Do you think he killed Joy?"

Jacob shook his head. "I don't like the bastard, but the creep has an alibi."

"He could have hired someone," Griff suggested.

"That's a possibility. My deputy is looking into his financials to see if he was in trouble or if he withdrew a significant amount of money lately, money he could have used for that purpose."

"How about insurance?"

"Joy's business was doing well. No major financial problems. Wayne was not a beneficiary on her insurance. She removed him from the policy when she filed for divorce. He also had no claims to the business."

"Maybe he was angry she cut him out."

"Could be," Jacob said. "But I have to start considering other persons of interest. I'm on my way to talk to Riley Thornton, the receptionist at the salon. Maybe she knows more about Joy's personal life."

"Tonight, I'll drop by the bar where Joy and I went," Griff offered. "Maybe the bartender saw her with someone else."

"Good idea. I'll meet you," Jacob offered.

Griff shook his head. "Let me go alone. Bartender might freeze up when he sees a uniform." Griff pointed to the ultrasound picture. "Besides, you have a family to go home to. How's Cora feeling?"

"Tired, but excited," Jacob said with a grin. "Nina's ecstatic about having a little brother or sister."

"I'm happy for you, brother." Griff suddenly felt antsy to leave. "Let me know what Liam uncovers about Ginny."

They agreed to stay in touch, and Griff left the office. Outside a few raindrops had started to fall, the clouds growing darker by the minute. He headed back to his truck, then decided to track down Ginny again.

Maybe she was back at the inn? He climbed in his truck, then drove past Mitzi's. Ginny's little sedan was there.

But she hurried out just as he neared the parking lot. He slowed and watched to see where she was going, his pulse hammering as he noticed her checking over her shoulder as she walked. She passed the mercantile and arts-and-crafts store, scanned the street as she walked. At one point, she ducked beneath an awning, then peered around the corner as if looking for someone.

Or…as if she thought someone was following her. What—or who—was she running from?

GINNY MADE HER way along the storefronts until she spotted the smoky ashes of Joy's Nail Salon, or what was left of it, which was a charred rubble of ash and burned materials. A cleanup crew had yet to clear the mess which seemed like a massive endeavor. Crime-scene tape flapping in the wind still cordoned off the area.

The businesses along the street nearest the salon included a barber shop, boutique, pet-grooming spa, novelty-and-gift store and a henna tattoo parlor.

Joy might have met a love interest from the barber shop. A frisson of nerves hit her as she entered the all-male establishment. The scent of aftershave and men's salon products wafted around her. Three chairs faced mirrors with barbers busy at work at their stations.

She offered the young man behind the desk a smile. He was probably early twenties, and sported a ponytail and a diamond stud in his left ear. She introduced herself as a journalist and asked if he'd known Joy.

"Seen her around," the guy said with a scowl. "Too bad about that fire. She ran a nice place. We coordinated some marketing efforts. Some of our customers' wives liked to get their nails done while the men got a shave."

Ginny cleared her throat. "Was she seeing anyone in particular?"

The phone rang, and he shook his head. "Not that I know of." While he answered the call, Ginny stepped over and spoke to one of the other barbers, a fortyish man with a thick beard. His gaze skated over her, then he smiled. But his smile faded when she explained the reason for her visit.

"I don't know about her personal life," he said. "I asked her to dinner once, but she turned me down. Guess I wasn't her type."

"What was her type?"

He shrugged. "Like I said, I don't know anything about what she did on her own time."

She laid a business card on his workstation. "Please call me if you think of anything."

She received similar reactions from the other two barbers. None of them claimed to have dated Joy or knew who she might be involved with.

When she left the barber shop, she headed inside the pet spa. A curly-haired blonde about Joy's age was leading a white miniature poodle to its owner at the desk. Ginny watched as the groomer accepted payment and petted the dog goodbye.

The girl's name tag said Katie. Ginny introduced herself and asked about Joy.

"She did my nails," Katie said. "They get such a mess here when I'm working."

"Did you two discuss your personal lives?" Ginny asked, striving for subtlety.

Katie stacked fliers about an upcoming Pet Rescue event on the counter. "I told her about my boyfriend," Katie said. "She was a good listener."

"Was Joy seeing anyone?" Ginny asked.

Katie tapped her fingers on the desk. "Why are you asking? Do you think someone she dated killed her?"

"I don't know," Ginny said. "The police are investigating. But I'm considering a human-interest angle for my story."

Katie seemed to mull over that statement for a minute. "Well, I think there was a new guy she was seeing, but she didn't tell me his name. Bragged that he was really good-looking and charming and knew how to treat a lady."

"Did she have a picture of him or describe him?"

"Nothing specific, just that he liked to take her to nice

places, expensive places, not like some of the losers she'd dated before."

"Where did they meet?"

Katie chuckled. "That was the funny thing. They met on a dating site. All my friends have been doing it, but all the men they connected with are creeps. A couple guys were into porn, one into guns and another into S & M."

"I've heard similar stories from other women," Ginny said. "Do you remember the name of the site she joined?"

Katie ran her fingers through her thick, sandy-blond hair. "I think it was called Meet Your Man. No, that's not right."

"You mean Meet Your Mate?"

Her eyes brightened. "Yeah, that's it."

Ginny's lungs strained for air. Tonight, she was supposed to meet a date from Meet Your Mate. Was Robert already looking for a replacement for Joy?

HE FLICKED THE lighter and watched the tip burst to life with a beautiful orange-and-red flame. He had been mesmerized by fire since he was a child.

Ever since the night he'd stood outside his own house and watched it burn to the ground with his mama in it.

The sound of the fire hissing transported him back in time.

HE WAS FIVE years old and his daddy dragged him outside and made him stand by the giant oak tree with the Spanish moss that dragged the ground like a witch's hair.

"Stay here!" Daddy shouted as he ran back inside.

But he didn't stay put. He sneaked up and watched his daddy and mama arguing in the kitchen.

"You'll never leave me," Daddy said. "Never."

"Give me the boy and let me go," Mama cried.

Daddy grabbed her arms and shook her. "You said till death do us part."

Mama tried to jerk free and run, but Daddy flung her backward against the wall. She stumbled and her head hit the counter. Then his daddy lunged at her and wrapped his hands around her throat.

He stood frozen. A scream of terror lodged in his throat as his daddy choked the life out of her. She flailed her arms and hands, struggling to yank free. But his daddy was too strong and mad, like one of the rabid dogs he'd seen running free on the deserted mountain roads.

The world blurred out of focus. Smoke filled the air. Or maybe it was the tears blinding him. He blinked and rubbed at his eyes, but they felt gritty.

When his vision cleared, Daddy shoved Mama to the floor. He held his breath to see if she got up, but she lay still, in a puddle on the black-and-white tile. Her red dress spilled around her like blood. Her eyes looked wide as she stared up at the ceiling. Her hands were curled by her sides. She didn't move.

Daddy lit the gas burner on the old gas stove, then tossed the match onto the flame. Then he turned and walked out of the kitchen.

A smile tilted Daddy's mouth and a calmness came over him like it always did after his father gave Mama one of the beatings. A loud boom sounded, then flames burst through the house. The windows exploded, spraying glass. Wood crackled and popped. The roof collapsed.

Daddy ran toward him. He snatched his hand in his and held it so tight it hurt. They stood silently, watching the flames eat up the old house and everything in it.

"That's what happens when your wife tries to leave you." Daddy said as he dragged him toward the old pickup truck. "She has to be punished."

He swallowed back a sob as his daddy pushed him into the truck. Daddy would punish him if he cried like a baby. "What about Mommy?" he finally whispered.

"Don't worry, son," Daddy said. "She should have listened like I told her."

Then his daddy started the engine and drove away without looking back.

He turned in the seat and watched the smoke float in the sky and the flames light the darkness.

He would miss Mama.

But the fire was so pretty he couldn't take his eyes off it.

Chapter Six

Griff felt like a stalker as he watched Ginny visit the barber shop and pet-grooming spa.

She was definitely investigating Joy's murder, not just a routine arson story. Could she have known Joy? If so, why not admit it?

His phone buzzed and he connected, hoping Jacob had more information.

"Where are you?" Jacob asked without preamble.

"I've been following Ginny," Griff said. "She came to Joy's Nail Salon, then went in and talked to people at the barber shop and pet-grooming spa."

"Stay close to her," Jacob said. "Liam said he couldn't find anything on her either. She must be using a fake name."

"The question is why," Griff muttered.

"Good question," Jacob said. "Meanwhile I talked to Riley. She's really torn up about Joy's death. Said a developer came in talking about buying up that entire row of businesses and wanted everyone to sell."

Griff's pulse jumped. "I take it Joy didn't want to sell?"

"No, apparently she was the only holdout. Owner of the barber shop said he'd already found another spot if he sold. But Joy liked the location and didn't want to have to start over. Besides, the apartment space above was a perfect fit for her."

"Who is this developer?" Griff asked.

"Some guy from Asheville named Thad Rigden. Liam is running a background on him, and I'm going to have a talk with him when I locate him."

According to Ginny's business card, she was from Asheville. Was there a connection?

Jacob's words echoed in his head. *Stay close to her. She must be using a fake name.*

Griff decided to try a new tactic with her. He'd play nice. Just like his mother used to say: *you catch more flies with honey.*

Hell, he'd drip honey if necessary to find out why that pretty little woman had come to town and tried to use him.

GINNY HAD A bad feeling that Joy's match date might have led to her death. Then again, if Robert had dated her, he could have met her at a bar or even walked into the barber shop for a shave, seen her next door and made contact.

"Did Joy mention having problems with anyone?" Ginny asked. "Maybe an old boyfriend?"

"Her ex was definitely an issue." Katie waved to a customer with a sheltie as she entered the store. "Oh, and she and that developer butted heads."

"Developer?"

"Yeah, Thad Rigden. He's a big real estate developer who wanted to buy up all our stores and build condos here. Joy refused to sell when he offered her a deal. She liked the location and said Whistler didn't need fancy condos. They needed to support local small businesses."

"Were you going to sell?" Ginny asked.

Katie shrugged. "The money was good, and I needed it, so yeah. He promised to help me find another location. In fact, everyone was on board except Joy. Even her business partner was in favor."

"Joy had a business partner?"

"Yeah, a private investor," she said. "Although she never told me who it was."

Ginny's instincts reared their ugly head. The real estate agent would know the name of this investor. "So, I guess this investor stood to gain if the place sold. Or if an insurance settlement came from it."

Katie fidgeted. "You think someone killed Joy for money over her shop?"

"I don't know, just exploring theories," Ginny said.

Either way, she intended to talk to the developer. Her mind pieced together a scenario. Robert had been business savvy and could have posed as the real estate mogul.

"Do you have his contact information?" Ginny asked.

The woman with the sheltie was approaching with a cart full of items including a dog bed and chew toys. Katie reached inside the drawer behind the counter. "He left some business cards," she said and handed Ginny one of them.

"Thanks." Ginny laid her own card on the counter by the register. "Call me if you think of anything else."

She left Katie to deal with her customer, stepped outside then called the number for the developer. The phone rang three times, then the voice mail kicked on, so she left a message saying she was interested in speaking with him about some property for a business start-up, and that Katie had recommended him.

Maybe he'd know if Joy's silent partner was Robert, or he could give her another name.

GRIFF WANTED TO talk to Ginny, but his phone buzzed. His boss.

"Sorry, Griff, I know it's your day off, but we need help. Another wildfire, up at Pigeon Creek this time."

Dammit. He was only a mile from the firehouse, so he drove over and joined the backup team just as the first on-call squad peeled from the fire station. He geared up quickly, hoping for rain to help drown out the fire. Though the dark clouds were ominous and threatening, they hadn't yet unleashed. Still, the wind had shifted and picked up, adding to the problem.

His buddy, Trey, the lead today, radioed the GPS coordinates from the first squad and suggested Griff's team take the east area where they believed the fire had begun. Team one would hit the center. The wind was carrying it fast, catching dried leaves and trees and moving in the direction of the new cabins on the creek.

"We have a squad near the cabins, already wetting the area down to ward off the blaze from reaching the houses. If this builds up momentum, we'll need to attack it from above," Trey said.

"Copy that," Griff responded into the mike clipped to his uniform.

Flames lit the sky as the truck screeched to a stop; the sound of wood crackling and timber falling rumbled. This one had gotten out of control quickly.

He and his squad launched into action, rolling out hoses, raising ladders to be able to spray into the heart of the fire and hacking away vegetation inch by inch to keep it from catching in case the wind took an abrupt shift and the fire moved the opposite direction.

Heat suffused Griff, the odor of charred wood and debris rising in the air. Sweat beaded his skin inside his uniform, and the smoke was so thick he could barely see through his protective hat and face mask.

They worked for the next two hours, and finally got the damn blaze under control. Still they dumped more water on the embers to ensure the wind didn't stir it back to life. Griff prayed no one was caught in the forest or trapped inside the blaze. The smoke alone could kill a person.

As the area where the fire started slowly died, he began searching for signs of the point of origin and an accelerant. Heat scalded him through his clothing, preventing him from traveling too deeply across the charred ground. He moved to the edge and scanned the area nearest the creek.

The sight of several empty beer bottles caught his eye, along with footprints. He shone his light into the brush and spotted a pack of matches. The fact that they were the same brand as the ones he'd discovered at the previous fire suggested they were dealing with one arsonist. Or if this was a bunch of teenagers, the same group of kids.

He bagged the matches and bottles to send to forensics. A few feet away, he found an empty bottle of lighter fluid.

He'd known these fires weren't accidental, but now he had proof. Hopefully forensics could find a print somewhere on the items he'd collected, and they could stop this arsonist before someone was injured or a fatality occurred.

GINNY HAD QUESTIONED all of the business owners in the strip with Joy's Nail Salon. Each one confirmed Katie's story that they were on board to sell to the developer. The description of the developer could fit Robert, although none of them had seen him in person. And no one else had insight into a silent partner. Apparently, a female working with the developer had visited the property and made the initial assessment, then reported back to him.

Still gritty and achy from the earlier fall, she decided to return to the inn and shower before she met Karl Cross at the bar. She checked her surroundings and over her shoulder as she walked back to her car, then slid inside to drive back to the inn.

Once again, she had the uncanny sense she was being watched. She jerked her head around and scanned the parking lot. A man in a dark hoodie walked hurriedly toward a green Lexus. Another man in a suit and raincoat ducked into a sleek black Cadillac, although she couldn't see his face.

Was she paranoid?

For months after she'd left Robert, and after Tess's death, she'd thought she'd seen Robert everywhere. On the street, at the grocery store, in a car passing by, at the coffee shop… She'd told the police, but without proof he was following her, they couldn't do anything.

At one point, she'd thought she was losing her mind.

But she'd been certain he was watching her. That he stayed in the shadows taunting her. He'd left dead flowers on her car once. Another time he'd written a message in lipstick on her mailbox.

Every time an incident occurred, she moved. Hid out in dive hotels. Hostels. Shelters. Anywhere she thought she might be safe. She'd lived in her Asheville apartment longer than she'd lived anywhere in three years.

She had no home anymore. No family. No one who cared.

Swallowing against the lump in her throat, she surveyed the street and watched to see if the sedan followed her as she veered from the parking lot. Dark clouds rumbled, the sky overcast and dreary just like her mood.

She parked at the inn, tugging the hood of her raincoat over her head as she grabbed her computer bag. Gripping it in one hand, she kept the other one over her weapon in her coat pocket as she hurried up the cobblestone path to the front door. The owner of the inn had decorated the front door with a handmade wreath, and bird feeders dotted the garden area to the right. A path led through a flower garden that supposedly featured the innkeeper's love of roses, although nothing was blooming now.

Tess would have loved the garden. She would have painted all the beautiful colors with its lush green foliage and the backdrop of the mountains and sharp ridges rising above.

Ginny ducked inside the door, her heart aching as she

climbed the stairs to her room. As she pulled her key from her purse and unlocked the door, an icy foreboding washed over her.

The cologne. She could smell Robert's cologne as if he was in the room.

Fear nearly immobilized her. If he had been here, was he inside? Had he picked the lock?

She held her breath as she poked her head into the room. The coverlet and pillows on the iron bed were just as she'd left them. Her suitcase lay open on the luggage rack. The welcome basket sat on the table, the ribbon still tied at the base.

It didn't appear anyone was inside.

Shoulders tense, she inched into the room. Had she left the bathroom door ajar?

She eased the hall door closed behind her, then pulled her gun at the ready and inched toward the bathroom. The door squeaked as she pushed it open and blood rushed to her head.

A message had been written in lipstick on the mirror just like the one Robert had written her before when he'd taunted her.

A message that said—*I'm watching, love. I'm always watching.*

GRIFF HAD JUST stepped from the shower when his phone buzzed. Jacob.

"Hey, man," Griff said as he connected the call. "Did you receive my message about the forensics I sent to the lab?"

"Yeah, I told them to fast-track the lab work. I want to stop whoever's doing this *now*." Jacob paused. "I set up a time for us to talk to the students at a school assembly tomorrow. 10:00 a.m."

Griff rubbed the back of his neck where his skin still felt scalded from the heat. "I'll be there."

A tense second passed, then Jacob cleared his throat.

"By the way, I questioned some of the shop owners by Joy's place. That reporter was all over town asking questions today just like you said."

Griff rubbed a hand over his eyes. "She's persistent at her job."

"Yeah, but she might just get herself killed nosing around. I'll pay her a visit and ask her to leave the investigation up to the law."

Griff dropped his wet towel to the floor and grabbed a pair of boxers. "Let me talk to her first," he offered. "She seemed spooked at the thought of talking to you."

"Probably because if she interferes, I can arrest her."

He hoped it didn't come to that. "I'll head over to the inn and talk to her now. Warn her that she needs to back off." Not that he expected her to listen. But it was worth a shot.

They agreed, and ended the call, then Griff finished dressing. He pulled on a button-down navy shirt with his jeans and combed his hair. He didn't know why he took the time with his appearance, but decided it was because he was headed to the bar to talk to the bartender after he left Ginny. Not because he wanted to impress her.

Five minutes later, he parked at the inn. A few raindrops pinged the ground just as he reached the porch. Wind chimes tinkled as the breeze stirred them, and the scent of rain filled the air. He entered the inn, then went to the desk and asked for Ginny's room.

The owner's eyes flickered with interest as if she thought he was there on a date.

He silently groaned then climbed the stairs and knocked on the door to the Sunflower room.

Seconds passed with no response, and he knocked again. "Ginny, it's Griff. We need to talk."

Another second, then two. Finally, her voice. "Just a minute."

Footsteps sounded inside, then the lock turned, and

Ginny appeared. The moment he saw her, he knew something was wrong.

Her face looked ashen, and a bandage on her forehead made his eyebrows raise. It was mostly hidden by her hair but visible when she tilted her head sideways. Her hands also looked bruised, the palms scraped.

What in the hell had happened to her?

Chapter Seven

Robert's message kept replaying in Ginny's head. *I'm watching, love. I'm always watching.*

She hadn't been paranoid. Whether or not Robert had killed Joy, he was here in Whistler. And he'd been inside her room.

Nausea threatened, but she swallowed hard, determined to pull herself together. She inhaled sharply, rattled by Griff's appearance.

Why had he shown up right now?

She needed time to assimilate the fact that Robert was close by. That she'd thought she was prepared to confront him. To kill him. But now her courage was waffling.

"Ginny?" Griff's voice sounded thick with worry. He gently took her arm, closed the door behind him and guided her over to the bed. Her knees felt so pathetically weak that she sank onto the mattress. On some level, it registered that she hadn't been alone with a man since Robert. And that Griff was big and muscular and could probably overtake her if he wanted.

But the fear fogging her brain had nothing to do with Griff.

He knelt in front of her, gently lifted her hands and examined her palms. "Tell me what happened. You didn't have these at the café."

She looked at her palms in a daze. She barely felt the

sting of the scrapes now, just the cold, hard terror of knowing Robert was two steps ahead of her. That she'd thought she might have control.

"What happened?" Griff asked again, his voice riddled with worry.

She looked into his eyes and saw genuine concern which nearly brought her to tears. But Robert had been a consummate liar, had pretended to care. Even after he hurt her, he'd kiss her and soothe her with tender looks and sweet nothings.

All lies.

She pulled her hands from Griff and straightened her spine. "I took a fall into the street earlier."

"A fall? It was an accident?"

"Of course," she said. "It was crowded, and I was crossing the street from the café after you left and wasn't paying attention and just tripped."

After hearing other abused victims' stories, she realized how lame her excuse sounded.

"That's why you're trembling now?" he asked. "That happened hours ago."

Ginny knotted her hands in her lap. She had to distract him from what had happened to her. "What are you doing here, Griff?"

Disappointment tinged his sigh. "I talked to Jacob. He said you were asking questions around town about Joy."

Ginny crossed her arms. "I did. And we've already discussed this. That's my job."

Griff cleared his throat. "Nosing around in a murder investigation is dangerous. You could get yourself killed." His gaze shot to her hands again, and Ginny lifted her chin.

"You're one to talk. You run into burning buildings and blazing forests for your job."

"I do it to save lives, not for some byline," Griff said, his voice taking on an edge.

Ginny's temper flared. "Maybe I'm doing it for the same reason. If I expose Joy's killer and he's a repeat offender, I might save another woman from the same fate."

Griff's eyes narrowed, and she wondered if she'd said too much. But he couldn't convince her not to finish this. Because this wasn't just a story or a byline she was after. She did want to save lives.

Including her own.

GRIFF STUDIED A fire methodically. Examined it for the point of origin. Analyzed the type of accelerant used to fuel the blaze. Utilized forensics to prove the arsonist's identity.

He needed to analyze Ginny in the same manner.

Obviously, logic was not working. And he'd bet his next paycheck that she hadn't fallen.

Warning her to back off had seemed like a wise idea. But she either was just stubborn, or...this case was personal to her for some reason. Had she known Joy?

Her statement about a possible repeat offender echoed in his head and strained his patience. "What do you mean, if he's a repeat offender? Ginny, do you know who killed Joy?"

Her mouth tightened. "No, I was talking hypothetical."

Dammit, he didn't believe her. But he stepped away to wrangle his temper under control. He'd frightened her earlier at her car when he'd caught her following him, and something else had frightened her afterward.

More than anything he needed to win her trust.

"You do realize that by asking about this killer, you're drawing his attention to yourself and he might come after you?"

She winced slightly, her only reaction. "I do. But if I help catch him, it'll be worth it."

"Why is it worth risking your life?" he asked. "Did you know Joy?"

She shook her head although a sad look passed across her face.

"Because you think whoever strangled her killed before?"

She looked away this time and absentmindedly rubbed her finger over the scar on her wrist. A telltale sign he was right. And one that made him more curious about how she'd gotten that scar.

Concerned about her now, he lowered his voice. "Ginny, tell me what you know." He reached for her arm to trace the burn scar with his finger, but she jerked it away and crossed the room to the window. For a moment, she stood staring outside at the rain drizzling against the window-pane and the dreary sky.

She looked pale, sad and frightened. But beautiful, like a lost child in a dark storm. The instinct to pull her in his arms pulsed through him, so strongly that he fisted his hands by his sides.

Pushing her would only make her run away.

GINNY ALMOST CAVED IN. Griff sounded so caring that for a moment, she forgot she couldn't trust him.

His brother was a man of the law. Griff saved lives.

They wouldn't approve of what she had planned for Robert.

But the idea of allowing him to comfort her teased at her resolve.

Even if Robert was here, he might not have anything to do with Joy's murder. There were other possibilities. She had to find the truth.

"Please, Ginny, I can't help you if you don't talk to me."

"I don't need your help."

"I think you do," he murmured.

Maybe she was out of her league. She needed to give

him an olive branch, a half-truth, because he didn't appear to be backing off.

"All right," she said. "Sit down and we'll talk." She gestured toward the wing chair in the corner while she claimed the desk chair, needing distance between them. "But this is confidential."

His thick dark brow quirked up in response. "Go on."

She inhaled a deep breath, planning the story in her mind. If she kept practicing, she might become as adept as Robert at bending the truth. Although her stomach knotted at that idea. She didn't like deceiving others.

But she also detested the fact that the police had let Robert get away with murder.

"I was recently contacted by a victim who claimed a man she was dating tried to strangle her and then set her house on fire."

Griff squared his shoulders. "She survived?"

If only she had. "Barely. She went into hiding afterward, because she was afraid he'd find her again and finish what he'd started."

"Did she report the attack to the police?" Griff asked.

"She did, but it didn't go well." Ginny fought anger at the way she'd been treated when she'd first reported Robert's abuse. "He escaped."

"What was his name? Where is he?"

"She claims she met him on an online dating site, but when the police investigated, the photo had been taken down. Apparently, the man was savvy enough to delete his profile and wipe it from detection by the authorities."

"What about the FBI? Cyber experts?"

"They found nothing. He probably used a fake identity and profile before, and he's most likely created a whole new persona for himself now."

Silence stretched between them for a tension-filled minute. "What about a sketch?" Griff finally asked. "Did she work with a police artist?"

Ginny bit her lip. "I don't know. She didn't give me one."

"My brothers are different from this other cop," Griff insisted. "They aren't incompetent and will get the job done."

"Maybe. But first I have to know if the cases are even connected."

"She called you when she saw the news about Joy's murder?" Griff said, piecing her story together.

"Yes," Ginny said. At least that was partly true. "That's the reason I wanted to know if Joy was strangled, if the MOs were the same. If not, I can move on somewhere else to look for this man. But if it's the same one... Well, I want to nail him to the wall."

Griff remained silent for another heartbeat, then heaved a breath. "All right. I'll help, too. Ask her to send a sketch and I'll show it around town myself. And if you'll tell me the name the man used on his dating profile, I'll ask Liam to look into it."

Ginny shook her head. "I told you this is confidential, Griff. This woman trusted me, not the police. If I find out he's the one responsible, I'll keep you informed."

Griff stroked her arm gently. "Ginny, if you're right and this guy is a serial predator, he's dangerous and won't have any qualms about coming after you."

"I don't care," Ginny said. "I'm going to find him and make him pay for what he did to her."

GRIFF TRIED ONE more time to convince Ginny to talk to Jacob, but she refused.

"I shared this with you in confidence. She wants to remain anonymous," she said, her gaze daring him to argue. "I expect you to uphold that confidence."

He debated on whether or not he could.

He'd never been a liar or a user, and he didn't want to

start now. Jacob had urged him to stick close to Ginny and see what he could learn, and he had. But now his interest was piqued in both what Ginny had relayed, and what she'd kept to herself.

That burn scar on her wrist meant she had been involved in a fire. She'd talked about an anonymous tip.

Had it been anonymous? Or someone she knew?

Or was it possible that she'd been a victim of the same man or some similar scenario?

Either way, the thought of her in danger disturbed him and roused his protective instincts.

He sat outside in his truck for a while, biding time until he went to the bar. But when Ginny hadn't ventured out of the inn a half hour later, he decided she'd play it smart and stay tucked in for the night.

He started his engine and drove to Whistler's Nightcap, hoping to glean more information about Joy's love life. The parking lot was filling up, a mixture of locals and tourists coming to the mountains for hiking and camping adventures. Soon the town would heat up with spring festivals and white-water rafting. Already hikers ready to explore the Appalachian Trail were piling in, gearing up at the local outfitters, sharing meals and drinks as they planned their excursions.

Most would never complete the two-thousand-mile trek from Georgia to Maine, but even a few hundred miles of the trail was an accomplishment that warranted a pat on the back and admiration from their families and friends.

Fletch would be busy rescuing half of them when they had accidents or suffered injuries or got lost, a common problem on the endless miles of forests and trails in the wilderness.

Griff secured his phone in his pocket, tugged his jacket hood up to ward off the drizzling rain and loped inside. But he couldn't shake the image of Ginny from his mind.

She'd looked so vulnerable and small and proud. Dammit, that pride stirred his admiration, but made dread curl in his belly.

Loud country music pulsed through the crowded interior of the bar while a band rocked out on stage. The dim light helped conceal flaws for hopeless drunks on the prowl for a good-time girl for the night.

Once upon a time, he'd played that game. Joy had been part of it.

He'd learned his lesson and hadn't engaged since. Two women at the bar, midtwenties, attractive and built, wearing skimpy outfits, gave him flirtatious looks. He shot them a half smile then walked to the opposite end and slid onto a bar stool to face the door so he'd have a view of the dance floor where couples gyrated to the music.

The bartender, a bearded, broad-shouldered gym rat named Boone, flicked his hand up in recognition, and Griff ordered an IPA. He waited until Boone brought him the beer, then motioned that he wanted to talk.

"What's up?" Boone asked.

"You heard about Joy Norris being murdered?"

Boone nodded. "Yeah, sorry to hear it. Didn't the two of you date for a while?"

"Very briefly," Griff said. "But I learned she was married at the time and that was it."

"Most of the dudes here don't give a damn if a woman has a ring." Boone made a low sound in his throat. "Truth is, half the women don't either."

A damn shame. His parents would still be married and faithful to each other if they were alive. He had a feeling Jacob and Cora, and Fletch and Jade would be the same. "Did you see Joy hanging out with anyone recently?"

Boone scratched his fingers through his beard. "She didn't come in that much. But she was here a couple of weeks ago with some guy in a suit. That's the reason it stuck out." He gestured toward the casual atmosphere. "He didn't seem to fit in."

"Were they getting along?"

"He was all over her," Boone said. "And seemed protective. Some other guy offered to buy her a drink, and the date turned all huffy and macho. I thought he was going to punch the poor bastard out."

Griff's suspicious nature surfaced. "What was the date's name?"

Boone scrunched his face in thought, then gestured to one of the waitresses that he'd work on her drink order. "Can't really remember. Something kind of uppity, like Winston or William."

"Can you describe him?"

Two guys leaned on the bar and called Boone's name. "You gonna get us a beer or talk all night?"

"Sorry, man, customers are waiting." Boone tossed the towel over his shoulder, picked up a mug and began to fill it from the tap.

"Just a quick description," Griff said.

"Tall, dressed well, sandy blond hair. Real intense guy. Not a body builder or anything but strong looking. He had these beady eyes. Kind of dude you wouldn't want to mess with."

The waitress appeared for the beer, and Boone hurried to take care of the guys who were calling his name again.

Griff stewed over the information as he studied the crowd in case the man Boone described was in the room.

But someone else caught his eye. A woman with ivory skin and soft black hair who'd just come in the door.

Ginny.

Dammit to hell, what was she doing here?

Chapter Eight

Ginny had not been on a date since her experience with Robert. Not that this was a real date, but she had to pretend.

Nerves tightened her shoulder blades as she surveyed the interior of the bar. The country music and relaxed decor didn't fit with Robert. Typically, he preferred more upscale places although Whistler wasn't exactly big-city living so the choices were limited. And it was possible he was trying to keep a low profile to avoid detection.

She headed toward the right to the adjoining dining area where the music volume was lower as were the lights, creating a more intimate atmosphere. White tablecloths, each adorned with a vase of a single rose, added a hint of romance.

Her stomach churned. Robert would choose the more intimate side.

The hostess for the restaurant side was a tall blonde who wore a simple black dress with glittery jewelry. Robert's type. Although he had told her he had a thing for redheads.

She requested a table facing the door, and the hostess escorted her to a small table in a dimly lit section.

Clutching her purse, which held her .22, in her lap, she seated herself so she could see anyone who entered or left.

Karl Cross said he'd be wearing a navy sport coat and khakis, a little underdressed for Robert, but it might be his attempt to fit into the town and not draw suspicion to himself.

She ordered water and a glass of white wine although she left the wine untouched. Didn't want alcohol interfering with her reflexes if she needed to defend herself. She sipped her water and waited, surprised at the number of single women crowding into the bar area.

She had never been a fan of the bar scene, had always thought it dangerous. The online dating site had been just as bad. The attractive profiles could easily sway a woman into believing she'd met her Prince Charming, yet in reality the person behind the face on-screen might be an amphibian beneath the facade.

A man with silver-tipped dark hair entered, then a cowboy in a Stetson. The cowboy headed toward the bar while the other man paused and looked around, then turned to the dining area. He was wearing a dark sport coat. She tensed as he scanned the room.

Not Robert. Was he Karl Cross?

She took another sip of water as he started to cross the room, but he bypassed her table and joined a middle-aged woman at the table near her. She was so busy watching the couple kiss that she didn't notice another man approaching until she felt his presence beside her table. A shadow moved into her vision, and she looked up, her chest clenching.

He was tall, dark haired, medium build, nice looking.

But he wasn't Robert.

He offered her a cocky smile. "June?"

"That's me," she said, itching to leave already. Although if Robert hadn't killed Joy, she could have met another predator online. This could be him.

He slid into the chair and raked his gaze over her. Her first instinct was to jut her chin up in challenge, but she was supposed to be quiet, shy, bookish June so refrained.

"A pleasure to meet you," he said. "You have an interesting profile."

She gave him a shy smile. "So do you. Do you live in Whistler?"

He shook his head. "I have a cabin in the mountains nearby, so I come here for relaxation between business trips."

"Do you travel a lot?"

The waitress appeared and he ordered a whiskey. "Just in the States, wherever the deals are to be made," he said as the waitress left.

"What kinds of deals?"

"Oh, a little of this and that."

Her distrust rose. He was being evasive. "Where's your home base?" Ginny asked.

"Charlotte. What about you?" he asked.

"I'm here visiting family, my grandmother," she said ad-libbing. Better he think she had someone who would miss her if she disappeared unexpectedly.

They made small talk for another few minutes, then she decided to broach the real reason she'd met him. "You don't look like you'd have trouble meeting women," she said. "Do you engage in a lot of online dating?"

He chuckled. "I *don't* have trouble," he said. "But I'm looking for a specific type."

Her skin prickled. "And what type is that?"

A flicker of interest sparked in his eyes. "Someone quiet. Humble. Women these days are flashy and forward. They don't appreciate a man taking care of them."

She barely resisted slugging him. He sounded like Robert. "Have you dated anyone else from Whistler?"

His smile disappeared. "What does that matter?"

"Just wondering if there's an old flame around who'd get jealous if she saw us together?"

"No one at the moment." His eyes darkened. "It pains me to say the last woman I was seeing died suddenly."

Ginny bit her lip to stifle a reaction. "Oh, my goodness. You weren't seeing that pretty woman named Joy, were you? I arrived in town the day after she died in that horrible fire."

The ice in his drink clinked as he lifted it for a sip. "Did you know her?"

She shook her head. "No, I just saw the news. I heard she liked to play around."

His hands tightened into fists on the table. "That's what I'm talking about. Women who aren't faithful. I can't tolerate that."

If the woman he'd dated was Joy, he'd just confirmed a motive for murder.

He reached for her hand and stroked her fingers. "But you wouldn't be like that, would you, June? You wouldn't lie to a man?"

She had had enough. He wasn't Robert, but he was despicable anyway. She pushed away from the table and stood. "You know, Karl, I don't think this is going to work."

He tightened his fingers around her wrist so hard she winced. "What? Aren't you going to give me a chance?"

She gritted her teeth. "I just don't feel like we're right for each other." She yanked at her hand to pull free, but his grip grew more intense.

"That's not fair, June. Sit back down—"

"Let the woman go."

Ginny gritted her teeth as she looked up and found Griff staring down at her and Karl with a lethal expression on his chiseled face.

NOTHING RILED GRIFF more than a bully manhandling a woman. And this creep looked as if he'd gone from friendly to psycho possessive in seconds.

The man released Ginny's wrist then angled his head and shot Griff a venomous look. "Who the hell are you?"

Griff fisted his hands by his sides. Resorting to physical force wasn't his style, but if it meant protecting Ginny and he was provoked, he wouldn't back down either. This jerk was decent-size, but he could take him in a skinny minute.

"A friend of the lady's," Griff said coldly.

Ginny shot him an irritated look and absentmindedly rubbed at her wrist, which was red from the man's tight grip.

"I can handle this, Griff," she said stiffly.

He arched a brow in challenge. Did she know this jerk? Was she actually going to defend him?

Karl shoved his chair back. "What is this? Some kind of hustle?" He narrowed his eyes at Ginny. "You plan a date, then your boyfriend jumps in for fun?"

Shock flashed across Ginny's face at the implication. "No. But this date is over."

She snatched her purse, threw it over her shoulder and brushed past Karl and Griff.

Karl stood as if to go after her, but Griff blocked his path. "You heard her. It's over. Touch her again and you'll answer to me, someone more your size."

Karl squared his shoulders, anger radiating from him. "Don't worry. She's not my type anyway."

Griff barely resisted the urge to punch the jerk. Instead, he stepped back and went after Ginny himself. The music blared louder from the bar area, and a line dance had kicked up, boots pounding the scarred wooden floor.

He hurried out the door and searched the parking lot. Ginny was climbing in her car, so he jogged over and caught the door just before she could close it. Her eyes widened, a sliver of fear darkening the depths that made him feel like a heel. He threw his hands up to indicate he meant no harm.

"Are you okay?" he asked gruffly.

Her breathing rasped out. "Yes. And by the way, I had the situation under control." Stubborn pride laced her voice.

"Of course, you did," he said. "But when I see a man roughhousing a woman, I can't help but step in. My father taught me to respect women."

His comment seemed to soften the defensive expression on her face. "Then thank you. But I really was fine."

He leaned closer to her in the open doorway of the car. "What was that about anyway? I thought you were just visiting town. Did you know that man?"

She cut her eyes away, avoiding him, then flexed her fingers around the steering wheel as if debating on how to respond. Finally, she sighed and looked back at him. "I don't want to talk about it here. Meet me back at the inn."

She bit her bottom lip, then started the engine. But she scanned the parking lot as she pulled away. Was she afraid the man inside would follow her?

Or was she was running from someone else?

GINNY DROVE TO the inn, relieved to see that Karl Cross didn't follow her. As stern as she might have been, Griff was much more intimidating.

Although why had he come to her rescue? She didn't think he liked her or wanted to talk to her. Had he followed her to the bar?

She parked and climbed out, her nerves on edge. Had Robert snuck back inside the room?

Griff parked behind her and walked over to her car. "Let's meet in the parlor," Ginny said. "There's wine and coffee at the buffet in the evenings."

Griff walked beside her as they made their way up the path to the porch. The earlier rain was dissipating, yet the wind had picked up again, blowing leaves across the lawn and sending the wind chimes on the porch into motion. The tinkling reminded her of the holidays when she and Tess had been children and had enjoyed their mother's endless litany of jingle bells that she strung everywhere. Her mother bought them silly Christmas socks every year to wear for their annual Christmas pajama photo by the tree. When she was six and Tess was four, they'd separated to choose each other's presents and ended up buying each other the same book of paper dolls.

Tears burned the backs of her eyelids. Each memory of her sister refueled her rage and anger.

Griff opened the door, and they entered the lobby, then made their way to the parlor. Thankfully it was deserted so they had the room to themselves.

She poured a glass of wine for herself, then offered Griff one from the buffet. He shook his head and chose coffee, then joined her in the seating area. The wine helped soothe her jangled nerves as she warmed herself by the fire.

Griff seated himself across from her in the big club chair. "Come on, Ginny. Who was that man?"

"I had a date," she admitted.

He raised a brow. "You came for a story and now you're dating? I don't understand."

He didn't have to, but he obviously wasn't going to let it go. Her plan to use him hadn't worked at all. He was too damn smart.

"I told you that I received a tip from an abuse victim," Ginny said. "She met the man online through one of those dating sites."

Griff's jaw tightened. "Let me guess. You joined that site hoping to meet that creep?"

Ginny ran her finger along the rim of her glass. "Like I said earlier, he disappeared. She's terrified he's looking for her."

Griff cleared his throat. "Did you get a description of the man?"

Ginny shifted. "Medium build, sandy-blondish hair, dressed well. He likes nice restaurants and wine."

Griff tensed. "The bartender gave a similar description of a man Joy was in there with once. He thought his name was Winston or William."

Ginny paused with her glass halfway to her lips. "He said his name was Karl Cross. He became defensive when I asked about Joy, and he said the last woman he dated died suddenly."

"I'll ask Jacob and Liam to investigate him."

Ginny traced a finger around the rim of her glass. "I told you I don't want to talk to the cops. Whatever I share with you is confidential."

Griff made a low sound of frustration in his throat. "For God's sake, Ginny, I'm just trying to help. You have to get over this paranoia about the police."

"That's impossible when this woman's attacker bought off a cop to find out where she was hiding, and he nearly killed her."

Tension charged the air between them. "I'm sorry that happened, but I assure you my brothers are decent. They'll do everything they can to track down this bastard and make him pay."

Ginny leaned forward, desperate to believe him.

But his brothers would only get in her way.

GRIFF STUDIED GINNY for a moment. Although he sensed she'd told him multiple lies, if what she'd said about the cop accepting a bribe was true, he understood her distrust of the law. Arguing with her would only push her further away. He'd learn more by keeping her close and agreeing to work with her. "All right, I'll keep your confidence," he replied. "But trust works both ways. You aren't allowed to print anything I tell you unless I clear it with Jacob first."

Ginny pasted on her game face. "Of course."

"Do you think the man you met tonight was the same one who attacked your source?"

She shook her head. "I don't know. But have your brother check him out. If he dated Joy, he might be the man you're hunting."

"What online dating site did you use?"

Ginny stretched out her legs. "Meet Your Mate."

Seeing that man put his hands on Ginny bothered Griff more than he wanted to admit. He told himself his reaction was simple protective instincts that he'd feel for any woman, but something about the pained note in Ginny's voice tore at his heartstrings on a more personal level.

"You're playing with fire by trying to lure this predator," he said huskily.

Ginny finished her wine and stood. "You're not going to change my mind. So, remember our deal."

He clenched his jaw as she walked away, removed his phone from his belt and punched Liam's number to ask him to dig up everything he could on Karl Cross and that dating site. He'd also ask him to look at other cases involving strangulation and arson.

Like it or not, he didn't intend to let Ginny use herself as bait and get herself killed.

Chapter Nine

Ginny watched Griff leave with a mixture of admiration and trepidation. He was a strong man. Could be dangerous. She'd seen that flare of temper in his eyes when he'd ordered Karl to release his grip on her. And he'd pinned her with a stare that made her feel uncomfortable.

Yet as much as she hesitated to trust him, she didn't think he'd hurt her. At least not physically. His protective streak seemed to be *for* her, not in a possessive way, but in the chivalrous way she'd only seen in the movies.

Could it be real?

It didn't matter. She was here for one reason and one reason only. To find the man who'd killed her sister. As soon as she reached her room, she'd call that real estate developer again. Maybe if she was persistent enough, he'd return her call.

Moving on autopilot, she scanned the main lobby of the inn as she approached the stairs. Not that she thought Karl Cross would have followed her here, but a woman could never be too careful. One lunatic in her life was enough.

Another reason to avoid men.

She'd just made a deal with one though. *To share information, nothing more.*

She mulled over the tidbit Griff had shared. The man Joy was with at the bar could have been Robert. If he'd gone by William or Winston, maybe she could find his profile on the dating site.

A light rain began to fall again, and fog formed on the picture windows in the front. For a moment, her vision blurred, and she thought she saw a man standing by the trees flanking the drive.

He wore a long dark trench coat and hat and seemed to be staring at her.

Robert?

Heart pounding, she slid her hand over her purse, then reached inside for her weapon. The wind kicked up, trees swaying outside. A tree branch snapped at the windowpane. Rain fell, fat drops splattering the glass.

She hurried to the front door but when she opened it, there was no one there.

Heaving a breath, she shut the door, turned and fled to-ward the stairs. Her foot slid on the slick wood, and she grabbed the rail to steady herself, then forced herself to slow down as she climbed to the second floor. If Robert was out there, he was gone. At least for the moment.

She glanced down the hall at the top of the stairs to make sure he hadn't somehow gotten inside, then hurried toward her room. Hands trembling, she fumbled with her key, then jammed it in the lock and opened the door. The cloying scent of Robert's aftershave still clung to the air. Or was it fresh?

Entering on shaky legs, she pulled her gun and scanned the sitting area then rounded the alcove to the bed. A cry lodged in her throat at the sight of the white lilies lying on the bed.

Lilies are for purity, Robert had said. *Just like I want you to be pure for me.*

Tears spilled over as she surveyed the room and eased toward the bathroom. A bath had been run. Rose petals floated in the water. A bottle of champagne sat on the bathroom counter with two champagne flutes waiting.

And then the note.

Sleep tight, love. Soon you'll be in my arms again. Very soon.

GRIFF PHONED JACOB to relay his conversation with Ginny as soon as he made it to his cabin.

"Did she mention where this attack happened? In North Carolina or another state?" Jacob asked.

Dammit, he should have probed her for more information, but his specialty was to extinguish and investigate fires, not serve as a detective in a homicide investigation. "No. The next time I see her I can find out. But since she's from Asheville, it's probable that it occurred in North Carolina."

"I'll ask Liam to look for a case that fits this scenario."

Griff entered his house and punched in the code to the alarm. "Anything on the forensics from the last fire?"

"The lab just called. They have a match on some prints. A couple of teenagers at the high school. A kid named Jerome Miller who was caught shoplifting cigarettes at a gas station, and Randy Henner. Randy was caught driving without a license."

"Both are petty crimes, and a big jump to escalate to arson," Griff said.

"I know. If these teens are already taking risks and looking for a rush, booze might have triggered their behavior to escalate."

"Boys will be boys getting out of hand," Griff muttered.

"Maybe. The assembly at the school is tomorrow at ten. I contacted the principal and told her I plan to question the boys afterward."

"I'll be there."

"One more thing, Griff. Bring a picture of Ginny if you

can get one, and Liam can run it so we can find out who she really is."

An uneasy feeling tightened Griff's chest. He didn't like spying on anyone behind their back. But Ginny was playing a dangerous game, and he didn't want her to get hurt, so he agreed.

Maybe Liam would confirm she was exactly who she claimed to be, and that he could trust her.

He told Jacob about the dating site. "If Joy met her killer on this site, we need to explore it."

"I'll call forensics again and see if they've been able to recover anything from Joy's computer." Jacob paused. "See you tomorrow."

Griff muttered agreement, then poured himself a whiskey. He needed some sleep, but how could he sleep when he was worried a killer might be targeting Ginny?

Ginny stood frozen and trembling, reliving every horrific memory of Robert in her head as the rose petals bobbed gently across the bathwater.

When they'd first met, Robert had turned her head with flattering compliments and sweet nothings he'd whispered in her ear. He'd wined and dined her and promised to support her while she finished her degree. He'd carried her shopping bags at designer boutiques and lavished her with expensive jewelry to ensure she dressed in style.

She'd insisted she didn't need fancy clothes or jewelry, that she was a simple girl who liked homemade meals and quiet nights, one who dreamed of a family of her own someday.

He'd given those words lip service, but three months into the relationship, he announced he didn't want children, and he certainly didn't want her body to be disfigured with a pregnancy. Appearances mattered to him. She had to work out. Diet. Learn how to dress and behave.

Be the perfect wife.

That meant looking good on his arm and entertaining his friends and clients in the home he intended to design for them. A glass house where she would have to tiptoe around on eggshells for the rest of her life.

She'd realized then that they weren't a match. Home was about family and loving each other, not being perfect or about surface appearances or impressing rich strangers who tossed money around like it was nothing.

That night she'd told him so, and he'd become irate. Told her she owed him and should be grateful for all he'd done for her.

That he would never let her go.

She lifted her fingers and traced them across her throat, a suffocating feeling overcoming her as she recalled his fingers pressing into her vocal cords. His words had hammered home her reservations and she'd decided she had to leave. When he'd found her packing, he'd announced she had to be taught a lesson then he'd tried to strangle her.

She'd screamed and fought him, but he'd dug his fingers into her windpipe and for a moment she'd almost passed out. But in the struggle, she'd managed to grab a lamp and she'd smashed it against his head. He released her and she'd run for the door, but he'd chased her down, then given her a beating she'd never forget.

A lesson she deserved, he claimed as she lay bleeding and hurting on the floor. Later, he'd pulled her against him, comforted her, then run her a bath and sat beside her to nurse her wounds as she'd shivered in shock.

But his plan had backfired. The rage had built inside her that night like a fire that couldn't be extinguished. Instead of coercing her as he'd planned, he'd done the opposite. The first strike across her face had cemented her determination to leave him and given birth to hatred.

Outside the wind banged against the glass, startling her

back to the present. She swallowed hard to chase the memories back into the darkness, then summoned her strength. Tess's sweet face flashed behind her eyes, and she wiped at tears.

She hurried to the bedroom door and locked it, then dragged the dresser in front of the doorway. Furious at Robert for unnerving her with his games, she let the bathwater run down the drain, threw the rose petals into the trash and poured the champagne down the sink. The bottle went into the trash, then she snagged the lilies from the bed and added them to the pile.

Fueled with adrenaline, she opened her laptop and began combing the dating site for a man named William or Winston who fit Robert's general description. Twenty minutes later, after scrolling through a dozen Williams, and three Winstons, she found a possible match. William Roberts.

Roberts? Could he have used his first name as his last in the profile?

Again, the man's face was hidden in shadows. He had a short beard, neatly trimmed, and stood by a Mercedes wearing a dark pin-striped suit. Enjoyed French wines. International cuisine. Had made his money in the stock market.

His profile fit.

She sent him a message saying she'd like to meet, then pulled on her pajamas, grabbed her gun and crawled into bed. She kept the bathroom light on and turned on her side, so she faced the door with her weapon gripped in her hand, ready to shoot if he decided to slip in during the night.

THE NEXT MORNING Griff showed up at the school assembly a half hour early to meet Jacob.

"No word from Liam yet," Jacob said. "But he's investigating Ginny Bagwell, murders and attempted murders involving strangulation and arson."

Griff had thought about Ginny all night. Something

wasn't right with her story. If Jacob uncovered information he could share with her, maybe she'd open up.

Both the principal and the school counselor, Linette Akron, met them in the gymnasium as the kids filed in. Griff was not a fan of public speaking, but this was a serious matter. He'd spent the morning compiling photos of the recent fires and had thrown a few less graphic shots of burn victims into the mix. His audience was young and impressionable, but God knows they'd become somewhat desensitized to violence and trauma from the news and school shootings and had to face the reality of the dangers of the fires. The counselor stood by in the event a student needed help or became emotional.

The principal called the assembly to order and explained the reason for the meeting, then introduced Griff. Jacob situated himself by the door nearest where the two boys in question had been strategically seated.

"We're here today because of a very serious matter," the principal began. "In the past few weeks, there have been a series of wildfires along the AT in our area, one of which was not far from the school and the town of Whistler." She gestured to Griff. "Today one of our local firefighters from station house 7 is here to discuss these fires."

Griff stepped up to the podium and cleared his throat, then opened with a general explanation of arson. The PowerPoint he'd prepared showed pictures of the actual fires and how close they'd spread to campsites and a residential area. When the photographs of burn victims and corpses appeared, shocked gasps reverberated through the gym.

"We're discussing this today because we need your help." Griff clicked to show a photo of the beer bottles and matchbook recovered from the scene. "These items were discovered near the point of origin of the fire." Another photo revealed the lighter fluid. "Although it's possible the fires were small campfires where someone was drinking and partying, then the fire got out of hand or wasn't extinguished properly, evidence suggests the fires were intentionally set."

The teens in the room began to shift and make noises of discomfort.

One of the boys in question looked panicked and glanced at the exit sign, but Jacob moved to the edge of the row where he sat, made eye contact with him and shook his head.

"We need you to let us know if you've seen or heard anything, any chatter, about these fires at school, off the school grounds or online." The students shifted again, fear and panic flitting through the group.

Griff adopted a nonconfrontational stance. "I'm sure none of you want to see anyone hurt or killed by these wildfires. If you have information, please tell your parents, the counselor, or call the sheriff. Because if there are injuries or casualties, the arson charge will be elevated to manslaughter or possibly homicide."

More gasps, indicating he'd gotten their attention.

The counselor stepped up to offer her services, emphasizing anonymity. She'd already established a special drop box for the students to report instances of bullying, drugs or weapons on campus, and urged the students to use it now.

As soon as the principal dismissed the assembly and the kids began to file out, Jacob cornered the two boys in question. Due to the fact that they were minors, their parents had been asked to meet in the counselor's office where the boys would be questioned.

Jacob assured Griff he'd keep him abreast if he got a confession, and Griff paced the entryway in the school.

All night he'd been haunted by images of Ginny being attacked or strangled.

He hoped to hell she was safe.

HE THUMBED THROUGH the photographs he'd snapped of Reese while she darted around Whistler asking questions about Joy Norris's murder. She'd thought she was hiding out all this time, and he'd let her believe it.

Decided time and distance might make her miss him. Appreciate him.

Laughter rippled in his throat as he traced a finger over her heart-shaped face. Joy had reminded him so much of Reese with her auburn hair that when he'd closed his eyes and pounded himself inside her, he'd imagined it was Reese.

But then she opened her sassy mouth to talk in that nasal like voice, and he saw her face. Makeup smeared and too-red lipstick. She'd looked ugly.

Just like the others. No one could replace Reese because she was perfect.

And she was his.

Once he got her back, he'd make sure she knew it. And she'd never leave him again.

Chapter Ten

Robert was toying with her. Playing hide-and-seek to frighten her. Enjoying keeping her on edge.

And it was working.

Ginny kept her gun in the bathroom while she showered and dressed. As she checked the dating site on her computer, her phone pinged that she had a message, and she quickly checked it. It was Thad Rigden, the real estate developer buying up the block of businesses housing Joy's Nail Salon.

The voice sounded slightly higher-pitched than Robert's, but if this man was Robert, he could have disguised it. He suggested they meet for coffee at Mitzi's at ten-thirty, so she agreed, then spent the next half hour scrolling through online dating profiles reviewing every William and Winston she could find.

The man she'd pinged the night before responded that he'd like to meet her for a drink around five. She confirmed, then stowed her gun inside her purse, grabbed her jacket and headed outside. She checked the hallway in all directions, then hurried downstairs. Pausing at the bottom of the stairwell, she scanned the entryway and parlor. An older couple was enjoying coffee and a late breakfast, and two young women dressed for hiking rushed out the door, backpacks slung over their shoulders.

A gusty breeze whipped her hair around her face as she

stepped outside, and a cigarette glowed near a tree at the edge of the woods.

Robert?

He hadn't smoked cigarettes when she'd known him but had occasionally enjoyed a cigar. She thought about the wildfires Griff had been putting out and wondered if Robert could possibly be responsible. Deciding she needed the exercise, she veered onto the sidewalk leading to the heart of town, keeping one hand securely on her purse to give her easy access to her gun if needed as she walked to Mitzi's.

A midmorning crowd filled the café, a mixture of retirees, campers and hikers preparing to set out on the AT. She waved to Mitzi as she entered, then started to take a booth near the front, but Mitzi motioned for her to follow her.

"That real estate developer is back here," Mitzi said as she led Ginny through the center of the café to a booth in the corner near the back.

Ginny's stomach tightened as they approached. The man was facing the rear wall with his face away from her. He had short, neatly groomed brown hair, and a gold signet ring glittered from his hand as he lifted his coffee cup for a sip.

Robert had worn a gold signet ring with the letter *R* etched in the design. The imprint of it on her cheek had lingered for days after he'd hit her.

GRIFF WAITED FOR Jacob in the entrance of the school while Jacob questioned the two boys he'd identified as persons of interest. Memories of attending Whistler High flooded back.

Griff had played defense on the high school soccer team and helped them make it to the state championships. School shootings and drugs and violence had not been part of his experience. Boys had roughhoused, enjoyed off-roading and met girls behind the bleachers to make out. Not one for online social media, he'd attended high school pep rallies, football games, dances in the gym and he'd hung out by the river with friends.

On camping trips, his father had taught him and his brothers how to read maps, fish and kayak. He'd loved the fresh air, outdoors and endless miles of forests. Sure, he and his brothers had sneaked a few beers in their day, but they'd been harmless and respected the land and the people in town.

His father had run for sheriff to protect the residents and had instilled the same values in him and his brothers. Each of them had become first responders to honor him.

Then that fire had taken his life. Gone in a minute.

Griff should have insisted his father stay outside that horrible day. His father hadn't been prepared to run into the fiery building. Hadn't been wearing safety equipment. No oxygen mask or helmet or fireproof clothing.

But the fire had created such chaos, and with so many lives in danger, his father hadn't thought once about joining the rescue attempts. Dozens of sick patients, disabled, people in wheelchairs and bedridden needed help. Mothers and children and babies were among the needy, too.

They'd tried to save them all. And even then, they'd failed.

Footsteps dragged him from the haunting memory. Jacob approached him, grim faced. Griff expected him to escort the boys to the jail, but he was alone. The teens' parents were accompanying the boys through the exit.

Jacob paused to shake hands with the principal and counselor, then joined Griff.

"What happened? Aren't you making arrests?" Griff asked.

Jacob motioned for them to go outside, and they left together, then walked over to Jacob's squad car.

Jacob scrubbed a hand over his chin. "Both boys admitted to drinking in the woods, to smoking a couple of cigarettes and building a campfire on two occasions. But they claim they covered the fire with mounds of dirt before they left."

"Could have accidentally started back up."

Jacob shook his head. "That's just it. Both kids have alibis for the nights of the wildfires that spread. Parents confirmed they were home studying for tests during the time of the first fire, and one of the teachers verified that the boys play baseball and had an away game during the time of that last one."

Griff muttered a frustrated sound. "If they didn't set the fires, maybe some other kids are responsible."

"That's possible, but I'm beginning to wonder if it was teens."

"Why do you say that?"

"The boys mentioned seeing a man in a long coat and hat with binoculars on a hill near the locations of the fires. They both insisted they'd seen his footprints around before, up around Raven's Ridge."

"I'll go back and search that area," Griff said. "If whoever they saw is our arsonist, he may have left some evidence behind."

GINNY SLID HER hand inside her purse and gripped her gun as she walked around the table. Her legs felt shaky, but anger heated her blood as she braced herself to face Robert once more.

The man stood and lifted his hand, the signet ring glittering beneath the overhead light. This man was the right height and build, but his eyes were set farther apart, his nose slightly longer, and his forehead not as high. Not Robert.

Relief mingled with frustration. Dammit, she wanted to get this over with. Make Robert confront her so she could… kill him? Could she really pull the trigger?

Tess's sweet face taunted her, and she swallowed hard. Yes, hell, yes, she could.

But this man hadn't killed her sister. She was wasting her time. Unless…he'd killed Joy and the similarities were coincidental.

The man extended his hand. "Thad Rigden. You're Ginny Bagwell, the woman who called about looking for property in town?"

Ginny nodded and claimed the chair across from him. Mitzi appeared, and she ordered plain coffee while he ordered a latte.

"Tell me about yourself, Ginny," Thad said. "Where are you from and what do you do?"

"I live in Asheville," she said simply. "And actually, I'm a journalist."

His eyebrow rose. "I thought you were looking for property for a business." He sipped his coffee. "Or did I misunderstand your message?"

"I'm sorry to mislead you," she said, deciding to opt for a half-truth. "I talked to Joy Norris's neighbors and they said you offered to purchase her property. That you had plans to rebuild the entire block."

His friendly smile faded. "That's true. Everyone except Joy agreed to sell. But I thought I could convince her to do so in time."

"Really?"

"Yes, I suspected she was holding out for more money, so I was working on securing a more lucrative deal for her."

"I see. But now that she's dead, it'll probably be easier to take over."

He narrowed his eyes. "Actually, that's not how it works. If she didn't have a specific will dictating who the property went to, it will go into probate. That could take months which will slow down the entire project."

That was true. "Did she have a will?"

Irritation carved frown lines around his mouth. "I don't know. Since the police ruled her death a homicide, nothing can happen until the investigation is complete."

"One of the other store owners mentioned that Joy had a silent partner. Do you know who that was?"

"No. If I had, I would have tried to convince him or her to talk some sense into Joy." He studied her with hooded eyes. "Now, Ms. Bagwell, why are you asking me these questions?"

Ginny knotted her hands in her lap under the table. "I had the impression the two of you were more than business acquaintances."

A flicker of unease settled across his features. "We had dinner a few times, but it was mostly business. I thought if I showed her my plans for the development, she'd be swayed into selling."

"But it didn't work?"

"No, she was stubborn," he muttered.

"That must have angered you, especially if your business plans relied on her cooperation."

A muscle ticked in his jaw. "If you're suggesting that I killed Joy because she refused to sell, you're way off base. Maybe you should talk to the sheriff instead of running around making accusations."

"I did speak to him, but he isn't sharing."

"That's for damn sure. I asked him what happened, but he shut me down. Even implied that I might have killed her to get hold of her property, just like you did." He released an angry sigh, stood and tossed his napkin on the table. "If I were you, Ms. Bagwell, I'd go back to Asheville. If you keep running around making accusations, you might end up like Joy."

GRIFF CALLED FLETCH, explained his conversation with Jacob and asked him to meet him at the put-in to the trail near Raven's Ridge. There, Griff led the way. Three miles in, they passed the point of origin for the latest wildfire.

The ridge overlooked the burned area, so the arsonist could have set it, then climbed to higher ground and watched it sizzle along the forest floor, eating up leaves, twigs and brittle grass as it spread.

Although crime-scene investigators had combed the area, he and Griff searched the territory again to make sure they hadn't missed something. When they were satisfied they hadn't, they climbed upward toward the ridge, following the path leading to the top. More rain threatened as dark clouds rumbled and swallowed the light from the sky.

Griff and Fletch hiked past trees so thick they had to turn sideways to weave between them. When they reached the top, the steep overhang jutted out over the woods below and offered an expansive view of where the fire had started.

The perfect place for an arsonist to watch his handiwork and bask in the glory as the flames licked higher and higher.

Griff and Fletch divided up and searched separate areas, the threat of bad weather forcing them not to waste time. Near a cluster of hemlocks leading away from the overhang, Griff spotted boot prints that had been somewhat protected from being washed away by the rain the night before. He shone his light along the edges and thought they might be able to make a cast, then noticed a path of crushed weeds a few feet from the prints.

He panned his light across the brush. Something shiny was trapped in the weeds. He pulled on gloves, and stooped to his knees. His fingers brushed over the shiny metal object, and he freed it, then held it up to examine it. A lighter—fancy, expensive, with the emblem of a black panther on the side.

Not one teens would own.

A hiker on the trail could have dropped it. But considering the location where he'd found it and the proximity to the latest wildfire, it raised suspicion. He bagged it and put it in his pocket, then strode over to Fletch where he finished making the cast of the boot print. They searched for another hour. Unfortunately, they found nothing else. Rain threatening, they hiked down the mountain to their vehicles.

"I'll run these by Jacob's office," Fletch offered.

"Thanks." The lighter might belong to the arsonist, but the fact that Joy's business and home had also burned down was seeming less like a coincidence. And more like they could be connected.

Which led him back to Ginny Bagwell.

She'd been shaken the night before. Had bruises where she'd fallen—or been pushed. He'd warned her she was flirting with danger.

What if something had happened to her while he'd been gone today?

GINNY SPENT THE afternoon at the coffee shop researching Thad Rigden on her computer. She looked for anything she could find indicating he was shady, dangerous or that he might have killed Joy out of anger over the fact that she refused to sell.

He had been through a nasty divorce settlement, which had gone public when his wife sued him for half of their assets, assets that amounted to almost a million dollars. The wife had filed a restraining order against Thad during the divorce proceedings with claims of intimidation tactics.

Had he used those tactics on Joy and the situation had spiraled out of control? Was he so desperate for the investment opportunity to replenish the money he'd given his wife that he'd resort to murder?

The clock on the wall ticked off the minutes to the next hour, and she realized it was time to meet her next date from Meet Your Mate. She hurried back to the inn and changed into a nice sweater and black slacks, then walked to the wine bar William Roberts had suggested.

As always, she checked her surroundings and seated herself to face the doorway. For the next hour, she watched couples and individuals come and go, but her date didn't show. Wondering if she'd misread the time and place, she checked her phone for messages and reviewed the original interchange. No. She had the date, time and place correct.

The creep had stood her up.

Annoyed, she polished off the one glass of merlot she'd allowed herself to sip while waiting, paid the bill, gathered her purse and headed outside. More dark storm clouds threatened, thunder rumbling, and she increased her pace hoping to make it back to the inn before another deluge of rain descended.

The sun had come and gone while she was in the wine bar, and night had fallen with the temperature dropping again, adding a crispness to the air. Just as she passed the alley between Mitzi's and the craft store, footsteps pounded behind her.

She halted, sliding her hand to open her purse, then spun around to see who was there. A shadow moved into her vision, then suddenly jumped her. She tried to steady herself, but two strong hands shoved her backward and she hit the brick wall and fell into the dark alley.

Chapter Eleven

A shadow in the alley just past Mitzi's caught Griff's eyes as he drove toward the inn. He slowed, wondering if it was a lost tourist or someone attempting to break in the back door of the café. Occasionally drifters or vagrants Dumpster dived for food outside the restaurants. With tourist season beginning, sometimes seedy or questionable loners crept in to hide out on the trail, so it could mean trouble.

He eased into a parking spot at the diner, climbed out and walked toward the alley. Sounds of scuffling and voices echoed from the dark corner.

"Get off me, you bastard!"

Griff's instincts roared to life, and he darted into the alley. Ginny. She was on the ground fighting off an attacker. Before he could reach her, she shoved the man off her. Then she raised her feet and kicked him hard. He flew backward with a grunt, then dove at her again. But she lurched to her feet and threw her arms up in a defensive move that looked as if she'd been trained in self-defense. The man went for her throat with both hands, but she balled her right hand into a knot and punched him in the face. He bellowed, blood spurting from his nose, and lunged at her.

Enraged, Griff glanced in the alley in search of a stick or something he could use as a weapon, but it was too damn dark to see. Clenching his hands into fists, he jogged toward the creep. The man must have heard him, because he turned his head toward Griff. Shadows clouded Griff's vision, and the dark hoodie the man wore hid his features. The only thing he could tell was that he was medium build and height and wore all dark clothing.

His sound of rage rent the air, then he darted down the alley in the opposite direction.

Griff ran toward Ginny, calling her name. She seemed startled to see him and was trying to push herself up to stand. Her hair was tangled, her clothes disheveled, her eyes wide with fear and anger.

He gripped her arms to steady her and surveyed her features for injuries. Blood dotted her lower lip, and her cheek looked red. The damn bastard had hit her. "Are you okay?"

She nodded, but she was trembling and swayed as if dizzy. He pulled her up against him and wrapped his arms around her. "It's okay. You're safe now." He rubbed slow circles over her back and dropped a tender kiss in her hair. "It's over. He's gone now and can't hurt you."

She gripped his arms, her breathing erratic and choppy. Griff soothed her again, then helped her to the bench in front of Mitzi's. "Stay here and call Jacob. I'm going after him!" He didn't give her time to protest. He squeezed her arm again, then took off running down the alley.

He jogged to the end, then checked both directions. A flash of something across the street caught his eye, and he raced across the intersection. By the time he made it to the other side, he'd lost sight of the figure. Halting by the streetlight, he scanned the parking lot and storefronts, but he'd disappeared.

Dammit.

Heaving a breath, he studied the area again, but the only people he saw were a couple walking their dog and an older man pushing his walker toward a Cadillac near the Italian restaurant. Frustrated but concerned for Ginny, he hurried back down the alley and found her still waiting on the park bench in front of Mitzi's. She looked shaken and angry as he approached her.

He dropped onto the bench beside her. "Did you call Jacob?"

She shook her head.

"Why not?"

She rubbed at the scar on her wrist. "I told you I don't like the police."

Griff had had enough of her stubbornness. "Ginny, you were just attacked. That man could have killed you."

When she lifted her head, the emotions in her eyes nearly brought him to his knees. "I know that. But I was prepared."

His mind raced. "You may have taken a few self-defense classes, but he still could have overtaken you. For God's sake, you've been asking questions about Joy's death. That could have been her killer."

"I'm well aware of that."

Griff pulled his phone from the clip on his belt. "We have to report this to Jacob. And this time I refuse to accept no for an answer."

She reached up and placed her hands over his. "Please, Griff, don't."

"I'm sorry," he murmured. "Jacob has to know."

The disappointment in her expression made guilt knot his belly. But he pressed his brother's number anyway. Like it or not, he didn't intend to stand by and watch men attack women in his town and get away with it.

GINNY'S FIRST INSTINCT was to run. She could flee town, drive to another place and start hiding out all over again.

But that was no life. And doing so gave Robert the power he wanted over her.

He'd said she'd never escape him. And even in hiding, she hadn't because he dominated her thoughts. She looked for him on every corner, in every store, in every restaurant or café she went to. He haunted her sleep at night and every waking minute of the day. His menacing voice whispered her name when she stepped outside, or even in the shower. Especially when she was alone at night.

She'd been alone now for three years. Ever since he'd taken Tess from her.

She straightened her spine. This time she would not run. She would stay and fight. For Tess. And for herself.

"Let's go to my truck," Griff said. "We can wait on Jacob there."

She nodded although she couldn't quite look at Griff. He might see through her if she did.

Now that the adrenaline of the attack was wearing off, pain racked her body. She rolled her shoulder to alleviate the soreness and flexed her hands. Suddenly cold through and through, she began to tremble.

Griff walked her to his truck and unlocked it, then helped her inside and started the engine. He retrieved a blanket from the backseat. "Come here." He leaned toward her and gently wrapped it around her. Tears burned the backs of her eyelids.

Tears she refused to let fall in front of him.

But his tenderness touched a chord deep inside her, and she allowed him to pull her up against him and hold her for a minute.

"Are you hurt?" he murmured against her hair.

Just her pride. But she bit back the words and shook her head no.

"Did you see his face?" he asked.

Had she? She closed her eyes and struggled to recall the details of the assault. She'd been so careful, watching everywhere she went. But he'd come out of nowhere and jumped her from behind. He was strong. About Robert's height and weight.

Had she smelled his cologne?

"Ginny, did you recognize him?"

"No," she said honestly. She had her suspicions but, she couldn't be certain it had been Robert. Robert would have said something more. He wanted her to know he was watching. He would have whispered her name to taunt her, or at least used his pet name for her.

Love.

His tone had been so endearing in the beginning that the nickname had made her heart swell with affection. She'd felt lucky that he'd chosen her.

God…

She'd thought he'd take care of her, be her partner for life. But the day she'd realized the true man beneath the facade, his tone had changed drastically.

If he was watching her and he saw her talk to the sheriff, he'd assume she'd told the police about him. That would only intensify his rage.

"Do you want to talk about the attack?" Griff asked gruffly.

She lifted her head and blinked away emotions she didn't want to feel. No man could be as tender and tough as Griff appeared to be. It wasn't real.

She couldn't allow herself to believe that it was.

GRIFF RUBBED GINNY'S BACK in slow, soothing circles. She felt so small and vulnerable in his arms that he wanted to keep her there where she was safe.

He hadn't liked seeing that man jump her. Hadn't liked it one damn bit.

She might think she was tough, but that man outweighed her by at least fifty pounds.

Jacob drove up beside Griff's truck, lights twirling, and Griff reluctantly pulled away. He couldn't become involved with Ginny when she was keeping secrets.

He opened the door, stepped out and met Jacob by his truck.

Jacob folded his arms and glanced at Ginny. "What happened?"

"I was driving over to check on her when I saw her in the alley. Some guy attacked her, and she was fighting him off."

Jacob raised a brow. "Did you get a look at him?"

Griff shook his head. "Not a good one. Medium height and build dressed in all dark clothing. Wore a hoodie that half covered his face."

"Does Ginny know who it was?"

"She claims she doesn't and that she didn't see his face."

"You believe her?"

A tense second passed. Then Griff cleared his throat. "I want to."

Jacob muttered a curse. "All right. Stay with her and I'll search the alley, then we'll go to the station to file an incident report. I'm going to ask a couple of my deputies to search around town as well."

Jacob retrieved his flashlight and crime kit from his car and headed down the alley. Griff got back in his truck. Ginny had recovered slightly, brushed through her hair with her fingers and looked a little calmer. Although she sported a bruise on her cheek now, and her knuckle was scraped. Anger at the sight churned in his belly, and he gritted his teeth. "Jacob wants to search the alley, then we'll head to the station to file an incident report."

"That's really not necessary," Ginny said. "The man is long gone, and I can't identify him."

"Maybe he left some evidence behind in the scuffle," Griff said. "Something that will help us nail the creep."

Ginny fidgeted and turned to look out the window. Silence stretched between them as they waited.

"What made you decide to go into investigative journalism?" he asked.

She pursed her lips in thought. "My father was a journalist," Ginny said. "He used to travel the world and un-cover stories about cover-ups with large corporations. I thought it was interesting that he helped people by expos-ing the truth."

Griff had never thought about journalism like that.

She shifted and twisted her hands together. "When I was little, I carried a notebook around and eavesdropped on people's conversations. Then I'd make up elaborate sto-ries about what they were talking about or where they were going." The memory brought a smile to her face.

"Your father must be proud of you," he said quietly.

"He died when I was twelve. A hit man for one of the companies he was investigating," Ginny said, pain lacing her voice.

Griff understood about wanting to please and impress your father. "I'm sorry you lost him that young. Did the man who killed him go to prison?"

"Yes, but it took a couple of years for the police to make the case." Ginny swallowed. "You lost yours in the fire that happened in Whistler, didn't you?"

"You did your homework."

"I'm sorry." Her tone grew soft, sincere. "He died a hero though."

"Yeah, but my brothers and I want justice for his death. And we won't give up until we get it."

THEY HAD MORE in common than Ginny thought.

His comment made her question herself though. Would her father be proud of her?

No. She'd been a fool to fall for a slick charmer and should have recognized the signs that he was abusive be-fore she agreed to the second date.

But she'd worn blinders and been snowed by his com-pliments, his gifts and attention. Tess had always been the pretty sister, the one the boys chased, while she'd buried her nose in a book and been more interested in researching stories on the internet than relating to students her own age.

And now Tess, his pretty little princess, had died because of Ginny's stupidity and foolishness.

Her father had also stood for good, had wanted to expose the seedy side of big corporations and help the underdogs who were unknowing victims.

What would he think about her plan to avenge Tess's death?

"Jacob is back," Griff said, cutting into her thoughts.

Ginny steeled herself against her emotions. Griff was a stubborn man. No sense arguing with him at the moment. He started the engine and followed Jacob to the police station. Ginny's nerves bristled as she entered, the memory of begging the police for their help hitting her with the force of a fist. The skeptical looks. The questions. The pitying stares.

The fact that she'd trusted them and one officer had betrayed her just as Robert had.

Who could she trust now?

Jacob led them past the receptionist and down a hall to his office. A deputy glanced up as they passed, a curious look in his eyes, unnerving Ginny even more.

Jacob gave her a visual once-over, his expression grim. "First of all, do you need a doctor?"

She shook her head. "I was just shaken, that's all."

"Your cheek is bruised, and your hands scraped," Griff cut in.

Ginny glared at him. She didn't need him pointing out that she'd nearly lost the battle with the man.

Jacob gestured for them to sit, and he returned a couple of minutes later with two coffees. He gave one to Griff and offered the other to her. Chilled from the ordeal, she took the cup and cradled it in her hands just to warm herself.

"This is a waste of time," Ginny said before Jacob could

speak. "I didn't see the man's face. I can't give you a description, and I don't know who he was or why he jumped me."

"You're nosing around into a murder investigation," Jacob said. "That sounds like reason to me."

The two men exchanged silent looks that Ginny didn't quite know how to read. A brotherhood bond, she guessed. Just like she and Tess had once shared as sisters.

"Walk me through your day." Jacob slid a legal pad in front of her. "Write down the names of anyone you talked to." His voice was blunt. "And don't leave out anyone. Including the men you met on that dating site."

Ginny barely stifled a gasp. "How did you know about that?"

Jacob shrugged. "Griff mentioned that's how your anonymous source met the man who hurt her, so that would be a logical place to start."

She let his comment slide. If Robert hadn't killed Joy, one of the men from the site or the real estate developer could have. Jacob could investigate them and free her up to deal with Robert.

Unless William Roberts had been Robert. He could have set up the date to lure her away from Griff, then watched from afar as she waited on him to arrive. Then he'd stood her up, followed her and attacked her in the alley.

She quickly jotted down the names, then pushed the pad toward Jacob.

He folded his arms and studied her. "Do you have a sketch or photo of the man this source of yours dated? The one who allegedly attacked her?"

Ginny stood, furious. "I'm working on it." She turned and glared at Griff. "This is the reason I said no police. I don't like being interrogated as if I'm a suspect."

"Miss Bagwell, I'm trying to find out who assaulted you

and solve a murder investigation," the sheriff said. "Without your cooperation, that's impossible."

She tapped the notepad. "There's your list."

She started for the door, but Griff cleared his throat. "Ginny, wait. Is there anyone else who would want to hurt you?"

HIS PLAN WAS WORKING. Reese, who called herself Ginny now, was on edge. By now, she must have seen the flowers he'd left for her in her room. And she'd gotten his message. Knew he was watching.

That he'd have her soon.

Rage knifed through him though as he remembered that big fireman rescuing her in the alley. Hell, he'd been on the verge of coming to her rescue when the bastard jumped in to be her hero.

Had she started hooking up with him? With other strangers?

Apparently so. She'd rejoined that damned dating site. He'd been monitoring it for months just in case she resurfaced.

Worse, the fireman seemed to be buddy-buddy with the sheriff. Mitzi said they were brothers.

Had Reese, Ginny, told the police about him? Had she shown them a photo from his first profile?

It didn't matter. He didn't look like that anymore. Even she wouldn't recognize him on the street.

Although she would remember when he got her alone. She'd remember everything.

Chapter Twelve

Griff's question echoed in Ginny's ears. *Is there anyone else who would want to hurt you?*

She hesitated, then pointed to the list. "I gave you the names of everyone I've talked to since I arrived. You can talk to them and then tell me if one of them attacked me." Head held high, she left the office and walked through the hallway to the front door.

Outside, the sky was dark, wind whipping through the trees and making the traffic light sway in the intersection. Rain still threatened, the temperature in the low fifties, although the wind chill made it feel more like thirty in the mountains.

She stepped outside, scanning the street, the hair on the nape of her neck bristling. Even though she'd left Robert, she felt as if he'd been with her, smothering her, his claws sunk deep into her psyche, every day since.

It had to stop.

She'd just reached the corner by the traffic light to cross the street when she heard Griff call her name. She tensed, bracing herself for a confrontation.

"You're not walking back to the inn alone," he said huskily.

The concern in his voice touched her. "Griff, I appreciate you coming to my rescue earlier, but I'm fine now. I just want to go to my room and rest."

"All right. But I'm going to make sure you arrive safely."

"That's not necessary."

"Yes, it is. You were attacked once tonight. What if that guy comes back for you?"

"He probably just wanted my wallet and is long gone," Ginny said as she quickened her pace.

"You don't believe that and neither do I," Griff said. "If he targeted you because you're asking questions about Joy's murder, he must want to stop you."

Ginny ignored the twinge of guilt she felt for fudging the truth with Griff. He seemed sincere, like he was really worried about her safety. Realizing there was nothing she could say to deter him from accompanying her, she lapsed into silence until they reached the inn.

She glanced up at the quaint two-story house, desperate to remember that beauty still existed amidst the ugliness that had become her life. But her breath caught at the sight of a shadow in her window. Her hand automatically moved over her purse, and she itched to reach inside and draw her weapon.

"Thanks for walking me back." She turned and headed up the porch steps, but Griff stayed on her heels.

"I'll walk you to your room," he said quietly.

The intensity in his eyes made her stomach flutter. "Griff, just go. I don't need a babysitter."

"More like a bodyguard," he said, his voice thick.

She had needed one three years ago. Had asked the police for one. But they hadn't had the manpower.

It was too late now to start over. And definitely too late to start anything with this sexy fireman.

If Robert was waiting for her in her room, she wanted to see him and get it over with so she could leave town before Griff had to find out the truth about why she'd come to Whistler.

GRIFF GENTLY TOUCHED Ginny's arm. Jacob had caught him as Ginny rushed out the door. Liam had found another case where a woman was strangled, and her house set on fire afterward to cover her death.

A woman named Tess Taggart from Raleigh.

He wondered if Ginny knew about the case. She'd claimed her source had survived, but if she'd done her research and found out about this other woman, that might have triggered her to make a connection to Joy.

"Come on," he murmured. "I want to take a look at those bruises. You might need medical attention."

"I don't," she said.

He chuckled. "Humor me. EMT training is part of my job."

"For goodness' sakes, you're a pest," she said, a note of irritation to her voice.

He chuckled. She was a feisty, independent little thing. "Aww, Ginny. A gentleman makes sure a lady gets home safe and sound, all the way to her door."

Ginny clamped her teeth over her bottom lip. "I haven't been with any gentlemen lately."

He raised a brow. Her comment raised more questions in his mind. "Well, my mama and daddy taught me to be one."

They'd reached the porch, and he opened the front door. Ginny fidgeted. "Thank you, Griff, but I'm inside now. I'll be fine."

"To your doorway," he insisted.

Anger flared in her eyes, and she sighed then walked past the parlor to the staircase. He followed, scanning the entry and room in case her attacker had slipped in and was posing as a guest. If the creep who'd assaulted her had done so because of Joy's murder, he'd probably been watching her and knew where she was staying.

Griff had also noticed her reaction when she'd looked

up at the window as if disturbed by something. Was someone in Ginny's room?

More curious than ever, he cupped her elbow with his
hand and guided her up the staircase. "I'll just make sure
you're tucked safely inside, then I'll leave for the night."

She shot him an annoyed look, then reached for her key.
Her hand trembled and for a moment, she simply stood
there as if afraid to go in. Or was she afraid he would?

Was she afraid of *him*?

His stomach clenched at the thought. Maybe he had
come on too strong. But he was only trying to protect her.

And find out what she was hiding. If she knew who'd
killed Joy, she needed to talk.

She fiddled with the keys and dropped them, so he
picked them up and unlocked the door. Through the open
doorway he spotted the bathroom door that had been left
ajar and the bed where a red lace nightgown lay. Had
she left out a gown to wear for a lover? Could that be the
shadow he'd seen in the window?

Maybe she had a boyfriend back home who'd decided
to join her in Whistler?

The scene in front of him certainly looked as if it had
been staged for a romantic rendezvous.

A sea of rose petals trailed the floor from the doorway
to the bed, then dotted the coverlet. Champagne sat chill-
ing in an ice bucket with two flutes beside it. A box of expensive chocolates was on the pillow.

He narrowed his eyes. Not just a box of chocolates. A
box with a photograph lying next to it.

A picture of a young woman who resembled Ginny.

The color drained from Ginny's face, and she staggered
sideways and gripped the edge of the doorway with a groan.

Griff grabbed her arm to steady her and caught her as
her legs buckled beneath her.

What in the hell was going on? If this was a romantic rendezvous, she didn't look happy about it.

THE PHOTOGRAPH... TESS... Her precious little sister.

Emotions clogged Ginny's throat, and the world blurred into a fog of memories. The last few times she'd seen Tess. Christmas. Three years ago. They'd made eggnog and sugar cookies and gorged on them as they watched their favorite holiday movie.

Then the spring festival in Boone where Tess had rented a booth to showcase her paintings. She'd been so excited that day to sell three of her original pieces to people who'd been enthusiastic enough about her style to mention her to local art galleries.

With their parents gone, it was just the two of them, and they'd pinky sworn to celebrate every holiday and birthday together.

After their father's death when their mother realized how fragile life could be, she'd made Ginny promise to take care of Tess if something happened to her.

But she'd failed her mother. Her father. Her sister.

Tess could have enjoyed a long, exciting and successful career as an artist. She'd dreamed of traveling to Paris one day and painting along the Seine River.

But all her dreams had been cut short. Her life snuffed out with senseless violence.

All because Ginny had allowed herself to fall for a slick psycho like Robert.

She should have been the one who'd died.

"Ginny, what's going on?"

Griff's hand at the small of her back was gentle but firm. So was his voice.

"Were you expecting somebody tonight?"

Was she? Yes. She'd known he was here.

She had to pull herself together.

Releasing a weary sigh, she stepped inside the room. Her fingers itched to pull the gun, but her gut instinct screamed that Robert was already gone. He was playing out his fantasy game of tormenting her.

"Ginny, please talk to me," Griff said in such a quiet, soothing tone that she gestured for him to come in and to close the door.

Angry at Robert for his sick need for control and at herself for allowing him to still rattle her, she stiffened her spine.

"Were you expecting someone? A boyfriend maybe?" Griff asked.

She dropped her purse on the table by the door, then strode to the bathroom and peeked inside. Another bubble bath waiting. More rose petals. The scented soap he'd chosen for her. The one she thought was so sickening sweet it was nauseating.

Griff was right behind her and looked over her shoulder. "Am I interrupting something?"

For the first time since she'd met Griff, relief that he'd insisted on following her flooded her. Yes, he was interrupting. But apparently it wasn't time for her to confront Robert face-to-face. The demented jerk was making a statement, indicating he would choose the time.

Just like he wanted to be in control of everything else.

A fit of anger overcame her, and she dipped her hand into the tub to release the water, then wiped her hand on the towel and hurried back to the bed. She snatched the picture of her sister and pressed it to her chest, then raked the rose petals onto the floor with one hand, crushing them beneath her boots.

Griff stepped back, hands raised, confusion marring his face. Then understanding, as if he realized for some reason she needed to vent.

She didn't need to simply vent. She needed Robert out of her life forever.

Exhausted from the fight with her attacker and emotionally drained from Robert's intimidation tactics, she sank into the chair in the corner. Griff stood by the door, shifting onto the balls of his feet, his steady breathing the only sound in the room.

She sat in silence, clutching Tess's picture in her hands as she tried to gather her composure. The clock in the room ticked away the minutes. Thunder rumbled softly outside. The creak of footsteps in the hallway echoed through the doorway.

Griff knelt in front of her. "I know it's been a helluva day. You were attacked. And now it's obvious someone was in your room. What's going on, Ginny?"

She shook her head, too tried to pretend any longer.

"Do you know who was here?"

She released a shaky sigh then looked into Griff's eyes. The kindness she saw reflected in the depths tore at her resolve to keep her secret. Damn Robert for putting her in this position. For changing her...

"Do you?" Griff asked in a low tone.

She nodded numbly.

"Who was it?"

She squeezed her eyes to stem tears, then shook her head. She didn't want to share her story with Griff. It was too humiliating.

He lifted her wrist and rubbed slow circles across her palm, then traced the burn scar on her wrist. "Does whoever it was have something to do with this?"

She gave a small nod.

He rubbed his thumb across her chin and lifted it, so their gazes locked. Robert's had been filled with seduction and lies.

Griff's were more serious, somber, filled with a quiet,

tender understanding and kindness that she'd never seen before in a man. He was strong. Tough. Dealt with life-and-death situations. Saved lives. He cared about others.

He could hurt her if he wanted. Not physically because he wasn't that kind of man. A rarity.

But emotionally. Because she liked him. Was starting to trust him.

Shame filled her. Would he help her if he knew the truth? Or would he look at her the way she saw herself—as the woman who got her little sister murdered?

GRIFF DIDN'T LIKE the pieces of the puzzle shifting and connecting in his head. Pieces of hidden truths he suspected had brought Ginny to Whistler that were personal.

She wasn't just chasing a story. At least not just *any* story.

He gently took the picture from her and studied it. The girl in the picture looked younger than Ginny. Hair a soft blond, hazel eyes, a slight pug nose. Similar, but different. A relative?

"Who is this?" he asked softly.

She ran her finger over the woman's face. "My sister. Her name was Tess."

Griff tamped down a reaction as the truth dawned. Tess Taggart, the woman from Raleigh who was murdered. "What happened to her?" he asked, desperate for her to explain.

"She's gone." She stood, wrapped her arms around her waist and walked over to the window. Rain began to patter the panes and fog blurred the view to the outside, cocooning them into the warmth of the room.

Although Ginny was shivering.

"What happened?"

"I don't want to talk about it."

Maybe not, but he sensed she needed to. He tried to recall everything she'd told him, deciphering through it for the truth in her story. "The man who set all this up? Did he kill her?"

She closed her eyes, her lower lip quivering. "He did."

"Was she dating him?"

She shook her head. "No. He didn't even know her."

Griff twisted his mouth in thought. He hated guessing. She'd told him about an anonymous source, had said the woman escaped. Had she lied? Was there really a source?

Liam's report echoed in his head. "How did she die, Ginny?"

Her eyes remained closed as if she was reliving the painful memories. Or maybe concocting another lie to tell him.

"She was strangled, wasn't she?" The truth made his stomach knot. "Like Joy? That's the reason you came to Whistler isn't it?"

She didn't have to answer. The gut-wrenching agony on her face told him everything.

He couldn't help himself. She looked so vulnerable and broken that he crossed the room and pulled her into his arms. "You believe the same man who killed your sister killed Joy. And he was in your room. He knows you're here looking for him?"

She nodded and leaned into him, her chest heaving up and down with emotions. "Yes. And it's my fault they're dead," she murmured. "All my fault."

Chapter Thirteen

Ginny's chest eased slightly as she finally confided in Griff. Shame followed.

She'd carried the burden of guilt alone for so long that it was more than humbling to admit it out loud. Griff would look at her differently now just as she looked at herself differently. The contempt she felt for her actions was overwhelming.

But at least now he knew, he'd be repulsed and leave her alone.

He slowly released her and looked into her eyes, his jaw clenched. "What do you mean? It's your fault?"

She folded her arms across her chest, bracing herself for his disgust. "Tess didn't know the man who killed her. She wasn't dating him. I was."

Griff arched a brow. "You're the anonymous source, aren't you?"

She nodded. She might as well confess everything now. "I met him on a dating site. All my friends were doing it and said it was safe, as long as we met in public."

His jaw tightened. "Go on."

"He was nice and charming at first, showered me with compliments and gifts, wined and dined me, bought me expensive jewelry and designer clothes."

"And then?"

"Then he became possessive." She drummed her fingers

over her arms. "He alienated me from Tess, from friends. All he cared about was how I looked on his arm and that I become the *doting wife*." Her skin crawled at the memories of his voice as he tightened his fingers around her wrists and crawled on top of her.

"One day I'd had enough and told him I was leaving, but he…didn't take it well."

Griff's lips curled into a frown. "He hit you?"

Shame reddened her cheeks. "He beat the hell out of me. But with the first blow, I knew I had to get away from him."

"God, Ginny." He reached for her, but she threw up her hands. She didn't want to be touched right now. Didn't want his pitying look. "Did you go to the police?" he asked.

She shifted from foot to foot. "I followed the rules and filed a protective order. But that only incensed him. He began stalking me. Following me everywhere I went. Showing up at the coffee shop and at school where I was enrolled in journalism classes. He left little gifts to remind me he was watching me. He was always watching." A shudder coursed through her. "When his gifts and notes and romantic gestures didn't work, he followed me to my apartment one night and broke in. That night I wound up in the ER. He told the doctors I fell down the staircase."

A muscle ticked in Griff's jaw. "Did the police arrest him?"

"Yes. He spent a few hours in lockup, but he had money and friends with deep pockets. By nightfall, he was back at my place and enraged that I had the gall to have him put in handcuffs. He said I'd pay." And she had.

With her sister's life.

Griff folded his hands together. "Then what happened?"

"I asked the police for protective custody, but they didn't have the manpower. I moved, created a new identity and thought I'd escaped, but he bribed a cop and found me again."

So that part of the story was true. "No wonder you don't trust the police," Griff said.

"That time, he tied me up and left me for days, so I'd learn my lesson." Her heart hammered. "Finally, I managed to untie myself and crawled out the window. I drove to Tess's to stay with her until I could figure out what to do. On my way though, he called and said he warned me I'd be sorry." Her breath caught in her chest at the sound of his sinister voice leaving that message on the phone. "When I got to Tess's house, it was on fire. I ran in to save her, but it was too late." Tears choked her voice as the image of Tess's pale, lifeless face surfaced.

"So, you see now. My sister would still be alive if I hadn't been such a fool and gone out with him."

GRIFF HAD SENSED Ginny was lying, that there was a story behind that scar on her wrist, but he hadn't considered she was an abuse victim or that a maniac had murdered her sister. No wonder she'd taken self-defense classes.

"Did the police investigate your sister's murder?" Griff asked.

"They did, but they didn't find his prints in the place or evidence proving it was him. Then he disappeared."

"And you think he came here, that he connected with Joy and murdered her?"

"It fits," she said in a pained whisper.

Griff gestured toward the flower petals she'd raked on the floor. "He did all this, too."

"He's cruel, likes to taunt me. He wants me to know that I can't escape him, and that he'll punish me again."

Griff raked a hand through his hair, his anger boiling.

"He has to pay," Ginny murmured. "I have to make him pay."

If someone had killed one of his brothers, he'd be out of his mind with rage and grief, too.

"He used to leave rose petals on my bed and in my bath," she said, her voice adopting a faraway sound as if she was trying to distance herself from the memories. "He also left a message on the mirror yesterday written in the same shade of lipstick he forced me to wear."

"Have you seen him in town?" Griff asked.

"Not exactly," she admitted. "I felt like he was following me. And when I fell the other day—"

"He pushed you?" Griff cursed. "Dammit, Ginny, why didn't you tell me?"

Emotions darkened her eyes. "Having a stalker is not exactly something to go around bragging about. Besides, I had to make sure he was here. That real estate developer might have murdered Joy because she was the holdout on his deal."

"Jacob is looking into that angle." Griff's mind raced as he added everything up. "The dating site—you went there to try to find him." Not a question, but a statement.

"He used it once. I thought he might try again, and I could find him."

"And then what?" He clenched his hands by his sides to keep from shaking her. "Dammit, Ginny, it's too dangerous."

"Someone has to stop him," she cried. "He murdered my sister in cold blood and ruined my life." She began to pace, swinging her hands frantically. "I changed my name, my looks, everything about myself, but he's still after me."

"Your name, it isn't Ginny Bagwell?"

Regret flared in her expression. "No."

Anger railed through him. What kind of life had she lived since her sister's murder? Looking over her shoulder at every turn just as she had when he'd seen her in town. Grieving over her sister's death. Probably tormented by guilt. And fear.

This man was dangerous. *Deadly* dangerous.

"I'm sorry for what happened to you," Griff said softly. "But you can't face him alone. Let me help you."

"It's not your problem," Ginny said matter-of-factly.

Griff inched toward her, careful not to touch or push her. Now that he understood her reticence, he didn't want to frighten her.

"I'm making it my problem," Griff said. "You may have dealt with dirty or incompetent cops before, but my brothers are not them. Jacob and Liam, he's with the FBI, will find this bastard and this time he'll pay for what he did."

She rubbed her fingers over her temple, the bruise on her cheek darkening to purple. "You don't understand, Griff," Ginny said, her voice laced with panic. "I don't want you involved. He'll kill you if he thinks you're helping me."

GINNY COULDN'T LIVE with another person's death on her conscience.

"I can take care of myself," Griff said. "But we have to talk to Jacob and Liam. If this man is in town, he has to be stopped before he hurts you or someone else."

Ginny's stomach fluttered. She had to do whatever necessary to keep him from killing another woman.

Confiding in the police would throw a kink in her plan for revenge, but saving lives took priority over her own need to see him suffer.

"Tell me his name, Ginny. And if you have a picture of him, that would be helpful."

She didn't want to involve them, but she saw no choice. "I knew him as Robert Bouldercrest, but I doubt he goes by that name now. I've looked for him on social media and dating sites and Googled him, but nothing shows up."

"Liam has sources at the FBI," Griff pointed out. "What did this man do for a living?"

"Investments," she said. "That's the reason I thought he might be posing as Thad Rigden, the real estate developer. Robert used to brag that he swooped in on failing businesses and small towns, bought up the property and turned it into gold."

"But you met Rigden and it wasn't him?"

"No, it wasn't. He seemed like a cutthroat business guy, but he definitely was not Robert."

"Do you have a picture of Robert?" Griff asked.

"I'm afraid not."

"You didn't take photographs of the two of you together?" Griff sounded surprised.

"We did, but the night he tied me up, he confiscated my phone. After I escaped, I bought burner ones hoping he couldn't track me down. And when I looked up his old profile on Meet Your Mate, he'd removed it."

"How about a sketch? Can you draw one?"

"I'm not a very good artist."

"Jacob's wife, Cora, is. If you can describe him for her, she can draw a composite."

Ginny hesitated. "I don't want to involve anyone else, Griff. He might hurt them."

"Trust me, we'll take precautions. I'd never do anything to jeopardize Jacob's family."

Trust had not been part of her vocabulary for years. But Griff sounded so sincere that she relented.

"I'll call Jacob and make the arrangements. We could meet here."

"He knows I'm staying at the inn," Ginny pointed out.

"True. Then we'll go to Liam's," Griff said. "He lives out of town in the mountains. He can come here and see if Robert left prints."

"The police already have his prints," Ginny said. "And I know it's him. He left a clear message for me."

A tense second passed, then Griff phoned his brother while she found a small broom in the closet and swept up the rose petals. She cleaned the bathroom as well, then glanced at herself in the mirror. The bruise looked stark on her cheek, her eyes glassy with fear.

Hating the fact that she looked like a victim, she retrieved her purse and dabbed powder on her cheeks to cover the bruise. She finger-combed the tangles from her hair, then found Griff waiting in the entry of the room.

"We're meeting in half an hour at Liam's. Are you ready to go?"

No. She'd never be ready. She'd have to hash over her story again. Face the sympathetic faces, the condemning looks. Tell them she'd gotten her sister killed.

Hatred for Robert mounted inside her. Still, if he'd killed Joy Norris, he might kill again—before he got to her. She couldn't take the chance on not cooperating.

She riffled through her suitcase, snagged a snow cap and scarf as a disguise, then followed Griff outside to his truck. She scanned the area, and so did he, but no one seemed to be lurking around. Although Robert could be hiding in the trees behind the inn. Or in one of the cars parked on the street.

She buckled her seat belt and kept an eye out as Griff pulled onto the road leading out of town. He repeatedly checked his rearview mirror. A black sedan seemed to be following them through town as they veered to the road winding toward the mountain. But Griff sped into a side street, and the car moved on.

Tension coiled inside her as he wound up the mountain road. The sharp drop-offs, ridges and switchbacks reminded her she was living on the edge.

"Tell me about Jacob's wife," Ginny said.

Griff cleared his throat. "Her name is Cora. She was married to another man a few years ago and delivered a baby girl, but that baby was kidnapped during the hospital fire that killed my father."

Ginny released a soft gasp. "That's horrible."

"It was," he said with a sigh. "Anyway, Cora's marriage fell apart after the kidnapping, but she never gave up looking for her daughter. A few months ago, my brother reopened the case and found her little girl, so she and Cora were reunited."

"And now she's married to your brother?"

"Yep. And expecting a baby."

At least Cora's nightmare had ended. Although Ginny couldn't imagine losing a child and all the years Cora had missed with her. Memories she could never get back.

A strained silence fell between them as he drove, and he seemed deep in thought. Or maybe he was just concentrating on the road.

When they finally reached the turnoff for his brother Liam's mountain home, she realized it was isolated. The two-story log house sat at the top of a hill with a spectacular view of the mountain ridges and river. Jacob's squad car was already parked in the graveled drive.

Anxiety tightened her belly as she and Griff walked up to the house. Trees swayed in the wind, the backdrop of the mountain so scenic that her heart gave another pang. Tess would have loved it. She would have painted it with wildflowers dotting the mountains and the front yard in soft shades of colors like a watercolor palette.

Griff's brother Liam greeted them at the door and introduced himself, then Jacob introduced his wife, Cora. She was pretty and kind looking. When she laid a hand on her pregnant belly, the joy on her face was undeniable.

"Griff explained the situation. I'm sorry for what you've been through," Liam said. "I'm already talking with analysts at the Bureau to see if we can track down Bouldercrest."

The agent's direct approach was comforting. Cora gestured for her to sit on the leather sofa by the fire and offered her hot tea. Ginny accepted, grateful for the warmth to alleviate the chill that had become a permanent part of her.

"I'm so sorry for everything that's happened to you," Cora said softly. "I can't imagine."

"And I can't imagine how you suffered when your little girl was missing."

Cora smiled. "We are a pair, aren't we?"

"We are." Ginny relaxed and sipped the tea. They'd both suffered in their own way, but Cora was strong and had survived.

She would survive, too. Keeping Robert from hurting another woman was key to that survival.

HE HAD BEEN watching her for days. Mitzi was friendly. Pretty. Talked to everyone and treated each customer like a friend.

He'd seen Ginny—Reese—with her in that café. Wondered what she'd told the other woman. If she'd warned her about men like him.

Laughter sounded in his throat as he lifted the lighter and flicked it. The short flame that burst to life made his body jump with excitement. Night had fallen. Ginny had found her presents.

He'd seen her with that same man again. The firefighter.

If she thought she could hook up with some other man, she was wrong. She had to be taught another lesson.

That if she didn't come back to him, he'd just keep killing.

Let her think about that tonight when she heard about poor Mitzi.

Chapter Fourteen

Griff jammed his hands into his jeans' pockets as he glanced at Ginny. She'd been riddled with anxiety on the drive over. Who could blame her?

Her psycho ex-boyfriend had abused her, stalked her and killed her sister. All in the name of love.

No wonder she had trust issues.

Before they got started, Fletch and Jade showed up to join them, and Griff introduced everyone.

"Fletch works search and rescue on the trail," he told Ginny. "And Jade is a detective. She has connections to people in Asheville."

Ginny said hello but twisted her hands together. "I didn't realize your entire family would be here."

"Our family works together when there's a problem," Griff explained. "If your stalker is hiding out on the trail, Fletch needs to know what he looks like so he can keep an eye out. He also knows places the jerk might hide off-the-grid."

"I can't imagine Robert camping or staying in the woods," Ginny said. "He has high-class tastes."

"I'll start researching hotels and inns where he might rent a room," Jade offered.

Ginny lapsed into silence, and Cora pulled a sketch pad from a quilted shoulder bag. "Why don't we get started now?"

Griff and his brothers stepped aside and gathered around

the breakfast bar where Liam had his laptop open. Jade joined them to learn the details of the case.

"I don't like the fact that she lied to you and to me," Jacob told Griff. "That she came here knowing who killed Joy and kept it to herself."

"She didn't know for certain it was him," Griff said in her defense. "How could she? It's not like he called her and admitted he killed Joy."

"She still should have come to me," Jacob said stubbornly.

Griff explained about Robert Bouldercrest bribing a cop to find her. "It took all my persuasive efforts to convince her to talk to you tonight."

Liam gave him a grim look. "I've pulled everything I could find on the Tess Taggart case. She definitely was strangled prior to the fire. There was no way Ginny could have saved her that night."

"Unless she'd stayed with Bouldercrest," Griff pointed out. "Which was not an option. Eventually he would have killed her."

"That's true," Jade cut in. "Abusers are narcissistic, obsessive and territorial. They treat women like they're possessions and have the mentality that if they can't have a woman, no one else will."

Relief tapped at Griff's mounting frustration. Protecting Ginny seemed daunting. But with his brothers' help, his tension eased slightly.

"Did she find proof that Joy was involved with this man Robert?" Liam asked.

Griff shook his head. "According to her, Joy resembled the way she used to look before she changed her appearance and went into hiding. That tipped her off to come here."

Liam turned to his computer and pulled up a photo. Griff's heart stuttered at the sight of the auburn-haired beauty on the screen. She looked young and optimistic, her green eyes glowing with happiness and the promise of a future.

"That was Ginny, aka Reese Taggart, five years ago," Liam said.

"Before she met Bouldercrest." And dyed her hair black. She must be wearing colored contacts, as well. He'd thought she was pretty when he'd met her, but she was stunning in that photograph. Had she intentionally played down her looks so as not to attract attention from Robert or any other man?

A well of sadness dug a hole in Griff's chest. What woman should have to live like that?

None. Certainly not Ginny.

Or Reese Taggart.

Anger at Robert Bouldercrest seized him. "She does resemble Joy," Griff said. Although Ginny was prettier. Sweeter. More sincere. Joy had cheated on her ex and lied to Griff.

Ginny had lied to him, but for different reasons. To protect herself.

If he'd been in her shoes, if someone he knew had killed his brothers, wouldn't he do anything to make that person pay?

"I did some checking," Jade said. "Her story about the cop being bribed to reveal her location is true. The cop who accepted that bribe has been suspended permanently. He cut a deal with the ADA to walk away quietly or face jail time."

"He could have gotten Ginny killed," Griff muttered in disgust.

Liam drummed his knuckles on the quartz countertop. "I had a feeling that if this man stalked Ginny, he might have done it before," Liam said. "I did some digging after I talked to Jacob and found another homicide investigation with a similar MO. This one was in Savannah, Georgia."

Griff went bone still. "Ginny wasn't his first victim?"

Liam shook his head. "I don't think so. I think we're dealing with a serial predator. And he's not going to stop until we catch him."

GINNY FELT A kinship with Cora that reminded her of her relationship with Tess.

She described Robert in detail, correcting Cora when she drew the mouth a little too wide and the eyes too slanted. His nose was more narrow, chin had a cleft. Robert hadn't looked evil in the least. He could have been a model for an entrepreneurial magazine or *GQ*.

"Nothing about him stood out as abnormal or dangerous," she told Cora. "Not until you crossed him."

"That's the worst kind," Cora said softly. "And the easiest to fall for."

"I was such a fool," Ginny said in a raw whisper.

Cora squeezed her hand. "This man was a predator, so don't blame yourself. You were trusting and had no reason to suspect he wasn't who he pretended to be. That's the nature of a sociopath. Just look at Charles Manson and all the women he charmed."

"But my sister died because I wore blinders," Ginny said in a raw whisper.

Cora squeezed her hand in understanding. "I'm sure she wouldn't blame you, and she wouldn't want you to blame yourself."

Probably true. Tess was selfless, full of life. Optimistic to a fault. And as trusting as Ginny had been.

She missed her so much her heart gave a pang.

Cora finished the sketch and turned it to face Ginny. "Is this close?"

Perspiration beaded on Ginny's neck at the sheer likeness of the drawing to Robert's face. "That's him."

Jade joined them and studied the photo. "We'll pass this to all local law authorities and issue an APB for him."

"He probably altered his appearance now. He knows the police are still looking for him in connection to my sister's murder and is like a chameleon. He fits in wherever he is and goes unnoticed."

Jade's determined expression didn't waver. "Don't worry. The Maverick men are smart, thorough and determined. They'll find him."

Cora squeezed Ginny's hand. "You can trust us. This family takes care of each other."

"Liam and Jacob are two of the finest lawmen I've ever known," Jade continued. "And Fletch…" A warm smile flickered in her eyes as she glanced at her husband. "He's honest and trustworthy and will do everything he can to track down this man."

"I…don't know what to say," Ginny whispered. "The lawmen I worked with before treated me like what happened was my fault." If she remembered correctly, they'd treated her mother as a suspect when her father was first murdered, too.

"I understand how it feels to be looked at with suspicion," Cora said. "When my daughter was kidnapped, the police acted as if my husband, at the time, and I did something to her. It was a horrible feeling and made me not want to work with the police."

Ginny wiped her clammy hands on her slacks. Cora did understand.

"And I know what it's like to be a victim," Jade added. "A few months ago, I was investigating a serial murder case when I was attacked and left for dead in the mountains in the middle of a blizzard. When I came to, I didn't remember my name or what happened."

Ginny gaped at her. "How did you survive?"

Jade smiled. "Fletch found me and carried me to a shelter to wait out the storm. Slowly my memories started to return. But I had nightmares for weeks afterward." She gestured toward Jacob and Liam. "Those men saved my life and helped me seek justice." Sincerity laced her voice. "They'll help you, too, Ginny. You just have to trust them."

A warmth seeped through Ginny, chasing away some of the chill. Both of these women had overcome trauma and seemed stronger for it. Could she do the same?

Jade reached for the sketch. "Let me give this to Liam so he can log it into the system."

Cora handed her the sketch and Jade passed it to the men. Griff scrutinized the sketch, then walked over to her with a grim expression. He probably wondered how she could have been so gullible to have entangled herself with a sadistic psycho like Robert.

She'd asked herself the same question a thousand times.

"Let me make some more tea." Cora excused herself and went to the kitchen.

Griff slid onto the sofa beside Ginny. "You okay?" he asked softly.

She nodded, although nothing about this situation was okay. "I can't believe I allowed this to happen."

"Don't do that," Griff said firmly. "Stop blaming yourself for being a victim."

"That's hard to do when my sister lost her life because of me."

A tense silence lingered for a moment before Griff spoke. "You weren't the only one who fell for him."

Ginny wrinkled her brow. "You mean Joy?"

Griff shrugged. "No. There was another woman before you. At least Liam found a victim who fit the same profile. She was from Savannah, Georgia."

Ginny's heart stuttered. "She was strangled?"

"And her house set on fire," Griff said. "Her name was Ava Frances. She was twenty-five. Her coworkers said she met a man on a dating site. His name was David Lakin. He was an investor."

"Just like Robert," Ginny said in a low voice.

Griff nodded. "One of her friends apparently became suspicious of his behavior. After they were engaged, Ava pulled away from her friends and family, even left her job to stay home and be the wife he wanted."

Goose bumps skated up Ginny's arms. "What happened?"

"One of the girlfriends confronted him, and he strangled her and burned down her apartment with her in it."

Oh, God. Images of Tess's dead body taunted Ginny. She thought she was going to be sick.

"A week later, the fiancée ended up dead, strangled and left in her car which he set on fire."

Ginny leaned forward with her elbows on her knees, lowered her head and took several deep breaths to stem the nausea.

Robert had done the same thing to another woman before her, and he'd killed her friend just like he had Tess. Who knows how many more women's lives he would destroy if they didn't stop him now?

He hadn't left any of his lovers, witnesses or anyone who'd crossed him alive.

Which meant he didn't want her as his wife as he'd said. He wanted to kill her.

Now THAT GRIFF understood the reason Ginny was running and her distrust of the police, her actions made sense. Hopefully, Cora and Jade had alleviated her anxiety over confiding in him and his brothers.

"Bouldercrest knows where Ginny's staying?" Jacob asked.

Griff nodded. "He's been in her room at the inn."

"Did she report the break-in to the innkeeper?"

"I don't think so. After what happened with that dirty cop, I don't think she's trusted anyone since."

Griff wanted her to trust him almost as much as he wanted to protect her.

"I can assign a car outside the inn," Jacob suggested. "If he shows up there, we'll grab him."

"Good. Although I don't think Ginny should stay at the inn tonight," Griff said. "It's too dangerous."

Jacob arched a brow. "What do you suggest?"

"She can stay in my spare room. My security system is state-of-the-art."

"True," Liam said. "Although if this guy saw you with Ginny, it could be dangerous for you."

Griff squared his shoulders. "I can handle myself. You forget I face danger every day on the job."

"This is different," Jacob said. "You aren't just dealing with an arsonist. This is a cold-blooded psychopath."

"All the more reason we make sure he doesn't get to Ginny," Griff said.

His brothers reluctantly agreed, and Jacob phoned his deputy about standing guard at the inn in case Bouldercrest showed. Liam scanned the sketch Cora had drawn of the man and entered it into the system to alert law-enforcement agencies to be on the lookout for him. Fletch took a copy to pass to the rangers on the AT and to use as a reference himself.

"Anything more on the teens and the wildfire arsons?" he asked Jacob.

"I don't think those boys are the perps. My guess is the arsonist saw where the boys had been partying in the woods and started the fires close by, assuming we'd instantly accuse the teens."

"Which we did," Griff muttered. "What if Bouldercrest set the fires to distract us from Joy's murder and from Ginny?"

"That's possible," Liam agreed.

Jacob patted Griff's back. "Don't let down your guard,

man. Bouldercrest has gotten away with four murders so far that we know of, and an attempt on Ginny's life. He's smart and methodical."

GRIFF PROMISED TO be careful and call Jacob if he noticed any sign Robert was following him. Cora and Jade gave Ginny a hug of encouragement before they left, and Griff's heart squeezed with affection for his sisters-in-law. His family had always come together in a crisis and were doing so now. He was a lucky man to have them.

Ginny was alone and had nobody. He couldn't let her down.

"We're going to find him and bring him to justice," Griff assured her as he drove to his cabin.

Ginny stared out the truck window. "I hope so. He's destroyed enough lives already."

He didn't know how to respond. She was right. It was her reality. But he had the sudden urge to pull her in his arms and assure her that no one would ever hurt her again.

She'd balked at the idea of staying at his place, but he insisted. "We should stop at the inn and let me pack a bag."

He shook his head. "Not tonight. He might be watching, and I don't want him to follow us to my place. I'll drive you back in the morning."

A sliver of fear flashed in her eyes. Was she afraid to spend the night at his cabin?

"Ginny, I swear you'll have your own room and privacy at my house. I have a state-of-the-art security system so no one can get in. And I won't bother you."

"Robert had a security system, too. He used it to keep me locked inside."

Griff inhaled a sharp breath. "I'm not him," he said, anger toward the monster who'd abused her throbbing inside him. "I just want you to be safe for the night. Jacob is stationing his deputy outside the inn, so if Robert shows up there tonight, we might catch him and this nightmare will be over."

She shivered and dug herself deeper inside her jacket as if the thin coat could hold the demons at bay.

He hoped she didn't see him as one of them.

Chapter Fifteen

In spite of Griff's reassurances, Ginny insisted he stop by and let her pick up her car. Call it a safety net, but it was important that she be able to come and go of her own free will. She would never let another man dictate her life or trap her again.

Griff didn't like the idea of going anywhere near the inn, but he agreed to a compromise and asked Jacob to have one of the deputies drop her car at his house. She'd been alone so long now that she'd forgotten what it was like not to be alone.

To have a family, people who came together and supported you when you needed it. People who'd literally do anything for you. Griff had that with his brothers. They obviously shared affection for each other and worked together.

What would it be like to have a family like that?

You had it with Tess. Except you let Robert alienate you from her.

Her lungs squeezed with her need for air. Griff parked in front of his log cabin, and she realized how much he must love these mountains and the town to have stayed after his father's death. She and Tess sold their family home after they lost their mother. It had been too painful to go inside the rooms where they'd grown up. Every place she'd turned she'd seen her parents, childhood memories, the love. The emptiness. That void had been overpowering.

"You must be tired," Griff said as they battled the wind up to his front porch. "How's your head?"

"I'm fine." Although she winced at the reminder of her encounter with her attacker. If Robert had jumped her, he would have said something to let her know if it was him, wouldn't he? Maybe she had angered Thad Rigden.

But he seemed too sophisticated to assault a woman in an alley.

"Your house is beautiful," she said as they entered. "It feels warm and cozy."

"Thanks," Griff said. "After we lost our folks, we decided to sell the old homestead and each of us built a cabin. It was too hard going back to the house."

Ginny smiled. "Tess and I sold our parents' home after my mom passed, too." Another thing they had in common.

Griff flipped a switch and the gas logs in the fireplace burst to life. The floor-to-ceiling stone fireplace and rustic features added charm, and the picture window and French doors leading to the massive deck offered a beautiful scenic view. Soft firelight flickered and danced, adding warmth and an ambience that would have been romantic if romance was part of her life.

"Did you do some of the work yourself?" she asked as she admired the millwork and rustic mantel.

"Yeah, it's kind of a hobby. I built the bannister and made my table out of reclaimed wood." Pride filled his voice. "And the columns were made from heart pine from my parents' property."

Impressive. "It's lovely that you brought a piece of history with you."

"My brothers and I all did."

Just like she'd kept the quilt her grandmother had made for her and carried it with her wherever she moved.

Griff set the alarm system, then offered her a drink. "I have whiskey or wine," he said.

"A whiskey would be great." And alleviate some of her anxiety.

He poured them both a finger in a highball glass, then handed it to her. She swirled the liquid around in the glass while he began pulling items from the refrigerator.

"I hope you like omelets," he said. "My specialty for dinner when I haven't grocery shopped."

"I hadn't thought about dinner," she admitted as she crossed the room to stare out the French doors. The trees shivered in the breeze, and stars fought through the storm clouds but failed, pitching the night into almost total darkness.

Exactly the way she'd felt for three years.

She glanced back at Griff, and her stomach fluttered. Before she'd been scarred and broken, she would have been attracted to him. Heck, she still was.

But she didn't belong here. Not in his home or with his family.

She didn't belong anywhere anymore.

GRIFF ADDED ONIONS, peppers and mushrooms to the pan, then watched them sizzle in olive oil until they softened before he stirred in the eggs and added cheese. The scent of bacon frying on his griddle made his mouth water.

He needed to distract himself from thinking about Ginny in his kitchen. As she stood by his window gazing at the inky sky and mountain ranges, she looked tormented. He loved the seclusion of the mountains and wilderness but considering Ginny's situation, he understood her wariness. Although for a moment, he'd seen longing in her expression, as if she wanted to be part of this beautiful place.

As if she was all alone.

He'd never thought about being lonely before himself, because he had his brothers. Although there were all kinds of lonely.

Two of his brothers had partners now, lovers and wives. He envied them. And tonight, sharing a simple meal with Ginny in his cabin felt intimate.

A self-deprecating sigh escaped him. He could not entertain fantasies about a relationship with her. For God's sake, she was a domestic violence victim with a stalker.

Anger at the situation and the bastard heated his blood and made him renew his vow to protect her.

He dished up the omelets and bacon, then grabbed toast from the toaster and set strawberry jam on the table. "It's ready," he said, wondering what she'd think of his culinary skills.

She turned and looked so vulnerable that his gut instinct whispered for him to sweep her in his arms and hold her until her fear subsided.

Don't do it. The exact worst thing he could do was to touch her.

"It smells delicious," she said as she joined him at the breakfast bar.

"Another whiskey?" he offered.

She shook her head. "I need to keep my wits about me in case Robert finds us."

Dammit, no woman should have to think like that.

He pushed the whiskey bottle to the back of the bar and filled glasses of water for them. He needed to stay alert himself. If this maniac found her here, he'd tear his damn head off. Then he'd call his brothers.

She seated herself at the counter, and he dropped onto the stool beside her, careful not to crowd her.

"You didn't have to do this," she said as she reached for her fork.

"I had to eat," he said. "Besides, I enjoy being in the kitchen. At the firehouse, we take turns cooking."

A smile softened her eyes. "My mother enjoyed cooking, too. She said it relaxed her."

He grinned. "Chopping vegetables is cathartic." A good way to release tension.

She smiled again, and he realized he'd been chopping ever since they returned to his place. He had to keep his damn hands busy so he wouldn't touch her.

"So, your mother liked to cook?" he asked to fill the awkward silence.

"She did." She forked up a bite full of the omelet and devoured it. "Delicious. Did you use fresh chives?"

"I did," Griff said. "You know your herbs?"

"Mom again. She was on a low-salt diet, so she substituted fresh herbs instead."

"Did she have a specialty?"

"Pasta dishes and desserts," Ginny said. "She treated pastries like an art form just like my sister did when she painted."

"Your sister was an artist?"

"Watercolor was her favorite medium," Ginny said thoughtfully. "She painted beautiful landscapes with vibrant reds and oranges and subtle blues and greens. She would have wanted to paint your view out back."

Griff allowed them to sit in the moment as she remembered her sister and they ate. "I can't imagine living anywhere but here on the mountain."

"I can't imagine being able to settle down," she admitted softly. "The past three years I haven't stayed in the same place for more than three or four months. I'd get nervous and feel like I was being watched, then move on to the next town."

Griff's stomach clenched. "That must be difficult," he murmured. Even after his father and mother passed, he still had family left. Ginny had no one.

A strained silence fell as they finished their meal. When she stood to clear the dishes, he shook his head. "I've got it. Go get some rest. It's been a long day."

She paused at the edge of the breakfast bar and looked up at him with a dozen emotions in her eyes. "Why are you being so nice to me? I lied to you. I…got my sister killed and may have gotten Joy killed, too."

Griff couldn't resist. He lifted his hands and gently rubbed her arms. "You did lie, but I understand the reason now. And you are not responsible for your sister's death or Joy's." He didn't know how to convince her to believe him. "This guy is a manipulator, Ginny. You saw what he wanted you to see. Once you realized who and what he was, you did what you had to do."

"But my sweet sister is dead because of it," Ginny said.

Griff squeezed her arm. "Your sister would have wanted you to leave an abusive situation." He lowered his voice. "She'd also want you to be happy now, too."

"I can't be happy as long as he's out there." She ran her fingers through her hair, then turned and walked into the guest bedroom.

A minute later, he heard her lock the door and the room went dark.

Ginny curled beneath the thick quilt in Griff's extra bedroom and listened to the wind beat at the roof and windows. March had swept in with a vengeance, keeping winter alive in the mountains and a foreboding chill in the air that lingered like the coldness in her heart.

For just a minute today, surrounded by Griff's loving family and the compassion of the two wives, she'd almost felt a crack in the veneer. Had almost felt like there might be a possibility for a future for her without a maniac breathing down her neck.

That there might a light at the end of the dark tunnel she'd fallen into when she'd held her lifeless sister in her arms.

She shivered and burrowed deeper beneath the quilt,

wondering what hands had lovingly stitched the log-cabin pattern. In addition to baking, her mother had loved quilting and so had her grandmother. When she was a little girl, she remembered sitting in her grandma's sewing room while she spread colorful swatches of dozens of fabrics across her worktable. Although Tess had been the artist, she'd enjoyed helping her grandma arrange the different swatches and colors into a design.

One year Grammy pieced quilts for her and Tess as Christmas gifts. They'd slept curled beneath them on cold winter nights and pretended their grandma's arms were lovingly wrapped around them. The quilts had become even more special after she'd passed.

Footsteps echoed from the living room, and she tensed, holding her breath the way she used to do when she heard Robert come home. Would he be in a loving mood? Demand her attention? Or would he be angry and vent his frustration on her? Had she done something to incense him? Had she left a glass on the counter? Forgotten to stack the dishes the way he'd taught her?

Forgotten to fold the afghan across the couch? Left the magazines scattered instead of stacked in alphabetical order?

She clutched the quilt edge, listening for the footsteps to grow closer. For the doorknob to jiggle.

But instead, they faded. Griff was out there, not Robert. Griff who'd promised to protect her.

Would she ever be able to enjoy intimacy with a man again?

The memory of Griff pulling her into his arms taunted her. It had felt so…good. Tender. Unlike Robert's possessive brute force.

She hated him for changing her. For ruining her trust and for making her skeptical of every man she met.

The anxiety inside her spread, and she curled lower beneath the bedding, savoring the warmth and comfort it offered. The house was quiet, the faint glow of a quarter moon seeping through the dark storm clouds and glowing gently in the room.

Exhausted from the attack, she closed her eyes and allowed herself to drift asleep.

In her dreams, she wasn't broken anymore. And the world was full of colors.

GRIFF STOOD OUTSIDE on his deck, counting his blessings and wrangling unwanted feelings for Ginny under control.

She deserved better. True happiness and relief from the suffocating burden of guilt weighing her down.

Damn, he wanted to fix all her problems. That meant protecting her, and helping his brothers track down the man who'd made her life miserable.

He gazed at the heavens, willing his father to send him strength and his mother her wisdom. Something rustled in the woods behind his house, and he tensed and scanned the trees. Hard to see much of anything at night. The moonlight barely created a dent in the darkness, and somewhere in the distance, a coyote howled.

He reached inside his den and snagged his night binoculars from the side table by the sofa, then returned and used them to scan the property. Leaves rustled and tree branches swayed in the wind.

His protective instincts for Ginny mounted as he pictured Robert Bouldercrest skulking around trying to frighten her. What kind of lowlife coward preyed on women and enjoyed their fear?

He'd never understand that kind of evil.

Senses alert, he kept watch for another hour. Finally, when he was satisfied the bastard was gone, if he was out there, he closed the door and locked it. Then he checked to verify that the security system was armed, shuffled into his bedroom and stripped down to his boxers. After he brushed his teeth, he climbed in bed.

But just as he closed his eyes to grab a few hours of sleep, his phone buzzed. He snatched it from his nightstand. His chief.

"Griff, we need you. A fire in town. Burgess just came down with some kind of bug and is puking his guts out. And Thomas sprained his damn ankle on the last job."

Griff sat up and instantly reached for his clothes. "Where's the fire?"

"Mitzi's Café."

His feet hit the floor. Would Ginny be safe if he left her here with the security system armed?

Chapter Sixteen

Griff hated to wake Ginny. But he didn't want to leave without alerting her that he'd be gone.

He quickly dressed, then checked out the windows again. Nothing seemed amiss, so he knocked on the guest-bedroom door. "Ginny?"

Except for the wind battering the house, everything seemed quiet. He waited a couple more minutes, then knocked again. "Ginny, it's Griff. I have to go."

Footsteps shuffled from inside the room, then he heard the lock turn and the door opened a fraction of an inch. Ginny looked up at him through sleep-glazed eyes. Her hair was tousled, her face void of makeup, making her look young and innocent and so beautiful his chest clenched. Although the bruise on her cheek reminded him that she was in danger.

"What's wrong?" she asked, her tone confused as if he'd woken her from a deep sleep.

"There's a fire in town," he said. "I have to go. I just wanted you to know where I was if you woke up and I wasn't back."

She blinked, her brow pinched. "A fire?"

"Yeah. In town. Mitzi's diner." He hesitated. "Go back to bed. I'll set the alarm. You'll be safe here for the night."

"Mitzi's? But I was just there."

"I know. It was probably just a kitchen fire, but the team

is short and needs me. The security system is synced with my phone, and you have my number. Lock the bedroom door again and go back to sleep. I'll be back as soon as possible."

She gave a little nod although she looked troubled by the thought of another fire. He didn't want to frighten her, but his own mind had gone to a dark place. Mitzi was single and lived alone. It was possible Robert could have targeted her as another victim.

He waited until she closed the door and the lock turned before he checked the security system. He grabbed his jacket and phone on the way out the door, then scanned his property before he climbed in his truck. Even as he started the engine, he surveyed the periphery and woods beyond in case Robert had discovered that Ginny had come to his house.

The road was deserted, the forest quiet, no lights burning in the darkness to raise suspicion. Once he hit the main road, he sped up and made it to town in record time. The guys from his station house were already on the scene, rolling out hoses and gearing up.

The fire looked somewhat contained to the back of the café where the kitchen was located. It was late so Mitzi would have gone home already.

He dashed to the truck, found an extra uniform and mask and geared up to go in.

"Any word on Mitzi?" he asked as he hurried over to Baxter who was in charge and doling out orders.

"No, but we just arrived."

"Who called it in?"

"Don't know," Baxter said. "There's the sheriff. Maybe he knows."

Jacob jogged over to him. "Didn't realize you were working tonight, Griff," Jacob said.

"Squad needed me. I'll check and see if anyone's inside. Find out if Mitzi is home and if she's all right."

"On it." Jacob patted his arm. "Be careful, bro."

Griff nodded, yanked his oxygen mask over his face and ran toward the burning building. Smoke billowed in a thick cloud, clogging his vision, but the front of the café hadn't yet caught. The scent of burning wood and metal was strong, and he scanned the room, but it was empty.

"Anyone here?" The crackling of wood and hissing of the blaze was the only response. Mitzi or even the janitor could be in the back, trapped or hurt. He dodged a patch of flames as he wove past the tables and through the door leading to the kitchen. When he opened the door, flames danced along the back wall.

He glanced at the gas stove and wondered if that had been the source of the fire. Had Mitzi left it on by accident?

Behind him, his men moved in. They began to douse the flames and he scanned the room, searching. "Mitzi? Anyone in here?"

No answer.

He inched around the wood cabinet by the pantry door and the entrance to the small office. A piece of burning board splintered down, and he knocked it away with gloved hands then plowed around another patch of flames. He shone his flashlight in the pantry and yelled again, but there was no one inside. The bags of flour and sugar and other food products were erupting as he stepped back to check the office.

Cookbooks and menu guides filled a shelf above the desk where a computer sat along with other stacks of papers. Thankfully the office was empty.

They worked for over an hour to extinguish and contain the blaze. Sweat beaded Griff's neck. He tasted ash as he finished up and searched for an accelerant. An empty lighter-fluid can lay in the corner of the kitchen near the stove.

Arson.

He asked Baxter to bag it for evidence and to look for other forensics once the embers died down and they could search more thoroughly.

With Ginny on his mind, he checked his phone. No word from her. Jacob had texted though.

Mitzi is not home. Looks like there was a scuffle. Blood on the floor. I think she was taken.

Griff's blood ran cold, and he ran to tell Baxter that he had to go. Then he jumped in his car and headed toward Mitzi's.

GINNY WAS SO exhausted she fell back asleep immediately. Being in Griff's house had lulled her into a sense of security she hadn't felt in years.

But an hour later, she woke with a start. A noise outside? Someone lurking at the window?

Grabbing her gun from her purse and her phone from the nightstand, she eased open the curtains. She peered outside, her breathing ragged.

On first perusal, no one was visible. But that didn't mean someone wasn't out there.

Fear knifing through her, she tiptoed to the bedroom door, pressed her ear to the wood and listened. No voices or footsteps. Her chest eased slightly. Griff had said he'd set the alarm, but Robert was tech savvy. If there was a way to disarm it, he'd find it.

She had to check the house before she could totally relax again. Griff's words drifted through her consciousness. A fire in town. Mitzi's diner.

She'd eaten at Mitzi's. Had talked to the pretty young woman. Had questioned other people in the diner.

What if Robert had been watching? What if the fire at the café was his way of getting her attention? Or…what if he'd seen her being friendly with the woman and decided to hurt Mitzi to punish *her*?

Fear squeezed at her lungs, robbing her breath. No…not Mitzi…not another woman hurt because of her.

Anger compounded her fear, and she clenched her gun, then eased open the lock on the bedroom door. Griff had left a light on in the kitchen, illuminating it in a soft glow. The curtains were drawn over the French doors. The front door closed.

No sign anyone was inside.

Still, Robert could be lurking somewhere on the property. With acres of woods, there were dozens of places to hide. Or he could be with Mitzi, playing one of his mind games or physically hurting her before he…killed her.

Choking back a cry, she eased into the room and scanned the space. Just as it had been when she'd gone to bed. She inched toward the French doors, holding her breath with every step. When she reached the curtain, she summoned her courage and gently pushed it aside just an inch to look out into the forest.

A tree branch snapped off in the wind. Storm clouds rumbled. A few feet into the woods and she thought she spotted a light. Just a tiny pinpoint, no bigger than the point of a sewing needle.

A cigarette? A lighter?

Heart racing, she blinked to clear her vision and narrowed her eyes. Yes, there it was. A small light flickering against the darkness.

And it was moving. Coming closer.

Her hands trembled. Her legs felt weak. But Tess's face flashed behind her eyes, and she raised her gun. *Come on, Robert. I'm waiting. If you're out there, just try getting to me.*

She steeled herself as she watched the light move closer and closer and closer. Then it was in the backyard.

She glanced down at her phone for a millisecond. Considered calling Griff.

There was no time. She had to handle this herself. Get rid of Robert forever.

GRIFF THREW THE truck into Park in front of Mitzi's.

Jacob's police car was parked in the drive, the lights in the house's interior shining. He hit the ground at a fast walk, then knocked at the door. "It's me, Jacob."

Jacob met him at the door. "Don't touch anything. I called for an Evidence Response Team to process the house. If Ginny's stalker kidnapped Mitzi, we have to follow the book. Any evidence we collect might help put him away."

"Got it." Griff wiped a hand over his sweaty hair. "I think the fire at Mitzi's was arson. We found a can of lighter fluid in the kitchen. He probably turned on the gas stove and lit up the place."

"How much damage?" Jacob asked.

"Mostly the kitchen and her office. Except for smoke and water damage, the front dining room is okay." If they found Mitzi and she was safe, she could rebuild.

He just prayed she was alive.

Jacob gestured for Griff to follow him. Griff avoided touching the walls or doorway or anything inside. The living area looked undisturbed, lamps and bookshelves and furnishings neatly kept. Cookbooks lined an open shelf beside the window that overlooked the backyard in the kitchen. A collection of pottery in a dusty green color filled one shelf, and a coffee station occupied a corner. A large island with a stainless steel counter completed the room, a cook's dream. Even the kitchen towels were lined up neatly and evenly on the towel rack on the side of the island.

"Everything looks intact," he commented.

"Until you reach the bedroom," Jacob pointed out. "That's another reason to suspect foul play. She seems particular about her belongings but look in here."

Jacob gestured to the open doorway into the bedroom, and Griff understood what he meant. The bedding was not only rumpled, but twisted and torn off the bed, dangling as if Mitzi had fought with someone. The bedside lamp was overturned, the glass base shattered. Blood dotted the floor beside it.

Had she grabbed it to defend herself?

Or had her abductor cut himself?

Jacob pointed to the rustic pine floor and the floral rug at the foot of the brass bed. More blood. "Looks like they fought, and he dragged her from the bed. Whoever was cut bled, but it's not a significant amount, so hopefully Mitzi's still alive."

"But for how long?" Griff grumbled.

"If we can match the blood type or DNA to Bouldercrest, we can confirm we're dealing with the same perp." Jacob narrowed his eyes. "Do you know if Mitzi was seeing anyone?"

"I have no idea," Griff said. "But her coworkers at the café might."

Jacob heaved a breath. "I'll canvass her neighbors and talk to her staff."

Griff glanced into the bathroom. It was just as neat as the other room. Whatever had happened had occurred in the bedroom.

A sick feeling knotted his stomach. The protective order Ginny had issued against Bouldercrest had failed. Griff stiffened his spine.

He would not fail her.

"If Robert abducted Mitzi, why set the fire at her café instead of her house?" he asked.

Jacob furrowed his brows. "To divide our manpower. We need people investigating here and at the café."

"Smart." Another thought occurred to Griff. "If he discovered Ginny is with me, he might want to lure me away." God. And it had worked.

"I have to get back to Ginny." He could call but he hoped she was sleeping and safe and sound.

"I have to wait on the ERT," Jacob said. "But if you get there and see him, call me for backup." Jacob pressed a hand to Griff's chest. "This guy is dangerous, Griff. Don't try to take him down yourself."

He wasn't a weakling. If Bouldercrest was there and threatening Ginny, he'd do whatever necessary to protect her.

"You will call me, won't you?" Jacob asked in the big brother tone he'd used to order him around when he was a kid. Jacob still thought it would work.

He almost laughed, but simply nodded. He didn't have time to argue. If Robert had kidnapped Mitzi, she was in danger. Jacob needed to work on finding her.

And if the bastard had set the fire to lure Griff away and divide law enforcement, he might be at Griff's place now.

Heart pounding, he hurried through the house and outside to his truck. He fired up the engine, tires squealing as he raced from her driveway and sped toward home.

Traffic was practically nonexistent in the middle of the night, except for a couple of truckers, and he maneuvered around them and wove onto the winding road to his cabin. With every mile, his fear intensified.

If Bouldercrest had kidnapped Mitzi, where would he take her? Would he kill her right away or keep her for his own sick pleasure? Where would he hide out?

Poor Mitzi. She was an innocent in all this. She didn't

deserve to be hurt or used as a pawn in a demented man's twisted game. And she certainly didn't deserve to die.

Neither did Ginny.

His phone buzzed. The alarm company. He snatched it and connected.

"Your alarm has been activated. You have ninety seconds to turn it off or 9-1-1 will be alerted."

Someone had triggered the alarm. He had to get to Ginny...

GINNY FROZE AT the sound of the alarm trilling.

She'd been staring at the backyard. The light was gone. No...on the steps. Moving upward.

Her hand wobbled. She pressed her finger over the trigger. Aimed.

Suddenly a loud noise startled her. Something hit the glass in the French doors. Instead of breaking, they rattled.

Then she saw Robert. His face pressed against the glass.

Chapter Seventeen

Griff barreled up the mountain road to his cabin, scanning the road and woods for any signs of Ginny's stalker. He phoned the security company and asked them to hold off on a police car, that he was almost home.

If he needed one, he'd call Jacob.

Darkness bathed the forest, night sounds echoing in the wilderness offering endless places for a predator to hide. His headlights caught sight of an animal in the road. A stray dog. He swerved to avoid running over it, tires churning on the graveled embankment until he righted his truck. Another mile, and he sped up his driveway.

No sign of trouble as he approached. The light in the guest room was off. Only the soft glow of the kitchen light above the window shone. He couldn't see his deck from the front, but he didn't spot a car or other vehicle on the property. But Bouldercrest could have come up from the woods or the river. Canoes and other small boats traveled behind the property and could put in at any number of docks or places along the way.

He flipped off his lights, not wanting to alert Bouldercrest if he was waiting in ambush. He slowed and parked in front of the house, then reached inside the dash of his truck and removed his pistol. A second later, he threw open the door, eased along the bushes toward his porch then climbed the steps as quietly as possible.

When he reached the porch landing, he peered through the window to the side. The light in the kitchen was still on, the fire in the fireplace glowing. Everything seemed still. Quiet. No movement.

Holding his breath, he punched in the security code to quiet it, then unlocked the door and eased into the entryway. He inched toward the living area/kitchen, keeping his gun by his side and ready.

Just as he passed the bench by the front door, he glanced toward the guest-bedroom door. It was open. Where was Ginny?

Heart hammering again, he crept toward the living room and scanned it. His pulse jumped when he finally spotted her. She was crouched behind the big club chair, a gun poised and aimed at him, her eyes wide and startled looking. Even in the shadows, he could feel waves of fear rolling off her.

"Ginny," he threw up his hands in warning. "Don't shoot. It's Griff."

Her hand trembled in the firelight, but she didn't budge. "Ginny, listen. It's me. The alarm went off and I came back to check on you." He stowed his gun in the back of his jeans, then reached out his hand and slowly moved toward her.

"You're safe now. Please put the gun down," he said in a low, soothing voice. Another step, another inch. Her breathing rattled in the tense silence.

"Look at me," he murmured. "It's me, Griff."

She blinked then his face must have finally registered, because she lowered her hand and let her gun hang to her side. He hurried toward her, knelt in front of her and eased the weapon from her hand where she was still clenching it.

His jaw tightened as he desperately tried to control his rage. He didn't like any stranger on his property, especially one who preyed on women.

"You're safe," he whispered as he cupped her face between his hands and forced her to look into his eyes.

"No," she said, her voice cracking. "He was here. He was outside. I saw him."

GINNY THOUGHT SHE could handle facing Robert, but she'd frozen up when she'd seen his sinister face through the window.

Dammit, she had to figure out a way to get the upper hand. Not to let him paralyze her.

"He was here?" Griff asked. "Where?"

"Out back. I saw a cigarette burning. Then movement. He crossed the backyard and just walked up onto the deck."

"Bold move." Griff rubbed her arms gently. "You're sure. You saw his face?"

She murmured *yes*. "He threw something against the French doors. It banged the glass."

"Did he try to break in?"

"No," she whispered. "The alarm was blaring, and he just smiled…then disappeared."

Griff frowned.

"He likes to play games," Ginny explained. "Taunt me. He did it before. Wanted to show me he could get close to me without being caught."

A tense second passed. "Let me see what he threw at the glass." He walked over to the doors.

Ginny followed him, anxious to know if Robert had really left or if he was lurking in the shadows. Maybe he thought she'd check outside to see what he'd thrown, and he'd snatch her.

Griff pushed the curtain aside and peered through the darkness, scanning the deck.

But he didn't see anyone. The woods were thick with trees and night shadows though, so it was possible he was still watching.

Although why hide in the woods when he'd accomplished his goal? If he'd wanted to attack her or hurt her tonight, he would have broken in when he was on the deck.

Griff unlocked the door, opened it and stepped outside. Ginny hugged the doorjamb and kept her eyes peeled for an attack while he shone a flashlight across the deck. His body tensed as he knelt. Then he pulled a handkerchief from his pocket, wrapped it around his hand and used it to pick up something on the deck floor.

"What is it?" Ginny asked as he stepped back inside.

Griff opened his palm and her pulse jumped. At first sight, it appeared to simply be one of the smooth river rocks. But as he spread his fingers, she noticed a piece of paper wrapped around it. Griff eased away the rubber band holding it in place, revealing a strand of hair.

"Oh, my God. Is that what I think it is?" she asked in a raw whisper.

"I think so." He angled the note for her to read it, and her stomach churned.

Mitzi says hello. Don't make me kill her.

GRIFF STARED AT the message in silence. He'd never met Robert Bouldercrest, but he hated the creep. He was not only dangerous, but he was downright cruel.

"He has Mitzi," Ginny said, her voice hoarse with emotions. She grabbed his arm. "Did you know, Griff?"

He made a low sound in his throat. "I wasn't sure," he said. "She wasn't at the café where the fire began. Jacob went to her house to look for her, but she was gone."

"Gone?"

"It looks like there was a struggle in her bedroom." He closed the door and locked it again. He drew the curtains, blocking out the sightline of the mountains and woods where Robert had been skulking.

But the message on that damn rock was imprinted on

his brain. And Mitzi's hair…what had he done to her? Was there still time to save her? If so, how?

Ginny looked frightened and angry at the same time. He couldn't blame her.

"Let me call Jacob," Griff said. "He needs to put this stone into evidence and verify the hair belongs to Mitzi. And Liam can get people searching the area for Bouldercrest."

Ginny's voice warbled. "He wants to torture me by making me imagine the evil things he's doing to her."

Griff muttered a curse. The man was an animal. And he knew Mitzi was with him now.

Griff rubbed her arms again. "Sit by the fire and warm up."

She sank onto the chair and dropped her head into her hands as he phoned Jacob. "I'm still at Mitzi's with the ERT," Jacob said. "What's going on?"

Griff explained about Robert's visit and the gift he'd left for Ginny. "She's certain it's him, and that he has Mitzi. We need to find her fast, Jacob."

"I'll call Liam. We'll get men combing the woods behind your house and set up roadblocks."

"He's not trying to get out of town," Griff muttered in disgust. "He wants to torment Ginny by keeping Mitzi close by."

"You're right. I'll organize a search team with the volunteer deputies in the county," Jacob said. "They can start searching abandoned buildings and cabins in the area. Bouldercrest has to be holed up somewhere. And we're damn well going to find him."

But would they do that before he killed Mitzi? Griff chewed the inside of his cheek to keep from voicing his concern out loud. He certainly didn't want to in front of Ginny. She was in enough agony already.

"I'll stop by in the morning to pick up the stone to send

to the lab," Jacob said. "Meanwhile you'd better stay there with Ginny. And keep your alarm system armed."

"Don't worry. I won't leave her alone again." He didn't intend to allow Bouldercrest to get to her on his watch.

THE PROTECTIVENESS IN Griff's voice warmed Ginny and helped to soothe her frayed nerves. Although anxiety over what was happening to Mitzi continued to nag at her.

Was Robert exacting his rage toward her onto Mitzi?

Griff hung up the phone and slanted her a worried look. "You okay?"

"I am, but Mitzi isn't." She paced in front of the fireplace. "I wonder what he's doing to her. If he'll keep her alive or—"

Griff stroked her back. "Don't go there, Ginny. I know you're terrified and I'm afraid for Mitzi, too. But Jacob and Liam will find her." He exhaled sharply. "Jacob is calling in emergency teams of deputies to search Whistler and its outskirts and Liam is on it. They'll pass the info on to Fletch so he can check places on the AT where Robert might hole up. We'll find him."

"What if we're not in time?" Panic made it difficult to breathe.

"Think positive," he said.

"You don't know Robert like I do." Ginny shivered. "He's cold and calculating. He gets pleasure out of inflicting pain."

"I'm beginning to realize just how depraved he is," Griff said in a voice tinged with disgust. "And I want to see him pay for what he did to you and Joy and every other woman he hurt."

"We need to do something. Robert has been playing games with me because he knew my weaknesses. I have to find out his and turn the tables on him."

Griff's brows shot up. "That's a good idea. What do you know about him?"

She searched her memory banks, filtering through the facade he'd presented and the few details he'd accidentally revealed. Were any of them true?

"Not much," she admitted. "Except that he lost his mother when he was young."

"Did he say what happened to her?"

She shook her head. "He refused to talk about it. Just said that she was gone and that his father raised him alone. He taught him everything he knew." A shudder coursed through her, but she stiffened her spine. "I thought he was referring to business, but what if he meant other things?"

"Like how he treated women," Griff filled in. "Oftentimes abused children become abusers."

"True," Ginny said. "The counselor I worked with after I escaped Robert gave me a ton of material to help me understand how an abuser chooses his victims. Predators are experts at reading others' weaknesses to use against them."

"He's violent and lacks self-control," Griff said. "What if he saw his father behave aggressively with his mother or with another woman?" Griff hesitated. "And the fire. Maybe…"

"Maybe what?"

"Perhaps his father liked to set fires, too," Griff said. "Or Robert could have been infatuated with fires as a child. If so, there might be a record of him starting fires as a child or as a juvenile."

He snagged his phone again. "I'll call Liam and suggest that he investigate that angle."

Ginny said a silent prayer they'd find something to use against him.

MITZI WAS SWEET. And so pretty. He'd watched her ever since he'd come to this hole-in-the-wall town.

But she wasn't Reese.

Sometimes he hated Reese. Wished he'd never met her. That she hadn't seduced him and made him love her. Made him want her so badly that he couldn't look at another woman without comparing her to his beloved.

Joy certainly hadn't measured up. Sure, she'd accepted his advances. Had let him crawl into her bed. She'd enjoyed his gifts and attention. But there had been a desperation about her that disgusted him. As if she knew she wasn't beautiful or smart enough. Her body was full of imperfections. Her face a little too made up and fake just like her personality.

She'd liked his money. He'd noticed that right away.

In the beginning, Reese had been impressed with his gifts, too. But after a couple of months, she'd said she didn't want them. Didn't want the fancy dinners or dresses he chose for her. She'd even given him back the diamond necklace and the blood-red ruby ring. When he'd offered to sweep her away to Europe for a romantic getaway for a month, she'd balked and declared she didn't want to be away from her sister that long.

Laughter bubbled in his throat. He'd fixed that, now hadn't he?

Mitzi looked up at him with wide, tear-stained eyes. Her sob caught in the gag he'd stuffed in her mouth. Her body shook with fear.

He sat down beside her where she lay tied on the bed and stroked her hair away from her face. The strands were damp from tears. And there was the missing chunk where he'd cut off a piece to send to Reese.

It wouldn't matter if her hair was long and pretty and perfect though. Not where she was going.

Chapter Eighteen

Ginny paced in front of the fireplace while Griff texted Liam about more information on Robert Bouldercrest.

As he hung up, he rolled his shoulders to alleviate his tension. He still reeked of smoke and soot from working the fire at Mitzi's Café.

The clock read four in the morning.

"Why don't you try to rest," he told Ginny. "Jacob has people searching for Mitzi. There's nothing else we can do until we get a lead or find more information on Bouldercrest."

"Maybe I could make a plea on the news, offer to exchange myself in return for Mitzi's safety," Ginny said with an urgency to her voice that made panic zing through him.

He shook his head, vying for calm when he wanted to shout, "Hell no."

"That's not going to happen, Ginny. Even if we set up a meet and exchange, you can't trust that he won't kill her."

Her face turned ashen, making him regret his harsh words. But he couldn't retract them because they were true. He certainly didn't intend to let Ginny offer herself up like some sacrificial lamb. Too many things could go wrong.

"I just feel so helpless," she cried. "Mitzi's with that maniac because of me and I'm just sitting here doing nothing."

Emotions overcame her and she sank onto the couch again and dropped her face into her hands. Her body trembled.

Unable to help himself, he crossed the room to her, sat down beside her and pulled her into his arms. "I know it's terrifying, but you're not alone now." He rubbed slow circles across her back, and she leaned into him and pressed her hand against his chest.

She was so small and delicate that he dropped a kiss against her hair and whispered soft assurances that everything would work out. She nestled against him and he closed his arms around her, praying he could deliver on his promises.

The warmth of the fire seemed to cocoon them into a more relaxed state, the sound of the crackling wood in the fireplace comforting. Her erratic breathing finally steadied, and she lifted her head and looked into his eyes. Griff's breath lodged in his throat.

In spite of the fear pounding in his chest, fear that mirrored hers, tension simmered between them. The kind of tension that stirred his desires and made him itch to be closer to her.

She placed her hand against his cheek, and he angled his head and studied her. The last thing he wanted to do was to frighten her or make demands upon her.

The tiniest inkling of sexual awareness flickered in her eyes, then they filled with longing and encouragement, and she parted her lips. He slowly leaned toward her. She leaned in at the same time, but he still hovered within an inch of her lips, determined to give her every opportunity to pull away if she wanted.

But she didn't pull away.

She tilted her head and pressed her lips to his. The kiss was gentle and so tentative that emotions he'd never experienced for another woman blossomed in his chest.

A second later, she threaded her fingers in his hair, drawing him nearer as she deepened the kiss. It took every ounce of his willpower not to lower her onto the sofa, climb on top of her and run his hands all over her sweet, supple body.

But this was Ginny, a woman who'd been bullied and abused and threatened. A woman who didn't readily trust.

He could not break the tentative bond he'd built, or the connection simmering between them.

Even if he couldn't have her, he'd protect her so that madman couldn't get to her.

GINNY HAD NO idea what had come over her, but every cell in her body screamed to kiss Griff. To let him hold her and chase away her demons, at least for a little while.

It had been so long since she'd kissed a man, or even wanted to kiss a man, that his lips sent a flurry of excitement and desire through her. Reservations whispered through her mind, but she ignored them.

Griff was nothing like Robert. He wasn't pushy or rough, hadn't tried to charm her pants off her. He'd done nothing except be honorable and protect her. Even now, in his arms, although strength and power emanated from his muscular body, his touch was tender and gentle.

She had no doubt that if she wanted him to stop, he would.

She just didn't want him to. Not yet anyway.

She craved the comfort of his arms and lips. Wanted to remember that once there had been joy in life, not just the mind-numbing fear, anger, grief and sadness consuming her for three years.

Griff stroked her back, their bodies rubbing together as he teased her lips apart with his tongue. She welcomed his sensual foreplay as the kiss became more frenetic. Hunger built inside her, heat and need making her cling to him, and she silently urged him to continue. He pulled away and looked into her eyes, questions lingering.

Affection for the handsome, sexy firefighter replaced the cautionary voice in her head, and she dragged his mouth back to her, taking what she wanted. His hands slowly roamed downward to her waist, and she ran her hands over his shoulders and back, reveling in the way his corded muscles flexed beneath her touch.

The sense that she had control emboldened her. She had the power to turn him on. To take without fearing he would force himself on her or explode violently if she decided to leave.

The realization was mind-blowing and cathartic and intensified her desire and her admiration for him.

As if he understood her needs, he trailed kisses down her jaw and neck, suckling the sensitive skin of her throat as his hand moved toward her breast.

She arched into him, her breath puffing out in tiny pants that burst into the stillness of the night. The sound of the wind battering the glass broke into that stillness though and shattered the fog of desire wrapping its tentacles around her heart.

Griff seemed to understand that, too. He traced a thumb over her cheek, then cupped her face in his hands and kissed her again. This time there was hunger, but also the tenderness of a man's understanding and respect.

He gently pulled away from her, his breathing erratic. "I smell like smoke. I'm going to shower. Lie down and try to sleep, Ginny." He pressed a kiss to her forehead. "I'll be here, and the alarm is armed. Hopefully, tomorrow Liam and Jacob will have answers."

He was right. She couldn't allow herself to fall into bed with him and forget that it was her ex-lover who'd kidnapped Mitzi. That Mitzi's life was in his cruel hands.

She had to focus on the reason she'd come to Whistler. And falling for Griff Maverick had no part in it.

GRIFF DOVE INTO the shower, anxious to cleanse himself of the acrid scent of smoke and soot. Granted, he was accustomed to the odor, but when he'd kissed Ginny, he'd realized he'd wanted to come to her fresh and clean, not covered in the remnants of sweat and ash from his job. Or the violence created by her stalker.

The cool water helped alleviate his hard-on, then he cranked the temperature up to a blasting hot to scrub his body and hair. Smoke tended to linger and cling to every possible surface of his skin. He didn't want Ginny to associate the odor with him.

Forget it, man. She only kissed you out of gratitude. And fear. You're protecting her and she was afraid. That's it. Period.

Sobering at the thought, he soaped and scrubbed himself until his skin felt raw and every vestige of lust was wiped from his mind. Yet as he climbed out, dried off and pulled on clean sweats, a more disturbing thought hit him.

It wasn't just lust with Ginny. He was falling for her.

Except Ginny wasn't even her real name.

He had to remember that. When Bouldercrest was caught and put away, she would return to her life. She sure as hell didn't need another man attaching himself to her. Dreaming up unrealistic expectations. Trying to tie her down.

She needed her space. And to feel safe.

He'd damn well give that to her.

He towel-dried his hair, brushed his teeth, then went to check on her. She'd curled up on his couch and fallen asleep in front of the fire. Only she was tossing and turning, murmuring protests as if she was running from that madman in her sleep.

Exhausted and hating to see her suffer, he slid onto the sofa, lay down beside her and wrapped his arms around her. She snuggled into his arms, and he rubbed her back and dropped kisses into her hair, soothing her nightmares until she settled into a deep sleep.

He closed his eyes and held her, forcing his fears about Mitzi at bay. He trusted Jacob and Liam to do their jobs. Tonight, he'd protect Ginny and get some rest.

He had to be prepared to help tomorrow if they got a lead on Bouldercrest. Or if Ginny decided to run again.

Exhaustion overcame him, and he drifted to sleep. But just like when he was on duty, he never truly relaxed. If the alarm sounded, he had to be quick on his feet.

Sometime later, sunlight crept through the curtains, jarring him to wake. He glanced at the clock. Seven thirty in the morning. He'd slept over two hours. Not bad considering the situation, he guessed.

Ginny sighed in her sleep, and he stroked her hair gently from her face. Lying on her side in his arms, she looked so peaceful that he didn't want to disturb her, so he hugged her tighter and lay there with her for another hour, listening to the wind blowing outside and the sound of birds chirping their morning song. Firelight flickered off her skin, making it look almost golden. Although the sight of the bruise on her cheek brought reality back with a vengeance.

"I'll take care of you," he whispered, willing his heart to be rational when it was already too late. Why had Ginny broken through the barrier around his heart now?

Especially when he and his brothers still needed to find his father's killer.

His phone buzzed on the coffee table. He stretched enough to snag it and checked the message.

Liam. Have information on Bouldercrest. Meet me in an hour?

Ginny shifted against him, and he struggled for control as her hips rubbed against his sex.

"Griff?"

Jacob's voice jerked him from his lustful thoughts.

He texted his brother in return. Stop by here. Don't want to leave Ginny alone.

A second passed. Then two. Liam responded that he'd be there in half an hour.

Griff eased himself from Ginny and laid her head on one of his throw pillows, then grabbed the afghan from the couch and draped it over her sweet body. Then he shuffled over to the kitchen and started a pot of coffee to brew while he hurried to take another shower.

A cold one to kill his morning erection before his brother arrived and started asking questions.

THE DELICIOUS AROMA of coffee brought Ginny out of a deep, exhausted sleep. She blinked to orient herself, then realized she was asleep on Griff's couch. The memory of his arms around her all night and his warm body pressed against hers taunted her.

She wanted to burrow into that place where she felt safe and…cared for.

Something she'd never felt with Robert. She had been a possession to him, someone to fill his needs. Hers hadn't mattered.

Footsteps from the kitchen brought her to a sitting position, and she saw Griff's back as he poured coffee into a mug. Firelight played off his broad shoulders and dark hair making him look sexy and tempting.

She had no business thinking about Griff and sex. "Coffee smells great," she said softly.

He turned to her with a small smile, then gestured to the mug. "Cream? Sugar?"

"Just black," she said. "I need something strong this morning."

"Me, too." He poured a second mug, then walked over to join her. He offered her a cup, and she took it, warming her hands with the hot mug.

Protective Order

"Liam is going to stop by in a few minutes. He has information on Bouldercrest."

Her pulse jumped. "Any word on Mitzi?"

"Not yet. I texted Jacob, and he said they're still combing the town and woods."

Ginny sipped her coffee. Every hour that passed dimmed the chances they'd find Mitzi alive.

"I'd better freshen up then." Suddenly self-conscious wearing the sweats Griff had given her to sleep in, she stood and carried her coffee with her to the guest bathroom. She closed the door, then studied herself in the mirror.

Hair tousled, eyes a little foggy from sleep, pale skin. What did Griff see when he looked at her?

A woman in trouble. One he was helping. *That's all.*

She splashed water on her face, then finger combed the tangles from her hair. Her color was starting to fade, her auburn roots showing through. Time for another dye job.

She needed another shower, too, but that could wait. Getting naked in Griff's bathroom with him and his brother nearby seemed too intimate. After they talked, she'd go to the inn, shower and change clothes. She needed a little distance between her and the handsome firefighter who made her suddenly want things she could never have.

She quickly dressed in the clothes she'd worn the day before, smoothed out the wrinkles on her shirt, then sipped her coffee as she returned to the den. Griff set a plate of cinnamon rolls on the coffee table.

"You made these?" she asked, impressed.

He chuckled. "They're from a can."

She laughed, which sounded foreign to her own ears.

The doorbell rang interrupting the moment, and he hurried to answer it while she refilled her coffee. His brother Liam appeared, solemn faced as he entered. Griff offered him coffee, and the men filled mugs then joined her in the den.

Liam spoke to her, then set a file on the table.

"Any word on Mitzi?" Ginny asked.

"Jacob thinks they found a cabin where Bouldercrest might have been staying, but he's gone. No sign of Mitzi at the moment, but Griff called in the SAR's dogs to track the scent."

Griff retrieved the baggie holding the river rock and Mitzi's hair and handed it to his brother. "This came last night. Somehow he found out Ginny was here."

Liam cursed beneath his breath, then reached for the file. "Let me tell you what I learned about Bouldercrest."

Ginny tightened her fingers around the mug as he opened the folder. "It took some digging, but I think this is the man you called Robert." He showed her a photograph, and Ginny confirmed that the image belonged to Robert.

"His real name is Ansel Holmes," Liam said. "His parents were Louise and Jimmy." Liam laid out a photograph of the remains of a burned house and then a picture of a small auburn-haired woman. "This is the mother. When Ansel was five years old, she died."

Ginny pressed her fingers to her mouth to stifle a gasp. His mother's hair was auburn...

"What happened?" Griff asked.

"Apparently the couple had marital issues," Liam filled in. "Neighbors reported domestic violence and police visited the house twice. According to a neighbor, the mother planned to leave her husband and take her son with her."

"But the father wouldn't let that happen," Ginny murmured.

"Right," Liam said. "Neighbor overheard Holmes tell his wife she'd never leave, and she certainly wouldn't take his son."

Ginny set her coffee on the table and twisted her hand in her lap. The conversation sounded too familiar.

"Then what happened?" Griff prodded.

"One night about a week after that incident, neighbors reported a fire at the house. When police arrived, they found the mother's body inside."

"Let me guess," Ginny said. "She was strangled?"

Griff cleared his throat. "And police speculated the fire was set to cover evidence?"

"Right again. But it gets even more disturbing," Liam said. "Police believe the son witnessed the murder."

A tense second passed. "Did they arrest the father?" Griff asked.

Liam shook his head. "He disappeared with the boy. That's when they became the Bouldercrest family."

"He learned to kill from his father," Ginny said under her breath. "And when I tried to leave him, it triggered the memory of his mother trying to leave." Because she had auburn hair.

And now in his mind, he was killing his mother over and over and over...

Chapter Nineteen

Ginny fought the urge to feel sorry for Robert. Witnessing his mother's abuse and murder had obviously traumatized him.

Yet not all kids from abused homes grew up to be killers.

"A profiler would say that he chose his victims as surrogates for the mother who he perceived abandoned him," Liam said. "It doesn't excuse his crimes, but understanding his thought processes can be helpful in finding him and eliciting a confession from him when we do."

"He doesn't think he did anything wrong," Ginny said matter-of-factly. "He functions on learned behavior and values. His father probably pounded it into his head that the man was head of the household, that the woman was subservient and supposed to obey."

"Archaic," Griff muttered.

His comment warmed Ginny's heart. Yet she was piecing together the dark corners of Robert's mental processes. "In his mind, he justifies his actions by how he was raised. He thinks he was good to me, to the other women, and that we were ungrateful for all he did for us."

"He's psychotic," Griff muttered.

"Narcissistic personality disorder," Liam said. "Combined with obsessive-compulsive disorder and the abuse. His father may have forced him to watch when he beat his mother, said he was teaching her a lesson and teaching him to be a good son."

"She was supposed to be the perfect wife," Ginny murmured. "I heard that more than once. Only I didn't measure up."

Griff squeezed her arm. "You do realize that it had nothing to do with you. That you weren't inadequate, Ginny. That none of this is your fault."

Her counselor had drilled the same sentiment over and over into her head. "I do. But when it's beaten into your skull, it's difficult not to feel that you did something wrong."

"Well, you didn't," Griff said. "Look at his past. His thinking is totally screwed up."

"Griff is right," Liam agreed. "With this type of disorder, nothing a woman or anyone else does can measure up to his twisted and unrealistic standards and beliefs."

"When someone really cares about you, they focus on the positive," Griff pointed out. "And on pleasing you. Not on what you can do for them or how they make you look."

Ginny sucked in a sharp breath. Griff was so much healthier mentally than Robert had ever been.

She tapped her foot on the floor. "So, what do we do now?"

"Our teams are looking for Mitzi, and my people are working to identify his aliases and locate him." Liam said. "Now that we have a profile and his picture, I'm going to release it to the media. Maybe someone in or around Whistler spotted him or has information about where he's staying."

"And where he took Mitzi," Ginny said.

"That, too."

"Let me make a personal statement on the news," Ginny offered.

Griff cleared his throat. "I told you no, Ginny."

She turned to Liam. "Please. Maybe I can reach him. After all, I'm the one he really wants."

Liam pulled a hand down his chin. "That's too dangerous. Give us a little time. If we don't find him, we'll consider setting that up."

She gritted her teeth. She appreciated the fact that he and Griff wanted to protect her. But what about what she wanted?

She was tired of men making decisions for her. If Mitzi died, she had to live with her death on her conscience, not them.

She'd driven to Whistler to find Robert. She would come up with her own plan and end this nightmare for good.

GRIFF WATCHED GINNY pace again as he stepped aside to talk to his brothers. "How do you think this information will help us find Bouldercrest?"

Liam shrugged. "It might not. But when we do locate him, we can use it to establish a personal connection. That connection could enable us to convince him to release Mitzi."

Griff hissed. *If* she was still alive. They had no idea.

"What can I do to help?" he asked.

"Ginny seems to trust you. Stay with her and make sure she doesn't do something stupid like go after Bouldercrest herself."

Griff wanted to argue that Ginny was smarter than that. And she was smart. But emotions could make a person do irrational things. And at the moment she was running on fear.

"We'll keep you posted if we hear something or find Mitzi."

Griff nodded and glanced back at Ginny as he closed the door behind his brothers. Her agitation was like a live force in the room.

She halted her frantic pacing with a sigh. "I need to go back to the inn and shower and change clothes."

"I'll follow you and we'll pick up your bags and bring them back here."

Her lips pressed into a frown. "All right."

He slipped on his jacket and retrieved his keys, turned off the gas logs and escorted Ginny outside.

The rain had passed although dark clouds still hovered, casting a grayness across the mountain. Trees swayed and the wind battered the bushes. The chill in the air hinted at another storm, maybe a tornado on its way.

Knowing Bouldercrest had been at his house, on his property, roused his anger. He scanned the yard and beyond for signs the maniac had returned. Maybe he hoped Griff would leave Ginny alone.

Not going to happen.

Traffic was minimal, but he kept his eyes peeled for trouble as he maneuvered the switchbacks on the winding mountain road back toward town. Ginny was right behind him in her car. When he pulled up to the inn, he noticed the deputy Jacob had assigned to stand guard for Robert at the inn parked in the drive in an unmarked car.

He threw up a hand in acknowledgement to the deputy, climbed out and walked Ginny up to the inn.

"You can go now," she told him when they stood on the porch.

"I'm not leaving," he said. "I'll walk you to the room then wait downstairs while you shower and gather your things."

She didn't look happy about it, but she didn't argue. They walked up the stairs together, and she unlocked the door. He placed his hand on her arm and insisted he enter first and check the room.

At first glance, everything appeared to be just as they'd

left it. He took a quick sweep of the bathroom and didn't see anything troubling inside, so returned to the door.

Ginny walked over to her suitcase and unzipped the bag.

His phone buzzed on his hip. Jacob. He punched Connect.

"Griff, there's another fire. This time behind your house."

Dammit to hell.

"I'll send my deputy inside to stand watch over Ginny while you go home."

"What's wrong?" Ginny asked as he hung up.

"A fire behind my house. Jacob's there. I have to go." He explained about the deputy. "Stay inside your room, Ginny. Bouldercrest could have set this fire to lure me away from you, so don't go anywhere until I come back."

He gave her a quick hug, hurried out the door, waited until she locked it then jogged down the stairs.

IT WAS ALREADY HAPPENING. Robert was targeting Griff because he was helping her. No one was safe if they got close to her.

Why had she let down her guard for even a moment?

Praying Griff's house was okay and grateful his brother was meeting him there, she locked the door, then stepped into the shower. That kiss with Griff taunted her. Sweet and tender, but she'd tasted need and desire, a potent combination.

Griff knew how to respect a woman. To give, not simply take as Robert had done. To step away if she asked.

She didn't want to ask. She wanted him to kiss her again. To feel his lips on her and his arms around her and to know that she wasn't alone.

The hot water usually calmed her, but anxiety felt like needles pricking her skin. She quickly rinsed off, then towel-dried her hair and hurried to dress.

Just as she opened her suitcase, the sound of a telephone

ringing echoed. She reached for her purse, then realized it wasn't her phone. A chill slithered through her as she felt in her bag. Buried beneath her underwear, she found a burner cell phone ringing.

Her heart raced, but she steeled herself as she answered. "Hello."

"It's good to hear your voice, love," Robert murmured. "I've missed you."

She closed her eyes and envisioned her sister's face in her mind. Felt her sister's terror as Robert had wrapped his hands around her throat.

Then Joy's face. She hadn't known the woman, but she imagined her shock and terror when she'd realized the man she thought charming was a sadistic animal.

And Mitzi, the sweet, friendly young woman who liked to bake.

"You took Mitzi, didn't you?"

"I warned you not to leave me."

"She has nothing to do with us, Robert. Please let her go."

"I can't do that now, love. You have to be taught a lesson."

Emotions thickened Ginny's throat. "I've learned my lesson. Just let her go."

His heavy breathing echoed over the line. "Not until you admit you belong to me. I told you that the first time we made love."

She swallowed hard at the memory. That night had started off tender and romantic. But when he'd held her arms above her head, looked into her eyes and declared that she was his, fear had rippled through her. The romance and tenderness had evaporated. In its place, she'd seen a dark, obsessive streak.

"I don't belong to you," she said matter-of-factly. "I told

you that when I left. But Mitzi shouldn't have to suffer because of me."

"And I told you that I'd never let you go."

His sinister tone made bile rise to her throat. "You killed Joy Norris, didn't you?"

A bitter laugh rumbled over the line. "She wasn't you, my love. No one else can ever take your place. Don't you know that by now?"

She inhaled slowly. "You need psychiatric help, Robert. Turn yourself in and get some counseling."

"There's nothing wrong with me, Reese. But when you make promises, you should keep them. And you promised yourself to me when you crawled in my bed."

He was twisting everything to his advantage. Her therapist had warned her that abusers were manipulative and made the victims feel as if they were at fault.

"I didn't promise to let you abuse me or murder anyone," she retorted. "Now let Mitzi go, Robert, and leave me alone."

"I will never leave you," he whispered darkly. *"Never."*

"But I don't love you." How could she love a monster?

"Because of that fireman," he said, his voice terse.

She breathed in and out again. "He has nothing to do with this."

"You spent the night with him," Robert said. "You cheated on me."

"We would have to be a couple for me to cheat on you," she quipped. "And we're not a couple and never will be."

A tense heartbeat passed. His breathing became more erratic. "But we will be together again. And this time it will be forever."

"That's not going to happen, Robert. Forcing me and killing my sister and other women won't make me love you."

"Because you're in love with *him*?" he said bitterly.

No, she wasn't. Was she?

"Once he's gone, you'll come back to me."

She opened her mouth to tell him that Griff meant nothing to her. She had to protect him. But the line went dead in her hands.

GRIFF HIT THE ground running as soon as he made it back to his cabin. Relief hit him when he realized the fire hadn't spread to his house.

But he spotted the blaze in the woods behind his property, ran around the cabin to the backyard and down the hill into the brush. The fire engine had managed to park in close proximity to the burning leaves and trees, and his team was already geared up and spraying the flames from the fire hoses. Smoke billowed above the treetops and floated into the sky, a thick gray that obscured the clouds above.

Jacob stood at the edge of the scene, a grim look on his face. "Those boys didn't start this," he said as Griff joined him. "I've already checked with their parents and they're at home. Seems the parents took action after the interrogations and are monitoring their movements."

"It's Bouldercrest," Griff said, his pulse hammering. "He was here before. Now he's leaving me a message." That lighter he'd found at the ridge probably belonged to him. And so did the boot print.

Jacob wiped sweat from his brow. Already the scent of burned lumber and grass permeated the air, and ashes swirled in the breeze, the fire threatening to spread to other areas of the woods as the embers fell onto dry land.

"Griff, this man is extremely dangerous. Now that he knows Ginny stayed here with you, he's gunning for you, brother."

Griff gritted his teeth. "Don't worry about me, Jacob. I can take care of myself." But Ginny...she was vulnerable.

"Let me help my squad, then I need to get back to her."

Jacob gave him a worried look, but his phone buzzed, and he answered it while Griff jogged over to the fire truck, geared up and joined his team. The wind howled off the mountain, causing the flames to spread from one tree to another and feeding the fire.

"We've set up a perimeter," Baxter said as Griff took over one of the hoses. "Hopefully we can keep it contained."

"Any sign of point of origin?" Griff asked.

Baxter pointed toward the edge of Griff's property where a gas can lay in the bushes. "You got lucky. If the wind had been blowing uphill, it might have spread to your deck."

Lucky? Maybe. So far, he was alive, and his house had been spared. But what else did Robert Bouldercrest have planned?

He and his squad worked for the next hour to get the blaze under control. By the time it had settled down and died out, he was sweating, angry and worried sick about Ginny.

Jacob had left with the gas can to send to the lab for prints. One of his team was assigned to stay and monitor conditions in case the wind sparked the embers and resurrected the fire.

He removed his gear and stowed it, then headed back to the inn. He called Ginny's cell phone on the way, but she didn't answer. He told himself she might be in the shower, but anxiety tightened every cell in his body.

By the time he arrived, he was in a state of near panic. He pulled into the drive and glanced at the unmarked car where the deputy was surveilling the inn.

His pulse jumped as he hurried to talk to the deputy. At first glance it appeared the man was sleeping on the job. His head was tilted to the side, and his body looked slumped.

Anger zinged through him. How could he sleep when

he was supposed to be watching out for Ginny? What if something had happened?

He tapped the glass, but the man didn't respond. He tried again, but nothing. Heart hammering, he yanked open the door, and touched the deputy's shoulder.

When he still didn't move, Griff leaned inside, and tilted the man's head sideways. Dammit.

Blood. On the deputy's shirt. Chest. Hands.

He'd been shot in the chest. And he was dead.

MITZI LOOKED UP at him with frightened, doe-like eyes. She was a pretty girl.

Just not Reese.

"You just won't do," he murmured as he stroked her hair from her tear-stained cheek.

She wiggled and squirmed, twisted her hands to try to break the ropes binding them together.

Watching her fight made his body harden. He did like a fighter. As long as she learned her lesson and then accepted her proper place.

But her hair was wrong. Not the right color.

He pressed a kiss on her forehead, and she went bone still, tensing as if she might let him have his way if he'd release her.

Silly woman. He'd told her she wasn't right. Even if he took her or she gave herself to him and said she loved him, she still wouldn't be.

He gripped her face in his hands and squeezed her cheeks so tightly her eyes bulged. "It's up to Reese now if you live or die," he whispered. The same for the fireman. "It's all up to my Reese."

Chapter Twenty

Ginny imagined Griff's beautiful house being destroyed by fire, a house he'd practically built with his own hands, and nausea clogged her throat.

He'd lost his father in a fire, and now he was working to save his own house. What if Robert had started the fire and was there now? He could have set a trap for Griff.

She snatched her phone to call and warn him, but hesitated. She grabbed the burner phone but couldn't remember his number. Panic setting in, she considered calling the sheriff's office, but Jacob was at Griff's so he would protect him.

At least she hoped he did, she thought as she paced the room. She could not allow Robert to hurt Griff or Mitzi or anyone else.

She'd promised Griff she'd stay inside the room, but how could she sit here and do nothing when Robert might be mapping out his attack?

A plan began to form in her mind. She had to take charge. Stop him herself.

Nerves tightened her shoulders as she retrieved her gun, pulled on her jacket and stowed the weapon in her pocket. Then she called the number Robert had phoned from in the burner phone.

The phone rang once, then twice, then a third time. Finally, Robert answered.

"I've been expecting your call, love."

Her skin crawled. "Please don't hurt Mitzi or Griff," she said. "I'll do whatever you want. Just tell me where to come."

A long pause filled with his breathing. "Did he put you up to this?"

"He has no idea I've talked to you." She just hoped he was okay.

"How about the police? Are you working with the sheriff?"

"No," she said emphatically. "I'm alone. I just want this to stop. No one else has to get hurt, Robert."

His heavy breathing echoed over the line. "All right. I'll text you the address where to meet me. But it has to be tonight. And no calling the police or telling that damn fireman or Mitzi is dead."

Ginny's lungs strained for a breath. Now that she understood what made him tick, she'd play his game until she found Mitzi and confirmed she was safe. "I understand. I'll do whatever you say."

"You'd better, Reese. This is your last chance."

A knock pounded on the door, startling her. "Send me the address. And don't hurt Mitzi or the deal is off."

She didn't wait for a response. She ended the call herself.

"Ginny, are you in there? It's me, Griff!"

She threaded her fingers through her hair, then rushed to the door and opened it. The sight of Griff's handsome face sent relief through her.

Robert hadn't managed to hurt him. At least not yet.

She intended to keep it that way. Which meant lying to Griff. Escaping from his watchful, protective eyes and facing Robert on her own.

"Thank God, you're all right." The strain on Griff's face eased a fraction, then he drew her into his arms. "I was afraid he'd hurt you."

"I'm okay." She curled her arms around him. "I was afraid he'd hurt you or burned down your house."

He eased away from her an inch, then brushed her cheek with his thumb. "My house is fine. But…"

"But what?"

"He killed the deputy watching the inn. I've already called Jacob."

Emotions flooded her. Sorrow. Guilt. Hatred for Robert. And a deep fear for Mitzi and for Griff that cemented her decision to meet Robert alone.

GRIFF'S HEART WAS hammering so fast he thought his chest would explode. He soaked in the sight of Ginny's beautiful face riddled with panic and fear, and sadness twisted at his gut.

"Oh, God," she choked out. "Another man is dead because of me."

He regretted telling her, but he'd had no choice. She had to know the lengths Robert had gone to today. That it was imperative she stay with him so he could protect her.

"The deputy understood the dangers of the job, Ginny."

"That still doesn't make it right." Tremors rippled through her body, and he hugged her tighter.

"I know it's not right. He was a good man."

She gulped back tears. "Did he have family? Was he married? Did he have children?"

"No, no and no," Griff said. "He was divorced, had just moved here. I don't think he had family either, at least not that I know of."

A small cry broke from her, and he rubbed slow circles along her back. "Shh, it's all right."

"Nothing about this is all right."

"I know," he murmured. "But he did his job and we will find Robert. I promise."

"How many more people have to die before he's caught

and locked away?" Ginny asked, bitterness darkening her tone.

"Hopefully no more." Griff pressed a kiss to her cheek. "I need to go back downstairs and wait on Jacob. I just had to make sure you were safe first." Although he'd left the body alone. That didn't sit well in his gut either. What if someone messed with the crime scene?

"What about the innkeeper?" Ginny asked.

"She's fine. The two guests who were registered checked out when they heard a policeman was stationed outside." He squeezed her arm. "Lock the door and stay in the room," Griff ordered.

Ginny shook her head. "I'll go with you."

"You don't need to see the deputy like that," Griff said. "I promise I'll return as soon as Jacob arrives." A siren wailed from outside, and she pulled away from him. "All right. Go. I'll be here when you get back."

He hoped to hell she was, and that she didn't do anything stupid like try to leave without him.

GINNY LOCKED THE door as soon as Griff left the room. Then she walked over to the window, pushed the curtain aside and watched as Jacob climbed from his police car and hurried to the deputy's car.

Griff met them just as a hearse appeared and parked. It had to belong to the ME.

God, the day kept getting worse.

The men gathered around the deputy's car, but Griff's body blocked her view of the man inside. A van veered into the parking lot, and a team climbed out, wearing jackets with ERT on the back. They would work the crime scene and collect evidence.

Her stomach knotted as they snapped pictures of the car and deputy, then began to take ones of the surrounding ground and area. She hoped they gathered conclusive evidence, although if she found Robert first, they wouldn't need it.

She'd take care of him herself.

The thought made her feel sick inside, but she couldn't live with people dying on her account.

Tears for the deputy spilled from her eyes, and she brushed them away angrily. Griff spoke to his brother, then glanced up at the window, and their gazes locked.

He was the kind of tough, stubborn strong man who made a hero. She could so fall in love with him if things were different.

She might even learn to trust again.

He left Jacob and the ME and search team and walked toward the inn.

The phone Robert had left for her taunted her from the nightstand. Griff would want her to confide about the phone call.

But sharing with him would only endanger him. Tonight, she'd meet Robert and take care of him then everyone else would be safe.

The thought of dying didn't frighten her. Her life the past three years had not really been living. She didn't want to go to prison, but justice for her sister and all the others whose lives had been destroyed by Robert would be worth it.

A knock sounded at the door. "Ginny?"

She inhaled a calming breath, then turned the lock. Griff looked so handsome and sexy and worried that she wanted him more than she'd ever wanted anything in her life. Just one night with him.

Anything could go wrong when she met Robert. He might kill her. She might kill him and go to jail.

She didn't want to do either without the memory of one blissful night in Griff's arms.

Granted, she didn't deserve to be with him.

But she reached for him anyway. "Griff?" Her voice broke. It was full of need and desire.

He pulled her to him and kissed her with such longing and tenderness that she used her foot to shut the door, then tugged him toward the bed.

GRIFF HAD BEEN so pent up with fear and frustration that he desperately wanted to hold Ginny and feel that she was alive in his arms. Her sweet lips moving against his triggered desires that heated his blood and nearly shattered his self-control.

No, he could control himself. If she wanted, he'd stop.

She teased his lips with her tongue, probing, searching, asking for more. Erotic sensations shot through him, stirring hunger and passion.

But the reminder of the dead deputy outside and how Ginny had suffered barreled through his brain at full speed, and he slowly ended the kiss and pulled away so he could look into her eyes.

"Ginny, I can't do this."

Her lips parted. Her breath panted out. "Why not? You don't want me?"

God, she was killing him.

"I do," he murmured. "But I like and respect you too much to take advantage of you after the way you've suffered."

She threaded her fingers through his hair, then rose on her tiptoes and kissed him again. "You aren't taking advantage."

"But Robert—"

"You're nothing like him and I know it." She traced her fingers along his jaw. "Please, Griff. I want to be with you, to replace all those bad memories with sweet, tender ones. Give me that."

He studied her for a moment. Felt the beating of her heart

as her chest rose and fell against his. No woman had ever touched his heart the way she had.

Or stirred his body to such deep desires.

"Ginny, are you sure?" he whispered.

Her lips tilted into a seductive smile, and she kissed him again. This time he didn't hesitate. He scooped her into his arms, carried her to bed then lay down beside her.

She curled into his arms, wrapped her leg around his thigh and pressed her body against his. Pleasure burst inside him, and he kissed her again, then plunged his tongue into her mouth, loving her the way she'd asked.

GINNY RAKED HER hands across Griff's muscular back as he trailed kisses down her neck and throat. Her body tingled with erotic sensations, and she urged him closer, savoring the feel of his hard body over hers.

He moved his hand to her breast, and she moaned in pleasure, whispering his name in a plea for more. Her breath panting out, she lifted her fingers and pulled at his T-shirt. He raised his body enough to yank it over his head and toss it to the floor.

"I smell like smoke," he murmured. "I should shower."

"I don't care." She cupped his face in her hands. "I want you now, just like you are."

The sexy smile he gave her sent tingles through her, and she pulled at his belt buckle.

His breath rasped out. "If you want me to stop at any time, just say the word."

"I won't want you to stop," she murmured. She'd never been more sure of anything in her life.

He helped her remove his clothing, shedding it in seconds, then he slowly undressed her, teasing her skin with gentle fingers and lips as he peeled her garments away.

Finally, naked, he kissed her again, then lowered his head and traced his tongue over her nipple. She moaned a little sigh of pleasure, then rubbed her hands over his back. His thick muscles bunched and flexed as he tugged her nipple into his mouth and suckled her. He loved one breast, then gave the other the same titillating treatment, and she wrapped her legs around him and stroked his calf with her foot.

He groaned, then moved lower and flicked his tongue down her body, teasing her with erotic kisses until he spread her legs and dipped his tongue inside her. Pure pleasure shot through her in such waves that her body began to quiver with sensations. He cupped her bottom in his hands and lifted her hips to give him better access, then drove her over the edge with his fingers and mouth until a million butter-flies burst inside her, and she cried out with her orgasm.

She whispered his name, begging him for more, and he climbed above her and looked into her eyes.

"Ginny?"

"Please." She slid her hand to his hard, thick length and stroked him. Hunger and pleasure darkened his eyes, and he moaned her name. He rolled sideways and disappoint-ment seized her. Was he was going to leave her?

Then he grabbed a condom from the pocket of his pants, ripped open the package and rolled it on.

She helped him, desire building again with the anticipa-tion of having that hard length filling her. Seconds later, he stroked her inner thighs with his sex, then pushed her legs farther apart and probed her womanhood.

One touch, one stroke, and pleasure soared to life again. He thrust into her, then pulled out, then entered her again, teasing and pleasuring her and building a rhythm that soon turned frantic with raw hunger. Over and over again, he thrust deeper and deeper each time until they were both panting, and their orgasms came together.

Groaning, he lowered his head and kissed her again,

deeply and intimately, as the waves of pleasure rocked through them.

Both sated and breathless, he rolled to her side and pulled her into his arms, then they fell asleep wrapped around each other.

Sometime later, Ginny woke to the sound of a small beep. Sunlight had faded and dusk was setting in, shadows filling the room. She glanced sideways and saw Griff's handsome, protective face and his strong jaw, relaxed in sleep.

Her heart thudded. God help her. She'd fallen in love with him.

The beep punctuated the air again. The burner phone.

She hated to leave the warmth and safety of Griff's arms, but Robert was calling. She could never have a life with Griff until Robert was out of her life permanently.

Not that she'd have one after she finished with Robert. But she had to finish…

Slowly, she extricated herself from Griff's arms. He must have been exhausted from the last few days of firefighting and taking care of her, because he moaned slightly but didn't wake. She slid from bed, grabbed the burner phone and checked the text.

Robert had sent an address, GPS coordinates.

Come alone or Mitzi dies.

Chapter Twenty-One

Ginny quickly dressed, stowed her gun in her jacket pocket, then snatched her purse and keys. Just as she was tiptoeing toward the door, Griff stirred from sleep.

He would try to stop her if he woke up. Thinking on her feet, she dropped her bag then hurried over and grabbed the end of the sheet that they'd kicked from the bed. She lowered herself onto the mattress, eased his arms above his head and slipped the sheet around his wrists and tied it high on the bedpost. Just as she was finishing securing the knots, he opened his eyes.

He looked startled for a moment, then surprised as if he thought she was playing some sex game. "What are you doing, Ginny?"

She hated to disappoint him, but better that than have him dead.

She tightened the knot, then dropped a kiss on his cheek. "I'm sorry, Griff. But I have to go."

His brows shot up in alarm. "What?"

She glanced at his naked body and wanted nothing more than to crawl back in his arms and make love to him again. Now that he'd awakened that part of her where she could feel again, it was hard to walk away from it.

But she couldn't stay with Griff. Robert was waiting. And if she didn't do as he said, he would kill Mitzi, then he'd come after Griff. She cared too much about him to let him endanger himself for her.

"I have to leave."

He raked his free hand through his hair. "You're not going anywhere. Robert could be waiting outside."

She squared her shoulders and stepped away from the bed. "He is waiting for me. And if I don't come to him, he's going to kill Mitzi."

Anger darkened his eyes. "Then we'll call Jacob. He'll track him—"

"No." She pulled the gun from her pocket. "He said to come alone, or he'd kill her."

"Ginny, please, listen to me. It's a trap, don't you see that?"

"Of course, I do. I'm not a fool. At least not anymore." She lifted the gun. "I'm going to play along then get him out of my life forever."

He jerked at the sheet and moved his legs to the side of the bed. "Untie me, Ginny. You can't face him alone. It's too dangerous."

"It's more dangerous if I don't do as he says." Her hand shook slightly as she trained the gun on his chest. "I'm not going to let Mitzi die because I'm afraid of Robert."

"Please, Ginny," Griff pleaded. "He'll probably kill her anyway, then kill you or abduct you and do God knows what."

Her anger rallied, swift and fast. "This ends tonight. I have to do it for my sister and Mitzi and Joy and all the other women he hurt or will hurt in the future."

He jerked at the binding around his wrists, making the bed post rattle. "Please, let me go. I can hide in the car with you. He won't even know I'm there."

Tears pricked her eyes. He was so brave, and strong and caring. He risked his life every day for others.

Today was not the day he'd lose his life. At least not for her.

"Thank you for last night," she said in a pained whisper. Then she turned and walked out the door and hurried out to her car.

She plugged the GPS coordinates into her phone, drove from the parking lot and headed out of town to meet the man who'd destroyed her life. She refused to allow him to destroy anyone else's.

GRIFF BELLOWED GINNY'S name as the door closed behind her. He couldn't believe she'd made love to him and now was leaving him here while she faced that monster alone.

And what did she mean—she was going to end it? What did she have planned?

He jerked at the sheet, but the knot was fast and tight. Furious and afraid for her life, he rolled sideways and struggled to reach the top of the bed post where she'd secured the knot. The little vixen had made certain it was secure and tied it in several places along the post.

Perspiration trickled down his neck as he stretched his body upward on the headboard and twisted his hands so he could reach the top. He wiggled and worked the fabric, slowly easing it loose and managed to release the first knot.

On to the second. With every moment he worked, Ginny was getting closer and closer to Bouldercrest. Why hadn't she let him go with her?

She had a gun, but did she know how to use it? He'd seen her fight that day the man attacked her on the street, but Bouldercrest could take her by surprise and she might not be able to fend him off, or get a shot in.

And what if he took the gun from her and shot her with her own weapon?

His heart pounded so hard he could hear the blood roaring in his ears. The second knot finally slipped free.

It took him another fifteen minutes to release his wrists from the post. By then the images bombarding him made his blood pulse with fear. With sweaty palms, he snatched his phone, pressed Jacob's number and reached for his clothes. When Jacob answered, he was dragging on his pants.

"Jacob, listen, Ginny heard from that bastard and she's gone after him."

Jacob heaved a breath. "Are you with her?"

Self-disgust ate at him. He'd let his emotions cloud his judgment and had slept with her. Had she seduced him so she could tie him up and get away?

"Griff?"

"No. Long story, but she's gone, and she has a gun. He told her to come alone or he'd kill Mitzi."

Jacob spewed a litany of curse words. "Did she say where she was supposed to meet him?"

Griff yanked on his shirt, fumbling with the buttons. "No. She just took off."

"All right, I'll call Liam and see if we can trace her phone."

"I'll meet you at the station."

Jacob agreed, and Griff shoved his feet into his shoes, then snatched his jacket and ran for the door.

GINNY'S HEAD WAS spinning as she veered down the narrow, winding road leading to the area where Robert requested they meet. Giant trees and brush enveloped her into an eerie world where the tunnel through the forest felt endless and eerie.

Robert would choose a remote location, some place he thought no one would find him.

Or hear her if she screamed.

She bounced over a rut in the road, making her stomach lurch, and struggled to tamp down her fear. The sweet taste of revenge roused her courage, and she plunged on, weaving around twists and turns until she reached a clearing that ended on a ridge. A small cabin sat near the edge, rustic and weathered, and the yard was overgrown with weeds encroaching on the patchy grass.

Wind beat at the loose shutters, causing them to flap, and making the deserted place look cold and desolate. Aware Robert would be hiding out, watching her approach, she scanned the area in search of him as she braked to a stop. Her hand automatically flew to her gun, an image of her sister's face flashing behind her eyes.

"Today is for you, Tess."

Resignation and determination washed over her as she climbed from the car. She turned in a wide circle, hoping Robert would be a man and meet her face-to-face.

Instead, the sound of a woman screaming echoed in the wind.

Mitzi.

Her heart jumped to her throat, and she took off running toward the house. She'd come here to save Mitzi and she wouldn't back down now.

She crossed the grass and climbed the steps to the porch, her eyes trained for Robert. But he was nowhere in sight. Probably skulking in the shadows like a coward.

She twisted the doorknob, and it creaked open. The interior was dark and dank, and wind whistled through the eaves of the old boards of the house. One step in and the wooden floor squeaked. She paused to listen for Mitzi again. A noise sounded from a back room to the right.

Scuffling? Mitzi crying?

Her heart wrenched.

She slowly eased toward the hallway, her hand over her gun in her jacket pocket, ready to pull it when Robert appeared. Another step and Mitzi's cry grew louder. She passed a small room that appeared empty, then a bathroom that was dirty and hadn't seen paint in a decade or more. Then a second bedroom. Just as she was about to enter it, the floor creaked behind her.

Her fingers wrapped around the handle of her gun. Before she could pull it from her pocket Robert wrapped his arms around her neck in a choke hold and dragged her into the room.

BY THE TIME Griff met Jacob at the sheriff's office, Liam had a trace on Ginny's phone. Jacob peeled from the parking lot and sped through town, siren blaring.

Griff's stomach knotted every time he imagined what Robert might do to Ginny.

She was tough and strong and a survivor. She deserved to be treated with love and respect. He had the desperate urge to be the one who showed her how a man should love a woman.

How could he have fallen for her in such a short time?

Especially when she'd lied to him.

Had she simply used him the night before to distract him so she could confront Robert on her own?

He didn't want to believe she would do that. She'd been abused and stalked to the point he'd worried she wouldn't want a physical relationship. Yet she'd come apart in his arms.

The connection he'd felt with her had to be real, didn't it?

"How did she get away from you?" Jacob asked.

Humiliation shot through Griff. "She pulled a gun."

"Dammit. Why didn't she call me?" Jacob asked.

Griff remembered the fear haunting her eyes. And the guilt lacing her voice. "She's afraid," he said.

"All the more reason not to go off alone."

"I know, but this bastard murdered her sister and she blames herself. She believes it's her fault he killed Joy and kidnapped Mitzi."

Jacob pressed his lips into a thin line. "Guilt is pretty powerful, isn't it?"

Griff studied his brother's deep scowl. They'd never really talked about their father's death. "It wasn't your fault that Dad didn't survive the hospital fire," Griff said. "I'm the firefighter. I should have insisted he stay outside."

Jacob made a low sound in his throat. "Don't do that, Griff. It wasn't your fault either. Dad did what Dad did, his job. That scene was chaotic, and lives were at stake. We needed manpower. None of us could have just stood by and watched without helping."

Griff's throat felt thick with emotions. Jacob was right. He'd blamed himself, but the only way he could have stopped his father from running into the hospital to help save lives was to have knocked him unconscious.

The Maverick men were protectors. That instinct had been bred into their blood when they were born.

Jacob swerved onto a graveled road that appeared to lead nowhere, and he sped around the winding curves as he followed the GPS coordinates Liam had sent. The storm clouds disappeared beneath the thick overhanging trees, casting the road into such darkness that Jacob had to turn on his headlights.

Three miles down the winding road, they finally broke into a clearing. Griff's heart stuttered at the sight of Ginny's car.

"She's here," he said.

"Stay in the car and let me handle this," Jacob said. "He might be armed."

"No way." Griff reached for the door handle.

Jacob held up a warning hand. "Then stay behind me and follow my lead. The last thing I want is for you to get shot by a stray bullet if Ginny fires at Bouldercrest."

Griff nodded, then said a silent prayer that Ginny was all right as they eased their way toward the house.

THE SOUND OF crying roused Ginny from unconsciousness. Reality crashed back with the force of a tornado, infuriating her. Robert had gotten the best of her.

After all her training and armed with a weapon, he'd won.

She blinked and tried to focus on her vision. No…she refused to give up. She had to think.

She felt something along her arm, then her cheek and opened her eyes. Robert. He was stroking her face with his fingers.

Her skin crawled.

For a moment, she considered spitting in his face, but that would do nothing except incite his anger. She had to outsmart him.

Think, Ginny, think.

Mitzi's muffled cry echoed nearby, and she glanced sideways. The young woman was tied and gagged, curled on a cot in the corner, her hands secured to the bedpost.

She'd left Griff the same way. Except she'd done it to protect him, not hold him hostage.

"Robert," she murmured.

"I'm here, love. I told you we'd be together soon."

Emotions threatened to make her ill, but she swallowed back the bile. *Use what you know about him. Get inside his head.* "I know why you were so upset when I left," she said softly. "I understand now."

His fingers stopped moving across her cheek. "What do you mean? You know?"

She feigned a smile. "Your father hit your mother, so she decided to leave him, didn't she? But he wanted her to stay."

Robert's jaw tightened, eyes flickering with a myriad of emotions.

"You watched him beat her, didn't you? He told you mothers and wives weren't supposed to leave. Then he killed her."

Razor-sharp anger blazed on his face. "They're not supposed to leave. They're supposed to be faithful and love you forever."

"That's the reason you tried so hard to hold on to me," she said in a low whisper. "I realize that now. Now that I understand, I think we can make it work."

His Adam's apple bobbed as he swallowed, his eyes shifting as if he was debating whether or not to believe her.

"We'll talk things through," she continued softly. "Everything will be different between us this time."

"How different?" he asked, his voice rough with emotions.

"We'll be together, and we'll talk. And I won't leave." She smiled at him again, although her stomach was heaving in protest. "Please untie me and I'll show you how much I've missed you."

He trailed his fingers over her throat, then around her breast, and she choked back a cry of revulsion.

"Please," she whispered. "I want to touch you and give you pleasure."

Desire sparked in his ugly gray eyes, and he slipped his fingers up and began to untie her while he kissed her neck and throat. Ginny closed her eyes and willed herself to play along, but hatred, deep and dark, bloomed like a cancer inside her.

Finally, he freed the last knot around her hands, then he held them above her head and crawled on top of her. Panic threatened. She had to reverse the situation.

She gripped his hands with her own, then flipped him over to his back. He looked startled, but she lowered her head and kissed his cheek to assuage his alarm. "I told you, I want to show you how much I missed you. Let me pleasure you first, then you can have your way with me just like you did when we first met."

Excitement and lust. A chuckle rumbled from him and

he rubbed himself against her. "I like the new Reese. Maybe I'll start calling you Ginny, too."

She smiled, clenched his hands and straddled him.

"You wanna play rough?" he asked.

"Just like you like it." She held his hands tightly, pushed her knee between his legs then suddenly kicked upward with her knee and jabbed him in the groin. He bellowed in pain and grabbed at his sex.

"What the hell?"

Taking advantage of the moment, she spotted her gun on the table across the room then dove for it.

He recovered and grabbed at her leg, but she kicked at his face and scrambled away. He chased her, caught her arm and flung her against the wall. Her head snapped backward, and she tasted blood, but she called on the skills she'd learned in self-defense and swung her arm up to deflect his assault when he came at her.

A swift thrust into his belly, and he doubled over. She kicked him in the groin again, then raced for the gun.

Breath panting out, she closed her fingers around it, turned and aimed it at his chest as he bellowed his rage.

Chapter Twenty-Two

Griff heard noises from the rear of the house the minute he entered the front door. Jacob had circled around the side of the house to the back to scope out the situation.

But Griff forged on. If Bouldercrest was armed, he'd deal with it.

The floor creaked as he eased down the hallway toward the source of the noise. He'd heard sounds that indicated a fight. A woman's muffled sobbing. Then Bouldercrest bellowing in rage.

He couldn't afford to waste a minute.

He crept to the door and peered inside to assess the situation. Mitzi lay on a cot in the corner, tied and gagged. He visually swept the room and found Bouldercrest against the far wall, his hands up in surrender as Ginny pointed a gun at him.

Instead of looking afraid though, Bouldercrest looked excited. The crazed look in his eyes indicated he was planning his next move. Twice Ginny's size, he could take her down in a minute.

"You deserve to die, Robert," Ginny said. "You killed Tess, the only person in the world I loved."

"That was your fault," Bouldercrest barked. "I told you you'd be sorry if you left me."

"I was not your possession." Ginny's hand trembled, the gun bobbing up and down. "And I never will be."

"You're such a liar," Bouldercrest said. "A few minutes ago, you said you missed me and that you'd do whatever I said."

"I said I'd show you how much I missed you and I'm going to." She took a step closer to Bouldercrest and aimed the gun at the man's chest.

"You won't shoot me," the bastard said calmly. "You don't have what it takes to pull that trigger."

The damn fool was taunting her, practically challenging her. "You're wrong," Ginny said, her voice calm but filled with a deep-seated hatred. "You changed me, Robert. I'm not that sweet, meek person you first met."

Her finger moved to the trigger, and Griff's breath stalled in his chest. He stepped to the doorway. "Don't do it, Ginny," he murmured.

Footsteps echoed on the wood floor, and Griff knew Jacob was behind him. "Let me handle it," Jacob said in a low voice.

Griff threw up a warning hand. "I've got it, Jacob."

"Go away," Ginny told Griff and Jacob. "He deserves to die."

"That may be true," Griff said. "And maybe he changed you in some ways. He made you tougher and more wary of people. But don't let him turn you into a killer."

Ginny made a strangled sound. "He has to pay for what he did. I need justice for my sister and all the other lives he destroyed."

"He'll get justice," Griff said. "I promise. He'll go to prison for the rest of his life."

"But my sister is gone forever," Ginny cried.

Griff barely breathed out. "I know, and I'm sorry. I understand what it's like to lose someone you loved. You know I do."

A tear trickled down her cheek. "What about Joy? And the deputy? They died because of me."

"No, Ginny," Griff said. "They died because this man is a sadistic cold-blooded killer. But you're not. You have love and goodness in you."

Bouldercrest released a sarcastic laugh. "You don't know anything about me. Only a man who can't get his own woman tries to steal another man's."

"I'm not your woman," Ginny shouted. "Griff is ten times the man you are. Real men don't have to bully women into being with them."

Bouldercrest stepped toward her, his hands clenched as if he wanted to choke her, and Ginny pulled the trigger. Bouldercrest froze as the bullet pinged the floor beside his feet.

"Move again and you're dead," Ginny snapped.

Jacob cleared his throat. "Ginny, let me have the gun. I'll arrest him and haul him to jail myself."

Her eyes darted toward Griff and Jacob, but she shook her head. "I came here to get justice for Tess. And I won't leave without it."

"Then think about your sister," Griff murmured. "What kind of person was she? What would she want you to do? Would she want you to commit murder in her name?"

EMOTIONS CHOKED GINNY as Griff's words hacked at her thirst for revenge. Her sister loved people, animals, children. She was an artist and saw the world through hopeful eyes, through her love of nature and its wonders.

Would Tess want her to destroy her life for revenge? To live with anger and hatred?

Her hand wavered. She couldn't breathe. Her sister was gone, and all the beautiful colors died with her.

"I understand what it feels like to want revenge," Griff said. "For a while after my father died, I wanted the same thing. I thought if I found the person who'd set that fire, I'd beat the hell out of him. But then one day when I looked at his picture, I heard his voice talking to me. Telling me to respect women and children and to protect others. That day I realized if I sought revenge, it would eat away at my soul. And I would be desecrating his memory."

Ginny clamped her teeth over her bottom lip, her hand shaking.

"So, I decided to honor his memory by being the kind of man he'd want me to be." He inched closer to her. "I never met your sister, but I can't imagine she'd want you to throw away your life by going to prison for murder. Would she?"

Pain and grief twisted at Ginny. "No, she wouldn't."

"I think she'd want you to live your life and be happy. To show this bastard that he didn't break you."

"He has to be punished," Ginny said.

"Yes, he does." Griff took another step closer to her. "He deserves to rot in prison. To have to face the people he hurt and live with that every day."

Emotions tore at Ginny, pulling her in different directions. Griff was right. But could she let Robert live? She'd wanted revenge for so long, she didn't know what to do with herself without it.

She heaved a wary breath. "How did you get past the anger?"

"I still get angry," Griff admitted. "But I have my brothers."

"That's just it," Ginny said in a pained whisper. "I have no one."

Griff placed a hand on her shoulder. "You're not alone, Ginny. You have me."

His soothing words helped heal her battered soul, and her rage dissipated. Griff was right. Her sister would want her to live her life for her.

She lowered the gun, but just as she did, Robert lunged toward her.

"Very touching, you tramp," he snarled.

Griff gripped Ginny's arm to pull her out of the way, then a gunshot sounded.

Jacob. Robert went down with a loud shout of pain, hugging his leg. Griff eased the gun from Ginny and covered Jacob while Jacob handcuffed Bouldercrest. Then he pulled Ginny into his arms.

When the bastard was secure, Jacob hurried to the cot where Mitzi lay, tied and gagged, her eyes wide in shock. He quickly untied her, then phoned for an ambulance.

Ginny pulled away from Griff, ran over to Mitzi and sank onto the bed beside her. "I'm so sorry, Mitzi. So sorry," Ginny whispered.

Mitzi was trembling, her cheeks red with tears, eyes swollen, her face pale. "He…was crazy."

"I know." She hugged Mitzi and held her, comforting her while they waited for the ambulance.

Two HOURS LATER, after Mitzi was transported to the hospital, examined, and doctors reported that she was fine physically, she was released and sent home.

Bouldercrest underwent surgery to have the bullet removed from his leg and was moved to a prison facility with medical care to await his trial.

Jacob went home to his pregnant wife and stepdaughter, and Griff drove Ginny back to the inn. She'd been quiet and withdrawn ever since they left the hospital.

Griff walked her to her room and escorted her inside. "It's over now, Ginny," he murmured.

"I know. It's hard to believe. Thinking about what he did and wanting to catch him has consumed me for three years."

He feathered a strand of hair from her cheek. "Maybe you can start to heal now."

She looked up into his eyes, but instead of peace, turmoil still streaked her face.

"I meant what I said back there," Griff said. "You're not alone. I'm here for you."

Her eyes narrowed. "I…appreciate you saying that, Griff. But you don't have to protect me anymore."

His pulse jumped. "What if I want to be part of your life?"

A wave of sadness tinged her eyes. "I need time."

Emotions roughened his voice. "What are you going to do?"

"I don't know. That's what I need to figure out."

He offered her a tender smile. "I could help you do that."

She shook her head. "Thank you for everything you've done, Griff. But I need to be alone for a while." She rose on her tiptoes and kissed his cheek, then walked him to the door.

Griff left, his heart heavy. Why did he sense that Ginny had just said goodbye to him?

Chapter Twenty-Three

Two weeks later

Ginny laid a bundle of sunflowers on top of her sister's grave and sank down beside it.

"It's really over, Tess," she whispered. "Robert Bouldercrest is in prison and according to the police, he'll never be free again. They've charged him with four counts of murder, kidnapping, stalking and assault." The gas can and the lighter Griff had found had Robert's prints all over them. So did Ginny's room at the inn. Robert confessed to setting the wildfires as a diversion.

Jade had called to report that the man who'd attacked her in the alley was a drifter who'd been passing through. They'd caught him assaulting another woman and trying to steal her purse outside a hotel on the edge of town and he was in jail.

As the news sank in, Ginny—Reese—had finally begun to relax again and had taken back her real identity. Although she'd probably always look over her shoulder and she fully intended to keep up her self-defense training, she'd started sleeping better and the nightmares were fewer and further between.

She'd stowed her gun in a safe and hoped she never felt the need to pull it out again.

"I'm so sorry I let you down." Tears fell freely from her

face, but she didn't bother to wipe them away. She pressed her hand over her mother's grave. "I'm sorry I didn't take care of her, Mother. I…wish I could turn back time. Be smarter."

Forgive herself. She was still struggling with that.

Suddenly sunshine burst through the dark storm clouds, and a rainbow streaked the sky, the colors dancing across her sister's grave.

Reese's breath stuttered. Then she looked down at the ground and saw flower buds beginning to push through the ground.

Flower buds in all different colors.

Emotions overcame her, and she pressed a kiss to her fingers then to Tess's tombstone.

Beloved Sister, Best Friend and Wonderful Artist.

Tess had brought so much life into the world, had loved and lived in the moment, had painted landscapes full of joy and beauty.

The rainbow, the flowers…was her sister trying to send her a message?

Looking up at the rainbow again, she felt a burst of hope for the future. She whispered that she'd be back, then hurried toward her car.

An hour later, she studied the mountains in the distance as she drove toward Whistler. She'd dreamed of Griff every night and wanted to talk to him again.

To see if a future for them might be possible.

The temperature warmed with each passing hour, and she noticed tiny flower buds on the trees dotting the mountainside.

Griff's words about honoring her sister by living her life were going to be her new mantra. Now that she'd decided what that path would be, she wanted to tell Griff about it.

Her car chugged around the winding mountain road, and she slowed as she approached Griff's cabin. It looked even more picturesque now with the wildflowers blooming on the mountain and the sun slanting off the dark green foliage.

Nerves gathered in her belly as she parked, climbed out and walked up to the front door. What if Griff didn't feel the same way about her? What if he didn't love her?

She almost turned around but stopped herself. She'd overcome her worst fears by facing down the man who'd terrorized her. That had taken courage.

She had to summon her courage now. Still, her heart was on the line.

But instead of running away, she wanted to run toward her future. She only hoped Griff would be in it.

She'd started by changing her hair back to its natural color. No more colored contacts either. No more Ginny Bagwell.

Feeling more like herself, she rang the doorbell and twisted her hands together as she waited. A minute later, the door opened, and Griff stood on the other side, looking so sexy and handsome that her stomach fluttered. Surprise flickered in his eyes, then a smile, bolstering her courage.

"I missed you," she said, then mentally kicked herself. That wasn't how she'd planned to start the conversation.

His smile widened. "I missed you, too."

Relief whooshed through her, and she offered him her hand. "I have things to tell you, but first I want to introduce myself. My name is Reese Taggart."

His gaze met hers, and he nodded. "Hello, Reese." Then he cocked his head to the side. "You remind me of someone."

"I do?"

He nodded. "Yes, someone I fell in love with."

"That girl, the one who wanted revenge and lied to you… she's gone."

"I hope she's found peace," he murmured.

"She has. I mean I have."

A smile glittered in his dark eyes.

"As a matter of fact, I've decided to use my story to help others. I've been working on a series of articles about domestic violence." She licked her suddenly dry lips. "I'm also studying counseling so I can become a victim's advocate for domestic violence victims."

"Really?"

She tucked a strand of hair behind her ear. "I talked to your sister-in-law Jade about it when she called to update me on Robert's case."

"I think that's a great idea, Ginny—I mean, Reese."

"I just wanted to tell you." She hesitated a minute. Her courage faltered, and she started to leave.

"Wait," he said. "Don't go."

She looked into his eyes and felt a connection that rocked her back on her heels.

"I fell in love with Ginny," he said, "and that girl was part of you. I think I'm going to love Reese even more."

Then he pulled her into his arms, closed his mouth over hers and kissed her.

Six weeks later, she said *I Do* to the man she loved in the gazebo Griff built for their wedding behind the home they would share together.

As she kissed her husband, she heard her sister's angelic voice singing to her from the heavens.

* * * * *

BURIED SECRETS

CAROL ERICSON

Chapter One

The dark clouds barreled over the Catalina Mountains, and the skies opened. The rain pelted the highway, steam rising from the scorched asphalt. The first monsoon of the season had hit the Sonoran Desert with a vengeance, gleefully dousing the hot, thirsty landscape.

Jolene slammed on the brakes of her truck, her back wheels fishtailing for a few seconds. She pounded one hand on the steering wheel and shouted. "Learn to drive!"

She couldn't risk getting into an accident right now, not with her cargo. Her cell phone rang from the console, and she glanced down at the display showing her cousin's name before answering and switching to speaker.

"Hey, Wade. What's up?"

"It's Gran."

"Gran, if you're just going to keep borrowing Wade's phone, why not let me get you one of your own?"

"I don't know why I just can't get my old phone back." Gran clicked her tongue. "This is not progress."

Jolene twisted her lips. "Landline phones were discontinued on the reservation, Gran. They figured everyone had a cell phone."

"They figured wrong." She coughed.

"Are you still congested?"

"It's nothing. I called to find out when you were coming over. Wade told me you left town for a few days."

Her pulse picked up speed. "What's wrong?"

"Nothing's wrong. Does something always have to be wrong? I just wanted to visit with one of my favorite granddaughters. Where did you go?"

Jolene took a sip of water from the bottle in her cup holder. "I was in… Phoenix, visiting friends."

"Rain's rolling in." Gran sighed. "I felt it in my bones two days ago."

"It's already hit up here, confounding all the drivers from out of state. I'm just south of Tucson, so it's following me down to Paradiso." She cranked on her defroster. "It's going to be a good soaking."

"Well, you keep track of those weather patterns more than I do." Gran sniffed and said something to someone in the background—probably Jolene's cousin Wade. "There have been a few changes in town since you left."

Jolene rolled her eyes. Gran loved to gossip. "In two days? I doubt that, Gran."

"You know that young Border Patrol agent, Rob Valdez?"

"Pretty face, pumped-up arms? Yeah, I know Rob."

"He's off the market."

"What market would that be, Gran?" Jolene clamped her mouth closed against the laugh bubbling against her lips. She knew exactly which market Gran meant.

Gran huffed out a breath. "The marriage market, Jolene. He and some young woman left on an extended vacation together."

"A vacation? You're kidding. That seals his fate right there. He might as well attach a ball and chain to his ankle."

"Oh, you can laugh, but he was an eligible bachelor, one of the few left in town."

"Nice guy, but not my type. Too young for one thing."

"I know your type, Jolene, and the loss of Rob isn't so bad given the other news I picked up while you were gone."

Jolene's jaw tightened for a second. "Don't keep me in suspense, Gran. What is this other blessed event that occurred to counteract Rob Valdez's vacation with a woman?"

Gran paused for maximum dramatic effect. "Sam Cross is back in town."

Jolene's hands jerked on the steering wheel, and a wall of water from the puddle she'd veered into washed over the side of her truck. She swallowed. "Sam's back?"

"I know Sam *is* your type."

Jolene gripped the steering wheel. "Sam is married. That is most certainly *not* my type."

"He's divorced." Gran moved the phone from her mouth and yelled, "Just a few more minutes, Wade."

Jolene snorted. "He's been back for two days, and you already know his marital status? I doubt it, Gran. He would never leave his daughter."

"He had lunch at Rosita's yesterday, and Rosie told me he wasn't wearing a wedding band and when she asked to see pictures of his daughter, he showed her pictures on his phone of the girl but none of his wife."

Tears stung Jolene's eyes, and she blinked them away. "That's it, then. No wedding ring and no pics of the wife. You and Rosie are quite the spies."

Gran lowered her voice. "You don't have to pretend with me, Jolene."

"Sounds like Wade wants his phone back." Jolene cleared her throat of the lump lodged there and said, "I'll drop by the rez tomorrow. I have something to do tonight when I get home."

"Drive carefully and come over any time tomorrow."

Gran must've handed the phone back to Wade without hanging up, as voices floated over the line before Wade cut off the call.

Jolene blew out a long breath. What was Sam doing in town? It must have to do with work. He wouldn't be in Paradiso long, and she could probably avoid seeing him. She hoped she could avoid seeing him.

She drove the rest of the way to Paradiso hunched over the steering wheel, the rain not putting her on edge as much as the task before her. She could do it. She *had* to do it. As her father had taught her, sometimes the ends did justify the means.

Twenty minutes later, as she rolled into Paradiso, the rain came in with her, lashing through the town, flooding the streets. By the time she pulled into her driveway, the storm had spent itself with the dark clouds rushing across the desert and breaking apart at the border, as if an invisible wall existed there.

She pressed her thumb against the remote-control button in her truck that rolled back the garage door. She slid from the vehicle and took a quick glance around her neighborhood before opening the back door of the cab. She pulled out her overnight suitcase and set it on the ground, and then she grabbed the duffel bag on the back seat with both hands and hauled it from the truck.

She hitched the strap of the bag over her shoulder and lugged it into her garage, wheeling the suitcase behind her. She stashed the duffel under a counter next to her ski boots and bindings, nudging it into place with the toe of her wet sneaker.

She locked her truck and closed the garage door, standing still in the middle of her garage for several seconds until the automatic lights went out. Her eyes picked out the duffel bag in the dim confines of the garage, and then she spun around and charged through the door connecting her garage to her kitchen.

There was no turning back now.

She unpacked her suitcase. She hadn't lied to Gran about spending a few nights away, but she'd been in Tucson, not Phoenix. Nobody needed to know where she'd been.

After she unpacked, she searched through her kitchen for suitable dinner fare and ended up grazing on hummus, crackers, a stale flour tortilla and a handful of trail mix.

She watched the time on her cell phone and the rain outside the window. When the digital numbers ticked over to ten o'clock and the remainder of the storm clouds skittered across the sky, she headed for her bedroom and changed into a pair of jeans and a dark blue T-shirt.

She grabbed a small purse and a backpack, leaving her phone charging on the counter. Stepping from the kitchen into the garage, she hit the lights and stuffed some gloves, a spade, a flashlight, a rope, wire cutters and a few other items into the pack. She opened the garage door and unlocked her truck. The purse went into the front seat and the backpack went into the back.

She returned to the garage and curled one hand around a shovel. She balanced it on her shoulder and approached the truck. The puddle of water in the bed rippled as she laid down the shovel.

Placing her hands on her hips, she pivoted toward the garage and eyed the duffel. She huffed out a breath and strode toward it, her boots clumping on the cement floor of the garage.

She dragged the bag from beneath the counter and hauled it over her shoulder. She swung it onto the floor of the truck's back seat and brushed her hands together—as if that were it. That wasn't it. That was part one.

She climbed into her truck and punched the remote with her knuckle. She watched her garage door settle into place before backing out of her driveway.

When she merged onto the highway, she flicked on her brights. The crescent moon didn't have enough power to light up the desert, and the road didn't have many travelers. When the odd car did approach from the oncoming lane of traffic, she dimmed her lights.

Finally, she didn't meet any other cars coming the other way, and she expelled a breath she didn't even know she'd been holding. Nobody else would be out here at this time of night.

Her headlights illuminated the mile marker on the side of the highway, and she glanced at her odometer to track the miles. At two miles past the marker, she eased off her gas pedal and peered over the steering wheel.

She spotted the break in the highway and turned onto an access road. Her truck bounced and lurched as it ate up the rough ground beneath its wheels.

If you didn't know the fencing was there, you could drive right into it, but she caught the gleam from the metal posts and the heavy-duty wire strung between those posts.

She pulled up next to the fence and cut her lights. Her flashlight would have do. She didn't want to advertise her presence on this land, just in case another driver saw her lights out here from the highway. She hopped from the truck, opened the back door and snagged her backpack first.

Flicking on the flashlight, she ran its beam along the length of the fence. It hadn't been designed to keep people out so much as to stake a claim.

She ground her teeth together and ducked between the two wires that stretched from post to post. At least nobody had thought to electrify this fence, but again they didn't have anything to protect—not yet.

She stumbled across the desert floor for about twenty feet, and then dropped to her knees at a slight dip. Her flashlight illuminated the area—no rocks, no cactus, no distinguishing features.

She wedged her pack in the dirt to mark the spot and jogged back to her truck. She grabbed the shovel and wrestled the duffel bag from the back seat. The items slowed her progress back to the perfect spot, but she still had enough energy to do what she came here to do.

She dragged the backpack out of the way and plunged her shovel into the sand. In and out, she dipped the shovel into the sand and flicked it out to the side.

Sweating, she pinched her damp T-shirt from her body and surveyed her work. How deep did it have to be? Enough to conceal but not hide forever.

She unzipped the duffel bag at her feet, positioned it at the edge of the hole…and dumped the contents into the shallow grave.

SAM PUSHED HIS laptop away and with it, the faces of the missing people. Gone without a trace. How did that happen? And all of them last seen near the Arizona border towns.

He didn't believe in coincidences.

He'd thought at one point that the bones of the missing might be found in the myriad tunnels that ran between the US and Mexican border, but Border Patrol had gotten a line on most of those tunnels and no bodies had turned up inside them.

Still, the Sonoran Desert provided a vast graveyard. He pulled his laptop toward him again and switched from the faces of the mostly young people to a map of the desert running between Paradiso and the border.

One area on the map jumped out at him, and he traced his fingertip around the red line that marked the location where the new casino was planned. That land, which belonged to the Yaqui tribe, had always been somewhat reachable due to the access road.

He stood up, stretching his arms over his head. He wandered to the window of his motel room and gazed at the drops of water glistening on the glass. The rain had stopped, nothing preventing him from his expedition now.

He grabbed his weapon and his wallet and marched out to his rental car. When did Border Patrol ever stop working? Especially when an agent didn't have anything better to do.

He pulled out of the motel parking lot and headed toward the highway. His headlights glimmered on the wet asphalt, but on either side of him, the dark desert lurked, keeping its secrets—just like a woman.

Grunting, he hit the steering wheel with the heel of his hand and cranked up the radio. Two days back and the desert had already weaved its spell on him. He'd come to appreciate its mystical, magical aura when he lived here, but the memory had receded when he moved to San Diego. When he left Paradiso, he'd tried to put all those feelings aside—and failed.

When he saw the mile marker winking at him from the side of the road, he grabbed his cell phone and squinted at the directions. He should be seeing the entrance to an access road in about two miles. A few minutes later, he spotted the gap and turned into it, his tires kicking up sand and gravel.

His rental protested by shaking and jerking on the unpaved stretch of road. He gripped the wheel to steady it. "Hold on, baby."

A pair of headlights appeared in the distance, and he blinked his eyes. Did mirages show up at night? Who the hell would be out here?

His heart thumped against his chest. Someone up to no good.

As his car approached the vehicle—a truck by the look of it—he slowed to a crawl. The road couldn't accommodate the two of them passing each other. One of them would have to back into the sand, and a truck, probably with four-wheel drive, could do that a lot better than he could in this midsize with its four cylinders.

The truck jerked to a stop and started backing up at an angle. The driver recognized what Sam had already deduced. The truck would have to be the one to make way but if this dude thought he'd be heading out of here free, clear and anonymous, he didn't realize he'd run headlong into a Border Patrol agent—uniformed or not.

Sam threw his car into Park and left the engine running as he scrambled from the front seat. The driver of the truck revved his engine. Did the guy think he was going to run him over? Take him out in the dead of night?

Sam flipped open his wallet to his ID and badge and rested his other hand on his weapon as he stalked up to the driver's side of the truck.

Holding his badge in front of him and rapping on the hood of the vehicle, he approached the window. "Border Patrol. What's your business out here?"

The window buzzed down, and a pair of luminous dark eyes caught him in their gaze. "Sam? Sam Cross?"

Sam gulped and his heart beat even faster than before as the beam of his flashlight played over the high cheekbones and full lips of the woman he'd loved beyond all reason.

Chapter Two

He growled. "Who is it? Who are you?"

He'd have to try harder than that to sound convincing.

"Oh, please." She shaded her eyes against the intrusive glare of the flashlight. "You know damned well who it is, so get that light out of my face."

He shifted the beam to the side so that it illuminated the ends of her silky ponytail. Bad move. His breath hitched in his throat as he recalled the way that hair had feathered across his bare skin.

"Jolene Nighthawk?"

"In the flesh, Sam." She cut her engine and turned on the dome light in her truck. "What are you doing out here at this time of night?"

"I already asked you that question. It's not safe."

"It's my land…indirectly." She set her jaw, and her nostrils flared. "What could be safer?"

He shoved his hands in his pockets and kicked sand at her tire. "So, the Yaqui are going ahead with the casino development on the property. Is this your cousin Wade's doing?"

"Wade and the others." She lifted her shoulders. "The tribe put it to a vote, and the Desert Sun Casino won."

"Were you just…surveying the land?" He flung an arm out to the side. "Planting a bomb?"

Jolene jerked her head, her dark eyes flashing. "What does that mean?"

"Just kidding." He held up his hands. "I know you're probably not too happy about the casino. Weren't you trying to prove that any disruption of the land would impact the three-toed tree owl or something?"

She chuckled, and the low sultry sound did something to his insides. "There is no such thing as a three-toed tree owl. I think you mean the elf owl, so points for being close."

He grinned like an idiot, just so damned happy to be in her presence again. "See, I was listening to your lectures."

"Those were supposed to be conversations, not lectures. And no, the environmental study I ordered didn't prove that the casino would disturb the elf owls' habitat, as it's farther west." She gripped the steering wheel with both hands. "In the end, I had nothing."

"That's a good thing, isn't it? I mean, that the construction site isn't going to impact the desert critters."

"It's not going to affect them as much as it would have to for any alteration in the plans."

"The casino will provide a lot of jobs and generate a lot of money for the tribe, right? I know Border Patrol is involved at some level because some of those new employees will be coming from the Yaqui tribe members in Mexico. The Yaqui governing body has already contacted us." He felt the need to keep talking as Jolene stared at the desert over her steering wheel.

She whipped her head around, her eyes narrowed to slits. "Is that what you're doing out here? Is that why you're in Paradiso?"

Whoa. Had he become the enemy? Who was he kidding? He'd become the enemy the day he'd left her... The day she'd pushed him away.

"I... Something like that." He didn't have to give her all the gory details of his assignment.

She tapped the steering wheel with her long slender fingers. "At this time of night, you're not going to get a very clear picture of the scope of the project, and ground-breaking doesn't start for another two days. The equipment's not even in place yet."

"The rain stopped me from coming out before. I could've put it off until tomorrow, but…it called to me. The desert called to me, and I wanted to see the land before all the hubbub started." Heat rushed from his chest to his face, and he gave thanks to the darkness for its concealment.

"Same." She fired up the truck. "Are you going to be at the ground-breaking ceremony?"

"I'll be there. You?"

"Of course." She threw the truck in Reverse and backed up farther off the access road into the sand. "It's my land."

As she wheeled around him and his rental car, she put her hand out the window and yelled. "Watch out for singing sticks."

Her words caused a chill to run up his spine. She was referring to the Yaqui legend about the boy who killed his brother and buried him in the desert. A small stick with a button on top grew out of the dead boy's head where he was buried. When an old man driving his mules found the stick and grabbed it, the stick sang to him of the boy's death.

The tires of Jolene's truck squealed as they gained purchase on the access road, and Sam watched her taillights until his eyes watered and all he saw was a red blur.

He hopped back into his car and continued on his way. If only all the dead people he was searching for had sticks to mark their burial places.

Two days after his encounter with Jolene, Sam slipped the green shirt of his Border Patrol uniform from its hanger and shook it out. He stuffed his arms in the sleeves and buttoned it to the collar.

It would be hot as blazes at the ground-breaking ceremony for the casino, but he'd be there in an official capacity and couldn't exactly wear shorts and flip-flops. He didn't care. The event would give him another opportunity to see Jolene.

He'd tried to catch sight of her around town, short of stalking her outside her house, but she'd been keeping a low profile. She could've been busy with her duties as a ranger for the National Park Service...but he had a suspicion she was avoiding him.

He didn't blame her, but he'd have liked a chance to tell her his situation now—not that it would make a difference to her. Their meeting the other night showed that she'd clearly moved on.

Looking in the mirror, Sam ran a hand through his hair and then rubbed his front teeth with the pad of his finger— just in case he got to talk with Jolene.

He exited his motel room, and hit the remote for the Border Patrol truck in the parking lot. He climbed inside and made the return trip to the future site of the Yaqui casino.

About thirty minutes later, he slowed down as a line of traffic clogged the highway. Two highway patrol officers were waving people over to the side of the road to park.

Sam rolled down his window and stuck his arm out, flagging down an officer.

A big guy with mirrored sunglasses approached the truck. "You can go around and park at the site. Visitors are parking along the highway and shuttles will take them in to the ground-breaking."

"That's smart. No way all these cars are going to trundle down that road. So, I can pull right in?"

"If you can squeeze through the protestors." The man smirked. "It's a spectacle."

"There are protestors?"

"On the highway. We won't let them go down the access road."

"The Yaqui?" Sam's heartbeat rattled his rib cage.

"Some of them. The ones who don't want the casino. But they've been overruled." The cop rolled his shoulders. "Don't know what they're complaining about. That casino means big money for the tribe and every Yaqui with a card."

"There are more important things than money to some." Sam wheeled around the officer and crawled along the other side of the highway. The infrastructure around here was going to have to change to accommodate the casino. This two-lane highway wouldn't cut it.

As he approached the access road, the decibel level rose and he rolled down his window. Members of the Yaqui tribe were out in force, garbed in native dress, carrying signs, yelling and beating drums. The drums reverberated in Sam's ears, and he held his breath as he peered out the window at the protestors. Would Jolene be one of them?

Sometimes these protests could get unruly and violent, and he didn't want Jolene in the middle of it—not that she would appreciate or even want his protectiveness. He couldn't help it. He couldn't help a lot of things when it came to Jolene Nighthawk. When he didn't see her face among the crowd, he expelled a long breath. Maybe Granny Viv had prevailed upon Jolene to skip the protests today.

He coasted through the divide the highway patrol had forged through the group of protestors. Then he tucked in behind one of the vans ferrying people to the site.

The shuttle turned into a large cleared-out circular area,

and Sam followed suit. Colorful flags, that weren't here the other night, drooped in the still air, looking sad instead of festive but that didn't deter the mood of the dignitaries.

A stage had been set up, and Wade Nighthawk, Jolene's cousin, occupied the center of it. He wore his black hair in a sleek ponytail, his only other nod to his Native American heritage, a loose-fitting white shirt embroidered with the animal symbols of the Yaqui, which replaced his usual tailored shirts and suit jacket.

The mayor and other major players clustered on one end of the stage. Sam spotted Nash Dillon talking to a well-dressed older woman. Sam stuck his hand out the window of the truck and pointed at Nash, who nodded back at him. Although Nash was a Border Patrol agent, Nash's family's business had a stake in the casino development, and the dark-haired woman with dramatic gray streaks in her hair was probably involved in the money side of the project.

Clay Archer, the agent in charge of the Paradiso Border Patrol station, gave Sam a thumbs-up from the stage. *Better him than me up there.*

Sam parked and exited his vehicle. He strode up to the stage and clasped hands with Clay.

"Do you have to give a speech or something?"

Clay rolled his eyes. "Just a few words about the Yaqui on the other side of the border and the accommodations we'll make for them to come over and work in the casino."

Nash joined them. "I'd give anything to get off this stage, but my parents insisted I be here and meet the representative for our business group backing the project."

As the woman Nash had been speaking to approached, Sam raised his eyebrow and gave a quick shake of his head.

Nash turned to the woman smoothly. "Karen, I'd like to introduce you to a couple of my fellow Border Patrol agents,

Clay Archer and Sam Cross. Sam's out of San Diego. This is Karen Fisher. She's representing the investors."

The attractive woman's smooth face didn't match her graying hair—neither did her strong grip. "Nice to meet you. Thanks for all you do to keep us safe."

Clay, ever the gentleman, said, "Just doing our jobs, ma'am."

Karen drilled Nash with her dark eyes. "What are you doing here from…?"

"San Diego."

"That's right. I suppose you have even more problems with drugs coming across the border there, don't you?"

"We do."

"Sam, welcome back." Wade leaned past the others, extending his hand, his white teeth blinding against his brown skin.

The guy had the smile of a politician. Sam pumped his hand. "Good to see you, Wade. Congratulations."

"Thank you. This is going to mean a lot for Paradiso, as well as the tribe. But then—" Wade cocked his head and his ponytail slid over his shoulder "—you don't live here anymore, so it won't mean much to you. Granny told me you were in town, though. Business?"

"Uh-huh." Sam shifted his gaze to the right and left of the stage.

"Doesn't mean you can't combine a little pleasure with the business." Wade winked. "Jolene's by the equipment to the right."

Before Sam could deny he was searching for Jolene, Wade stepped back and slapped the back of Mayor Zamora. Total politician.

"I'm going to head over there." Sam tipped his head in the general direction of the heavy equipment ready to gouge the earth.

Clay raised his eyebrows. "You do that. I'm gonna practice my speech."

"We should probably take our seats." Nash cupped Karen's elbow and she nodded in Sam's direction.

Sam wended his way through the crowd of people, his step picking up when he saw Jolene helping Granny Viv into a seat. Granny Viv could be his excuse, not that he didn't want to see the old lady anyway. He'd been a favorite of hers—until he'd broken her granddaughter's heart.

He licked his lips as he walked up to the women, his tongue sweeping up grains of sand.

He squeezed Granny Viv's shoulder. "Finally, I get to see my favorite person in Paradiso."

Granny Viv cranked her head to the side. "You sound like Wade now. Nothing stopping you from dropping in at the rez for a visit."

"Been busy with work." Sam gave the old woman a hug. "You don't look a day older since I left."

"You *are* just like Wade." She wagged a gnarled finger at him. "Are you just going to ignore him, Jolene?"

"Gran, sit." She patted the back of the chair where she'd placed a cushion for her grandmother. "Hello, Sam. How are you?"

Oh, they were playing it like that—like they hadn't run into each other in the middle of the night at this very place the night before last. Two could play that game.

He wrapped his arms around her and pulled her in for a hug. Her soft body yielded to his for a second before she stiffened in his arms.

"Good to see you, Jolene. I was glad I didn't spy you out front with the protestors—for safety's sake."

She reared back from him until he dropped his arms. "Protest is futile. Clay giving a speech up there?"

That hug had affected him more than it had her, and

his tight throat made it hard to speak. "Something about the Yaqui on the other side of the border."

Granny Viv patted the chair next to her. "Sit here for the festivities."

Jolene gripped the back of the chair. "I thought I was sitting next to you, Gran?"

"I see you all the time. Let Sam sit here, and you can sit on the other side of him."

Sam plopped down in the seat to claim it before Jolene could, as if playing a game of musical chairs. "No place else I'd rather be."

With no other choice, Jolene sat next to him, crossing one long leg over the other, her eyebrows creating a V over her nose.

Mayor Zamora stepped up to the mic and tapped it. "Everyone enjoying the food and the dancers?"

He paused for the scattered applause and launched into his speech about the importance of the Yaqui tribe to the area and its cultural contributions.

The mayor's words flowed over Sam, one running into the other. Sam's attention was fully focused on Jolene's leg kicking back and forth. She usually favored jeans and boots, but today a light skirt rippled around her calves and each time she kicked out her foot, the slit in the skirt parted to reveal the smooth skin of her thigh.

Her elbow jabbed his shoulder. "Are you even paying attention?"

"What? Yeah, cultural contributions." He adjusted his sunglasses and peered at the stage where the flags had started flapping.

"I said, I wasn't sure how a gambling casino was a Yaqui cultural asset. They'll probably decorate it with our icons—ugh." Her full lips flattened into a snarl.

"Shh." Granny Viv reached across Sam and poked Jolene's arm. "Your cousin's up next."

Wade took the mayor's place at the mic and gave a loud whoop. The crowd went nuts and answered him in kind.

Jolene rolled her eyes and pointed at the darkening sky. "Looks like it's going to rain on their parade."

The wind had picked up and the once-pathetic flags snapped in the breeze, clapping along with the audience. Wade knew how to work a crowd, for sure. Little eddies of sand swirled on the desert floor, a sure sign of the oncoming monsoon.

He tilted his head toward hers. "Maybe they'll get through all the pomp and circumstance, and the mayor and Wade can toss a shovelful of sand over their shoulders before the big machines get to work."

"Will the excavators still work in the rain?" She folded her hands over her knee, twisting her fingers.

"Sure. After all this, they'll want to get started on the big dig."

Her restless hands moved to her skirt where she pleated the material, released it and pleated it again.

Jolene might've been happier out there with the protestors, but after the death of Jolene's father, Wade took the reins of the Nighthawk family and the family members had always been part of the Yaqui governing board. Bad optics for one Nighthawk cousin to be in here cheerleading the casino and the other out there carrying signs.

Clay did his part up there, and then the speeches ended. Both Mayor Zamora and Wade raised their ceremonial shovels and stepped from the stage. Someone came forward with wire cutters and snipped the wires between the posts, creating an opening for the two dignitaries.

They both plunged their shovels into the sand at the

same time, as a cheer rose from the crowd and the cameras came out.

Jolene sat stiffly beside him, barely taking a breath.

Sam touched her shoulder. "Did you get anything to eat? Do you want something from one of the food trucks?"

She flashed a smile at him that nearly knocked him off his chair. "Yeah, that would be great."

He hadn't expected that response. He figured she'd want to hightail it out of here as fast as she could. He asked Granny Viv if she wanted something to eat and she sent him and Jolene off in quest of some chili.

As they sauntered toward the food trucks, Jolene took a deep breath. "That rain is coming, but I think they'll be able to start digging before the deluge, don't you?"

"All of a sudden, you seem anxious for them to get to work." He shot her a glance from the side of his eye.

"It's like a bandage. Peel it off all at once." She jerked her thumb toward a food truck to the right. "I think this one has the chili Gran wants."

They shuffled in line until they reached the window, and Sam ordered three cups of chili and some bottles of water. He grabbed a straw when he picked up the food, and on their way back to Gran, he and Jolene squeezed their way through the people gawking at the excavators gulping up the sand and spitting it out in big piles.

When they reached Granny Viv, Sam placed the chili in her hands and put the bottle of water with the straw sticking out of it on the empty chair next to her. "Watch out. It's hot."

A clap of thunder boomed in the distance as if to emphasize his precaution.

The chatter level seemed to rise with the echoes of the thunder, and a mass of people began to surge toward the build site, knocking over a few chairs in the process.

"What's going on?" Jolene poked him in the back. "You're tall. Can you see what's happening? Something other than the thunder got all these people excited."

"I'm not sure." Sam peered above the bobbing heads. "A couple of the workmen are shouting and running toward the stage."

"I hope nobody's hurt." Granny Viv held her spoon full of steaming chili suspended in the air, halfway to her mouth.

Sam placed his food next to the water on the chair. "I'll check it out."

"I'm coming with you." Jolene added her bowl to the collection on the chair and hooked a finger in his belt loop. "Lead the way."

If she were willing to follow him, he'd lead her wherever she wanted to go.

Sam plowed through the clutches of people, with Jolene right behind him. When he reached the stage, he grabbed Clay's arm. "What's going on, Clay?"

"Not sure." He nodded toward the piles of sand and dirt. "The work crew found something, I think."

Sam edged closer to a couple of guys throwing their arms around and talking a mile a minute.

One shouted in Wade's face. "We have to stop. We have to stop."

A flush rose to Wade's cheeks. "Don't be ridiculous. It's nothing. Keep going."

The driver of one of the excavators dug his work boots into the sand. "I won't. I won't continue."

The other worker crossed himself and said, *"Dios mio."*

Jolene called out, her voice rising above the din. "Wade, what's wrong? What is it?"

Wade's head whipped around, a scowl marring his smooth face. "It's nothing. Nonsense."

The mayor shook his head. "Well, I'll be damned. Seems like the boys dug up some bones. We might've just stumbled on a graveyard."

Chapter Three

Jolene folded her arms across her midsection. "Bones? Human bones?"

"That's just it, Jolene, it could be anything, one of those extinct animals you care so much about." Wade flicked his long fingers toward the two workmen. "Do these guys look like archaeologists to you?"

"Are you?" She slashed a hand through the air, figuratively trying to wipe the smirk from Wade's face. "Watch your tone. They know what they saw."

Sam whistled through his teeth and murmured in her ear. "That's going to put a crimp in old Wade's plans, isn't it?"

She whispered. "He's right. Those bones could belong to anything."

"Or anyone." Sam's jaw tensed. "Didn't the mayor mention a graveyard? More than one set of bones?"

"Whatever it was, it shook up the crew." Jolene put a hand on Sam's back as he made a quick turn. "Where are you going?"

"I figure Clay and I know a human bone when we see one." He waved his arm in the air at Clay. "Hey, Clay!"

Clay joined them. "Did you hear that? They dug up some bones?"

"Are you thinking what I'm thinking? Let's go have a

look. It doesn't seem like anyone else wants to investigate."
He squeezed Jolene's shoulder. "Wait here."

"No way." She strode after the two Border Patrol agents.
"You don't think I know animal bones when I see them?
Ruling out is as important as identifying."

Sam cranked his head over his shoulder. "I know better
than to try to stop you from doing anything."

He couldn't stop her from loving him, either. But then,
he hadn't tried that hard.

The three of them trudged through the sand toward
the heavy equipment, its jaws suspended in the air, wide
open and frozen. They stopped at the edge of a hole in the
ground and peered down into it.

Clay jabbed a finger toward the sand. "There. It's a long
bone. Looks like a femur."

"Could be a coyote, a sheep." Sam slapped at a big drop
of rain that had fallen on the side of his neck.

Jolene's gaze darted between the bones in the pit, and
then she twisted her head over her shoulder and surveyed
the ground to the side of the excavator. A smooth crescent
protruded from the sand.

She broke away from Clay and Sam and wandered toward the pile of dirt the excavator had dumped after a few
digs. Crouching down, she brushed the sand away from
the white dome and called over her shoulder. "You think
this is from a coyote, too?"

Both men strode toward her and peeked over her shoulder at the human skull next to the wheel of the excavator.

Clay got on his phone. "I'm calling Paradiso PD. They
should have a car out here anyway, monitoring those protestors."

"I'll give Wade and Mayor Zamora the bad news. This
construction has to stop now. This could be a crime scene."
Sam pivoted in the sand and scuffed toward the stage.

Jolene's heart pounded, and she tugged on the back of his shirt. "Crime scene? What do you mean a crime scene?"

"Those bones could belong to a murder victim." His eyebrows snapped over his nose. "You're the one who found the skull. You know it doesn't belong to an animal."

"A murder victim?" She swiveled her head around, taking in the swirl of activity—the colors, the voices, the smells—and tilted to the side.

Sam grabbed her around the waist. "What's wrong? Are you feeling faint? Did the bones upset you?"

"The crush of people is getting to me. I'm going to collect Gran and get out of here." As she whirled away from Sam, Wade stormed up to her and pinched her upper arm between his thumb and forefinger. "What did you do?"

She yanked out of her cousin's grasp and stumbled into Sam. "Me? I didn't do anything."

"You were out there. I heard you found the human skull." He jabbed a finger into her chest. "Why do you have to go nosing into everything? I could've handled the guys. We could've…"

"What, Wade? Swept it under the rug? Kept it hidden?"

Sam had been on the phone during her exchange with Wade and when her cousin had gotten up close and personal, Sam swung around and smoothly stepped between them. "Whoa, Wade. You need to calm down. There was no hiding those bones. Do you think if Jolene hadn't discovered the skull, Clay and I wouldn't have seen it? The gruesome discovery shook up those workmen. They never would've kept quiet."

Wade stretched his lips, his plastic smile melting into a sneer. "You have no idea the effect a few bucks can have on a man's nerves."

"I wouldn't be spouting off about your bribery skills if

I were you, Wade." Sam held up his phone. "I called the Paradiso PD, and they're sending a car back. They're gonna put yellow crime scene tape up to replace your multicolored ribbons. Then the Pima County Sheriff's Department is going to send their CSIs out here to collect those bones."

Jolene swallowed. "What are they going to do with the bones?"

"Test them, measure them, analyze them. Maybe discover the identity of the person." Sam smacked Wade on the back. "Don't look so bummed, Wade. Once they clear out those bones and check the area for more, your project should be able to get back on track—in a year."

"This isn't going to deter us." Wade smoothed a hand over his face, putting his calm, unruffled facade back in place. "You should take Gran home, Jolene."

"That's what I was just going to do." A fat raindrop splashed on the back of her hand. "And not a minute too soon."

"I'll come with you." Sam cupped her elbow and guided her through the thinning crowd. "Wade's a piece of work."

"He's a piece of something." She shook him off. "You don't have to protect me against Wade—or anything else."

She'd been getting too comfortable with Sam's little gestures—the touches, the consideration, the fawning over Gran—scratch that last one. Gran adored Sam and reveled in the attentions he gave her.

When they got back to the chairs where they'd left Gran, two teens were sprawled across them, their noses buried in their phones.

Jolene recognized one of them. "Andrew, did you see my grandmother here?"

He lifted one eyebrow without raising his gaze from his phone. "Yeah, she left with my grandmother. They told me to stay here and let you know when you got back—and they took your car."

"They took my car?" Jolene peered at the sky. "Why'd they do that?"

Andrew shrugged one shoulder. "Me and my friend wanted to stay, so Granny Viv told my grandma to take your keys and your car so they could leave. I can drive you."

Jolene snagged her purse from under the chair. "That's okay, Andrew. I'll get a ride…"

"With me." Sam looked down his nose at the boy. "You're old enough to drive?"

"Got my license and everything." He socked his friend in the arm. "Let's go see if we can get a look at those bones."

As the boys slouched off, Sam turned to Jolene. "Do you mind waiting until I talk to the Paradiso PD? They'll probably want to talk to you, too."

"Me?" Her voice squeaked and she cleared her throat. "Why would they want to talk to me?"

"You found the skull."

"I didn't find it. The skull was lying on the ground." She adjusted her purse over her shoulder and folded her arms. The less she was involved with this, the better.

"It wasn't lying on the ground. Clay and I wouldn't have missed it if it were." He placed a hand on her back. "They're here."

Jolene glanced up at the officers talking to Wade and the two workmen. Wade had recovered his equilibrium and had the appearance of complete cooperation with the work stoppage. His wife, Cerisse, would get a whole different perspective at home tonight.

Sam greeted the cops and told them how he and Clay had gone out to look at the bones, just to see if they were human. He jerked his thumb toward her. "And the minute Jolene found the skull, we knew what we had."

The officer didn't have many questions for them and Jolene convinced Sam to leave before the sheriffs came on the scene.

"We left our names with the officer. If the sheriff's deputies want to contact us, they can." She tipped her head back to take in the darkening sky. "Besides, we're going to be caught in the deluge in a few minutes."

"At least we don't have to wait for the shuttle." He pointed out a Border Patrol vehicle parked behind the food trucks. "I got preferred parking."

As he opened the door of the truck for her, the rain started coming down in earnest. She ducked in quickly, and he slammed the door.

By the time he slid behind the wheel, his shirt was already soaked.

"It's going to be another monsoon like the other day."

"It is the season for them. How was the summer? Any rain then?"

"Not much. Looks like the clouds are making up for the dry months."

Sam followed one of the shuttle vans down the access road and swerved around it when they hit the highway.

He gestured toward the phone cupped in her hands. "Do you want to call Rosie and see if she and your grandmother made it home okay?"

"I'll give them more time to get there. I don't want to distract Rosie if she's driving. It's bad enough that her grandson Andrew is out here on the road."

"You didn't tell Granny Viv that we ran into each other the night before last." He slid a glance her way, and then concentrated on the road.

"I didn't want to worry her."

"Because she knows how upset you are about the casino going in?"

"Oh, I'm not that upset." She smoothed her hands over her skirt. "Progress, right? Wade told me how many jobs the casino will bring to the area…and our people. That can't be a bad thing. I understand Nash Dillon is involved in the project."

"Yeah." Sam rubbed his chin. "I think he's more involved with his job with the Border Patrol than he is with his family's business, but he was at the ground-breaking with the rep for one of the big financial backers."

"His family has that silent partner—the one who invested in the pecan-processing plant with them. I think he has a financial stake in the casino."

"Not him, personally. It's that Karen… Fisher who's repping the consortium. Nash has his hands full with the baby he and his fiancée are adopting."

"Yeah, Nash with a baby." She stared out the window at the rivulets of water squiggling down the glass—just like tears. She should ask him about his own child, his daughter. Her throat tightened, and she rested her forehead against the window.

"My wife and I are divorced." He blurted out the words, and they hung in the car between them.

Should she pick them up or let them settle and dissolve?

"I heard that one before." She put a hand over her mouth to stop any more accusations from flying out.

"Jolene, I never told you I was divorced." The truck hit a puddle and water splashed the window causing her to jerk back.

"Separated, divorced. You told me they were the same thing." She held her left hand out to the side, palm out. "I know. I believed what I wanted to believe."

"I thought my marriage was over, Jolene. I wanted it

to be over. I wanted to be with you." He slammed a fist against the dashboard.

Her fingers plucked at the material of her skirt. "I know you had to choose your daughter over me. I understand. Neither of us would've been happy if you'd abandoned your baby."

"And yet, here I am." He cranked on the defroster as the windows started fogging over. "Working out of state, my daughter in San Diego. Babies can't save failing marriages."

"You had to try." Her eyes followed the slapping windshield wipers, their motion almost hypnotizing her. "Wh-what's her name?"

"Jessica. I call her Jess." His fingers flexed on the steering wheel, and his tight jaw relaxed. "She just turned two."

Jolene knew exactly how old Sam's child was. It had been over two years now since he'd left her and broken her heart. She could've stopped him. He'd been waiting for her to stop him, but he would've hated himself and eventually he'd have hated her, too.

His own father had abandoned Sam, his brother and mother when Sam was just three years old. He could never do that to a child of his own.

Whatever had happened between him and his wife when he went back to the marriage must've been intolerable for him to end it.

She swiped a hand beneath her nose. "Is Jess talking?"

"Nonstop words and babble." He made the turn onto her street.

"Do you want to come in for a little while? There's someone who'd like to see you."

"Chip? You still have Chip?"

"Of course." She wouldn't tell him she'd soaked Chip's fur with her tears every night after Sam had left. Only she and Chip ever had to know that.

He pulled into her driveway, and she hopped out of the truck before he cut the engine. She ran to her covered walkway, holding her purse over her head to deflect the rain.

She stopped halfway to the door and cocked her head. "Do you hear that?"

"Sounds like a wild bear trying to claw his way outside."

"Chip knows you're here. He never gets that excited when I come home." She nudged a flowerpot to the side and stooped down to pick up her house key. As she pounded on the door with the heel of her hand, she said, "You'd better settle down in there. You should be on your best behavior."

She cracked the door open and Chip thrust his wet nose into the opening. "Are you ready, Sam?"

"Bring it on." Sam crouched down, bracing himself.

When Jolene swung open the door, Chip hurtled himself toward Sam and nearly bowled him over. Wagging his tail, Chip put his front paws on Sam's chest and bathed his face in dog kisses.

"Look at you." Sam hung his arm around the dog's neck and patted his side. "He's so big now. Is he a good guard dog?"

"The best. Can't you tell by the greeting he gave you?" She tugged on Chip's collar. "C'mon, you silly boy."

She widened the door, but Chip wouldn't budge until Sam rose and strode over the threshold.

Shutting the door behind them, she placed the extra key on the table in the entryway and hung up her wet purse on the peg next to the umbrella she could've used earlier. "Do you want something to drink?"

"Just water." He pulled the shirt of his uniform out of the waistband of his pants. "You know what I'd really like?"

Her heart fluttered and her mouth got dry as she watched Sam's fingers undo the top button on his shirt. She couldn't go there with him again, no matter how desperately her body yearned for his touch.

He raised an eyebrow. "If it's not too much trouble, I'd like to borrow your dryer for about twenty minutes before I go back to the station. This wet shirt is really uncomfortable."

"Of course, yes." She ducked down to pet Chip, letting her hair shield her warm face.

"The T-shirt, too?"

She glanced up at Sam, his shirt gaping open over a white V-neck T-shirt.

"I'm soaked to the skin."

"No problem." She scratched Chip behind one floppy ear. "I don't have anything you can wear unless you want to put on a robe. It's black but it does have flowers on it. I won't take pictures, I swear."

"It's not exactly cold, is it? I'll pass—not that I don't trust you."

She flicked her hair over her shoulder. What did he mean by that?

He shrugged out of his shirt and yanked at the hem of his T-shirt, peeling the wet cotton from his torso.

With the T-shirt over Sam's head, Jolene drank in the sight of his lean, muscled body. Her fingertips tingled with the memory of his smooth, warm flesh and the need ached in her gut.

He pulled the shirt off his head, and she turned toward the kitchen. "I'll get you that water and stuff those things in the dryer for you—as long as you don't expect me to iron anything."

"Lucky for both of us, the uniform doesn't need ironing." He followed her into the kitchen, holding his damp shirts in his hands in front of him, like an offering, facing her across the small center island.

"You can put those on the counter." She nodded toward the island as she reached for the cupboard and grabbed a glass. "We never got to finish our chili, did we? Are you hungry?"

"I'll pick up something on my way back to the station." He perched on a stool, only his bare chest visible above the edge of the counter.

If anyone had told her this morning she'd have Sam Cross half-naked in her kitchen by the afternoon, she'd have…thanked them.

She filled the glass with ice and water from her fridge and set it before him with a tap on the counter. Wiggling her fingers, she said, "Why are you still holding those wet things? Give them to me."

"Didn't want to get your gleaming counter all wet." He held out the bundle of clothes to the side, and she circled the island to take them, her gaze avoiding all that bare male flesh in front of her.

She took the shirts with both hands and walked back through the kitchen to the laundry room. "Perfect timing. I have some things in the wash that need to go in the dryer. We can save on electricity."

"I don't want my shirt to get your stuff dirty."

"It's fine. It's just a few towels and…other things." She tossed Sam's shirts in the dryer and then piled her own clothes in after. She plucked a dryer sheet from the box and threw it in with the rest. She jabbed a few buttons, took a deep breath and returned to the kitchen.

"You never told me what you were doing in Paradiso? Some case you're working?"

"Yeah, a case." He ran the side of his thumb down the sweating glass. "And that's why I want to thank you, Jolene."

"Thank me?" She poked a finger into her chest. "For what? How did I help your case?"

Sam gulped back the rest of the water and smacked the glass on the counter. "By planting those bones at the construction site."

Chapter Four

Sam narrowed his eyes, as he watched a rosy flush creep up Jolene's face. She'd just confirmed his suspicions.

"You think I planted those bones at the construction site? That's what you think I was doing there the other night?" Her long lashes fluttered with every blink of her eyes. "Wh-why would I do that?"

"C'mon, Jolene. What do you take me for?" He crossed his arms over his chest, probably losing a little of the high ground without his shirt. "You're out there in the middle of the night, a shovel in the bed of your pickup and a set of bones appears on the day of the ground-breaking for a casino you detest."

"That's crazy." She swept his glass from the counter and spun toward the sink. "Where would I get bones, anyway?"

"You're a resourceful woman. I'm sure it didn't take you long to figure out how to get your hands on a set of bones. And—" he leveled a finger at her "—you made sure we found the skull, because you knew it was there."

Pulling back her shoulders, she tilted up her chin. "You can't prove anything."

"Give me a month or two, and I'm sure I could prove it." He rested his arms on the counter and hunched his shoulders. "But I'm not interested in nailing you for planting bones. I'm not sure that's even a crime."

"Why not? Why even bring it up if you don't care?" She set the glass in the sink and turned, gripping the edge of the counter behind her.

"I didn't say I didn't care. Didn't I thank you for doing it?"

"You're not making any sense. I'm not admitting to anything, but why should you be happy if *someone* left bones there?"

"Because that helps my case." He scratched his jaw. "Can I have some more water, please? All this explaining is making me thirsty."

"That's funny. I don't hear you explaining much of anything. You're throwing around accusations and talking about some case. You still haven't told me why you're here." She snatched up his glass from the sink, and his leftover ice tinkled as she filled it again.

"Missing people."

Her hand jerked as she set the glass down, and the water sloshed over the side. "Missing people?"

Drawing an invisible line on the counter with this finger, he said, "There was a cluster of missing people southeast of San Diego at about the same time we saw an influx of a particularly pure form of meth, pink meth. We saw a similar pattern here in Paradiso from a few years ago. As I'd worked in this area before, my commander sent me here to look into it."

"I don't get it." She dabbled her fingers in the puddle of water on the counter. "People go missing all the time. Why do these folks warrant closer scrutiny than all the other missing people?"

He formed a circle with both of his hands. "This is a cluster. It's a higher than average number of people who have gone missing. They all disappeared close to the border—here and in San Diego—and they vanished at a time when we started seeing this new meth on the street."

"How is the discovery of bones in the desert going to help your investigation?"

Sam rubbed his chin. "On the border in California, out in the desert, we found a graveyard of bones. We're still identifying them, but so far they belong to the people who disappeared at the same time the pink meth showed up. It makes me think there's a similar graveyard out here, and I want a chance to do some digging, literally, before that casino comes in and covers it all up."

"What makes you think it's in that location?" Jolene hugged herself and rubbed her arms.

He'd gladly hold her in his arms to do the hugging, but even though she'd been the one who had insisted he return to his pregnant wife, she hadn't forgiven him for leaving... yet. He swallowed. "A tip I received."

"You're not going to tell me what it was?"

"I'd rather not, but now I can use the discovery of the bones you dumped there to turn this into more than a wild goose chase. Question." He shoved his glass toward her and splayed his hands on the countertop. "What's your plan once the experts figure out the bones you buried don't belong to some ancient member of the Yaqui tribe? That the land is not a sacred Yaqui burial site?"

Her full lips parted, and her lashes swept over her eyes. Then she squared her shoulders and tossed her hair over her shoulder. "I hadn't thought that far ahead. My goal was to halt the immediate ground-breaking—and I did."

Progress. Sam eased out a breath. He'd had no proof that Jolene had planted the bones at the construction site, so the fact that she'd admitted it to him signaled a thaw in the icy chill she'd maintained since seeing him again.

"That you did." He winked at her. "I'm not going to ask

you where you got them because I know you have friends in high places…or at least academic places, but how'd you know the exact place to put them? They could've started digging anywhere."

A small smile twisted her lips. "I have a map of the construction site, which includes phases, including where the first hole was going. It's all very specific."

"Let me guess." He ran a hand over his chest, and Jolene's gaze followed the movement like a feather across his skin. It made him hard. If just a look from her luminous dark eyes could do that to him, he was in more trouble than he'd expected coming back here.

"Yes? What's your guess?" She quirked an eyebrow at him.

"Umm…" he shook his head "…that you got it from your cousin somehow."

"I did. Gran is always using Wade's phone. I took a peek at it, saw the plans and printed them out from his phone. I hadn't formulated my scheme yet, but seeing those plans gave me a few ideas." She snapped her fingers. "And it worked."

"For now. It's not going to take forensics long to figure out those bones are not part of a Yaqui graveyard, especially with Wade and his backers pushing for results." He nudged a sleeping Chip with the toe of his boot, and the dog thumped his tail once.

"Nash Dillon? Do you think Nash will be pushing him?" She wrapped a lock of hair around her finger. "Do you think Nash can do anything to stop the casino? Would he?"

"I don't know if he would or not. Most people around here think the casino is a good idea, Jolene."

"Most people don't have a father who was murdered out there." Her bottom lip quivered, and Sam pushed up from the stool.

He skirted the counter and cupped her face with one hand. "I know. I'm sorry, and I'm sorry nobody was ever brought to justice for that crime. Is that the reason you're against the casino?"

"If Joe Blackhawk were alive today, there would be no question of a casino going on that land." She cinched his wrist with her fingers. "Don't you see, Sam? The two events are linked. My father was murdered to clear the way for the casino."

"What are you saying? You think Wade killed your father?"

"I don't know." She released his arm, made a half turn and braced her hands against the counter. "It's like your missing people. It's just too much of a coincidence."

He reached out to touch her back, and then pulled away at the sound of the buzzer on the dryer. "The authorities put your father's murder down to the drug trade—he saw something or someone he shouldn't have seen out there."

"I know what they say." She straightened up and squeezed past him, her filmy blouse brushing against the bare skin of his chest. "I just don't believe it."

He watched the sway of her hips in the floral skirt as she walked away from him, and he squeezed his eyes closed. What would Jolene think of him if she knew he was consumed by visions of her in his bed while she was talking to him about her father?

"I don't think you're going to have much luck with Nash. His family business is part of some consortium that makes investment decisions over which he has little to no control. He just sits back and reaps the profits."

She floated back into the kitchen with his shirts draped over her arm. "It was just an idea. Nash has always been so easygoing—and I know his fiancée's father was also killed, in the line of duty. I thought she might be sympathetic."

"I'm sure she would be. I'm sure they both would be, but like I said, Nash is carried along with the business with little control over the decisions. His parents set it up that way, as neither Nash nor his sister had much interest in the day-to-day running of the corporation."

She dangled his shirts from her fingertips. "All dry."

As he swept them from her grasp, a pair of black lacy panties loosened from his T-shirt and drifted to the floor. He plucked them up between two fingers and waved them in the air. "Damn, busted. I didn't think I'd taken these off, too."

She snatched them back from him and crumpled the silky material in her fist. "Very funny. I told you I put your things in with my laundry."

Chuckling, he pulled the warm T-shirt over his head. As he poked his head out of the neck, he said, "I think I can help you with the second part of your plan."

"You're going to use the discovery of the bones to launch an investigation into that construction area as a possible burial site for those missing people."

"Exactly." He shook out his uniform shirt and hung it on the back of a kitchen chair. "It won't carry the same weight as a sacred site, but it will definitely cause delays in the construction."

"Does that mean you're not going to tell anyone that I dropped those bones there?" She swept her tongue along her bottom lip.

"Why should I? The interruption you caused will give me some time to poke around that land. Then when forensics discovers the bones are…whatever they are, I'll have another reason to halt the project. Maybe I'll make a similar discovery in Paradiso as we did south of San Diego." He put his finger to his lips. "And you won't tell anyone about my plans, either, right?"

"My lips are sealed."

He stuck out his hand. "Then we have a deal."

"Deal." She curled her hand around his, her smooth flesh sending tingles up his arm.

She started to pull away, but he held fast, running the pad of his thumb across the back of her hand. "How have you been, otherwise? You look good."

She left her hand in his. "I'm fine. I still enjoy my work. The extended family is doing well. Chip's my constant companion."

He'd already asked around about Jolene's marital and dating status, and he'd been relieved to find out she was single and not dating anyone special. He squeezed her hand before releasing it. "Happy?"

"Outside of the garbage going on with the casino? Yeah, happy. And you? What happened to your marriage?"

He shrugged. "What didn't happen? I knew it was doomed the minute I moved back there...or at least after the birth of Jess."

"Aimee didn't change after Jess was born?" Jolene placed a hand against her heart.

"Nope—still the life of every party."

"Is she still using?" Her fingers curled against her blouse. "Not while she was pregnant?"

"She stopped at first, but I think she was taking drugs at the end." He slammed a fist on the counter. "I should've seen it, but she hid it from me. Lied."

"And Jess?" Jolene's eyes widened. "Is she okay?"

"She was premature and low birth weight. She's been a little slow with certain milestones. That's when I knew for sure Aimee had been using, even though she still denied it. She made a show of attending NA meetings, but that all fell apart when I followed her once and caught her in some guy's car smoking meth after the meeting."

"Oh, my God, Sam. I didn't realize it was so bad. What about Jess now? Is she with Aimee?"

"Aimee's mother is staying at the house while I'm gone. Aimee dumps Jess on her mom most of the time it's her turn to have her, anyway. I can trust Aimee's mom. Jess is in good hands."

"That must be so hard on you, Sam. So hard for Jess." She touched his shoulder. "I'm sorry."

He flinched. He didn't want Jolene back because she felt sorry for him.

"It's my fault. I should've known what I was getting into when I married Aimee, but then I was her partner in crime in those days."

"But you changed. You gave up the drinking. You grew up, and she didn't." Jolene tucked her hair behind one ear. "Do you think you could ever get full custody of Jess? Is that something you'd want to do?"

"I've started looking into it. We've been separated over a year, and the divorce was finalized a few months ago." He held up two fingers. "I swear."

"I believe you." She dipped her head once. "Maybe you could give me a ride to Gran's house, so I can pick up my car. I don't know what she was thinking taking off like that."

"I hope she wasn't feeling ill." Sam flicked his shirt off the chair, not unhappy with the abrupt change of subject, and punched an arm through one sleeve. Granny Viv was most likely scheming to get him and Jolene back together. She was always solidly rooting for the two of them—until he'd betrayed Jolene by lying about the last time he and Aimee had slept together.

He hadn't thought that detail would matter. He'd been trying to make himself more marketable to Jolene by distancing himself from his marriage. He never dreamed

Aimee would get pregnant, especially as she'd assured him she'd been on the pill during her recovery.

That had been one of the hardest things he'd had to do in his life—tell Jolene that the wife he was separated from, the wife he supposedly hadn't been intimate with since their separation six months before, was three months pregnant with his baby.

He smoothed his shirt over his chest and buttoned it up. "Do you mind if I have a look at that map?"

"If you think what you're doing can delay the project, then of course. I can make a copy of it for you on my printer, or you can take a picture of it with your phone." She held up her finger. "It's in my office."

She crossed the living room to an open door near the front entrance where she'd set up a small office. She called out. "It's just an eight-and-a-half-by-eleven sheet of paper, but it's detailed. Showed me where the first dig was going to be, anyway."

As Sam tucked in his shirt, he heard banging and rustling from the office. Maybe Jolene was making him a copy.

He buckled his equipment belt around his waist and strode to the office door. Poking his head inside, he said, "Are you making that copy?"

Jolene spun around, gripping her empty hands in front of her, her eyes dark pools. "It's gone, Sam. Somebody came in here and stole that map."

Chapter Five

Jolene dropped to her knees and rested the side of her face on the cool floor as she reached out with one hand to feel beneath the desk. "Maybe it fell to the floor."

Her words sounded hollow to her own ears. It hadn't fallen to the floor. She'd left it in the top right drawer of her desk.

Sam walked into the room, his boots clomping on the tile. He loomed over her. "Where did you have it?"

She sat up, bumping her head on the underside of the desk. "I put it in the drawer."

"Is the drawer full? Could it have gotten stuck?" He yanked open the drawer, and a couple of pens rattled. He shuffled through the sticky notepads, a few business cards and some slips of paper with usernames and passwords scribbled across them.

"It's gone, Sam." She sat cross-legged on the floor, rubbing the side of her head. "Someone broke into my house and took it."

"Is your head okay?" He extended his hand to her, and she grabbed it, more to steady her nerves than for assistance getting up.

"The head's fine. I'm not." She swept her hands across the neat desk. "Who would want that map? Why wouldn't he or she want me to have it?"

"And how'd this person even know you had the map?" Sam leaned his thigh against the desk. "Obviously, someone didn't randomly break into your house, see a map in a drawer and steal it on a whim, unless…"

"Unless what?" She pressed a hand against her stomach, trying to still the butterflies there—and this time they had nothing to do with Sam's touch.

"Is there anything else missing?"

She twisted her head from side to side. "Not that I noticed."

"When was the last time you consulted the map? If you looked at it this morning, the theft occurred when you were at the ground-breaking." He tapped a knuckle against the desk. "Did you happen to take a picture of it with your phone?"

"I should have, but I didn't." She balled her hand into a fist. "I haven't seen the map since the night I dumped the bones at the construction site. I had it with me that night."

"Could you have lost it there? Left it in your car?"

"I wish." The corner of her eye twitched. "I had it in my backpack when I went out there. When I came home, I unloaded my pack and put the map back in the drawer. I'm sure of it."

"So, somebody broke in at some point after that night." He swept his arm out to the side. "Have a look around. See if anything else is gone. Maybe it was just a common thief burglarizing your place, saw the map and thought it was buried treasure or something."

"Really?" She put a hand on her hip. "X marks the spot?"

He flicked a finger beneath her chin. "I'm exaggerating. Maybe he thought he could use it to blackmail someone. Look around."

"Computer's still here." She tapped the top of her closed laptop. "Printer."

She yanked open the top drawer of a two-drawer oak filing cabinet and thumbed through some files. "My passport, birth certificate, social security card, all here."

"Forget that stuff. What about valuables? Money? Jewelry?"

"Jewelry? You know I don't own any expensive pieces of jewelry." She held her arm in front of her and jangled the wooden bangles on her wrist. "I do have a safe with some cash and a few weapons."

Sam's head jerked up. "Weapons?"

"A couple of pieces my dad left me. If he'd have had one of them the night he was murdered, he'd probably still be here." Her eyes stung as she spun away from Sam. "The safe's in my bedroom closet."

He closed the desk drawer and followed her out of the office.

When she walked into her bedroom, she made a beeline for the walk-in closet and flicked on the switch on the wall outside. She pulled open the door, shoved aside some blouses hanging from a lower rack and crouched in front of the safe, which had been bolted to the floor.

She tapped out the combination and the lock clicked while a green light flashed twice. She swung open the door of the safe and lifted out a .45 and a 9mm Glock. "Hold these."

Sam took the weapons from her, holding one in each hand, weighing them. He whistled through his teeth. "Nice."

Thumbing through two stacks of bills, she said, "It doesn't look like anything was taken from the safe."

"I suppose you don't have a camera inside or outside?"

"Nope." She sat back on her heels. "But maybe I need one."

"Not a bad idea." He held out the guns to her, handles first.

She placed the .45, a heavy piece, on top of the cash and slammed the door shut. She entered the combination again, and held her finger on the lock button until it beeped.

"You forgot the Glock."

"No, I didn't." She stood up to face him, clutching the gun in her hand. "I'm keeping this one with me."

"You do know how to use that thing, don't you?"

She slid open the chamber, checked the bullet nestled inside and closed it with a snap. "Sure."

"Do you think Wade found out you printed the map and broke in here to take it back? Did he have to break in? Does he know about the key under the flowerpot?"

"If he does, I never told him. His sister knows, but she wouldn't blab about that." She made a move to exit the closet and he stepped to the side.

Their little dance set her clothes into motion, the hangers clicking, the material whispering.

"And how would he know I printed out the map?" She exited the closet, the gun dangling at her side. "That's why I printed it instead of sending it to myself. *That* he would've noticed, but I don't think there's any trail when an image is printed from your phone, is there?"

"I don't have a clue." He pressed his thumb against the closet light switch. "Why wouldn't he want you to see the map? In fact, why did you go all cloak-and-dagger to get the map? You could've just asked him for a copy."

"I didn't want him to think I had any interest in the project beyond my initial rejection of it. That's why I was secretive about it. I don't know why he would be—unless there's something on that map he wants to keep hush-hush." She sank to the edge of her bed, thankful she'd had time to make it this morning.

He sat next to her, causing the mattress to dip and her

shoulder to bump his. He didn't move. "Something illegal about the construction maybe? Did you notice anything about the map?"

She scooted away from him. "I don't know construction. I wouldn't have noticed anything like that. It was a building-phase map, which is why it helped me because it pinpointed exactly where the workers were going to start digging."

He patted his pocket. "I think your phone is ringing in the other room. It's not mine."

"It's probably Gran wondering what happened to me." She bounced up from the bed. "You can give me a ride?"

"Of course."

She snatched up her ringing phone on the counter, the call coming from Gran's friend Rosie. "Hello, Rosie?"

"Hi, Jolene. Viv is wondering when you're going to pick up your car. I'm still here with her, so can you give me a ride back to town? Or I can drive the car to your place, and you can give me a ride home from there."

"I want to check in on Gran anyway, so I'll go out there. Sam can drive, and then take you home. He gave me a ride to my place. Is Gran okay?"

"A little wet, but just fine. We were wondering the same about you. Do they know where those bones came from?"

"That'll take a while, Rosie. Construction has been halted in the meantime."

"Okay, we'll wait for you and Sam."

Gran yelled in the background. "Tell her not to hurry."

Jolene rolled her eyes at Sam. "We'll see you in a little while, Rosie."

Sam scratched Chip's belly. "Granny Viv and Rosie took your car, leaving Rosie's grandson to take her car, leaving you to catch a ride home only to drive to the rez, get your car and give Rosie a ride home. Did I get that straight?"

"Maybe the scheme didn't work out quite the way Gran wanted it to, but at least we got to admit our secrets to each other and forge a plan."

"We forged a plan?" Sam stopped rubbing Chip, who kicked his legs in the air to show his displeasure.

"Of course we did, Sam Cross. We're going to delay the Desert Sun Casino project long enough to find out if the land is the graveyard of missing people and why my father was murdered there."

AS SAM PULLED his truck up in front of Gran's house, he tapped on the window. "Wade's here. That could be trouble."

Jolene narrowed her eyes as she stared at Wade's yellow Humvee. "Why does he drive that abomination?"

Sam shrugged. "I don't know. It must be good for maneuvering in the sand."

"Wrong answer." Jolene punched his rock-hard bicep. "Maybe I can hint around that I think someone broke into my house and watch his reaction."

"Not a great idea." Sam cut the engine on his truck. "Don't get into it with him at all. The man's gonna be on edge."

"The better to trap him." She yanked on the door handle and slid from the truck, avoiding a puddle of rain in the dirt.

As she and Sam walked up to the porch, her cousin stepped out of the house, all smiles.

"That was quite a ground-breaking ceremony this morning, wasn't it? Ended in dramatic fashion with a monsoon." Wade shook out his umbrella.

Jolene raised one eyebrow. "And a pile of bones."

"Well, it *is* the desert, right, Sam? There are bound to be bones buried in the desert." Wade skirted several pools of water with his expensive cowboy boots on his way to the Humvee. He grasped the handle and turned. "You know it's funny, though. We did survey that land thoroughly and didn't find any bones before, especially so close to the access road."

"Maybe your surveyors did a lousy job." She waved from the porch. "I'm sure you'll be back in the saddle in no time."

Wade touched his fingers to his forehead. "Count on it, cuz."

The Humvee's engine rumbled as Jolene grabbed the handle of the screen door.

Sam touched her ear with his lips. "He sure is cheery."

"It's a facade. He's running scared." She pulled open the screen door and knocked on the front door once before pushing her way in. "Gran, it's me."

Rosita rose from a chair, holding two coffee mugs. "We just had some tea. Do you want some?"

"I think Sam needs to get the truck back to the Border Patrol station, and I need to get my car." Jolene strolled to her grandmother's chair and dropped a kiss on top of her head. "Was I taking too long for you to wait for me, Gran?"

"I knew that storm was going to break any minute, and I figured you and Sam might want to catch up." She tilted her head back to look into Jolene's face. "I was right. You two took a while to get here."

Sam took the cups from Rosita's hands and carried them into Gran's small kitchen. "I stopped by Jolene's house to see Chip…the dog."

"How was Wade after that debacle at the ground-breaking ceremony?" Jolene perched on the arm of Gran's chair. "We just saw him outside, and he seemed to be taking it in stride."

"He was upset when he came over here to check on me,

but he made a few calls and seemed to feel better after." Gran patted Jolene's knee. "He seemed to think you had something to do with the bones out there, Jolene. He came in here ranting and raving."

"Right. Like I have a spare skeleton in my closet at home." Jolene snorted. "Look, the Yaqui council voted, and they decided to go with the casino on that land. Nothing I can do about it."

"Your father could've stopped it." Gran clicked her tongue. "The rest don't have the backbone to stand up to Wade."

"Good thing Dad was conveniently murdered." Jolene blinked her eyes.

Gran's fingers turned into claws on Jolene's leg as she dug them into her flesh. "Wade loved your father, Jolene. He looked up to him. Learned from him. Please don't say those things to me."

"I'm sorry, Gran." Jolene kissed her grandmother's weathered cheek and stood up as Sam returned from washing the dishes in the sink. "Sam's going to give Rosie a ride back to her place, as they're heading in the same direction."

"Are you ready, Rosie?" Sam captured Gran's hand and kissed her gnarled fingers. "I'll see you later, Granny Viv."

"You can come by any time if you're washing dishes."

Rosie gathered her umbrella and purse and waved at Gran getting out of her chair. "Take a seat, Viv. We can see ourselves out."

Outside, Sam took Rosie's arm and steered her around the puddles to his truck as Jolene watched them, a hand on her hip.

After he handed Rosie into his truck, he approached Jolene. "What are you staring at?"

"You're such a gentleman…to the old gals."

"Hilarious." He placed his hands on her shoulders.

"Be careful. Wade, or whoever, wanted that map back for some reason."

"Maybe he just wanted to make sure I didn't pull any stunts like the one today. I beat him to the punch, and now he's over it." She took a step back into Gran's house, hanging on to the screen door.

"Why wouldn't he just approach you? Tell you he's aware you took the map from his phone, planted the bones and he's going to out you to the authorities?" He brushed some hair from her eyes. "There must be something else on that map he's hiding."

"Not sure I'll have another shot at it now." She waved to Rosie in the passenger seat of Sam's truck. "Thanks for the ride, Sam. Remember, I won't tell if you won't."

He pressed a finger to his lips and strode to his truck. She watched while Sam climbed in his truck and pulled out. As he peeled away from the house, he beeped his horn.

Jolene returned to Gran and spent the next hour giving her evasive answers about her and Sam. When she stood up and stretched, she gazed out the window at the rain coming down in sheets.

"I'd better get going, Gran. Do you need anything else?"

Gran patted her arm. "Just for you to be happy, Jolene."

She dropped a kiss on her grandmother's head. "Always that."

Outside, the rain lashed her as she ran to her car. She folded herself into the driver's seat and blasted the defroster. She rolled slowly along the roads of the reservation, and then turned onto the highway. The wipers on her car could barely keep up with the onslaught of water pouring across her windshield.

She sat forward in her seat, hunching over the steering wheel, easing off the accelerator. The car seemed to be floating underwater, the landscape a blurry, watery tapestry.

She picked up speed as she headed down an incline. She tapped her brakes and mumbled a few obscenities beneath her breath. The water had made her brakes squishy. She tapped again, putting a little more force into it.

As she stepped on the brake, the car whooshed forward, going even faster. She jerked the steering wheel harder than she wanted as she coasted into a slight curve in the road.

She tried the brakes again, and this time her foot hit the floor. Her back tires hydroplaned and the car began to fishtail. Gripping the steering wheel with one hand, she fumbled for the hand brake with the other.

The car lurched and skidded, and the rain-soaked scenery blurred into a kaleidoscope of colors as she careened out of control.

Chapter Six

Sam rolled to a stop in front of Rosie's neat Spanish-style house, the tiles on the roof dyed to a deep red from the torrent of rain, now moving sideways.

"Hold on a minute." He grabbed Rosie's umbrella and came around to the passenger side of the truck to let her out.

He held the umbrella over her head as he walked her to the front door.

Her grandson threw open the door. "Hurry, *Abuela*, before you get swept away."

Rosie turned to Sam on the porch. "You can take my umbrella back to the truck with you."

"That's okay." He handed the pink-and-red umbrella back to her. "I'm already wet. A little more rain isn't going to make much difference."

Head down, he jogged back to the truck. When he got behind the wheel, he flicked down the visor and slicked his hair back from his face, dripping with water.

He scowled at his reflection. "So much for drying your clothes at Jolene's."

It was a good ruse for taking half his clothes off at her place, anyway. Not that it did him much good. If he wanted to get back into her good graces…and her bed, he'd have to take things slowly. He'd burned her once, and she wasn't

the type of woman who trusted easily—her mother's aban-
donment and her father's death had seen to that.

Then *he* had to pile on.

He shook his head like a dog, flinging drops of water
inside the cab of the truck, and continued driving toward
the station.

As he turned down the main street, he had to pull to the
right for some emergency vehicles racing off to a call. A
lot of people didn't know how to drive in a storm like this.

He started forward again and turned into the parking
lot of the Border Patrol station, small compared to the one
in San Diego, but Paradiso saw lots of action.

He nabbed a parking spot near the front door, as a skel-
etal crew was on Sunday duty, and half of them had been at
the casino shindig. He ducked into the building and hung
the keys to the duty truck on the appropriate peg.

One of the new agents popped his head up from behind his computer monitor, his eyes wide. "Can you believe this storm?"

"It's monsoon season. Get used to it and enjoy the rain
while it lasts."

Sam pulled up to his desk and brought up a map of the
Yaqui land earmarked for the casino. He couldn't find
anything online about the casino plans—at least nothing
detailed. What could've been on that map that someone
hadn't wanted Jolene to see?

He dug into his missing persons again, looking for any
new links, but he just kept coming back to their involve-
ment in the drug trade. They had to be dead, and their
bodies had to be somewhere in the desert.

The phone jangled Sam's nerves even more, and Agent
Herrera picked up. The agent's excited voice carried across
the room.

When he hung up the phone, he scurried to Sam's desk.

"Big accident on the highway. Car skidded off the road and went into the wash, which happens to be swollen right now."

Sam whipped his head around. "Did this just happen? I saw emergency vehicles on my way in."

"That was something else. This is a car in the wash."

A muscle ticked at the corner of Sam's mouth. "The highway north? Because I came from the rez, and I didn't see anything out that way."

"Yeah, north and this happened after you arrived."

"Do you know the make and model of the car?"

"Heard it on the radio—black truck."

Sam's heart thundered in his chest. "License plate?"

Herrera strode back to his desk and tapped his keyboard, a crease between his eyebrows. "No plates. The truck's partially submerged in water."

"Jolene Nighthawk drives a black truck, and when I left her, she was planning to head north on the highway." Sam snatched the keys from the peg where he'd left them just about an hour ago. "I'm taking the truck out to the accident. Let me know if you hear anything else."

"Will do."

Sam flew out of the station and got back in the truck. It took all his self-control not to speed off in the rain. He didn't need to get into an accident on the way to the site of one.

He swatted at a bead of sweat rolling down his face. Just because it was monsoon season in the desert didn't mean the temperatures dropped. The temps hovered in the high eighties despite the skies breaking open.

And he was feeling the heat.

As the storm moved through, the rain slacked off but his wipers were still working furiously to keep up with the water coursing across his windshield. He spotted the lights of the emergency vehicles before he could actually make out any shapes.

He eased off the accelerator and rolled to a stop behind a highway patrol car. Scrambling from his truck, he yanked out his ID and badge. As he passed the orange cones, an officer approached him and Sam flashed his badge.

"Any fatalities?"

The officer shook his head. "The woman escaped from her vehicle before it filled with water. It could've been a lot worse, but the wash isn't deep enough yet for a car to be completely submerged."

"Woman?" Sam got an adrenaline spike that made him dizzy. "She's okay?"

"She's a bit banged up, but she's fine." The officer pointed to two EMTs hovering at the back of their ambulance. "Over there."

Sam strode to the ambulance, glancing to his right at Jolene's black truck sitting upright in the water. As he approached, one of the EMTs stepped away to reveal Jolene sitting in the back of the ambulance, her feet dangling over the side.

Her eyes widened when she saw him. "Sam! What are you doing here?"

Warm relief washed through his body and he ate up the space between them in two long strides. He took her hands in his and brought them to his lips. "Are you all right? I heard about the accident involving a truck north of town and immediately thought of you. What happened?"

Her gaze darted toward the EMT unwrapping the blood pressure cuff from her arm. "I skidded off the road. I think my brakes locked up."

"Didn't I tell you to get a new car the last time I was here?" His nerves caused his voice to come out louder than he'd intended and with a sharp edge.

Jolene disentangled her hands from his. "You told me a lot of things the last time you were in Paradiso."

The EMT threw a sideways glance at Sam and said, "Ma'am, are you sure you don't want to go to the hospital?"

"I'm sure. The car slid off the road into the water, my airbag deployed and I was able to crawl out the passenger window. Just a few bumps with some bruises to follow, I'm sure." She held up her arms, displaying a red rash from the airbag. "You checked my vitals and I'm fine, right? I didn't hit my head, so no worries about a concussion."

A crane lifted her car from the wash and water poured out the windows and cascaded from the chassis.

The EMT pointed to the mess. "You're not driving off in that."

"I've got a Border Patrol agent right here with his official truck to take me home." She patted his arm. "Right, Sam?"

"Absolutely, as long as she doesn't have any injuries and you don't think she's going to suffer any ill effects from the accident."

The EMT shrugged. "Just bruising, like she said. She has a few scrapes from squeezing through the window and clambering up the cement walls of the wash, but she acted fast—buzzed down that window and got out."

"Then we're good." Jolene hopped off the back of the ambulance and winced.

Sam caught her around the waist. "You sure you're okay?"

"Trent here already checked out my ankle. I just twisted it." She grimaced.

"Then you shouldn't be jumping around on it." Sam refused to release his hold on her, even though her body coiled away from his. "Do you need to talk to the cops?"

"They already got my statement—one car accident and no damage to public property."

"In that case…" He swept her up in his arms and carried her to his truck while she chattered in his ear.

"This is ridiculous, Sam. I don't need to be carried. Put me down, please."

He swung open the door of his truck and placed her inside. He hovered over her, hanging on the frame of the vehicle as the last of the storm spit out its final raindrops on the back of his neck.

"Let someone else take charge for a change." He leveled a finger at her. "You, sit."

He stomped off to find the cops investigating the scene of the accident and grabbed the first one. "Do you need Jolene anymore?"

The officer asked, "Is she leaving in the ambulance?"

"She doesn't want to go to the hospital. The EMTs cleared her, and I'm going to take her home. What happened out here?"

"Pretty much what she told us. She was driving in the rain, going downhill so her speed probably picked up. Her brakes failed, she applied her parking brake and the car spun out and landed upright in the wash. She was lucky. She called in the accident herself."

"That's good to hear. Her car being towed to the yard?"

"Yeah, they'll contact her, but it's probably totaled."

"Thanks." Sam pivoted away, took a few steps and called over his shoulder. "Brakes failed, huh?"

"That's what it sounds like."

Sam's boots crunched the soggy gravel as he returned to the truck. He climbed in and gripped the steering wheel with both hands. "Your brakes failed?"

"I stepped on the brake when I started going down the incline. Instead of slowing down, my car sort of whooshed forward. I didn't want to stomp on the brake pedal in the rain, so I eased my foot down and when it hit the floor, I knew I was in trouble."

A pain throbbed against his temple. "Were the brakes feeling squishy before? Squeaking?"

She tucked her hands beneath her thighs, and she hunched her shoulders as if warding off a shiver. "A little squishy, but I thought that was the rain."

"Your car's going to be towed to the police yard. It's totaled."

"The officers told me that. The tow truck driver gave me his info in case I need him for insurance purposes." She tapped a damp business card on the console. "What are you implying? About the brakes, I mean?"

He started the truck's engine and backed away from the patrol car before pulling onto the rain-slicked highway. "Brakes don't usually up and fail. You know it's coming. The pads go first, and you have that squishy, gummy feeling when you step on the brake. Brakes usually tell you they're failing by squeaking."

"So, if my brakes didn't gradually go bad on their own, you're thinking someone made them go bad all at once?" Her knees started bouncing, and he placed a hand on one of them.

"Your car was sitting at Granny Viv's place while Wade was just there. Doesn't he know something about cars?"

"He has a few classic cars he tinkers with." She tilted her head. "I don't think my cousin would try to kill me. Besides, I saw him leave Gran's."

"He could've come back or had someone else do it. You didn't die. He couldn't know the brakes would go out in that spot by the wash, or that your car would spin out."

"If he wasn't trying to kill me, you think he was trying to warn me?"

That prospect didn't seem to bring her any comfort, as she laced her fingers together and twisted them.

"Maybe scare you off from interfering in casino business. He seems to know you were the one who planted the bones at the construction site. He knows you got your hands on that map and used it to throw a a into his opening ceremony." Sam shoved a wet lock of hair from his forehead. "Wade Nighthawk is a man on a mission—and I don't think he's going to allow you or anyone else to stand in his way."

"If he knows I left the bones there, he has to know they're not going to come back as some ancient Yaqui."

"He also knows you, Jolene. He knows you're not going to give up. Maybe that accident was a little push to convince you to back off and leave it alone."

"Why doesn't he just tell me to my face?"

"Didn't he try that already?"

"Yes."

"He's never going to admit that he's behind any of this. He has a public persona to uphold, but make no mistake. If he had someone tamper with your brakes, he's fired a warning shot."

She gathered her hair in a ponytail and twisted it, squeezing out the water from the wash. "He should know better than that. I'm a Nighthawk."

As JOLENE LET Sam into her place, an ecstatic Chip circled their legs, his wet tail thumping out his welcome against the wall.

She patted his head. "He's been outside. I must've left the dog door open."

"Don't worry about Chip." He plucked at the sleeve of her blouse. "You're soaked to the bone. I don't care how warm it is. It's not a good idea to walk around in wet clothes."

"You should talk. I let you dry your clothes here and you got them all wet again." As she straightened up from petting Chip, a pain stabbed the back of her neck and she grabbed it, squeezing her eyes closed.

"Whiplash?" He cupped her elbow and led her to the couch. "That's why you go to the hospital when you're in an accident like that one."

"It's fine. I just feel a little banged up." She sank to the edge of the couch, her damp skirt clinging to her legs.

"You need a warm bath and a glass of wine." He backed up, tugging on Chip's collar. "Do you have any Epsom salt?"

"You're serious. You're going to run me a bath?" That's what worried her about Sam. He was all in—until he wasn't. He'd treated her like a princess, until he told her about his wife's pregnancy. A wife he'd supposedly separated from six months before, even though she was just three months pregnant.

"You don't climb out of an accident like yours and continue on as usual." He removed his gun from his holster and unbuckled his equipment belt.

"Oh, you mean business."

"I do. Stay there and relax."

She called after him. "No Epsom salts."

As Sam banged around in her bathroom, she twisted her head from side to side. Didn't feel like whiplash to her. She'd tried to relax her body when it became clear her car was going into the wash.

Could Wade really be responsible? She could see him issuing a warning, but he'd never try to seriously hurt her, would he? His ambition knew no bounds. He had his eye on politics, and he moved in the right circles.

"Look what I found." Sam returned to the living room with a pair of green Border Patrol sweats low on his hips, his upper body bare—again. When had he become such an exhibitionist?

She narrowed her eyes. "Where'd you find those?"

"Stuffed in your linen closet." He tugged at the waistband, pulling them even lower. "I remember giving you a few pairs of these."

"Yeah, I used to wear them." She got up too fast and clutched the back of the couch in her dizziness.

"You're not okay, Jolene. Are you sure you don't want me to take you to the emergency room?"

"No, thanks. You end up sicker from those places than you were when you walked in. I'm just a little rattled."

He joined her at the couch and slipped an arm around her waist. The brush of his bare skin against her arm overwhelmed her senses and her dizziness returned with a vengeance.

She leaned into him, and he tightened his hold on her.

"Let me help you."

He walked her into the master bathroom connected to her bedroom, past the pile of his wet clothes. A lilac-scented steam rose from the tub, foaming with bubbles.

"A bubble bath?"

"It's the closest thing I could find to Epsom salts. You can inhale the lilac like an aromatherapy thing." He'd flipped down the toilet seat and helped her sit.

When he reached around to unhook her skirt, she placed a hand on his arm. "I think I can get undressed by myself, Sam."

"Really? I'm not going to leave you and then hear a thud as you keel over, am I?" He unhooked and unzipped her skirt. "It's not like I haven't seen it all before."

She rested two fingers at the base of his throat where his pulse throbbed. "But you lost the privilege of seeing it all."

His dark eyebrows jumped, and his pulse beat faster against the pads of her fingers. "I did—and it was a privilege."

He stood up and started to back out of the bathroom. "Call me if you need help. I'll return with your wine."

He shut the door before she could tell him he didn't have to bring the wine—not that she didn't need a glass or two about now. But she didn't want to tempt him if he were still on the wagon—and it looked as if he was.

She finished undressing and slipped into the silky water, releasing a long breath as the bubbles enveloped her.

When she'd met Sam two years ago, he'd just stopped drinking. She'd seen him at her cousin's AA meeting. She'd gone to a meeting with Melody to support her, and pretty much couldn't take her eyes off the blue-eyed, black-haired man who'd looked so indestructible as he talked about the problems alcohol had brought to his life.

Her own father had won his battle with the bottle and had been the strongest man she knew.

Melody had played matchmaker, and her first date with Sam had morphed from a coffee to dinner and three hours of conversation. She'd been wary at first. When hadn't she been wary with men? But Sam had won her over without even trying. Maybe it had been her desire to fix him. What grounded woman went into a relationship with a person battling addiction, even one in recovery, who'd just separated from his wife?

Sam tapped on the door. "Are you in the tub? No mishaps?"

"I managed to undress all by myself and climb in without toppling over."

He nudged the door open with his toe, carrying two

glasses—a red wine for her and some iced tea for him. He sat on the edge of the tub, and she scooted farther under the bubbles.

He handed her the glass. "How does that feel? I didn't want to make it too hot."

"It's perfect, thank you." She wrapped her fingers around the stem of the glass. "You didn't need to bring me wine. Iced tea would've been okay."

"Don't worry about me." He took a sip of his tea and shook the ice in his glass. "Twenty-seven months sober. Not even a slipup."

"Congratulations. Melody, too." She tipped some wine into her mouth, letting it pool on her tongue before swallowing it. "Do you still go to meetings?"

"I hadn't been, but I'm not going to lie. I started attending more regularly at the time of the separation. It was hard leaving Jess, leaving her just like my old man left me, but your mother abandoned you, too, and you didn't turn to booze."

"Different situation, wasn't it?" She traced her finger around the rim of her glass. "I had my father and an extended family support system. Even though Dad turned to booze when Mom left, his illness gave me purpose. One of us had to be functioning."

Sam scooped up some bubbles, cupping them in his palm before turning his hand over and watching them dislodge and float back into the tub. "Is that what you saw in me? Someone to fix like you'd fixed your dad?"

She caught her breath. Had he been reading her mind? She sliced her hand through the water like a shark's fin. "No. You'd already started your journey to recovery when we met."

"Ah, but it's a rocky journey filled with potholes and backtracking. Alcoholics are never really fixed, are we?"

"The minute I met you, I knew you'd be successful. I didn't think you'd need saving." The bubbles across her chest melted into the water, putting her closer to exposure. Did she care? What if she got in deep with Sam, and he left again? He had a daughter who had to take priority.

Could she have a fling with him while he was here? While they were in each other's confidence? Could she forget him once he left?

Sam dipped his hand in the water and swirled it dangerously close to her hip. "You're losing your bubbles, and this hasn't been very relaxing for you—digging up old stuff. Drink your wine with no guilt. Stop thinking about your dad, stop thinking about my problems."

"Stop thinking about my own?" She touched her glass to his and took a sip of wine, slipping farther beneath the lukewarm water. She reached out a hand and ran it down his bare chest to the waistband of the sweats. "There's plenty of room in here."

His Adam's apple bobbed as he swallowed. "You know I want that more than anything. I want you more than anything."

"But?"

"I want you to be sure. You hardly rolled out the red carpet when you saw me."

She lifted one eyebrow. "Consider the circumstances. I had just dumped some bones in a shallow grave."

"It was more than that." The tips of his fingers played along the peaks of the bubbles. "I hurt you. I lied to you. I broke your trust."

"I'm the one who told you to go away and be with your daughter."

"Because…"

Chip's barking interrupted him, and she was almost relieved. She didn't want to go down this road with him again. Either she could trust him or she couldn't...or it wouldn't matter either way.

She heaved a sigh. "Chip must've gone outside again. I hope he's not even more wet, or worse, muddy."

"I'll take care of Chip. Finish your wine and your bath." He pushed up from the side of the tub. "You should take some ibuprofen."

Chip's claws tapped across the tile floor, and he appeared at the bathroom door with something dangling from his mouth.

"What is that, Chip? Sam, what does he have?"

His tail upright and wagging, Chip advanced into the bathroom, his trophy clutched in his jaws.

Sam jumped back from the dog. "It's a snake."

Chip dropped the snake on the floor, and Jolene rose from the tub, her mouth hanging open. "It's not just a snake. It's a snake with an arrow through its head."

"What the hell?" Sam prodded the reptile with a bare toe. "At least it's dead. Who would kill a snake like that?"

Goose bumps raced across her bare flesh. "Someone sending a warning to another Yaqui."

Chapter Seven

Sam felt the hair on the back of his neck quiver. Someone out there was serious.

"Get it out of here, Sam."

He glanced at Jolene standing in the tub, water sluicing from her skin and bubbles clinging to strategic areas of her naked body.

Chip whined and pawed at the dead snake, so Sam gave him his due and patted his head. "Good dog. Good boy."

"Never mind Chip. Get that thing out of my bathroom."

"I got it." He stepped over the mess on the floor and took Jolene's slippery arm. "Sit back down. You're getting chilled."

"I think that's more from the snake than the air hitting my body." She glanced down, and a pink flush rushed from her chest to her cheeks, as if realizing for the first time she was standing naked in front of him.

She plopped back down in the water, creating waves that edged over the side of the tub.

"What does it mean? The dead snake?"

Crossing her arms on the edge of the tub, she hunched forward. "The legend of the snake people tells us that snakes can take the form of humans so to kill a snake, unless it's in self-defense, is evil. The arrow through the snake's head is a warning to all who see it that evil walks among us."

"So, someone delivering that dead snake to you is a message that you're dealing with some shady characters."

"Something like that. It's not a good sign any way you look at it." She slid back into the tub.

"I'm going to get a plastic bag and pick that thing up with a paper towel—just in case there are fingerprints. If this is a warning, then we need to know who's behind it."

"It's obvious, isn't it?" She scooped up water in her hands and dumped it on her chest. "Nobody but a Yaqui is going to understand the significance of a snake with an arrow through its head. It was Wade."

"Then it's time to confront him." Sam hooked two fingers in Chip's collar and pulled him out of the bathroom before the dog could destroy the evidence.

Sam pulled open a kitchen drawer and grabbed a plastic bag. He ripped a sheet of paper towel from the roll and returned to the bathroom where Jolene was standing in a draining tub, a towel wrapped around her body.

He crouched next to the snake and picked it up by the arrow lodged in its head. He dropped the whole thing in the bag. "I'm gonna have prints run on that arrow, and then we'll have him."

"*If* he left prints." Jolene stepped out of the tub, avoiding the spot where Chip had dropped the snake. "This is ridiculous. If my cousin thinks he can get away with tampering with my brakes and leaving this warning, he's forgotten who I am."

"That's strange." Sam twisted the handle of the bag, tying it in a knot. "Why would Wade fix your brakes and then run over here and leave that message?"

"It's like you said." She tucked the corner of the towel under her arm. "He didn't expect my brakes to fail so spectacularly and maybe already planned to follow up with the snake warning as kind of a double whammy."

Sam scratched his chin. "You know what else is weird?"

"Besides you standing there making excuses for Wade?"

He jiggled the bag. "If nobody other than a Yaqui would understand the meaning behind the snake with the arrow, would Wade really do something so obvious?"

"You're asking these questions like my cousin is a normal person. He's unhinged. Why else would he act this way?" She pushed past him, the ends of her wet hair flinging drops of water at him.

"I don't think he's unhinged, Jolene. There's a lot of money at stake with this project. He's not about to watch it fail. That's why I don't think he'd do something as blatant as sending you that snake." He followed her into the bedroom. "I wonder where Chip found it."

Jolene turned in the middle of the room and flicked her fingers. "Out, please. I let you have a peek once, but don't get used to it."

He chuckled. "Yes, ma'am, but if you're running off to see Wade, I'm coming with you."

He exited her bedroom, dropped the bag with the snake on the counter so Chip couldn't get at it and returned to the bathroom to clean up. He rinsed out the tub and scooped up Jolene's wet clothes and dumped them in the hamper.

Turning, he nearly bumped into Jolene at the door. She'd changed into a pair of denim shorts and a red University of Arizona T-shirt. "Thanks for straightening up the bathroom. I heard the buzzer go off for the dryer. You can change out of your male stripper clothes and back into your uniform."

He spread his arms. "You think this is male stripper material? You need to get out more."

She tugged at the elastic waistband and let it snap

back in place. "You don't need to wear these so low on your hips."

"I do if I want them to cover my ankles." He held up his foot. "No wonder I gave these to you."

He headed toward the laundry room and scooped his warm clothes from the dryer. He shook out his slacks and shirt and draped them over his arm.

"I'm going to get dressed in your room, if that's okay."

Jolene looked up from toweling off Chip. "Go ahead. Do you think Chip will lead me to the spot where he found the snake?"

"Maybe, but does it matter? You don't have a security system here, no cameras. Wade, or whoever, left it on your front porch or in your backyard or your driveway. He probably knew Chip would grab it."

She snorted. "Can you really picture Wade shooting a snake with a bow and arrow, and then creeping around my house with the thing in his hand? He had someone plant it. I'm sure of that, just like he had someone fix my brakes at the rez. There are plenty of young people who want to get in the good graces of Wade Nighthawk."

"We can always ask your neighbors if they saw someone lurking near your house."

"I'll ask around." She pointed to his uniform. "Get dressed. Then we'll pay a little visit to Wade."

Sam ducked into her bedroom and peeled off the sweats. He had a ways to go to win back Jolene's trust, but at least she'd put away those daggers that were in her eyes—a shared goal always helped.

When he came out of the bedroom tucking his shirt in his pants, Jolene greeted him, his equipment belt hanging from her fingertips.

"Hurry, this is heavy even without the gun."

"You *are* in a rush." He took the belt from her, looped

it through his pants and reached for his weapon on the counter. "What's the hurry?"

"I want to catch Wade and Cerisse before they go out." She hitched her purse over her shoulder and slid the cover over the dog door. "I don't want Chip dragging in any more dead reptiles."

"You're really going to stride right up to his door and accuse him of killing snakes?" Sam opened the front door and poked his head outside. "Storm passed."

She pushed past him onto the porch. "One storm passed but Wade has a whole other type of storm heading his way."

Twenty minutes later, Sam's truck navigated the curvy road up to the foothills. He tapped on the window. "If your brakes had failed on this road, you really would've been in trouble."

"Sliding into the wash wasn't enough trouble?" She crossed her arms. "I could've drowned."

"Don't remind me." He squeezed her thigh. "When I heard a black truck had been in an accident, my stomach dropped."

She threw him a sideways glance. "Really?"

"What do you think?" He snatched his hand back from her leg. "Did you imagine I stopped caring about you... ever?"

Massaging her right temple, she said, "I don't know what to think, Sam. I guess I never expected to see you back in Paradiso, and let's be honest. You didn't come here to see me. You're in Paradiso for your case, which happens to coincide with my interests."

He released a long breath. Too much, too soon. "Is Wade's house around the next bend?"

"The only one on that stretch—beyond the white gates.

He's so pretentious." She huffed through her nose and dug her fingers into her biceps.

"Is this his money or Cerisse's? I know her family is wealthy, but Wade did all right in the real estate business."

"A combination of the two. Her father got him started, and Wade took off."

"Is she Yaqui?"

"Half on her mother's side."

Sam slowed his truck and made a sharp right turn into a driveway bordered by towering saguaro cactus. He hunched over the steering wheel and whistled. "Nice place. I don't think I've ever been here before."

He pulled around the circular driveway behind Wade's Humvee and a shiny Tesla. Before he cut the engine, Jolene hopped out of his truck, the bag with the snake swinging at her side.

He scrambled after her, not sure what she had planned for her cousin. He stepped onto the porch behind her just as the last tones of the doorbell echoed on the other side of the double doors.

Cerisse opened the door, not a dyed-blond hair out of place, a serene smile curving her plumped-up lips. "Jolene, Sam, so nice to see you. Wade said you were back in town. To stay?"

"Border Patrol business. How are you, Cerisse?"

She parted her lips to answer, but Jolene pushed past her. "Where's Wade?"

Cerisse lifted one sculpted eyebrow. "Is he expecting you, Jolene?"

"Why? Do I need an appointment? He's my cousin. I knew him when he was sitting in the dirt, splashing in a rain puddle on the reservation."

"Jolene?" Wade trotted down the curved staircase, his

long, thin fingers trailing along the polished bannister. "What's going on?"

"This." She ripped open the plastic bag Sam had carefully tied earlier to preserve the evidence, and dumped the dead snake on the floor. The point of the arrow clattered on the tile.

A scream pierced the air, and Sam jerked his head around as Melody flew down the stairs. "What is *that* doing in the house?"

"Ask your brother." Jolene clamped a hand on her hip. "He left it for me—after he tampered with my brakes."

Melody directed her wide-eyed gaze at Wade. "Wade? What is she talking about?"

"That's what I'd like to know." Wade spread his hands helplessly. "Sam?"

Cerisse touched Jolene's shoulder. "Do you want to sit down and explain, Jolene? You seem…overwrought."

"Oh, no you don't." Jolene shrugged away from Cerisse. "Somebody did something to my brakes today so that my car skidded in the rain, and I landed in the wash."

Melody gasped, covering her mouth with one hand. "That was you? We heard about the accident."

"You think I fixed your brakes…" Wade smoothed a hand over his glossy ponytail "…and then doubled down by putting a warning on your porch?"

"I didn't say it was on my porch. Chip brought it in." Jolene tapped her toe, a staccato beat on the floor that only added to the tension in the room.

"Why would I do that, Jolene?" Wade hooked a thumb in the pocket of his black jeans.

"Y-you know." Jolene bit her bottom lip.

She hadn't thought this through enough to realize she'd have to admit to burying those bones at the construction site.

One corner of Wade's mouth lifted. "I don't. Please enlighten me."

"Those bones today." Jolene threw out a hand. "You think I had something to do with that. You think I'm trying to sabotage the casino project."

"Did you? Are you?" A slight twitch at the corner of his eye broke the smooth facade of Wade's face.

"Of course she didn't, Wade." Cerisse patted Jolene's back gingerly, as if Jolene were some kind of feral creature and one wrong move could set her off.

Sam didn't blame Cerisse one bit.

"I didn't plant those bones, but you know I'm unhappy about the casino. My father wouldn't have wanted it, either."

"We've had this discussion before, Jolene. The casino will bring jobs. It'll improve the school on the reservation. All those things you *claim* to care about."

"My father died on that land. Don't you care about that?"

"I do, of course." Wade nudged the snake with the toe of his boot. "Could you please put this away? You're freaking Melody out."

"You can deny all you want, Wade, but I know you're behind these threats, these warnings." Jolene started to crouch down to shove the snake back in the bag, but Sam stopped her.

He bent over and pinched the snake's tail, dragging it back into the bag. The fewer fingerprints on this thing, the better.

"Cuz, if I thought you were interfering in the casino project, I'd just talk to you. In fact, I thought we already had that talk. You gave the impression that you were fine with it, or at least resigned to it."

"Just…" she shook a finger in his face "…watch yourself."

She spun around and charged outside.

Sam secured the bag again and shrugged. "She's upset about the accident. She had to squirm through the window into the water to get out of her car."

"That's terrible." Cerisse put a hand to her slender throat. "I'm glad you're back, Sam, if only for a short time. You always were the only one who could calm her down."

"She'll be fine." He raised his hand to Melody still clinging to the bannister of the staircase. "Good to see you again, Melody."

Always the gracious hostess, even in the most awkward of occasions, Cerisse showed him to the door with a smile. "Come back again under more pleasant circumstances."

Sam marched back to the truck where Jolene was already stationed in the passenger seat, her face tight. He'd better not tell her what Cerisse had said at the end there. She'd really explode.

He got behind the wheel, and placed the bag in the back seat. "That didn't go well. What did you expect? He wasn't going to admit it, even if he was responsible."

"If?" She pushed the hair from her flushed face. "You believed that smooth SOB?"

"Weren't you the one telling me after the accident that Wade wouldn't try to kill you?"

"Kill." She pounded a fist against her chest. "Do I look dead? He is trying to scare me off, though."

He cranked on the truck's engine and it rumbled in the circular driveway as he snapped in his seat belt. "Your feelings are out in the open now, so maybe that's not a bad thing."

"It's on you now, Sam. You have to find the bones of those missing people out there to put a stop to the construction."

"If I do find those remains, it'll halt the construction,

but it's not going to stop it—not like it would if it were a sacred Yaqui burial site." He wheeled around the fancy cars in the driveway and rolled down to the street.

"I know that, but if the project goes on hiatus, I'll have some time to look around for clues to my father's murder. Once that casino goes up, any evidence is going to be lost forever." She sniffed and pulled one leg up to her chest, wrapping her arm around it.

"I know you think something's out there, Jolene, but the Pima County Sheriff's Department did a thorough investigation." He brushed a knuckle across her cheek.

"There has to be more. What was my father doing out there that night?"

"Maybe like you, he was searching for something that might put an end to the casino project." Sam lifted one shoulder.

"And maybe he found it."

He turned to face her, wondering if he should dissuade her from this line of thought or encourage it.

"Look out!" Jolene jerked forward and smacked her hand against the dashboard.

Sam slammed on the brakes before he twisted his head front and center. Melody waved from the side of the road.

"What the hell is she doing out here, and how'd she get here so fast from the house?" Sam eased off the brake, and the truck crawled toward Melody.

"She must've gone out the side of the house and bypassed the driveway, taking the shortcut to the road." Jolene buzzed down the window. "Are you crazy, Melody? We almost hit you."

Folding her arms, Melody tucked her hands against her sides and approached the truck. She ducked her head and peered at them through the open window, her dark hair with the pink streak creating a veil around her face.

"I wanted to come out here and warn you to stop nosing around the casino project, Jolene."

"Great. You, too? I already got that warning, loud and clear, but it's not going to stop me. Something happened to Dad on that land, and I'm going to find out what it was before it's all covered over with slot machines."

"You don't understand, Jolene." Melody glanced over her shoulder. "Anyone who asks questions about the casino winds up dead—and you will, too."

Chapter Eight

As Sam pulled away from the side of the road in front of Wade's driveway, Jolene adjusted her side mirror to watch Melody grow smaller and smaller.

"What do you think about what she said? When we asked her, she couldn't name anyone else who had died as a result of snooping into the project. Do you think she's overreacting because of the snake? It really spooked her, but then Melody was always attuned to the old legends and myths."

"I hate to break it to you, Jolene, but Melody was drunk."

She tilted her head to the side to take in his profile. "Are you sure? She didn't seem drunk to me. Didn't smell drunk."

"Melody always favored vodka as her poison because it's hard to detect on someone's breath, but I saw the signs. You thought she was going to step in front of my truck because she was unsteady. Her eyes looked glassy, she slurred some of her words and...she was talking nonsense."

"You think so?" Jolene rubbed her hands against her bare thighs. "I wonder why she's drinking again. She told me she'd been clean and sober for years."

"Drunks can lie—and I should know. I'd be happy to go to a meeting with her while I'm here."

"What if she's telling the truth, Sam? Have there been any deaths associated with the casino project?"

"You're asking me? I haven't been in Paradiso for two years." He drummed his thumbs on the steering wheel. "But I can look into it. I haven't heard about any murders, except those associated with the drug trade."

"They wouldn't be classified as murders, would they? We can look for accidents, disappearances—I mean recent ones, not the ones you're looking at." She sat forward in her seat. "Where are we going?"

"When I heard about the accident on the highway, I took off in this Border Patrol truck. I still have my rental car at the station, and I want to drop off this bag—" he jerked his thumb over his shoulder "—to see if we can get any fingerprints from the arrow. Wade would have a hard time denying he put that on your property if we lifted his prints."

"What about me?" She trailed her fingers along one arm that was showing signs of bruising from the airbag. "I don't even have a car."

"Will your insurance company give you a rental? Have you even reported the accident?"

"I was on the phone to my insurance agent one minute after I called 911 and two minutes after I crawled from the wash like some swamp creature, before you came on the scene. They'll pay for a rental."

"This has been a helluva day, starting with the casino opening ceremony. Have you eaten anything since those few spoonfuls of chili you scarfed down at the groundbreaking?"

"No, but our day isn't over yet." She dug her phone out of her purse, which was still wet from the accident. "We're going to check out those deaths."

He pointed to her phone. "Does that still work?"

"It was zipped inside my purse when I brought it to

the surface with me. I used it to call 911." She flashed it at him. "And now I have a text coming in from my insurance company."

"You could do a commercial for that phone. And when I mentioned looking into the deaths, I didn't mean right this minute."

"No time like the present."

He grunted, which she took as agreement.

She glanced at him as he made the turn onto the main street running through town. Was he agreeing to all this because he believed her, believed Melody or was he doing it to stay close to her? Did it matter?

"All of this can only help your own case. You can't go digging around private Yaqui property, a construction site, because you have a hunch. If we discover additional…irregularities with the casino project, we can delay it even further."

"Okay, we're here." He pulled up to the Border Patrol station and parked the truck with the other official vehicles.

She had her own government truck with the National Park Service, but she didn't use it for personal transportation, either. Rubbing the side of her head, she said, "I have work tomorrow."

"Don't be ridiculous. You were in a bad car accident today. Call in sick for a few days." He tapped his head. "Does that hurt?"

"I do have a headache."

"So much for relaxing in a warm tub with a glass of wine." He cocked his head. "You sure you don't want to see a doctor?"

She pulled at the door handle and said, "I want to get to the bottom of what's going on at the property."

Once inside, Sam darted around the mostly empty office, preparing the snake and arrow for a fingerprint request and packing up his laptop.

After Jolene called her boss at the Park Service, she wandered among the desks. She picked up a framed photo of Nash Dillon, his fiancée and their baby.

"Have you seen Nash's baby yet? He and his fiancée are adopting."

"I heard that and couldn't believe it. I sort of thought he was a confirmed bachelor."

"The baby's mother was murdered—involved with a drug dealer. Jaycee Lemoin, she was from Paradiso, but not while you lived here." She put the picture down and sighed. "So much misery."

"I know about that situation." He shoved his laptop into his case. "I'm ready to get out of here, but I need to eat and change, not necessarily in that order. If we go out, I need to change first."

"Can we pick something up or order in? I'm really anxious to see if there have been any other unexplained deaths lately."

"Any others?"

"Besides my father." She leveled a finger at him. "And don't start with me. I never believed he was killed by drug dealers. Why? He was on Yaqui land. Why would the cartels be out there?"

"Good question." He placed a hand over his chest, over his heart. "And I wasn't going to say a word. There's definitely something going on with that project."

"Y-you haven't heard anything about the bones yet, have you?"

"Nothing." He slung his computer case over one shoulder. "You didn't leave anything that can be tied to you, did you?"

"No." She put a finger to her lips and rolled her eyes toward the other agent on the phone.

Sam called out to him and raised his hand. "Out of here, Herrera."

The agent waved them off and kicked his feet up on his desk.

As Sam opened the door for her, he said, "I don't think he was listening to one word we said, not that he could hear us."

"It's better to be careful. I don't want to be arrested for…illegally dumping bones."

He squeezed the back of her neck. "Nobody is going to arrest you."

"Desperate circumstances call for desperate measures, and that's all I could think of doing to halt that construction short of sabotaging the equipment."

"That—" Sam beeped the remote for his rental car "—*would* get you arrested. Promise me you won't do something like that."

"I promise. I'm not sure I would even know how to go about doing that."

"I'm sure you'd think of something." He opened the passenger door for her. "Pick up or delivery?"

"I'm okay with a pizza delivery. You?"

"I'm so hungry I could've eaten that dead snake." He slammed her door and opened the other side seconds later.

As he pulled out of the parking lot, he asked, "Is it just because your father died there that you want to stop this construction? From everything I hear, it's going to provide jobs. If there were any endangered species on that land or the construction was going to be a threat to any species, you'd know that by now, right?"

"That's right. The studies have been done. I even participated in them. Nothing's going to suffer out there. My

father was opposed to it because he wanted the desert to
remain in its natural form, but even he recognized the
importance of the jobs. I think he would've come around
eventually. That's why I can't understand what happened.
Wade and his cronies would've had a more difficult approval process had my father been alive, but I think even
Wade knew my father would have given in eventually once
all the studies came back."

"You think he might've been killed for some other reason?"

She lifted her shoulders to her ears. She couldn't explain her conviction to Sam. She had no facts, just feelings. "Maybe."

"Drugs."

"We're back to that?" She pulled her phone from her
purse and cupped it between her hands.

"Because it makes sense, Jolene. He could've witnessed
something, found something. There's a reason the sheriff's department came to that conclusion." He tapped her
hand. "Are you going to order that pizza?"

"Do you want anything else? Salad?"

"Basic pepperoni is fine or whatever else you want on
it. I don't need salad."

Sam pulled into the parking lot of his motel and cut the
engine. "Do you want to come in? I'll be just a minute."

"I'll wait in the car and order the pizza."

As he hustled to his room, she phoned in their order for
a large pepperoni pizza. Two minutes after she ended the
call, Sam appeared in the parking lot, his green uniform
swapped out for a pair of light-washed jeans and a dark
blue T-shirt she just knew matched his eyes.

He settled behind the wheel and asked, "Pizza ordered?"

"One-track mind. Yes, I ordered the pizza. Let's get
back to my place so we can start our search."

"One-track mind."

As they drove past the scene of her accident, Sam rapped a knuckle on the window. "This is where your car went off the road. I can just make out the skid marks. That was a close call. What do you think of Wade's response when you accused him of fixing your brakes?"

"Deny, deny, deny." She kicked off her sandal and wedged a bare foot on his dashboard. "I didn't expect anything else, but I put him on notice. When are you going to return to the construction site? You'd better make a move before the powers that be discover the bones today don't mean much of anything."

"I'll make my way out there. Don't worry about it." He rolled up to her house and swung into the driveway. "Are you going to get yourself a rental car tomorrow?"

She patted the side of her purse where she'd stashed her phone. "I've already made arrangements through text."

He parked the car, and she jumped out to search the porch before unlocking the front door. "No more presents."

She eased open the door, and Chip stuck his nose in the crack. "Yes, I brought Sam back with me. Don't worry."

As Sam stepped through the door, Chip pranced around his legs, wagging his chocolate brown tail a mile a minute.

How easy it was to be a dog. Chip could show his unbridled enthusiasm for having Sam back without risking heartache. It just wasn't feasible to have unconditional love for someone, not if you wanted to protect yourself.

And she wanted to protect herself against Sam.

Sam hauled his laptop onto her kitchen table. "We'll work here until the pizza comes."

"I'm going to feed Chip while you're setting up. Are we going to be able to see all deaths in the Paradiso area for the past two years? I think that's what we need to look at."

"We can do that." He flipped up the cover on his laptop. "We can also search for Desert Sun Casino opposition."

"Good idea." She ducked into the laundry room where she kept Chip's dog food in a plastic bin. She scooped out two cups for him and brought his dish into the kitchen where she added some warm water to the kibble.

She nudged his furry body with her knee. "You think you should be rewarded for bringing in that snake, huh?"

Sam looked up from his computer. "He can have some pepperoni from the pizza."

"That's not good for him. No wonder he lost a little weight after you…left." Her voice hitched, and she balled up a fist and pressed it against her stomach. Chip hadn't been the only one who'd lost weight.

Sam made kissing noises in the air. "Aww, what's the matter boy? Your mom doesn't spoil you?"

Chip turned his back on his food and trotted over to Sam.

"Do you mind? I'm trying to feed him." She gave a sharp whistle and shook Chip's bowl before setting it down on the kitchen floor.

Chip twirled around and made a beeline for his dish.

Jolene eyed the bottle of red Sam had opened earlier, and then pulled open the fridge. "Do you want something to drink with your pizza? Iced tea, lemonade, soda, water?"

"Water's fine—and stop making goo-goo eyes at that wine and pour yourself a glass. Do you think the smell of alcohol is going to make me relapse?"

"It's not rude?"

"Was it rude before when we were…dating? You drank then, and I didn't have a problem with it. I'm further along in my sobriety now, and it's even less of a problem."

She uncorked the bottle and plucked the wineglass she'd used earlier from the dish drainer. She poured half a glass, glanced at Sam hunched over his laptop and splashed in a few more gulps.

As she filled up a glass of water for Sam, the doorbell rang, setting Chip into a frenzy.

Sam hopped up from the table. "Settle down, Chip. We don't wanna scare away the pizza guy."

He got the door and paid the bill. As he carried the box to the kitchen, Chip went back to his own food.

Sam dangled a plastic bag from his fingers. "Paper plates and napkins?"

"I asked for those, too. We don't need to worry about dishes on top of everything else." She flipped open the box and loosened two slices from the whole. She plopped them onto a plate and put another two onto the other plate.

"You can add a few more of those for me." Sam rubbed his hands together. "Pizza from Mr. Pizza—one of the many things I missed about Paradiso."

"There's no pizza in San Diego?" She loaded Sam's plate with another two slices and carried the food to the table while Sam grabbed the drinks.

He said, "There are some things in Paradiso that you just can't get in San Diego."

She jerked her head around and raised her eyebrows. "You're pretty slick, Sam Cross."

"Don't get too full of yourself, Jolene Nighthawk." He raised the glasses. "I meant the pizza and… Chip."

She placed his plate next to the computer and took a seat.

"If you think I'm going to ruin my dinner by working, you don't know how hungry I am." He shoved the laptop to the center of the table and stationed himself in front of his food.

He wolfed down one piece before coming up for air and taking a drink of water.

Jolene swirled her wine. "I don't think I've ever seen anyone inhale a slice of pizza that fast in my life."

"Did I mention I was starving?" He plucked a circle of pepperoni from a slice on his plate and fed it to Chip, waiting patiently by Sam's chair.

"Hey! Chip doesn't need pepperoni."

"Look how happy he is." Sam patted Chip's head, and then wiped his hands on a paper napkin. "Now that the edge is off, I can take a look at this database—over another piece of pizza."

Still seated, she scooted her chair around next to his. "Are these the deaths for the past few years?"

"Sorted by most recent, first." He poked his finger at the screen. "Name, address, manner of death—so, homicide, suicide, accident, natural causes and some other stuff that I can collapse."

She tore the corner off her pizza with her teeth and loomed over Sam's shoulder, scanning the lines that contained too much information. "This is confusing."

"You're getting crumbs on my laptop." He blew on the keyboard. "And you're chewing in my ear. Give me a few seconds to get rid of some of these columns we don't need to see. When we pare this down, we can click on the file number and it'll take us to another database with more information about the details of the death."

Drawing back, she reached for her wine and took a sip. "You're not going to get into trouble for logging in and using these programs, are you?"

"I'm in Paradiso to investigate links between some missing people here and the remains of the missing people we located in the desert east of San Diego. Why wouldn't I be accessing these databases?" He clicked around the page, cleaning up the table, distilling it to the pertinent information.

She waved her hand at the screen. "Do you think we should eliminate the people over a certain age who died of natural causes?"

"We can do that." He scrolled down the list. "Here's an eighty-six-year-old woman who had a stroke."

"Yeah, like those." She squinted at the cause of death column. "More homicides than you'd expect outside of Tucson and Phoenix."

"Courtesy of the border and the drug trade."

They worked on the database together for over an hour and managed to polish off the pizza at the same time.

Jolene had limited her wine consumption to one glass, even though she could've used another. She collected the paper plates and the glasses.

"I think we have a good list to start going through. We already know we can ignore the murders of Jaycee Lemoin, her boyfriend, Brett, and the social worker he killed. Those didn't have anything to do with the casino project."

"Maybe none of these did." Sam lifted his head. "Is that your phone or mine?"

"Oops, mine." Jolene tossed the plates into the empty pizza box and grabbed the phone, flashing an unknown number. "Hello?"

"Jolene?"

"Yeah, who's this?"

"This is Eddie, the bartender at the Sundowner."

She raised her eyebrows at Sam. "Yeah, I know you. What's up, Eddie?"

"Your cousin Melody is at the bar and she's lit. I tried calling Wade, but he's not picking up."

"What's she doing?" She mouthed Melody's name to Sam. "Can you call her a rideshare?"

"Normally I'd do that but she's in bad shape, Jolene. I'm afraid to let her out the door by herself, and I don't trust any of these guys here tonight. They're not much better off themselves. I'd take care of her myself, but I have another two hours of work and she can't stay here in her condition."

"Okay, I'll be right over. Thanks, Eddie." She ended the call and tapped the phone against her chin. "You were right. Melody's fallen off the wagon—and in spectacular fashion. Sounds like she's drunk and disorderly in the Sundowner."

"Great." Sam logged off the computer. "I'm coming with you. Maybe I can talk her down."

"Let Chip out for a few minutes while I clean up the kitchen." She shoved the napkins in the pizza box. As she walked past Sam, she handed him the box. "Can you throw this in the trash outside, please?"

When Chip came back inside, Jolene locked up the house and grabbed her purse. As they walked out to Sam's rental car, she said, "I'm so disappointed in her."

Sam opened her car door and placed a hand on her shoulder. "You're not more disappointed than Melody is. Remember that. She already feels like a failure. Don't make it worse for her."

"You're right." She twisted her head to the side, and kissed the hand that rested on her shoulder. "I'm glad you're here."

Sam's eyes flickered for a second.

She'd meant it, at least for now.

The Sundowner had been a staple of Paradiso nightlife when Sam lived here two years ago, not that it was ever a place he frequented. He'd already stopped drinking and had separated from his wife by the time he moved here.

When she'd met him, he'd fallen off the wagon once, three months into his six months of sobriety—and that misstep had resulted in his ex's pregnancy. He'd told her about going back on the booze, but had failed to mention the hookup with his ex.

Not that she'd known him at the time. They'd gotten together a few months after that, and had had a few more blissful months until he announced that his ex was pregnant, which had signaled the end of their love story.

Sam nudged her shoulder. "It's at the end of the block, right?"

"The place with the blue-and-red neon sign."

"It's busy." Sam cruised past the front and all the cars parked along the curb and a rideshare double-parked, waiting for its rider.

"I'll make a U-turn." He turned the car around at the end of the block and parked across the street.

They got out of the car, and Sam grabbed her hand as they ran to the other side of the street.

Smokers had spilled out of the bar onto the sidewalk where live music from a country rock band blared. They squeezed past a drunk stumbling out the front door.

"I hope she's not in the same condition as that guy." Jolene jerked her thumb over her shoulder.

"If she is, we can handle it." Sam peered over everyone's heads.

She tugged on his sleeve, as the bass from the band reverberated in her chest. "See her?"

"No, let's head to the bar and find Eddie. Do you know what he looks like?"

"Big guy, shaved head, long beard and pumped-up, tattooed arms—can't miss him."

"Got him. He's a busy guy. Nice of him to take the time to call you." Sam steered her through the crowd, and they edged up to the bar.

Jolene raised her hand. "Eddie!"

The big guy nodded once as he topped off a beer. When

he finished with his customer, he moved down the bar and stopped on the other side from them, folding his massive arms. "She's gone."

"Gone? Where?" Jolene scanned the heads around her, hoping to see her cousin's pink-streaked black hair.

"She ordered a rideshare on her phone. I told her you were coming, but she didn't want to see you." He swiped the counter with a white cloth. "You know, she's been hitting the bottle for a while, but didn't want you to know."

"I'm not here to judge her. I just wanted to make sure she's safe." Jolene hugged her purse to her chest. She was pretty sure she'd vented to Melody about drunks who relapsed when she found out about Sam and his ex—maybe once or twice.

"She was coherent enough to order the car?" Sam braced his hands against the bar.

Eddie answered, "I helped her when she made it clear she was going home by herself, even though I tried to talk her out of it. You just missed her."

"Thanks, Eddie. I appreciate it." Jolene slipped her phone from the side pocket of her purse and called Melody's number. She listened to three rings before Melody's voice mail answered.

"She's not answering—probably because she saw it was me."

Sam cocked his head. "How many people use rideshare around here?"

"From the bar?" Eddie tugged on his earlobe, elongated with multiple piercings. "A good number. Hey, I gotta get back to work. Hope Melody is okay. I got a soft spot for that crazy girl."

Sam turned and leaned his back against the bar. "Does Melody live with Wade?"

"No, she has her own place. We should stop by, huh?"

"For sure. When Eddie called you, he didn't seem convinced Melody could make it home on her own safely. I think it's a good idea to check in on her."

"I agree." She tipped her head toward the band on the stage. "They're not bad."

Sam cut a bigger swath through the crowd than she could, so he led the way while she hooked a finger in the back pocket of his jeans.

As they burst onto the sidewalk, Sam dragged in a deep breath. "That smell makes me sick now."

She stepped off the curb, and he grabbed her arm.

"Hold on. That rideshare car is still waiting." He strode down the sidewalk and ducked down to the open passenger window of the car. "Who are you picking up?"

The driver pointed at Jolene standing next to Sam. "Are you Melody?"

Jolene put a hand to her throat. "You're waiting for Melody?"

"Is that you?"

"She's my cousin. I came to pick her up, but the bartender said she'd ordered a car. You're telling me she never came out here?"

"I don't know if she ever came out here or not, but nobody named Melody ever claimed the ride." He tapped the phone mounted on his dashboard. "I gave her fifteen minutes, so I'm gonna bounce and pick up another ride— unless you need a lift."

"N-no."

She and Sam backed away from the car and stared at each other.

"What does it mean?" She licked her lips. "She ordered a car and didn't take the ride?"

"Maybe someone she knew saw her and took her home."

Sam placed his hand on the small of her back. "Now we really need to go to her place."

She swept her arm to encompass the people scattered on the sidewalk. "Should we ask them if they saw her?"

"We can try."

With Sam at her elbow, she questioned the people on the sidewalk, but nobody remembered seeing a woman with pink-streaked hair, although one of the smokers remembered her from inside the bar.

He flicked his cigarette butt into the gutter and grinned. "That chick was wasted—tequila. Had to be tequila."

"But you didn't see where she went when she left the bar?"

"Sorry, no. She left before I did."

Jolene's heart hammered in her chest as she crossed the street with Sam. "I hope she's home safe, but why isn't she answering her phone?"

"You tried again?"

"I can't." As she settled in the car, she pulled out her phone and shook it from side to side "It's dead. Maybe it did get damaged in the accident."

"Use mine. I think I still have her number in my phone if you don't have it memorized." He handed his phone to her and then went around to the driver's side.

Jolene found Melody's number in Sam's phone and tapped it. This time it went straight to voice mail with no ring.

When Sam got behind the wheel, she grabbed his arm. "Sam, I think her phone is off now. It went straight to voice mail without ringing. Why would her phone be off?"

"Maybe it died when she got home. Maybe she turned it off."

"That girl never turns off her phone. It's attached to her hand."

"She's drunk, Jolene. It could mean anything." He started the car. "Which direction is her place?"

She guided him to Melody's apartment in one of the new buildings that had gone up to house workers coming in for the pecan-processing plant.

"She's on the second floor." She pointed through the windshield as Sam parked the car near the edge of the parking lot, away from tenant parking. "That's her place up there. She has a light on."

"She's probably passed out on the floor, or maybe she got lucky and made it to her bed. Worst-case scenario, she's clutching the toilet seat, puking her guts out."

"I'll take that worst-case scenario."

Sam's mouth tightened as he walked up the stairs to Melody's. Did he really believe his own worst-case scenario?

When they reached the second-floor landing, Jolene gasped. "That's her door, the one that's open."

Sam put his arm out. "Stay back for a minute and let me check it out."

With her adrenaline coursing through her system, Jolene pushed past Sam and charged through Melody's front door.

"Melody?" Jolene tripped to a stop and smacked her hand against a wall to steady herself. "Sam, she's been hurt. She passed out. There's blood."

Sam eased past Jolene and crouched next to Melody. He put two fingers against her throat.

"How bad is it? We need to call 911." Jolene took a step toward Sam.

"Stop. Don't come any closer. Melody is dead."

Chapter Nine

Jolene's face turned white, and her hand slid down the wall as she collapsed to a crouch. "Are you sure?"

"She doesn't have a pulse. CPR isn't going to help at this point." Sam put a finger on Melody's chin, her flesh still warm, and tipped her head to the side. Blood from a deep gash matted Melody's hair. "It's a head injury."

Jolene plunged her hand into her purse. "I'm calling 911."

"Your phone's dead." He held out his phone to her. "Try not to touch anything in here, Jolene."

As Jolene spoke a rush of words to the 911 operator, Sam swiveled his head to take a look around the room. As far as he could tell, nothing had been disturbed. Then he noticed blood on the edge of a glass coffee table. Squinting, he leaned in, careful not to touch it.

Jolene ended the call. "They're on their way. What happened, Sam?"

"There's blood and a few strands of hair stuck to that table. It's the right shape. She could've fallen and hit her head on the table."

"That would be enough to kill her?" Jolene sawed at her bottom lip with her teeth, her eyes wide and glassy.

"Do you see Melody's phone? Her purse?" Sam inched away from the body. He had to get Jolene out of here. If there was any foul play, they didn't want to be tromping around a crime scene.

Still gripping his phone, Jolene asked, "Do you think this was some kind of robbery gone wrong? Melody walked in on someone, and he pushed her? Took her purse?"

"I don't know. Do you see the purse?"

"Melody always carried a small cross-body bag, It's not…on her?"

Sam glanced down at Melody's still form, her pink-streaked hair fanning across her face. His gaze tracked across her blouse, bunched around her waist, her skirt demurely smoothed over her thighs and her feet with one sandal on and one off. "I don't see a purse."

Jolene twisted her hair into a knot over her shoulder. "How could this happen? We just missed her at the bar."

"Things happen when you're drunk. Things happen when you're drunk…and know too much." Sam pushed up to his feet. "I hear the sirens. We need to step outside."

Jolene seemed frozen in place. "Do you think someone killed her? That was my first thought, but I didn't want to come off as paranoid."

"Then we're both paranoid." Sam held out his hand. "C'mon. You already got your prints on that wall."

"I'm a visitor here. My prints are going to be all over this apartment." She grasped his hand with her cold fingers and he drew her up as the sirens ended in the parking lot below.

"We'll let the police figure it out."

"Like they figured out my father's murder?" She shook her head. "They'll take the path of least resistance. Her purse is missing, and she was drunk. That will be their main focus."

"Whoever took her purse and phone must've turned it

off. That's why you couldn't get through the last time you tried from my phone."

Footsteps clumped up the stairs, and Sam led Jolene out of the apartment just as the first responders made it to the landing.

Sam raised his hand. "Over here."

The next thirty minutes were a blur of activity. The EMTs didn't try to revive Melody, as they'd discovered the same thing he had—no pulse.

How had that happened so fast? Melody had lost a lot of blood, but not enough to bleed out in twenty minutes. The blow to her head could've done her in immediately. Had someone hit her and then smeared her blood and hair on the table to make it look like an accident?

How many other deaths in that database were conveniently accidental?

Jolene had wandered back into the apartment when the EMTs called it quits on Melody. The crime scene investigators from the sheriff's department were too busy to notice her presence. He hoped she wasn't in there contaminating evidence. Maybe she just didn't want to leave Melody alone.

The officer Sam had been talking to came up the stairs again. "The medical examiner is on her way. I don't have anything else for you or Ms. Nighthawk. You have my card, and I have your phone numbers. We'll be in touch if we need anything else."

Sam pointed to the eaves running above the apartment doorways. "Too bad there are no cameras here."

"We might be able to get something from across the street, and even though we don't have her phone, we'll get those records and see if she ordered another car."

"I'll be in Paradiso for a while on my case, so keep me

apprised. Jolene, Ms. Nighthawk, is understandably devastated by the death of her cousin."

"She's Wade Nighthawk's sister, too." The deputy pointed down to the parking lot where Wade was talking to a uniformed cop. "Wade has friends in high places. Someone must've told him."

Sam hustled back to Melody's apartment and called to Jolene, who seemed transfixed by the CSI guys going through Melody's living room.

She jerked her head to the side. "I—I just don't want her to be alone."

"I know." He crooked his finger at her. "Come here a second."

She gave a last look at Melody and approached him, tears streaking her face. She must've come out of the shock that had gripped her when they first discovered Melody.

He wrapped his arms around her and whispered in her ear. "Wade's here."

Her body stiffened, and he patted her back. "Don't make any wild accusations against him—not here, not now. That's his sister lying there."

She nodded and buried her face in his shoulder. "We should've done more."

"I know."

As Sam drew her out onto the landing, Wade shouted. "What are you two doing here? They won't let me pass."

Sam steered Jolene toward her cousin. "We found her, Wade. The bartender at the Sundowner called Jolene to pick up Melody, and we got there too late."

"How'd she get home? Who did this?" Wade's smooth face had tightened into a mask. His dark eyes glittered with anger.

Jolene hugged her cousin. "We don't know, Wade. We think she took a rideshare home. H-her purse is missing."

"I told her not to live here on her own." Wade smacked a fist into his palm. "She could've lived with us."

With her arms still wrapped around Wade, Jolene asked, "When did she start drinking again?"

Sam held his breath.

"Don't blame me for that. If you weren't so busy running around with your head in the clouds, you would've noticed. I couldn't make her stop." He thrust his hand out toward Sam. "Ask your boyfriend there if anyone can get an alcoholic to stop drinking."

Sam clenched his jaw, and then rolled his shoulders. The man had just lost his sister. "He's right, Jolene. Nobody is to blame for Melody's drinking except Melody."

"You're both accusing me of something I didn't even say." Jolene folded her arms. "I'm not blaming you. If anyone's to blame, it's me. If we had gotten to the Sundowner faster, we could've given Melody a ride home. Sam would've seen her safely inside."

"Look, I'm sorry. Sorry, Sam." Wade wiped his brow with the back of his hand. "I'm upset, lashing out."

Wade smoothed his hand along his ponytail, and his chest heaved as he took a deep breath. The smooth politician emerged. "Do the police think it was a robbery or an accident? All they told me was that she died from a head injury. Did she fall, or did someone hit her? They didn't tell me her purse was missing."

The medical examiner's white van pulled into the parking lot, and Sam touched Wade's arm. "Let's go downstairs, and let them finish their work here."

Wade gestured to the neighbors poking their heads out their doors. "Did anyone hear anything? See anything?"

Jolene answered, "We don't know, but the officers questioned them. They wouldn't tell us anything. The apartment next to Melody's is vacant. I remember when her neighbor moved out of there a few months ago. The management company hasn't rented it out yet."

They reached the bottom of the stairs and stepped aside for two people from the medical examiner's van carrying a stretcher.

Jolene averted her face as Wade swallowed, a struggle to maintain control twisting his features for a minute.

"The officers said they might be able to get something from the cameras over there." Sam pointed across the street.

"This damned building didn't even have a security system or cameras." Wade squeezed his eyes closed. "I told her. I told her."

Jolene took her cousin's hand. "Was Melody seeing anyone? Would someone else have picked her up from the bar?"

Wade's lids flew open. "What are you saying? Don't the police think this is either an accident or a robbery? You're not suggesting someone murdered Melody, are you?"

"I don't know." Jolene shrugged. "I'm just asking a question, and it's still murder if it was committed during a robbery."

"You would probably know more about Melody's dating life than I would. She didn't tell me anything like that, not after…"

"Not after you chased off the last guy." Jolene held up her hands. "I'm just saying."

"He was bad news, and you know it, Jolene. He's probably the one who got her drinking again."

"Is that true, Jolene?" Sam's hands curled into fists. "If so, Wade's right—bad news."

"I don't know. I don't think so. Melody and that guy split up almost six months ago. I don't think she'd been drinking that long." Jolene ran a hand through her hair. "Or maybe I'm just clueless."

"I don't know." Wade stared over Sam's shoulder, his eyes blinking. "I have to go up and see Melody's…body. I want to see her."

"Of course you do." Jolene squeezed his hand. "Let me know if we can do anything."

They both watched Wade's stiff back as he walked to the apartment's staircase, still swarming with cops.

Melody rubbed the back of her hand across her nose. "He seemed upset—or Wade-upset, which is a little different from everyone else's upset."

"I don't think Wade would murder his own sister—pay her off, threaten her, coerce her—but not murder." Sam pinched the bridge of his nose. "I have a headache, and I can't even imagine what you're feeling. I'm sorry about Melody, Jolene. Like the bartender said, I always had a soft spot for Melody, too. She's the one who introduced me to you."

He hit the remote for his car, and Jolene glanced at him from beneath her lashes before following him to the passenger side.

As he opened her door, a hissing sound came from the bushes bordering the parking lot. Sam pivoted and peered into the foliage, as Jolene tucked her fingers in the waistband of his jeans.

As he stepped in front of Jolene, Sam barked, "Who's there?"

A pair of eyes gleamed from a face that appeared between two bushes. "Hey, you ain't the po-po, are you?"

Sam knew how to answer that question under these circumstances. "No, I'm not a cop. Why? Who are you?"

The man shuffled from his hiding place, twigs and

leaves clinging to his bushy hair and beard. "I'm Tucker. Tucker the trucker."

Jolene moved closer to Sam, pressing her body against his.

Reaching back, Sam opened the car door for her, but she didn't move. "What are you doing out here, Tucker the trucker, and where's your truck?"

The man laughed, displaying a set of teeth with a few gaps. "I don't have it no more, man. No more truck."

Tucker was missing more than his teeth. "What do you want, Tucker?"

He raised a grubby unsteady finger, pointing over Sam's head. "I live there."

Sam's heart rate ticked up. "You live in that apartment building behind me?"

Tucker nodded, putting the finger to his lips. "I'm not supposed to, but the place is empty. I got in there once, so sometimes I squat there."

"Really?" He must mean the empty apartment right next to Melody's.

"Nobody's there. What's it to you?" Tucker puffed out his scrawny chest.

"Easy, man. I don't care." Sam twisted his head over his shoulder and whispered to Jolene, "Get in the car."

"And miss this? No way." She grabbed the top of the car door, peering over it at Tucker. "Did you know the woman who lived in that apartment? The one where all the cops are?"

"Pinky?" He grinned. "Yeah, I know her. She promised not to tell no one about me living there. She gave me beer sometimes."

"Did you see Pinky tonight, Tucker?" Sam shoved a hand in his pocket. "Did you see what happened?"

Tucker scuffed the toe of his filthy sneaker in the dirt. "Do you have beer?"

"I don't have any beer, but I have some money. If I give you some money, will you tell us what you saw tonight?" Sam pulled a crumpled ten from his pocket and bounced it up and down on his palm in front of Tucker.

When Tucker reached out for it, Sam formed a fist around the bill. "You gotta give me the goods first, Tucker."

"She's dead, huh? Pinky's dead?" The man's nose turned red, and he blinked his watery eyes.

Jolene sniffed. "Yeah, Pinky's dead."

Tucker cackled and slapped the thigh of his raggedy black pants. "I saw who killed her."

Chapter Ten

Jolene's fingers curled around the door, and she caught her breath. She felt like grabbing Tucker and shaking him, but she didn't want to scare him off. The guy seemed ready to blow away with the next breeze.

"You saw what happened to Pinky?"

"I heard." Tucker tapped his head. "I was dreaming in my pad."

"Dreaming?" Sam turned his head and rolled his eyes at her. "You mean you were sleeping?"

"I was sleeping and dreaming." Tucker started combing his fingers through his unkempt beard, not a gray hair visible, but he looked old enough to be Sam's father. "Big loud noise woke me up."

"Did you hear voices?" Sam allowed the ten-dollar bill to peek through his fist, and Tucker's gaze followed every one of Sam's gestures. "Yelling? Screaming?"

"Just a yelp, like a yelp, yip, yap. Big loud noise. Scraping sound like furniture moving." Tucker narrowed his eyes. "Then he left."

Jolene's heart jumped. "You saw the man who killed Mel… Pinky?"

"I heard footsteps—clomp, bomp, stomp. I eyed, spied though the blinds and saw a man leaving. Stocking cap on his head. It's hot. Nobody needs no stocking cap."

"This rhyming is giving me a headache." Sam rubbed his temple with two fingers. "Did you see what this guy looked like, Tucker? Other than the stocking cap? Beard? Long hair? Clothing?"

Tucker tore at his shirt. "It wasn't me. No beard. It wasn't me. Don't take my thumb, don't take my thumb, don't take my thumb, drum, crumb drive."

"Damn." Sam dragged a hand through his hair. "I didn't say it was you, Tucker, and we're not going to take your thumb. I'm asking what the guy looked like."

"Dark clothes, black clothes. Dark, stark, weird beard." He waved his hands. "Not me, not me. Not my thumb."

"We know that, Tucker." She tugged on Sam's sleeve. "Give him the money for God's sake."

Sam held on to the bill and asked, "Did you see him get into a car? Hear a car?"

"No car. Like me, no truck. But not me." Tucker started hopping from foot to foot. "It wasn't me. Not my thumb."

Sam smacked a hand against his forehead. "I don't know how much more of this I can take."

Jolene hunched over the car door. "Tucker, can you talk to the police? Tell them what you told us? You want to help Pinky, don't you? She was good to you, and that man hurt her."

"They'll get me for staying in that place when I ain't supposed to. They'll take my thumb drive. Pinky gave me that."

"You're not there now. The cops aren't going to arrest you for anything. They're trying to find out what happened to Pinky." Sam held out the balled up ten to Tucker. "I'll make sure they don't arrest you. Just tell them what you saw."

Tucker snatched the bill and opened his voluminous coat, wet from the rains, to find a place to put the money.

As he tugged open one side of his coat, a purse fell to the ground.

Jolene covered her mouth. "Sam, that's Melody's purse."

Tucker made a grab for the purse and shouted, "Not me. Not me. No thumb. In the floor."

He scrambled toward the bushes, and Sam lunged forward and tackled him, pinning his arms behind his back. "That's it, Tucker. Game over. Jolene, go get the police down here."

"Sam!" Jolene clutched her stomach as Tucker wailed. "You don't really believe he killed Melody, do you?"

"He has her damned purse, Jolene. Go get the cops before I have to hurt him." Sam flipped Tucker over and planted a knee in the middle of the frail man's back.

Jolene jogged across the parking lot and grabbed the first officer she saw. "We ran into a homeless guy near our car. He admitted to squatting in the apartment next to Melody's, and he has her purse."

Another cop overheard her and the two sheriff's deputies hustled toward the edge of the parking lot.

When they arrived, Sam looked up from the squirming Tucker. "I'm Border Patrol. I have my weapon but no cuffs. I didn't have to pull my gun, but you need to take him into custody."

Tucker thrashed on the ground. "You told me you wouldn't call them. Where's my ten bucks? Tucker, trucker. Tucker, trucker."

One of the officers swore. "Oh man, it's Tucker Bishop."

"You know him?" Sam panted. "He's wriggling like a fish on a line over here."

"We pick him up occasionally, mostly for a seventy-two-hour hold in the psych ward. He's usually not violent."

"Yeah, except he's in possession of a dead woman's purse. He told us he heard someone in Melody's apartment and saw him walk by, but I don't know how much we can trust him."

The deputies approached Sam and Tucker, one of them drawing his weapon. "Stop struggling, Tucker. We're gonna take you to the station and find out what you know, give you a cot and a hot. Why do you have that woman's purse?"

"She gave it to me. She gave me stuff."

Sam finally relinquished control of Tucker to the sheriff's deputies. Standing up, he brushed off his clothing. "I'm going to have to do more laundry."

Jolene spotted Melody's purse on the ground and crouched down, reaching out for it.

"Don't touch it, Jolene. Let them bag it for evidence and test it for prints. The fewer people touching it right now, the better."

She snatched her hand back. "I don't see her phone."

"What?" Sam took a knee beside her.

"Her phone." Jolene poked at the purse with a stick she snatched up from the parking lot. "She'd usually stick it in this side pocket."

Sam pushed to his feet. "Check Tucker's pockets for a phone."

One of the deputies snapped on a pair of gloves and asked Tucker to remove his coat. He searched through the pockets of the coat, and then patted down Tucker.

"Nothing."

Jolene approached Tucker, his hands cuffed behind him, his lips moving with mumbled words. Her heart ached for him. Melody would have been kind to him because Melody had a thing for lost causes.

"Tucker? Did you take Pinky's phone?"

He shook his shaggy head and spittle nestled in his beard. "No phone. No zone. No drone."

"Watch out, Ms. Nighthawk, we're taking him in. We'll ask him about the phone."

As the deputies bagged the purse and hauled off a subdued Tucker, Jolene plopped down in the passenger seat of Sam's car, her legs hanging over the side. "What the heck do you make of that? You can't possibly believe that poor confused man killed Melody."

"You said it. He's confused, Jolene. We don't know what's going on his head. We don't know what drugs he's on. I was willing to play along up until the minute Melody's purse fell out of his coat. He could've heard her come home, gone next door, asked for a beer. Maybe Melody invited him in, he saw her purse and decided to take it. She fought back, fell and hit her head." He shrugged in a way that encompassed everything else.

Jolene pinned her hands between her knees. "I don't know. If Tucker did kill her, why did he accost us in the parking lot? We didn't know he was there. He could've disappeared with Melody's purse. Nobody would've known of his presence. The cops might not have even discovered that he'd been in the apartment next door. Why implicate himself when he didn't have to?"

"Really, Jolene?" Sam raised his eyebrows. "You're acting like Tucker the trucker is a reasonable, rational human being, instead of a drug-and-booze-addled vagrant."

She dropped her head to her knees. "Oh, Melody, why'd you start drinking again?"

Sam stroked her hair. "I'm going to get you home—before something else happens."

When Sam got behind the wheel, Jolene tapped his forearm. "Is Melody Nighthawk going to be another person in that death register whose death is marked down as accidental? We need to comb through those names."

"Not tonight. Do you need to call someone, Granny

Viv, or will Wade take care of that?" He plucked a charger from the cup holder. "I don't think this will work with your phone."

"Wade will tell Gran. I'll charge my phone when I get home." She ran a finger down the thigh of his jeans. "Do you have to go back to your motel? I—I'm still rattled after everything that went on today. I'd rather not be alone— even with Chip there."

"I had no intention of leaving you alone tonight."

Jolene eased out a sigh and slumped in the seat. Was she inviting trouble by asking Sam to stay? Could she have him in her home and not her bed?

She'd find out soon enough.

When he walked into her house, Sam removed his weapon from his waistband and set it on the kitchen table. He pinched his T-shirt between two fingers and pulled it away from his body. "Every time I step into your home, there's something wrong with my clothes."

Jolene searched the counter for her phone charger. "What is it this time?"

"Did you get a look at Tucker and his clothing? He and it weren't too clean, and I had to tackle the guy." He pulled his T-shirt up to his face and sniffed it. "Yeah, this definitely has to go in the wash."

"I should start charging you for laundry." Jolene walked to her bedroom and plugged her phone into the charger on her nightstand.

When she returned to the living room, Chip had joined in on the sniffing. His nose was twitching as he checked out Sam's jeans.

"Even Chip notices." Sam patted the dog's head. "Good boy."

Jolene dropped onto the couch. "I can't believe Melody is dead. Gran is going to be heartbroken."

"Should you call her? You can use my phone again."

"I'll let Wade handle it. He might not even want to wake her at this hour to give her the news. We'll see her tomorrow." Tears pricked the back of Jolene's eyes, and she covered her face.

Sam rubbed a circle on her back. "I wish I had confronted her about drinking when she waved us down. I didn't want to get in her face, you know?"

"I know, and I feel like we could've gotten to the bar faster." She dropped her hands. "Was cleaning the kitchen so important? Changing clothes?"

"We didn't know what was going to happen, Jolene. Who could predict how this night would end?"

"Did she seem scared to you earlier? She did warn me."

"If she was so frightened, she wouldn't have gone out drinking on her own. She would've stayed at her brother's place, his gated home with the security system. Wade could've kept her safe if she was afraid."

"Unless she was afraid of Wade." She twisted her head around and met Sam's blue eyes. "Why are you hovering back there? Have a seat."

He thumped a hand against his chest. "You don't wanna get too close to this. I'm going to shower and put on those sweats I dug out of your closet earlier. Is that okay with you?"

"Go ahead. Do you want some tea, coffee, water?"

"I don't need anything to keep me awake. I'm already wired. You?" He yanked the T-shirt over his head, and she gulped.

She had the same visceral reaction she'd always had to the sight of Sam Cross's body—tingling excitement now mixed with an ache of longing.

"Same." She pushed up from the couch, trying to put distance between her and Sam's bare chest. "I'm going to make myself a cup of herbal tea. I'll make you one, too. You want it. You just don't know you want it yet."

"If it can help with the pounding in my head that was going on before we were subjected to Tucker the trucker and then got worse when I talked to him, I'm all for it." He pointed to the hallway. "Clean towel in the linen closet?"

"Help yourself, and you can stuff your clothes in the washer while you're at it."

She banged around in the kitchen, pulling tea bags and mugs from the cupboards, while Sam banged around in the hall closet. She hoped he wouldn't follow her instructions literally, and take off all his clothes and put them in the wash before he got in the shower. Sam shirtless had already tested her defenses. Sam naked would bring her walls crumbling down around her.

Jolene let out a long breath when she heard the water in the shower. She filled the mugs with water and stuck them in the microwave.

Two minutes later, she dredged the tea bags in the boiling water of each cup. If Sam didn't want the tea, she'd have a second cup.

She hunched over the counter, burying her chin in her palm. How had everything gotten so complicated? She'd planned to dump the bones she'd gotten from her friend in the U of A archaeology department at the construction site to muck up the work over there and do a little more digging into her father's death. How had it ended in Melody's death?

Of course, Melody could've been doing her own snooping that led to her death. Or maybe she'd taken a tumble and hit her head all by herself. She and Tucker could've gotten into a tug-of-war over the purse.

Sam stepped into the kitchen dressed in nothing but those Border Patrol sweats again, droplets of water shimmering on his chest, his clothes bunched in one hand. "Do you have anything you want to put in with these?"

At least the sweats seemed to be pulled up higher on his waist.

Chip trotted into the kitchen, his claws tapping on the tile floor. Sam bent over to scratch Chip behind the ear, and the sweats dipped a little more.

"No, knock yourself out. I have a short cycle, though, so you should use that to save water." She cleared her throat and held up one of the steaming mugs. "Tea?"

"I'll give it a try." He disappeared into the laundry room off the kitchen and turned on the washing machine with several beeps.

When he came out, she handed him a cup of tea. "That sounded like way too many beeps for the short cycle."

"I had to make a few corrections." He held the mug under his nose and closed his eyes. "It smells good, anyway, but most tea tastes like slightly flavored hot water to me."

She pushed at his back, his skin smooth beneath her fingertips. "It's soothing. Give it a try. Do you want some ibuprofen for your head?"

"That warm shower did the trick." He wrapped one hand around the mug and tilted his head, a damp lock of hair curling over his forehead. "How do you feel? It seems days instead of hours ago that I ran a bath for you to relax after your accident. How are those bruises on your arms? Your neck?"

She ran a hand across the back of her neck. "My neck's a little stiff, but I'm okay. Bruises are coloring up nicely. I just wish I could dial back the clock to the moment when Melody ran out to the street to warn me."

"Me, too, but that's futile. Believe me, I've wanted to turn the clock back many times." He touched his mug to hers. "Let's sit down and drink our tea—never thought I'd hear myself saying that. C'mon, Chip."

"You might like it." She strolled into the living room with Sam right behind her and Chip right behind him, his devoted follower. She sat on one side of the couch, grabbed the remote and turned on the TV. She didn't want any awkward silences between them.

Sam took the cushion next to her and noisily slurped his tea. "Yep, flavored hot water, but it's kind of minty."

She aimed the remote at the TV. "Have you seen this show?"

"Heard about it, haven't seen it." He stretched his arm across her shoulders and pulled her close. "It's okay now. Everything's going to be okay."

"But Melody…" She rested her head on his shoulder. Maybe she didn't want to put her trust in Sam for the long term, but for right now he represented something solid.

"I know." He smoothed the hair back from her forehead, his fingers tickling her skin.

Chip curled up on her feet, and Sam ran the sole of his foot across Chip's back. "See? Chip's here for you, too. We both are."

Jolene took another sip of her tea and set the cup on the coffee table. She turned to Sam and cupped his lean jaw in her hand. "I don't know what I want from you, Sam—maybe nothing. Maybe you're not prepared to offer anything."

He opened his mouth, and she put a finger to his lips. "But right now, I need you."

She replaced her finger with her lips, kissing his mint-flavored mouth.

He slipped his arms around her and deepened their kiss,

his hands sliding down her back. He murmured against her mouth, "I love you, Jolene. I never stopped loving you."

"Don't." She skimmed her hands across his shoulders, and then dug her fingernails into his flesh. "You don't have to tell me anything right now. You don't have to convince me of anything. I just want to be with you. Can we do that? Just be?"

He cinched his hands around her waist and pulled her into his lap so that she straddled him. "We can do whatever you want. I'm yours."

His words caused a thrill to race down her spine. Her fingertips buzzed, and she trailed them over the sculpted muscles of his chest, circling one brown nipple before she kissed it. She ran a finger along the waistband of the sweats.

"Easy on, easy off. How convenient." She tugged at the sweats, discovering Sam had stripped off his underwear, too. "*Very* convenient."

"I aim to please." He nuzzled her throat, planting a line of kisses on her shoulder. Then he peeled her T-shirt from her body, as she lifted her arms.

"I aim to please, too."

"You don't have to do anything to please me." He fumbled with her bra. "Except take this off."

She obliged and threw the undergarment over her head.

Chip scrambled to his feet and went to investigate.

"He's not going to chew that up, is he?" Sam had stopped caressing her breast as he eyed Chip across the room.

"Don't worry about him." She tried yanking down the sweats, but she was still sitting on Sam's lap and didn't get very far. "Should we take this into the bedroom...away from the watching eyes of Chip?"

"Definitely."

He scooped her up in his arms, both of them topless now, and she pressed her bare skin against his. She'd missed the feel of him.

He carried her into the bedroom and kicked the door closed behind them. "In case Chip gets any ideas."

She slid off his body and stood on her tiptoes, as he kissed her by the side of the bed, one hand placed at the back of her head. She didn't even mind the slight shaft of pain that needled her neck.

Her fingers slipped into the waistband of the sweats and tugged them down over the curve of his backside. Her hands kneaded his muscled buttocks, which he flexed for her benefit. "Someone's been running."

He stepped out of the sweats and kicked them across the floor. Then he reached for the button on her jeans.

"Wait." She grabbed his hand and, placing the palm of her other hand against his chest, she pushed him back a few steps. "I want to see what I've been missing these past few years."

Always the goofball, Sam folded his hands behind his head and posed, his erection on full display. The glow from the moon coming through the window played across the planes and bulges of his body.

"Is there enough light in here for you to get the full effect of my manliness? All we have is your charging phone and the moon."

She snorted and slid a hand along his shaft. "I couldn't miss this with a night-light."

As she caressed him, he closed his eyes and caught his breath. "Your hands feel like silk, but you know what I really miss?"

She dragged her nails down his chest. "This?"

He gasped. "No."

She knelt before him and ran her tongue along the length of him. "This?"

"Oh." His body shuddered. "No."

She took him in her mouth, sucking him hard, her own pleasure heating her blood. When she finished, she looked up. "That?"

He growled. "All of it, but what I really miss is how you used to trail your hair down my body. I can fantasize about that in the middle of the day, and it never fails to make me hard."

"Must make chasing bad guys a little...hard." She smirked at her joke.

He fell across the bed. "Come here and make my fantasies come true."

Crouching beside him, she whipped her hair back and forth, and then proceeded to lean over him, the ends of her hair tickling his flesh. "Like this?"

"It's even better than I remember, but why do you still have your jeans on?" He unbuttoned her fly and yanked down the zipper.

In one move, he swept her onto her back and pulled her pants and underwear off the rest of the way.

His eyes gleamed in the semidarkness. "You're right. There's plenty of light in here to see all the good stuff."

Nudging her legs apart, he kneeled between them. He bent over her and took possession of her mouth, kissing her hard. He skimmed his hand over the top of his head. "I'd run my hair over your body, but I think it'd be prickly instead of sensuous. I do have other tricks at my disposal, though."

"Did you always talk this much during sex?" She rubbed her hands against the flared muscles of his thighs.

"Must be nerves." He took one of her nipples between

his lips and suckled her, as his fingers moved between her legs.

He played with her throbbing folds just enough to get her squirming. Then he switched his attentions to her other peaked nipple.

She sucked in a breath and lifted her hips from the bed. She gritted her teeth and said, "You know what my fantasy has been since the minute I laid eyes on you in the desert?"

He stopped teasing her breast, but his fingers kept toying with her. Resting his scruffy chin on her chest, he said, "What?"

"You, inside of me."

"Like this?" He shoved two fingers into her core.

She thrashed her head to the side and bit her lip. "While that's nice…"

"Nice?" With his fingers still inside her, he dragged his thumb across her swollen flesh.

A low moan wrenched from her throat. "More than nice, but I want that other part of your anatomy inside me. You know, the bigger part."

His lips twisted and before she even had time to prepare herself for the onslaught, he plowed into her.

She clawed at his back. Already driven to the pinnacle by his touch, she held her breath as he thrust against her once, twice, three times.

Her toes curled and all her muscles coiled the second before the first wave of passion coursed through her body. Other waves followed, each a little less intense than that first crash, each flooding her with warmth.

Before she got too relaxed, Sam's body stiffened and in a hoarse voice, he demanded, "Open your eyes."

Her lids flew open to meet his intense blue gaze. He stared right into her soul as he came inside her. As his body shuddered, he bent his head and kissed her mouth, just a gentle touch of his lips.

Still connected to her, Sam dug an elbow into the pillow next to her head and braced his chin against his palm. "Did your fantasy go something like that?"

She screwed up her mouth and rolled her eyes to the ceiling. "*Something* like that. I think we'll have to try again later to see if we can get closer."

He rolled off her body and nestled his front against her side, draping one heavy leg over her hip. "You've gotten demanding over the years."

Pinching his chin, she said, "My resolve went right out the window the minute I saw you in those sweats this afternoon."

"What resolve was that?" He sucked her thumb into his mouth while he cupped her mound.

"You're doing it again." But she didn't pull away. She wriggled in even closer to him so that his fingers dipped between her legs.

He scraped his nails against the flesh of her inner thighs. "I can always stop."

"Don't you dare." She climbed on top of him, straddling his hips.

The light from her phone, charging on her nightstand, drew her gaze. "Oh, God. It looks like I have texts. I hope Wade didn't wake up Gran to tell her about Melody. Her nerves don't need that."

He patted her bottom. "Go ahead and look. I'm going to hit the bathroom."

Reluctantly, she slid from his body, and then a twinge of guilt needled her brain. Her cousin had died tonight and here she was rolling in the sheets with Sam.

As Sam clambered from the bed and staggered to the bathroom door, the sheets twisted around his ankles, Jolene curled her legs beneath her and snatched her phone from the charger. Drawing her brows together, she tapped the first text and blood pounded against her temples.

"Sam! Sam!" She brought the phone close to her face, the words from the text swimming in front of her eyes.

"What's wrong?" He came charging out of the bathroom, his hair wild, his eyes wide.

She held out her phone to face him. "I got a message from Melody."

Chapter Eleven

Sam rushed toward the bed, tripping on the sheets and kicking them out of the way, adrenaline pumping through his system.

He dropped onto the bed and grabbed the phone from her. "What do you mean? From Melody or her phone? What does it say?"

"It's nonsense. The text says *El Gringo Viejo*."

Sam's blood ran cold in his veins as he stared at the phone's display, unable to see the text. And now he *had* to see this text.

He handed the phone back to Jolene. "You must've clicked off the text when you gave the phone to me. Get it back. When was it sent? Did she send it or did the person who took her phone send it?"

Jolene covered her mouth. "I don't know. I didn't look."

She swept her thumb across the screen. "The text was sent two minutes after midnight. What time did we get to the Sundowner?"

"We were there around midnight. She'd already left, gotten a ride from someone. You'd called her by that time, but she didn't answer. The next time you tried calling, your phone had died. She must've sent you that text when your phone was dead."

Jolene threw the phone into the jumbled bed covers. "If my phone hadn't died, we might've been able to help her."

"Maybe not, Jolene." Sam retrieved the phone to make sure she'd read the text correctly. "She wasn't asking for help, was she?"

"No, but at least she'd contacted me."

He read the words on the display disbelievingly. "You're right. She texted *El Gringo Viejo*."

"What the hell does that mean? Old white guy?" She dug her hands into her hair. "Do you think that's who killed her? Some old white guy? Why would she text that in Spanish?"

"Jolene—" Sam cupped the phone between his hands "—El Gringo Viejo is a drug supplier in Mexico."

"What?" She collapsed against the headboard and rubbed the back of her head after banging it. "Why would Melody text that? What does that even mean? How would she know this man?"

"She must've known something about him, something about his dealings on this side of the border." Sam scratched his chin. "I don't get why his name is even coming up. Last month, we were able to finally identify him. Turns out, he's a guy named Ted Jessup. We got his prints and everything, found out he'd been holing up in Rocky Point."

"Rocky Point?"

His eyes must've been wandering, as she dragged a pillow into her lap to cover up all the good naked parts.

"I'd hardly call that holing up. Rocky Point is a tourist destination."

"The point is, nobody knew what he was doing there. He was just another rich gringo with a villa in the cliffs overlooking the sea. Then a couple of people made him, and the FBI was able to descend on his place—but he'd already escaped."

"He must be back in business." She flicked her fingers at him. "Could you put some clothes on? All this is distracting as hell."

He crawled over her legs to reach over the side of the bed and swipe up his sweats.

She wiggled her toes beneath the weight of him. "That's not helping."

He plumped a pillow against the headboard and flopped down next to her, pulling up the sweats. "Is that better?"

Glancing at the soft material covering his crotch and visible lump there, she said, "Marginally."

"I can't help it." He plucked at the sweats to hide his erection. "You're still naked."

"Is that all it takes to set you off? A naked woman with a pillow in her lap?" She crawled to the foot of the bed to retrieve her underwear, and he reclined against the pillow to enjoy the view.

"Is this a test?" He swept his hand over the curve of her derriere, her skin like silk beneath his fingertips. "Because you're flashing me, and no man in his right mind could resist that."

"Can we get back to the subject at hand?" She snatched up her panties and wriggled into them, clutching the pillow to her chest. "Why would Melody text me this man's moniker? She was warning us about looking into the casino project. Do you think this El Gringo Viejo could have anything to do with it?"

"Come back up here." He patted the mattress next to him. "I promise I'll keep my hands to myself and stay on topic."

She joined him, unfurling her long legs in front of her,

twisting her hair behind her head into a bun. "Could he be involved?"

Sam crossed his hands behind his head to keep them off Jolene's body and took a deep breath. He'd been drunk on making love with her, and even though Melody's text had sobered him up, Jolene's nearness was more intoxicating than a sip of Chivas.

He closed his eyes, his mind running over his case. The people they'd discovered dead and buried in the desert near San Diego had all died from a single shot to the head—execution style, drug-cartel style, even though their heads were still attached to their bodies. Their deaths had coincided with the appearance of a pure form of meth flooding the streets of southern California, pink meth.

That same meth had made its appearance in Arizona and New Mexico about four years ago—at the same time, a spate of missing persons had been reported in the area. Could El Gringo Viejo be behind the production and distribution of that meth?

He'd been active in Arizona for a number of years—not so much in California, but the appearance of the potent meth in Cali probably coincided with EGV feeling the heat in Rocky Point. Maybe he expanded his business to get out of Arizona where it had gotten too hot for him.

"What are you doing?" Jolene poked his ribs. "Are you sleeping?"

He grabbed her finger and kissed the tip. "I'm thinking."

"Are you going to let me in on your thoughts or does just talking to me about any subject in bed turn you on?"

Opening one eye, he turned his head. "Yeah, that's pretty much it, and you're still topless."

"I'm hugging a pillow."

"Lucky pillow."

She hit him over the head with the pillow and scrambled from the bed. She threw open her closet door, grabbing the first thing in front of her and pulling it on. Then she jumped back on the bed, the loose-fitting blouse floating around her.

"Better?"

His gaze raked her top half and the way the blouse settled around the curve of her breasts, her dusky nipple visible through the light material. "Yep, that's it, totally turned off."

Truth was, Jolene could wear a burlap sack and they could be discussing the national debt, and he wouldn't be totally immune to her charms and the sexual tension that buzzed between them like a living thing—and she knew it.

A rosy blush seeped into her cheeks, as she crossed her legs beneath her. "Okay, let me in on your thoughts about this character."

He gathered his wits again, and explained the connection between the bodies and the powerful meth hitting the streets. "We had the same occurrence in Arizona about four years back, before I was assigned to this sector but I read all about it. When that meth surfaced in San Diego and it coincided with our discovery of a dumping ground for drug couriers, I remembered what happened in Paradiso. Only difference is, we never found the bodies here."

"Do you think El Gringo Viejo could be responsible for that meth?" She pinned her knees to her chest, wrapping her arms around her legs.

"Border Patrol, FBI and DEA thought so at the time, but they could never pin it on him. He's always been more of a facilitator between the cartels and the suppliers. He wouldn't want the cartels to know he was selling and encroaching on their business."

"And you think the dumping ground here for those bodies could be the Desert Sun Casino construction site."

"It's similar to the other location in California in many ways. That's why I went out there the night I ran into you. I'd been looking at a map of the desert, and that site jumped out at me."

"We need to search that land, Sam." She rested her chin on her knees. "Now it's not just my father's death I have to investigate, it's Melody's."

"That's what law enforcement is for." Even as the words left his mouth, he knew Jolene would never accept them.

A light kindled in her dark eyes. "You don't even have enough proof to justify a search of the land. What chance do I have to convince anyone? That's why I buried those bones out there. I may be found out soon, but that discovery caused enough of a delay to buy us some time."

"I'd planned to do the search on my own." He swung his legs over the side of the bed and launched forward to collect the mess of sheets on the floor.

"You wouldn't even have had the opportunity to get on that property if it hadn't been for my scheme." She yanked on the edge of the top sheet as he handed it to her and smoothed it across the bed. "You owe me."

"Okay, we'll go out there together, but it has to be at night." He tucked the edge of the sheet under the mattress. "Now let's get some sleep before the sun comes up."

"I'm dreading the day ahead. Gran is going to be devastated by Melody's death. Do you think Tucker confessed yet?"

"So, now you think he did it?"

"Of course not, but that doesn't mean the poor soul isn't going to confess to it." She rolled out of bed. "I need to brush my teeth…and stuff. Do you want a toothbrush?"

He tapped his front tooth. "Before you got that text, I was in the bathroom rubbing toothpaste over my teeth with my finger."

"I have extra toothbrushes. You could've asked." She

padded to the bathroom, looking sexy as hell with that blouse floating around her.

While she ran the water in the bathroom, he straightened the covers on the bed.

"Here you go." She tossed him an unwrapped toothbrush as she exited the bathroom, and then pulled the bedroom curtains tight, shrouding the room in darkness.

He brushed his teeth and left the new toothbrush on the edge of the sink. Should he read anything into the toothbrush?

She'd already admitted to him she didn't know if she could trust him for the long haul. He'd have to change her mind. In the meantime, the short haul had been deeply satisfying.

He crept into the bedroom to find Jolene under the covers, one bare shoulder visible. At least she'd gotten rid of the blouse. He stripped off his sweats and crawled into bed naked, nestling up to her back. She'd left her underwear in place.

She reached behind him and skimmed her knuckles down his hip. "What happened to your clothes?"

"I only put those on so we could think." He wrapped an arm around her body and cupped her breast, dragging his thumb across her nipple while the breath hitched in her throat. "We don't have to think anymore, do we?"

She turned around within his embrace, and pressed her lips to his. She murmured against his mouth, "If I thought about what I was doing, I might stop."

And as he didn't want to think about what she had just said, he thrust his erection against her belly and proceeded to make her his own...while he still could.

THE NEXT MORNING, Sam carefully extricated himself from Jolene's limbs tangled with his. Before he slipped out of bed, he paused to study her face. A small bruise had formed over her left eyebrow, and her bottom lip looked slightly swollen—of course that could be from all the kisses they'd shared. He couldn't get enough of her.

He tiptoed from her bedroom and into the laundry room where he retrieved yesterday's clothes from the dryer. He got dressed in the living room, and set about making coffee.

He checked his own phone charging on the kitchen counter—a few texts from Aimee's mother about Jess and a call from work, but nothing as dramatic as Jolene's text last night. If only Melody could've given them more than El Gringo Viejo's name. Maybe she didn't know anything more about him—or maybe she was too drunk to know what she was doing.

The coffee started to drip in the pot, and he raided Jolene's fridge for eggs, butter, milk, cheese and a leftover pepper and onion. Since the separation from Aimee—the second separation—he'd gotten pretty good in the kitchen.

As the first omelet bubbled in the frying pan, Jolene scuffed into the kitchen, the blouse from last night hanging off her, the first several buttons undone. "Smells good, but it's lunchtime. I slept so late."

"You were in a car accident yesterday. I think you deserved to sleep late." He jiggled the pan. "I'm making omelets."

"I'm impressed." She yawned. "But my accident is not the reason why I slept late. I think that had something to do with the man in my bed."

"At least I'm properly dressed now, which is more than I can say for you." He waved the spatula at her. "Whoever told you that was a modest blouse was lying, especially when it's open to your navel."

She clutched the top of the blouse and yanked the two

pieces together. "I'll go take a shower and get dressed. Don't get any ideas about joining me in the shower. I'm sore."

He wiggled his eyebrows up and down. "I'm that good, huh?"

She picked up a balled-up paper towel from the counter and fired it at him. "My muscles are sore from the accident. Look at my arms."

He eyed the bruises from the airbag on her arms. "I saw those, but that airbag probably cut down on the damage to the rest of your body."

"I suppose so." She wrapped her hair around one hand. "I already have a million calls from Gran and Wade and everyone else this morning, so I guess what happened to Melody was not a bad dream."

"I'm sorry it wasn't." He slid the first omelet onto a plate. "Any chance you can get into Melody's apartment today?"

"What do you mean? Isn't it a crime scene? The sheriff's department arrested Tucker yesterday. They already had the crime scene tape up before we left last night."

"You stole onto a construction site and planted some bones. You can't figure out how to get past a little crime scene tape and into your cousin's apartment?"

"You're encouraging me to break the law, Agent Cross?" She folded her arms and tapped a bare foot on the floor.

"You need encouragement?" He cracked two more eggs into the bowl. "Go get dressed, and I'll finish breakfast."

"If you think we might find something useful at Melody's, I'll get in there. I have to see Gran and the rest of the family first. Do you think you can find out what's happening with Tucker?"

"Yeah, I'll do that."

Jolene slipped out of the kitchen, and a few minutes

later, he heard the shower running. He'd have liked nothing more than to join her, but she needed sustenance and painkillers right now—not another tumble in the sheets.

He finished cooking the second omelet, shoved some bread in the toaster and poured himself a cup of coffee. He even set the table and fed Chip.

When he looked up from placing the silverware next to the plates of food, Jolene was studying him, one hand on her hip. "You've become quite domestic."

"Now that I have Jess on my own, my apartment is immaculate."

One corner of her mouth lifted. "Never thought I'd see the day. I—I'd like to see you with your daughter someday."

"She's funny right now—and bossy." Should he be bragging to Jolene about Jess? He wanted to share his daughter with Jolene, but it hurt him that Jess wasn't hers.

"It's a cute age—which I know from my cousins' kids." She grabbed the back of a chair and sat down, picking up a fork. "I know where Melody hid a key to her place, so if the cops aren't watching her apartment, I can get in. How long will they designate it as an active crime scene?"

He shrugged and took a seat at the table. "Depends on what Tucker's been telling them. They were already searching her place. May have taken her computer and other electronic devices."

"I wonder if they found her phone? She must've texted me on her way home. I wish she would've told me how she was getting there." She wrapped both hands around her coffee mug and stared into the cup.

"Maybe she thought she was in the app car." Sam sawed into his omelet and stabbed at the piece of egg with his fork. "She called for a car, she was drunk and didn't realize she was getting into some random car. It's happened before."

"You mean someone was waiting for her. Knew she'd called for a car and took advantage of her inebriated state." She took a sip of coffee. "We need to talk to Eddie, the bartender. Maybe he saw someone hanging around her."

"We still need a motive. Tucker has a motive. He had her purse. He also had opportunity and the means."

"Do you really think that scrawny guy could've overpowered Melody?" She plunged her fork into the omelet and raised it to her mouth, a string of cheese hanging off the end.

"She was drunk, Jolene. Wasted, according to Eddie—and he should know. Maybe she did hit her head on the edge of that table while she was struggling with Tucker. She pulled away from him and fell. Tucker wouldn't have had to do anything."

"Why are you trying to convict Tucker? I thought you were going with the fake driver story." She dragged a paper towel across her mouth, but the cheese clung to her chin.

Sam reached over and dislodged the cheese with a dab of his finger against her face. "I'm playing devil's advocate. Tucker's motive was robbery. The fake driver's motive could've been knowledge."

"You mean Melody knew too much. Maybe part of what she knew was that El Gringo Viejo was involved in the casino project…and maybe some deaths connected to the project."

"Could be, but why didn't she go to the police? She could've laid out everything she knew for them and gotten some protection. A woman one of our agents is dating knows too much about El Gringo Viejo and she's under protection."

Her eyes widened. "Rob Valdez's girlfriend? That woman who showed up in Paradiso with amnesia?"

"That's the one, Libby James." He put his fork to his lips. "But you're not supposed to know that. It's life and death for her. Do you understand?"

"Of course. Didn't my cousin just get killed for the same reason?" She crunched into her toast and a shower of crumbs rained down on her plate.

"You came to that conclusion quickly. We were still discussing Tucker's guilt."

"I just don't believe it. I know you law enforcement types have to go with the evidence instead of feelings, but the cops don't know what we know about Melody and the casino project." She dusted her fingers together. "Should we tell them?"

"Not yet." Sam shook his head. "I can't believe I'm saying this, but I don't want to tell them until I have a chance to search that construction site. You talk about feelings over evidence? I've had a hunch about the connection between the missing people here and the bodies we found east of San Diego for over a month now, but I can't get a search warrant for that property based on my hunches. Doesn't work that way."

"So, you're going rogue. I like it."

"And the food? Do you like the food?" He aimed his fork at her half-eaten omelet.

"It's hard to talk and eat at the same time. It's great. Even Chip wants some." She nudged Chip with her foot. "You got dressed without taking a shower. Do you want to shower here? I have to get over to Gran's."

"I'll clean up at the motel. I need to go into the station, and that means I need my uniform. Besides…" he ran a thumb across her bottom lip "…I still have the scent of you on my skin."

"If you need to get to the station, and I definitely need to go to Gran's house, you'd better stop saying things like that." She pressed her lips together. "I'll clean up since you cooked."

"I'll let Chip out again. Should I leave the dog door open?" He strode to the sliding doors that led to the back, whistling for Chip.

Jolene picked up his cell phone. "Your phone's ringing. It's the station."

Sam slid open the door to set Chip free, and then turned to grab his phone from Jolene. "Cross here."

"It's Clay."

"Hey, Clay. What can I do for you? I was planning to come in this morning."

"This is really just a courtesy call, Sam. You know that transient who was arrested for having Melody's purse? The guy you held for the police?"

Sam's mouth got dry, and his pulse drummed in his ears."

"Yeah? What about him?"

"He's dead."

Chapter Twelve

Jolene furrowed her brow as she watched Sam clutching the phone with white knuckles, his chest heaving.

She whispered, "What about who?"

Same held up a finger at her. "How the hell did that happen, Clay?"

He paused, but whatever Clay was telling him was winding him up even more, as two red spots formed on his cheeks and lights flared in his blue eyes. "That's negligent. That's criminal. What did he say during questioning?"

Jolene twisted her fingers in front of her. Were they discussing Tucker? Had he confessed?

"This is unbelievable. They're gonna have to do a full investigation and heads should roll." His jaw tightened and Jolene could almost hear the teeth grinding from the kitchen. "Yeah, yeah."

He ended the call and held the phone in his hand, staring at it.

"What is it? What happened?"

Shoving the phone in his back pocket, he joined her in the kitchen. He put his hand on her arm and now her heart was galloping.

"Tucker Bishop killed himself in his jail cell this morning."

Her knees weakened and she grabbed the edge of the counter. "How?"

"He hung himself with the bedsheets." Sam tossed the leftover coffee from his cup into the sink and brown liquid marred the spotless porcelain. "How the hell did the deputies allow that to happen?"

"D-did he confess to murdering Melody before he killed himself?"

"No. He wouldn't cough up anything. Seems he told them less than he revealed to us. We probably know more than the police do about what Tucker was doing there and what he saw and heard." He cranked on the faucet and rinsed down the sink—busy work for agitated hands.

"Now we're not going to learn any more of what Tucker knew." She pressed a hand to her face. "Sam, do you think someone got to Tucker in jail? Does that kind of thing happen?"

He hunched over the sink, his T-shirt clinging to his tightly coiled muscles. "That stuff happens all the time, especially if the guy wasn't on suicide watch."

"Would Tucker have been on suicide watch?"

"Not unless he made statements that would indicate he was suicidal, which I guess he didn't."

"That's ridiculous. The man was obviously not in his right mind. Wouldn't that be considered suicidal on its surface?"

"Doesn't work that way. He didn't even confess to harming Melody."

"Because he didn't." Jolene folded her arms over her stomach. "But he knew who did, and that's why he was silenced."

"Whoa!" Sam spun around. "You're jumping fast and hard to some serious conclusions."

"C'mon, Sam. That's exactly what you're thinking. I saw it on your face when you were talking to Clay on the phone."

He plowed a hand through his hair. "What you're suggesting would require several things to happen—none of them complimentary to the Pima County Sheriff's Department."

"I'm not saying a deputy murdered Tucker, but you know how he was—highly unstable."

"That's an understatement."

"It wouldn't have taken much to drive that poor man over the edge completely—haranguing, suggestions, lies."

"You're implying someone was paid off to take him over that edge?" He rubbed his chin. "If so, we're in trouble. I'm going to have to be careful about my interest in the construction site, and the sooner I have a look, the better."

"The sooner *we* have a look, the better. There's no way you're keeping me away from that land."

Sam opened his mouth and then snapped it shut when he took in Jolene's flaring nostrils and the martial light in her eyes. When she got that look, nobody could tell her anything.

She wore that same look when he'd told her about his ex's pregnancy, and she'd ordered him to go back to his wife and unborn child and to forget about her…as if that were ever going to happen.

AT THE END of the day, Jolene collapsed on her couch, drained and depressed. Not even Chip licking at her hand could bring a smile to her face.

Chip had already been hard at work trying to cheer people up, as she'd brought him to Gran's house where the family had met to mourn Melody and discuss arrangements. All the relatives believed it was a robbery gone wrong with Tucker Bishop as the culprit. His suicide in jail had confirmed their beliefs.

Who was she to dissuade them? It had brought them a measure of comfort on a dark day.

As Sam had mentioned, they needed to keep a low profile regarding their suspicions about the casino project and what Melody may or may not have known about it. They didn't want to alert anyone to their interest any more than she'd already done so via her stunt with the bones.

And if those bones came back to her, it could all be dismissed as her concern for the land as a Yaqui.

She plucked at her skirt. She should probably change before Sam got here. He was coming over with dinner, and then they were heading to the construction site to have a look around.

Instead, she closed her eyes and patted Chip's head as he rested it against her knee. Two seconds later, a knock on the door made her jerk upright.

Chip whined and scampered to the front door. If he wasn't barking, he must know Sam was on the other side of that door. She glanced at her phone and jumped up from the couch. She'd been asleep for almost an hour.

She peeked through the blinds at Sam holding bags of food. Nudging Chip aside with her foot, she cracked open the door. "Come on in. I fell asleep on the couch."

"Get back, Chip." Sam pushed his way past the excited dog. "Chinese, is that okay?"

"I could've cooked something." She closed and locked the door, and then took a plastic bag twisted around Sam's fingers.

"You must've had a rough day if you fell asleep on the couch." He placed his bag on the counter. "How'd it go with the family? How's Granny Viv?"

"Heartbroken."

"It must've been a hard day for everyone." He reached

for a couple of plates from the cupboard. "Are you sure you want to come with me tonight?"

"Oh, no you don't." She waved a fork at him. "Don't try to dissuade me. I'm coming with you. I know where my father's body was found, and that's where we're going to start. It's a big piece of property. You can't just wander around in the dark, staring at the ground."

"I don't know what I expect to find there. Hasn't all that land been prepped for the construction? Isn't that why Wade knew there was something fishy about those bones?" He dipped into one of the bags and pulled out a carton of rice.

"Yeah, that was an amateur move on my part, but I had to put those bones where they'd be discovered during the ground-breaking ceremony." She plunged a couple of spoons into the other containers. "There's a part of that land that hasn't been prepared yet, though. They're holding that aside for a golf course, or something like that. Can you imagine green grass out there, and the amount of water it would take to keep it that way?"

"Other resorts out here have golf courses."

"Oh, so this is a resort now? Wade won't stop until he's built up a theme park for the whole family—Yaqui World."

Sam snorted. "I doubt that. So, there's untouched land bordering the construction area?"

"Yeah, and you need me to find it. So, don't get any ideas about leaving me out." She carried the food to the kitchen table. "We could eat this in the living room, but Chip would be all over us."

"Kitchen table is good."

They settled at the table with the open cartons of food in front of them and Chip at their feet.

"The whole family believes Tucker Bishop killed Melody to steal her purse. Did you learn anything more about his suicide?"

"I did." Sam scooted the peppers from his kung pao into a little pile on the edge of his plate. "The security camera in the jail cell isn't working."

Jolene dropped her chopsticks, flicking grains of rice into the air. "You're kidding."

"I wish I were. The deputies checked the security footage for that row of cells, and all they saw was fuzz. There was some trouble with that camera before, which makes the malfunction slightly more believable. But why put prisoners in those cells when you've already had issues with the cameras? It's not like there was no room in the cells."

"This stinks, Sam. It sounds like someone was on the take, ordered to keep Tucker quiet one way or the other."

"It's not my department. I can't order an investigation." He picked up a piece of chicken with his chopsticks, but it fell back to his plate before he could get it into his mouth. "Problem is, Tucker was a transient. He doesn't have anyone to demand that investigation."

"That's just sad." She held out a fork to him. "I can't stand to watch you anymore. You're going to starve using those chopsticks."

"I got this." He balanced the same piece of chicken on the ends of the chopsticks and hurried it into his mouth. "Did you get a chance to visit Melody's apartment?"

"No time, but I set myself up to go in there by offering to pack up her things. I can probably get in there legally instead of trying to sneak in, don't you think?"

"The sheriffs will probably let you in even if the yellow tape is still up. It might still be designated a crime scene, but it's most likely no longer active. They've ransacked the place by now—dusted for prints, collected blood and other DNA samples, taken her computer." He shrugged and shoveled some rice into his mouth. "If there's anything left for you to discover, it's going to be something that has no significance to law enforcement."

She held up a chopstick. "They don't know what we know, so what has no meaning for them might mean a great deal to us."

"This garlic chicken is making me thirsty." Sam pushed back from the table. "Can I get you something to drink?"

"Just water."

When he brought two glasses of water back to the table, she took a few gulps and shoved her plate away. "I'm done. I meant to change clothes when I got home. I'm not going to go digging around in the desert in a skirt."

"You had about two bites."

"No appetite." She crossed her chopsticks on the edge of her plate.

"You change and I'll finish eating. Then I'll feed Chip." Sam held up two fingers. "No garlic chicken for him, I swear."

"You'd better not. Dogs aren't supposed to have garlic." She placed a fork in front of him. "Use this, please, or we'll be here all night as you chase that chicken around your plate."

"I *am* getting kind of hungry." He grabbed the fork and plowed into the food.

She waved her hand over the table. "You're feeding Chip, so I'll clean up. Leave all this for me."

She spun around and headed toward the bedroom, averting her gaze from the bed. She couldn't look at it without a hot blush rushing to her cheeks. She'd been so darned easy after all her resolutions, but just because she'd taken Sam back into her bed, didn't mean she was letting him back into her heart—he had to earn his way back there.

She changed into the same outfit she'd worn to dump

those bones—dark jeans, dark T-shirt and boots. She wanted to blend in with the night, just in case.

After she brushed her teeth and pulled her hair into a ponytail, she went back into the living room. "Did Chip eat?"

"Every morsel. I let him out back." Sam flicked a dish towel over his shoulder. "Cleaned up, too."

"You didn't have to do that."

"You know these newfangled inventions like a dishwasher and refrigerator make it easy. I just stuck the cartons into the fridge and put the dishes in the dishwasher." He narrowed his eyes. "You look ready for a covert operation."

"Isn't that what this is? We're taking this seriously, aren't we?" She shoved her hands in her back pockets and dug the heels of her boots into the floor. "You're not doing this to humor me, are you?"

"Humor you? It's gone beyond that with Melody's death." He flipped up his shirt to expose the gun at his waist. "Does this look like I'm not taking it seriously?"

She swallowed. "All right, then. Let's go."

Sam went to the sliding doors and whistled for Chip. "Is his dog door closed?"

"I keep it closed at night once he's inside." She raised her eyebrows. "Afraid I'll get more warnings left on my porch?"

"If all you got were a few dead snakes with arrows through their heads, I'd be happy. Just keep your house locked up and Chip on guard."

Jolene grabbed a backpack with a flashlight, a spade, a bottle of water and some other essential items for creeping through the night in the desert.

She tripped to a stop on the porch when she saw Sam's Border Patrol truck parked behind the rental car that had been delivered to her today in the driveway. "You're on Border Patrol business?"

"Our agency isn't as particular about company vehicles as yours is. Did you think I was going to take that little rental into the sand? We'd get stuck in two minutes." He strode to the truck and opened the back. "Throw your stuff in here, and open your garage door so we can take a few tools."

"Tools?" She entered the code for her garage door.

"Don't tell me you dug through the sand to bury those bones with your two hands. I know you have a shovel. I saw it, remember?"

She ducked under the garage door before it finished opening and grabbed the shovel she'd used earlier in the week. "Anything else?"

"That's good enough." He took the shovel from her and threw it in the back of the truck.

As she climbed into the truck, the wind picked up and snatched at her ponytail. She tipped her head back and sniffed the air. "I hope there's not another monsoon on the way."

"Wouldn't surprise me." Sam slammed her door and went around to the driver's side. He started the truck and rolled down her driveway.

They rode in silence for a few miles with the radio playing in the background. Jolene gazed out the window and took a deep breath. "You never showed me any pictures of Jess."

"You never asked."

"D-do you have some on your phone?" She folded her hands in her lap. "I'd like to see them…her."

"I do." He snatched up his phone on the console and entered his passcode with his thumb. He dropped the phone in her lap. "If you go to my photos, you'll see a whole folder dedicated to her."

With unsteady hands, Jolene picked up his phone and accessed the folder called *Jess*. In the first picture, a bright-eyed toddler with curly dark hair grinned back at her.

Jolene's own lips stretched into a smile almost involuntarily. "She looks like you…and she looks full of mischief."

"She is." Sam's chest almost puffed up. "She's still small for her age, but her pediatrician says she'll catch up. She likes books. She likes anything with wheels, and she loves dogs. I showed her a picture of Chip when he was a puppy, and now she calls every dog Chip."

Tears pricked the back of Jolene's eyes, and the next picture of Jess riding a plastic Big Wheel blurred before her. "Sounds like you'll have to get her a dog."

"I will when she's older. I…" Sam stopped and his hands tightened on the steering wheel. "She's funny. She makes me laugh."

Jolene swiped through several more photos of the happy little girl. She'd made the right choice letting Sam go. Would he have been able to have the same kind of relationship with his daughter living apart from her? Living in another state? And with Aimee using again, he'd have never known a moment's peace.

She let out a sigh and placed his phone back on the console. "She's adorable."

"I want you to meet her, Jolene."

Tapping on the window, she said, "It's coming up. We can take the access road to the casino construction site, and then I'll guide you in from there."

Sam slowed the truck, but they didn't have to search for the entrance to the access road this time. A huge orange-and-yellow sign had gone up on the road, proclaiming this the future site of the Yaqui Desert Sun Casino.

The sign made her stomach churn. Her father had died here and it meant nothing to the people he'd led and counseled most of his life. She licked her lips. "Cheerful sign, huh?"

Sam glanced at her. "If you like that sort of thing."

As he pulled onto the access road, sand pinged the windshield of the truck. "It's windy out here tonight. If it brings in a storm, we're gonna abandon ship and do this another night."

"Yeah, well, I'm sure we're going to have a limited number of nights before the bones are dismissed as a stunt." She sat forward in her seat. "The equipment is still here. The builders must think they'll be back to work soon."

"Maybe they will." The truck crawled to a stop, idling at the edge of the construction site, the out-of-commission equipment hulking in the darkness like the bones of some extinct creatures. "Where to?"

She closed her eyes and mumbled a few words, tracing lines in the air with her fingertip.

"What are you doing? Is that an old Yaqui spell?"

She punched his arm. "Remember the map that was stolen?"

"Of course—the map you didn't accuse Wade of stealing because you didn't want him to know you had stolen the map from him in case he didn't realize you'd stolen the map. That map?"

"Yes." She tapped her head. "I memorized it—or at least the construction areas. There were other sections shaded in blue that were not yet earmarked for building. I think we should start there."

Sam peered over the steering wheel out the window. "You're going to know where to go from here without a compass, exact measurements and surveying equipment? We don't even have light."

"I have something better. The land has already been divided and marked. This open plot is all for show, for the ground-breaking, to make it look like this is the first time the developers are dipping into the land. Of course, it's not." She smacked the dashboard. "Drive forward. We'll see posts with markings on them that indicate the different areas of the casino. The buffet restaurant is at the south end of the complex and beyond that? Wasteland."

"I do have a compass in this truck, and we'll head south." He put the truck into gear and cranked the wheel to the left.

The truck went off the road, dipping and tipping along the desert floor. Neither Sam's nor her rental would've been able to navigate this terrain.

She grabbed his forearm. "Stop. You see that post up ahead with the reflective lights?"

"Uh-huh. One of the markers?"

"Yeah. I'll jump out and see what it says." She reached into the back seat of the truck and yanked her backpack into her lap. She dug into the main compartment and pulled out her flashlight. "I'll be right back."

She launched from the truck and rushed to the post. The less time she spent out here with the snakes and scorpions, the better—and she didn't mean the reptile and bug kind. Those she could handle.

She aimed her flashlight at the post, the beam picking out the letters. Then she scurried back to the truck and hopped in, panting just a little. "That's the lobby and customer service area. As I recall from the map, we can keep following this outer edge to the buffet. Do you see the temporary fence along here?"

"Yeah, I'll try not to veer into it and take it out."

As the truck trundled along what would be the west side of the casino complex, Jolene sat forward in her seat, taking note of each signpost. Their cessation would signal the end of the planned structure.

Sam whistled. "This is going to be a big place."

"Is that a post up ahead?" She squinted into the area flooded by the truck's brights. "It looks shorter and thicker. Don't hit it."

"I'm not going to hit it." He crept up to the post and threw the truck into Park. "Check it out."

Once more, she slid from the truck, the wind whipping her hair as she approached and lit up the four squat posts. Her fingers traced over the letters, her heart thumping.

When she got back in the truck, she turned to face Sam. "This is it. Those posts indicate the end of the dining area and the end of the building."

Sam tipped his head. "Then it's no-man's-land ahead."

"Yep."

"We're close to the border. I guess that makes it easier for the Yaqui in Mexico to come across and work in the casino."

"That's the idea." Jolene squashed down the niggling guilt she felt about the excitement the Yaqui on the other side of the border had about the coming project and their part in it.

"Yaqui land stretches right to the border and beyond, doesn't it?"

"That's why we need to be careful in your Border Patrol truck, Sam. Border Patrol has no jurisdiction at this border."

"Don't I know it. The map detailing the tunnels the cartel Las Moscas constructed along the border stopped short of Yaqui land."

She rapped on the window. "This is definitely the shaded area on the map—the no-go zone for construction."

"I wonder why." Sam drummed his thumbs on the steering wheel. "I think this is where we need to investigate."

As she grabbed the door handle of the truck, Sam put his hand on her arm. "Is this the area where your father's body was discovered?"

She nodded and pushed open the door.

The wind gusted, and she shielded her eyes against the grains of sand zinging through the air. Sam had left his headlights on, creating a lighted area.

With her head down, Jolene plowed through the sand toward the spot flooded with light. She studied the ground for anything unusual, any disruption to the plants or the rocks scattered about.

Sam had joined her, flicking his flashlight along the edge of the lighted region. "They haven't done anything to this section yet."

Scuffing along the ground, Jolene said, "You'd think they'd want to utilize the entire property, but I think they do plan on making a resort out of the place and this land figured into that."

Sam jerked his head up. "Did you hear that noise?"

Jolene held her breath, cocking her head to one side. When the wind blasted, she could hear a whooshing sound and the sand pinging Sam's truck, and when the wind died back down, the plaintive hoot of an owl echoed across the landscape.

"Nothing. What did you hear?"

"Thought I heard a buzzing sound." He kicked at a rock. "At least there's not much trash out here from the highway. Maybe the builders pick it up after a stiff breeze like tonight—just to keep on everyone's good side."

"They're not on my good side." Hands on her hips, Jolene scanned the ground, bit by bit, to the edge of the lighted area.

"I don't see anything, do you?" Sam had already turned back toward the truck.

"Nothing that would scream graveyard, anyway." She followed in his very large footsteps. "Keep going?"

"I want to continue to the border. See if it's more of the same."

When they both got into the truck, Sam put it into gear and eased it forward. "We don't need to get stuck out here. That would be a lot for me to explain."

The truck rumbled ahead, and Sam made a beeline for the border only he saw in his head. "It should be along here in less than a mile. They're gonna have to make some accommodations for the people coming over from Mexico to work in the casino."

They bounced along for a few more minutes before Sam slowed down and stopped. "Let's take a look."

As they stood outside the truck, Jolene asked, "Do you know where the border is?"

"It's beyond that ridge. When the land officials drew these borders, they didn't necessarily follow any geographic patterns—unless they could."

Sam raised a pair of binoculars to his eyes, more interested in the land beyond than the land below their feet.

Jolene aimed her flashlight at the ground, skimming it along the foliage. Every time the wind kicked up, flurries of sand danced in circles and bits of debris rolled along the desert floor.

Her light caught a piece of plastic or something that a Saguaro cactus had caught, and she crept toward it to peel it from the plant's spines.

As she reached for it, a loud report buffeted her ears, followed by something whizzing past her head.

Sam shouted, "Get down. Someone's shooting at us."

Chapter Thirteen

Sam hit the ground and twisted around to locate Jolene, hunched down by a large cactus. He yelled at her as another gunshot blasted from the ridge, along with a flash of light. "Down! Flat on the ground. Get behind that cactus, if you can."

He army-crawled toward her, shifting the binoculars onto his back and reaching for the weapon on his hip. Sand needled his eyes and slipped into his mouth as he made his way to Jolene.

Glass exploded as a bullet hit one of the truck's headlights. Sam dug in faster to reach Jolene, half of her body behind the saguaro and her legs jutting out, exposed.

He wrapped a hand around her ankle and she squealed.

"It's me. We're gonna crawl back to the truck. Stay as low as you can, burrow into the sand as much as possible. The shooters aren't too bright. They already knocked out one of the headlights, giving them less visibility."

He finally got his gun free, and he twisted his body, raised the weapon and shot out the other headlight. "There. They're gonna have an even harder time taking aim at us."

Placing himself between Jolene and the ridge, which was the source of the shooting, Sam crawled, using one elbow to propel himself while clutching his gun in the other hand.

They didn't stop moving and Sam didn't stop panting until they reached the truck. He'd left the doors open, so he half shoved, half lifted Jolene into the passenger seat. "Keep your head down. Are you okay?"

"I'm fine, terrified, but unharmed."

"Don't shut your door until I'm in the truck. I don't want to give them any sound to follow until I can gun this vehicle." He slinked back to the ground and crawled underneath the truck to get to the other side.

The shooting had stopped, but he didn't trust that the gunmen weren't on their way to the truck right now to continue their assault.

As he pulled himself up, the buzzing sound he'd heard before grew louder, and Jolene yelped.

"It's…it's… There's a drone, Sam. A drone is hovering above the truck."

"Damn." The drone glinted for a second, and then dipped out of view.

Sam hunched behind the wheel and said, "Shut your door now."

They both slammed their doors at the same time and Sam cranked on the engine. As much as he wanted to floor it and get the hell out of there, he didn't want to get stuck. He threw the gear into Reverse and eased on the gas pedal.

Even though he still had his head down, he didn't have to worry about hitting anything out here…except maybe a cactus. The truck rolled back, and he applied more pressure to the accelerator. The wheels ran over something, and then he shifted into Drive and took off in the direction of the construction area and the access road.

Several seconds later, his head popped up and the dark landscape loomed in front of him. "I can't see much without the headlights."

Jolene answered in a muffled voice, "Can I come up for air now?"

"I think we're okay." He glanced in his rearview mirror and didn't see anything coming—no light, no more gunfire. "We're good."

She straightened up, clutching her flashlight. "Do you have your flashlight? I can use both of them to shed a little light on our exit route."

"It's in my backpack, which I forgot is still on my back." He leaned forward. "Can you get it?"

She tugged at the pack, and he released the steering wheel so she could pull it from his arms. She dug into it and retrieved his flashlight.

"Let me try this." She rolled down her window and aimed both flashlights at the ground in front of the truck. "Does that help?"

"At least I won't go plowing into a cactus. Are we almost out of no-man's-land? We can follow the reflective posts back to the access road."

"Shouldn't be too much farther." She reached out and tapped the side mirror with one of the flashlights. "Do you think they'll come after us?"

"Doubt it. They know I'm armed, at any rate. Maybe that'll be enough to keep them away unless they want to engage in a gun battle."

"I should've brought Dad's gun with me."

"We don't need any more bullets flying." He jerked the steering wheel to the side. "Is that the edge of the casino?"

"Yeah, you've got this."

Tense silence loomed in the truck as Sam navigated his way out of the construction area and back onto the access road. He glanced at Jolene's ramrod-straight spine as she held the flashlights to help him navigate the terrain.

They both let out sighs when the truck tires gained

purchase on the dirt road that would take them out to the highway. Once on the asphalt, Sam floored it and the truck lurched forward, eating up the road beneath them.

"Do you still need the flashlights?"

"I'm good. I know this section of the highway like the back of my hand." He punched on the emergency lights. "Just for some extra visibility, although I don't think we'll meet many cars at this time of night."

"I hope we don't meet anyone." She flicked off the flashlights and collapsed against the seat, rubbing the back of her neck.

"Is your neck still bothering you?"

"I think it's just from holding my muscles so tight." She wound her ponytail around her hand. "What happened back there—I mean besides the obvious?"

"Someone's patrolling that area with a drone and I'm guessing that drone has a camera attached to it."

"It's not you guys?" She sucked in her bottom lip.

"We have drones on the border, but Yaqui land is off-limits to us." He nudged her shoulder. "You know that. Your father was one of the most vocal voices against our patrolling that section of the border, partly because he didn't feel the Yaqui needed any division between the Mexican tribe and the American tribe."

"Yeah, that was Dad. He had an almost childlike faith in humanity—never mind that the Yaqui across the border weren't all that interested in mingling with us."

"They are now." Sam swiped a bead of sweat from his forehead. "Maybe Wade accomplished with the casino what your father couldn't accomplish without it."

"You're probably right." She wedged her hands between her knees. "So, someone—not the Border Patrol—has drones on the border. Do you think it's the builders? And do you think they caught us on camera?"

"It might be the developers, but if they have armed guys shooting at trespassers instead of calling the Sheriff's Department, they're not going to want to admit they're the ones monitoring the drone footage."

"So, you think that's how they knew we were there? They were checking the video from the drone and saw us?" She brushed dust and sand from her jeans, and it settled in a fine layer on the truck mat. Stirring it with the toe of her boot, she said, "Sorry."

"Yeah, I think I have bigger problems with this truck than a little sand on the floor." Sam beeped the horn at a car coming at them in the other lane. The car honked back and flicked his lights on and off. "If the developers are the ones with the drones, their guys overreacted."

"Unless they weren't shooting to kill. Maybe they were just shooting to scare us off."

"Every time you have a gun in your hand, there's a chance someone's going to end up dead, so that's a stupid plan if that's the case." He wiped the back of his hand across his mouth, but he'd need to rinse with some water if he hoped to get the sand out of his teeth. "Or these shooters are not connected to the developer—and they're watching that land for another reason."

"You mean like there's something buried there they don't want anyone to find?"

"Maybe." Sam screwed up his mouth and chewed on the inside of his cheek. "There was something about that terrain."

Jolene slapped his arm. "Don't do that with your mouth. It's a bad habit."

"One of many." He banged his fist on the horn again as another car approached. "I'm going to have to take the back way into town to avoid rolling down Main Street with two busted headlights on my Border Patrol truck."

"What are you going to tell them?"

"A half-truth." He lifted one shoulder. He hated admitting to Jolene that he planned to tell a lie, even half of a lie. "I'll tell them someone shot out the headlights, but I won't tell them the circumstances. Because once I tell them the circumstances, my interest in that property is going to be common knowledge."

"Don't tell them…if you can get away with it, and you won't get into any trouble."

"Lies always cause trouble, don't they?" He ran a hand down the thigh of her dirty jeans. "Scared the hell out me when I realized someone was taking potshots at us. All I could think of was that I couldn't lose you after I'd…we'd, after I'd seen you again."

He snuck a peek at her profile, stony and mute, her lips pressed together.

He blew out a breath. "Anyway, I'm glad you weren't hurt."

"Me, too. I mean, I'm glad you weren't hurt."

He'd take that. He swallowed, the grains of sand scratching his throat.

When he finally turned onto Jolene's street, his shoulders dropped and he tried to roll out the tightness. They could've been killed out there.

He parked the truck behind her rental, and they dragged their stuff out, shaking the sand off in her driveway. The wind had settled, but a fat raindrop hit the back of his hand.

"Looks like the wind brought in another storm."

Jolene folded her arms across her zipped-up hoodie and tilted her head back. "It's a good thing we got here before the rain started. Driving with no headlights was bad enough but doing it on slick roads would've made it ten times worse."

He followed her to the garage door, and she opened

it using the keypad on the side. As it creaked open, Sam ducked under and returned her shovel to the corner.

Jolene jingled her keys as she walked up to the door that connected the garage to the house, Chip scratching and whining all the way. She unlocked the door and pressed her thumb against the control to close the garage.

"God, what a night." Sam tossed his backpack onto the floor. "All that shooting made me crave Chinese. Do you want some leftovers?"

"Yeah, but I refuse to eat it cold, like you usually do." She drew up close to him, practically touching her nose to his and his pulse jumped. She dabbed at his cheek with her fingertip. "You have a little dried blood there. Did the glass hit you?"

"Probably." He scraped at the spot and winced at the stinging sensation.

"You just made it bleed." She yanked a piece of paper towel from the holder and ran some water over it.

Closing his eyes, he held still as she pressed it gently against his face. He wanted to take her in his arms right now and lose himself in her kisses. Revel in her warm body when he could've lost her out there.

She took his hand and replaced her fingers with his on the paper towel. "Hold it there for a few seconds. It'll stop bleeding. It's just a little ding on that otherwise perfect face."

His eyelids flew open. Was that a come-on?

"Ugh, I have sand everywhere from crawling on the ground." She grabbed the zipper on her hoodie and yanked it down. The hoodie crackled as she peeled it from her body. She hung it over the back of a chair as she smacked some kind of plastic wrapper on the kitchen table.

Sam raised his eyebrows. "What is that?"

"It blew across the ground and got stuck on that cactus.

I grabbed it right before the shooting started and stuffed it inside my sweatshirt. I don't know why. It was just the biggest piece of trash out there."

"Let me see that." He tossed the wet paper towel sporting his blood into the trash, and smoothed his hand across the heavy plastic. "There's a label on this."

Jolene sidled up next to him and peered over his shoulder. "What's it say?"

Sam swiped away some of the dirt, careful not to smear the letters, which were neatly typed out like a label printed from a computer. The black lettering jumped out at him, and a spike of adrenaline jacked him up.

Jolene ran a finger beneath the words. "There's a date, and the words say… *Pink Lady*. There's a drink called Pink Lady. What is this, packaging for some booze?"

She flicked the edge of the plastic wrapping and turned away.

"Jolene, this is the type of label the cartels use to wrap and ID their product."

"What?" She spun around, knocking into a chair.

"Pink Lady is the meth I was telling you about, the meth that's connected to those dead bodies. Do you know what this means?" He grabbed the plastic and shook it.

She nodded once. "The cartels are using Yaqui land to smuggle drugs."

Chapter Fourteen

Jolene sank to the chair. "Maybe the Pima County Sheriffs were right all along. Maybe my dad's murder *was* related to the cartels, but he did more than stumble across a few mules, didn't he?"

"This connects a lot of dots." Sam slammed the packaging back on the table and paced to the corner of the room and back, Chip trotting at his heels. "You know how I was looking at that ridge and the landscape with my binoculars before the gunfire?"

"You mentioned you noticed something about the land out there, but never finished the thought."

"We got our hands on a map of tunnels the Las Moscas cartel was using to smuggle drugs into this country. The agents in this region have been going out to each tunnel to close it and destroy it. I had the chance to study all of the tunnels, and they shared some common features."

"A ridge, some brush."

After watching Sam's back-and-forth, Jolene pushed back her chair and grabbed Chip's collar. "Get on your bed, Chip."

The dog gave Sam one hopeful look before slinking to his bed in the corner, fluffing it up with his paws and plopping into it.

"Good boy." Jolene gripped the back of a kitchen chair.

"Pink Lady? Didn't you tell me the pure form of meth that accompanied the disappearances in San Diego was pink in color?"

"Yeah, that's it. On the street, they call it Pinky."

"Pinky?" Jolene dug her nails into the chair. "That's what Tucker called Melody."

"Sad coincidence." Sam tripped to a stop. "Melody hadn't added drugs to her other bad habits, had she?"

"Not that I know of, but what *do* I know?" She picked up the chair and settled it closer to the table. "I had no idea she was drinking again. I was a terrible cousin and friend, and on the very night she died, I was romping it up in bed—with you."

"Great, now you're adding guilt to the myriad reasons why you shouldn't have slept with me."

Jolene clenched her jaw to keep it from dropping open. Was that what he thought? That she regretted hooking up with him? Didn't she?

Casting her eyes down, she said, "Doesn't it feel wrong now?"

"Being with you would never feel wrong to me. Look at it this way." He folded his arms and wedged a shoulder against the sliding door. "Melody introduced us. She wanted us to get back together. Maybe she was leading us to each other."

She blinked. Sam had a fanciful side? "One thing I am going to do is try to make sense of her death, and I'm going to start by searching her apartment tomorrow."

"Then you'd better get to sleep tonight. I'm going to figure out a way to search for a tunnel on that property."

"Wade would never allow that." She ran her hand over the plastic packaging. "You think the cartels have a tunnel from Yaqui land on the Mexican side of the border to our land, and they're smuggling drugs...or *were* smuggling drugs through this tunnel?"

"I do think that. The group that's manufacturing this pink meth and putting it on the street requires such anonymity they're willing to kill off their mules to make sure they keep secrets."

"That's what happened in San Diego?"

"All the bodies we found and identified matched up to suspected mules. Someone met them when they made it across the border, and then murdered them to keep them quiet."

"Why do that? Cartels have used mules for ages. Sometimes they do go rogue, but the cartels have always been able to deal with those people."

Sam tugged on his earlobe. "This particular group... or person wants to lay low. I wonder if Melody knew El Gringo Viejo was behind Pink Lady. That would explain a lot. He wouldn't want the cartels to know he was infringing on their business."

"How would she know that, Sam? Melody didn't hang out with that crowd." She put two fingers on her lips.

"What? Did you remember something?"

"That relationship she had, the one Wade broke up. The guy was bad news. I think he may have been involved with the drug trade. Maybe she learned something from him."

"Do you remember his name?"

"Gabe, Gabe Altamarino. I think he's in Tucson, now."

"I think we need to pay him a visit and tell him the sad news about Melody."

"And the casino? What does this all have to do with the casino?"

"I'm not sure yet. It has to do with the land, doesn't it? Maybe the cartel is holding something over the investors."

Sam rubbed his eyes. "I'm done. I don't even want the Chinese food anymore. I just want a soft bed and sleep."

"About that…" Jolene wrinkled up her nose "…I need more time to think about that, about us. I'm sorry if I led you on last night."

Sam bent over and scratched Chip behind the ear. "Don't worry about it. It's all good, no expectations. Can I have the spare room, or should I leave?"

She'd hurt him, disappointed him. "Of course, you can stay here. I'm not going to kick you out to your truck with no headlights, especially since you saved my life tonight."

"I couldn't have gotten that truck out of there without you." He held up his hands. "And I promise I won't even use your washer and dryer this time."

"Have you seen the spare room? I turned it into a combination office and gym. There's no bed in there anymore."

He eyed the couch with Chip now curled up on one end. "The sofa's fine. Not much left of this night, anyway."

"You don't have to sleep out here…with Chip." She walked into the kitchen to hide her warm face. "I mean, you can share my bed, if…you know."

Inviting a man like Sam Cross into her bed with no promise of sex was like expecting a dog not to scratch his fleas. Bad analogy.

"You are irresistible, Jolene, but I think I can manage to keep my hands…and everything else…to myself in your presence."

Her cheeks flamed as she spun around. "I didn't mean it like that."

A grin spread across his handsome face. "I'm teasing you. I'd much rather share a bed with you than Chip, so I'm accepting your offer, strings and all, but I'm gonna need a shower first. I have sand in places that, well, you're never gonna discover tonight."

"I do, too. I'm like that cartoon character with a permanent cloud of dirt over my head."

"You first. I have a few things to check on my phone."

"Deal." She escaped the uncomfortable conversation and hightailed it to the bedroom.

She stripped off her clothes in the bathroom, leaving a pile of sand on the tile floor. Keeping her hair in a ponytail, she soaped up and rinsed off, showering in record time.

She pulled on a pair of pajamas—tops and bottoms— and slipped between the sheets.

Sam tapped on the door. "Everyone decent?"

"C'mon in."

He pushed open the door. "Everything's locked up. I let Chip out once more, and I started the dishwasher."

"Thanks, Sam. The bathroom's all yours." She yawned in an exaggerated manner. "I'm going to fall asleep in about two minutes."

"I'll keep it down." He moved silently across the room to the bathroom and clicked the door closed.

Her ears tuned in to every rustle and scrape from the other room. When the water started, she squeezed her eyes closed, visions of water sluicing over Sam's hard body making her mouth water.

She didn't have to worry about Sam controlling himself. She had to watch herself. When had she ever been able to resist that man? Only at the end, when she knew he had to be there for his baby.

The water stopped, and she clenched her muscles, holding herself still. By the time he exited the bathroom on a rush of citrus-scented steam, she was wide-awake.

He flipped back one corner of the covers and crawled into bed behind her, his warm, slightly damp skin giving off some kind of magnetic wave to pull her in.

She held her breath as he settled in, managing to avoid

all contact with her body. Then she cursed herself for holding her breath because she had to let it out.

She puckered her lips and blew it out. It sounded like a gale-force wind, but Sam didn't move a muscle. As she lay there listening to his breathing, it deepened. Sam didn't snore a lot or loudly, but a few snuffles and snorts indicated that he was off to dreamland. Wish she could say the same.

About an eternity later, Sam shifted and his knee wedged just beneath her bottom. When he didn't move it, she knew he'd reached nirvana—sound asleep while she still tossed and turned, or at least tossed and turned in her mind because she was in the exact same spot she had been in when Sam joined her in bed.

They should've just made love—she'd be asleep by now—asleep and satisfied and no more confused that she was now.

JOLENE JERKED AWAKE the next morning and scrambled out of bed. Sam had gotten up before her again. He'd obviously gotten more sleep than she had.

His voice, sounding way too cheerful for morning, greeted her from the kitchen. "I found some pancake mix. You want some pancakes?"

She tossed her grungy ponytail over her shoulder. "You've turned into a regular Suzy Homemaker. I don't remember you cooking one thing when…we were together."

"I told you, Jess changed everything. Full disclosure—" he held up a spatula "—I do have a housekeeper who comes in once a week, and I drop Jess off at day care when I'm working."

"Is it hard?" She tipped her head. "Is it hard being a single dad? Because that's what you are. How much time does Jess spend with Aimee?"

"As little as I can possibly get away with." His lips twisted and he flipped a pancake. "I made coffee, too."

She lifted her nose and sniffed. "I smell it."

"Sit down and eat." He held out a plate stacked with pancakes. "Do you have syrup in the fridge?"

"I think so." She took the plate with one hand and a coffee mug with the other. "Chip?"

"Fed him."

Hearing his name, Chip thumped his tail twice, obviously too sated to even get up and greet her.

"You're spoiling that dog." Jolene pulled out a chair. "How'd you sleep?"

"Great. I was beat." He pulled out the chair across from her and sat down with his own plate. "You?"

"I slept really well, too." She could lie with the best of them. "Do you need to go into the station today? My boss heard about Melody and told me to take another few days off, and I figured we… I could go to Melody's place this morning."

"I can join you. I have to bring the truck back and make some excuses for its condition. I also want to pick up that map of Las Moscas tunnels." Sam squeezed a puddle of syrup onto his pancakes.

"But that map didn't show a tunnel on Yaqui land, right?"

"I'm sure the tunnel I suspect is on Yaqui land is not one of Las Moscas'—or it *would* have been on that map. It's someone else. Someone who wants to maintain a covert presence, someone who doesn't want to upset the cartels. In short, El Gringo."

Jolene stirred some milk into her coffee. "The appearance of Pink Lady must've upset the cartels if it was that pure. It must've demanded a high price, higher than the regular meth coming across."

"Oh, it did, but it showed up in small quantities. It wasn't replacing the lower grade stuff by a long shot."

"Is it still on the street in San Diego?"

"It is." He cleared his throat before sawing into his pancakes. "They got to the mules *after* they crossed the border. The product had been taken off them before they were killed."

"That's so brutal." She shivered and took a sip of the hot coffee. "It's like he wants to wipe out everyone who knows about the origins of Pink Lady, but that can't be Melody."

"Maybe Melody didn't know about the origins of Pink Lady, but she had an idea of how it was connected to the casino and she'd heard about El Gringo Viejo." Sam stuffed the last of his pancakes in his mouth. "I'm going to head out to the station now and then go back to my motel to shower and change. I'll pick you up later, and we'll try to get into Melody's place."

As Jolene watched Sam back his truck out of her driveway, it felt like someone had punched her in the gut. No affection from him this morning, no kiss, no double entendre about sharing a bed—no nothing.

Had she just made the biggest mistake of her life?

An hour later, she blew out a sigh of relief when she saw Sam's rental car pull up in front of her house. Not that she doubted he'd return—he *did* want to get into Melody's place—but the last time she'd rejected him, he'd taken her at her word.

She patted Chip's head and said, "I get him all to myself this time, buddy."

She stepped out onto the porch and waved before Sam had a chance to leave his car. When she dipped inside the car, she said, "How'd it go with the truck?"

"I didn't have to answer too many questions—about that."

She shot him a glance from the corner of her eye. "What then?"

"If I'd found anything yet to justify my presence in Paradiso. I was appropriately vague." He patted his bag in the back seat. "And I got a copy of the tunnel map, courtesy of Nash Dillon." He lifted an eyebrow. "Nash invited me to the big bash in Tucson tomorrow night celebrating the casino. I'm sure you were invited. Why didn't you tell me?"

"I wasn't planning on going, and I wasn't sure they were still having it. They must be confident those bones I buried there aren't some long-lost Yaqui."

"They must be." He started the car and pulled away from her house. "Anyway, we're going."

"We are?"

"It might be an opportunity to find out more about the investors in the casino."

Jolene covered her mouth. "I almost forgot Nash's consortium has an investment in the Desert Sun Casino. Do you think he knows anything about a connection to the cartels?"

"Nash?" Sam snorted. "If Nash thought there was anything fishy about that property, he'd pull out. Truth is, he has more to do with the pecan-processing business than the other investments. He and his family leave that up to the partners."

"The gala tomorrow is a fancy dress-up thing. You ready for that?" She eyed his broad shoulders. She'd never seen Sam dressed to the nines before—and she'd like to.

"I can rent a tux in Tucson. It might not be a perfect fit, but I'm sure I'll be presentable."

He'd be more than presentable. "Then it's a date."

"Are *you* ready for it? You didn't plan to go."

"I have a few things that'll work. I wonder if Wade is still going."

"I'm not saying Wade's a cold dude, but I don't think the death of his sister is going to keep him from this. He's been waiting too long."

"I think you're right." Jolene sucked in a breath. "The crime scene tape is still up. Is it off-limits?"

"They're done collecting evidence from her place. There are no cops watching it, and you know where Melody kept a spare key, if it's still there. I say, we go for it."

He parked the car at the edge of the parking lot in front of the building, just like he had the previous time. Then they'd been accosted by Tucker. Who knew what would happen this time?

Jolene strode across the parking lot, not looking left or right, putting on a casual, noncommittal face—the type of face you wouldn't wear when attempting to search your dead cousin's apartment.

She tripped on the first step, and Sam grabbed her arm. "Hold on. You're acting like you're on your way to a demolition. Slow down. Take a few deep breaths. You're here to find suitable clothing for Melody's burial—if anyone asks."

Nodding, she filled her lungs with air, realizing that she'd been holding her breath all the way across the parking lot. She continued up the stairs without a mishap, or maybe that was due to Sam's steadying hand on her back.

He was still here for her, even though she'd relegated him to a tiny, cold corner of her bed last night, although he seemed to have minded it less than she had.

When they reached Melody's door, Sam ran a finger along the crime scene tape and held it out while Jolene crouched beside the middle pot in a row of wilted plants. She dug the key from the dirt, blew it off and held it up to Sam. They both ducked under the yellow tape, and Jolene clicked the door shut behind them.

As she turned to face the room, her nose twitched. Melody hadn't been dead long when they'd discovered her body, but the room still smelled like death. She made a wide berth around the red stain on the tile floor next to the coffee table.

"Where do we start?"

"With these." Sam dug in his backpack and pulled out two pairs of gloves. "Just in case. We don't need any more of our prints around here."

Jolene waved at the little table in the corner of the room, printer cables dangling over the edge like spiders' legs. "That's where she had her computer. So, I guess we can't check that."

"Drawers, shelves, pictures, closets. You might notice something that escaped the cops' attention." Sam snapped on his gloves. "I'll start in here. Why don't you hit the bedroom? One or two?"

"Just one bedroom, one bath." Crossing the room, Jolene tugged on the gloves. She stepped into Melody's bedroom, her gaze tracking across the unmade bed and the closet and drawers spilling their guts. "The police did a number in here."

Sam called back, "They're not paying a social call."

Jolene mumbled under her breath as she plucked the comforter from the floor. "They could be a little more respectful."

She yanked open a nightstand drawer and pulled out a dog-eared paperback. She tossed it on the bed, no better than the cops who'd trashed the place earlier. The book had been covering a box of condoms and some… Jolene picked up the silver bottle and squinted at the blue label— intimacy lotion. Jolene dropped the bottle. Good thing she was wearing these gloves.

Whatever Melody had been up to, she'd been getting more action than Jolene had.

As she shoved the drawer back into place, it stuck. Jolene jiggled it, but the drawer wouldn't close.

She pulled it out as far as it would go, and then stuck her arm into the drawer, her fingers wiggling toward the back and through the space at the end.

The folded edge of a piece of paper met her touch. She couldn't fit her thumb into the gap, so she pinched the paper between the pad of her middle finger and the top of her index finger, the gloves giving her a little traction. She worked it loose and pulled it free.

"What are you doing in here? I called you three times." Sam appeared, framed in the doorway, grasping the door-jamb on either side with gloved hands.

"Trying to get this piece of paper wedged behind the drawer." She shook it out, and scanned a list of names, most of them crossed out. Melody's ex's name was on the list, conspicuously not crossed out. "Ugh, I hope I didn't just stumble on a list of Melody's conquests, although it must've been before she bagged Gabe because his name isn't marked off—and it looks like she was into girls, too. Maybe it's something else—AA members or something."

"Can I see that?" A crease forming between his eye-brows, Sam launched into the room and snatched the paper from Jolene's hand.

"No need to get grabby. I'm happy to show you the paper, Sam…"

"Shh." He flapped the notepaper at her. "Jolene, this is a list of mules."

Her heart skipped a few beats, and she pressed a hand against her chest. "Drug mules? What was Melody doing with this list? Her name's not on it, is it?"

"It might as well be." He flattened the paper on the bed and smoothed his hand across it. "These are the people whose bodies I'm looking for—this is the list of the dead."

Chapter Fifteen

Sam stared at the familiar list of names, as Jolene gasped and dragged a pillow into her lap.

"*Missing*. You said they were missing persons."

"They're dead, Jolene. We know they're dead." His mouth twisted.

"Gabe Altamarino is on your list? Melody's ex-boy-friend?"

"This list is slightly different from mine. She has names on here that aren't crossed off, and yet they're on my list. She has others, like Gabe that I don't have at all."

"What's she doing with these names, Sam? Melody was no drug mule." She dropped the paperback book into the drawer and slid it closed.

"She wasn't but Gabe was, and she definitely knew what was going on at the construction site." He backtracked to the bedroom door and picked up the item he'd dropped. "I made my own discovery. That's why I was calling you."

"An arrow?" Jolene's hands curled into fists. "The same kind of arrow in the snake head Chip brought inside."

"Looks like Melody, not Wade, was trying to warn you away from interfering."

"But at the end, she texted me *El Gringo Viejo*. She must've had second thoughts, or was so wasted she wasn't thinking at all."

"Maybe once she knew I was helping you, she figured she'd drop his name." The feathers tickled his fingers as he ran his hand along the end of the arrow. "We need to find Gabe Altamarino."

"I always had a suspicion Melody never stopped seeing Gabe, despite Wade's best efforts." Jolene flicked her finger at the paper. "With his name on this list, do you think he's in hiding? How'd he get away if he was carrying Pink Lady across the border while the others disappeared? That was over two years ago, and he certainly wasn't in hiding when he was dating Melody."

"I don't know. Maybe he was one of the first, and the dealer wasn't being as thorough at that time." Sam lifted his shoulders. "Do you think Melody stole the map from you for the same reason? I'd feel better knowing she was the one skulking around your house."

"I would, too, but I doubt she was the one who fixed my brakes, so someone other than Melody wants me to back off...us, wants us to back off after what happened last night." Jolene carefully folded the sheet of paper. "I'm sticking this in my purse."

Sam had a strong urge to snatch the paper from her again and burn it. He didn't want Jolene to be in possession of any of this stuff. "Don't go waving that around. Put it in your safe."

"I can do that."

Sam nodded at a suitcase in the closet. "As long as we're here, you should probably go ahead and pack up some of Melody's clothes. Maybe pick out something for her burial and make good on that lie."

Jolene's dark eyes sparkled with unshed tears as she nodded. "Are you going to try to find Gabe? Like I said, I think he moved to Tucson after the breakup, or the pretend breakup."

"I'll use the resources back at the station. I can drop you off at Granny Viv's with Melody's suitcase, if you want to go there." He waved the arrow. "I'm going to toss this."

Ten minutes later, Sam took Melody's suitcase from Jolene and carried it down the stairs. He stashed it in the trunk of his car and they drove to the reservation.

He pulled up beside the Nighthawks' shiny Tesla and cut the engine. "I'll help you with the suitcase, but I'm not going inside—and if Wade's in there, it wouldn't be a good idea to spout off at him again."

She ran her fingertip along the seam of her lips. "I'm not saying a word to him about anything—not even Gabe, unless you want me to do some prying."

"No prying. The guy had a record, right? It should be easy to track him in the system and get a current address on him. If Tucker the trucker hadn't landed so conveniently in the laps of the police, they probably would've run down Gabe and questioned him, anyway."

"Yeah, I just can't shake off the guilt that we put Tucker in their sights."

"Tucker put himself there by taking Melody's purse."

"But not her phone."

"Phone's still missing." Sam popped the trunk and exited the vehicle. He hauled the suitcase from the back and wheeled it over the gravel to Granny Viv's front door. "Give my best and condolences to everyone and stay out of trouble."

"I'll do that." She placed her hand on his arm. "Pick me up later?"

"Sure, and if you get a ride back to your place before that, dinner?"

"I'll be sick of casseroles by that time." She jerked her thumb over her shoulder. "I'm sure the neighbors are delivering food to Gran and Wade's family."

"No casseroles, then. I'll be in touch." He spun around, leaving her on the porch. He could've gone inside, but he didn't do well with emotions like that. He'd pay his respects to Melody in his own way by attending a meeting here in Paradiso—the same one where he met Melody, who then introduced him to Jolene.

He owed her that.

As he pulled into the station, a team was headed out in the trucks. He called out the window to Clay, who told him one of the drones had picked up some suspicious activity at one of the sealed-off tunnels.

Yeah, he could tell Clay a thing or two about suspicious activity.

The call made the station quiet, and Sam waved to just one other agent moored to his desk, his ear glued to the phone.

He dropped into the chair behind his temporary desk and logged in to the computer. First order of business was to pull up the map to the Las Moscas tunnels and see which one was closest to the Yaqui land.

With the map in front of him on the display, he studied the red dots indicating the closed tunnels. His finger hovered over the one that was farthest west and closest to the casino property. He zoomed in on it and brought it up in an aerial view to analyze the landscape. He'd seen similar formations along the Yaqui land—right before someone started taking shots at him and Jolene.

He drew some boundaries on the screen and printed out the highlighted section of the map.

He'd need the tribe's approval to go hunting for a tunnel along the border of its property—and that meant Wade's approval. Would Wade really want that stigma attached to his casino project?

He stood up, stretched and retrieved his sheet of paper

from the printer. On the way back to his desk, he stopped by the vending machines and got a soda. He needed the caffeine.

Sleeping next to Jolene with the hands-off directive had been hell last night. Did she think he was made of stone? Hard, cold rock? He'd been rock hard, all right, but there'd been nothing cold about it.

She hadn't fooled him for a second. She hadn't been able to sleep, either. When Jolene slept, she threw arms and legs around, grabbing and bunching covers, crowding his space. Last night, she lay there like a log, not moving a muscle. It had to have taken great control on her part to pull that off.

The question remained, why'd she do it? Why'd she shut him down? She'd slipped up the night before. Desire had taken over her common sense, or maybe Melody's death had shaken her up so much she needed someone close. That didn't mean she wanted him back.

He snapped the tab on his can and chugged half the soda before taking his seat in front of the computer again.

This time he accessed the NCIC and entered *Gabe Altamarino*. He stared at the blinking cursor and the blank screen. Hunching forward, he entered *Gabriel Altamarino*. The system gave him no love—kinda like Jolene.

He took a few sips of his drink, cradling the bubbles with his tongue. Then he tried various spellings of *Altamarino*. Got a hit for Gabe Marino, but his picture and profile didn't match someone who'd be involved with Melody.

How'd that happen? One of the reasons Wade had been hell-bent against Melody's relationship with this guy was because he had a record. So, where was his record? Drug crimes as an adult could not be expunged. Maybe Gabe had been a juvenile when he'd committed these offenses.

Sam rubbed his eyes and dug into his email from his office in San Diego.

Jorge, the other agent in the office, approached his desk with a thick file. "Thought you might be interested in seeing this."

"What is it?" Sam pushed back from his desk and propped up his feet.

"It's the preliminary crime scene report from the Melody Nighthawk murder. You're the one who found her, right? Nabbed her killer?"

Sam wouldn't bet on that second statement, but he nodded. "Yeah, I knew Melody. She was my friend's cousin."

Jorge plopped the file on Sam's desk next to his feet. "The sheriff's office sent it over earlier. Basic autopsy, no toxicology yet, prints and other trace evidence."

They'd missed the list of drug mules in her nightstand drawer.

"Thanks, man." Sam dropped his feet from the desk and wheeled his chair in, flipping over the cover of the file folder.

He ran his finger down the first page of details, and then began shuffling through the pages. He stopped at the one listing the number of fingerprints found in Melody's apartment—looked like a list from Grand Central Terminal.

His prints were identified, as well as Jolene's, Wade's, Tucker's, a bunch of unknowns and several sets ID'd but not familiar to him—probably Melody's friends. The police had probably zeroed in on Tucker's prints being in the apartment and called it a day.

He glanced through the preliminary autopsy report. Time of death had already been nailed down, but a cause of death hadn't been determined yet. The medical examiner would want to look at the toxicology report before making anything official.

The rest of the pages slipped through his fingers as he thumbed through them until he got to the autopsy photos. He spread a few of them out on the desk and studied Melody's head wound. Must've been more than the blood loss that killed her.

The medical examiner had taken photos of the tattoos on Melody's body. Sam's throat got tight when he made out one on Melody's thigh that said *survivor.* Damn, he should've intervened when he saw her drunk.

He peeled up another photo from his desk of a tattoo across Melody's lower back. Squinting, he read out loud, "Chris."

Who the hell was Chris? Was that Melody's sponsor's name? Family member? Sam ticked off Jolene's family members on his fingers but didn't recall a Chris. One of her friends?

Friends. He shuffled back through to the beginning of the file, and pulled out the list of fingerprints in the apartment. Hadn't he seen a Chris on this sheet?

His gaze tracked down the page and stumbled over one name—Christopher Contreras. How had this guy been in Melody's apartment enough to leave several prints and merit ink on her body without anyone knowing about him? Jolene had never mentioned a Chris to him.

If the police had ID'd Contreras's prints, he had to be in the system, and Sam would bet good money the guy wasn't in there for being a teacher or public servant.

The keys on his computer clacked as he accessed the NCIC system again. He entered Contreras's name and got a hit. He brought up the guy's information, his blood humming as he read through Contreras's priors and his current address in Tucson.

He stabbed the key to send the file to the printer and picked up the phone.

Jolene answered breathlessly on the third ring. "Sam?"

"Are you ready? We're going to pay a visit to Gabe Altamarino, aka Chris Contreras."

Chapter Sixteen

Jolene stepped onto the porch of her grandmother's house, fanning herself. It almost felt cool out here compared to the heat generated by the family inside.

As Sam's car rolled in front of Gran's driveway, Jolene launched off the porch, a thousand questions bubbling at her lips. She grabbed at the car door before Sam even put the car in Park.

He popped the locks and she swooped inside, pulling the seat belt in after her to save time. "Who the heck is Christopher Contreras?"

"Chris Contreras is Gabe Altamarino."

"How do you know that?" She snapped on her seat belt and rapped on the dashboard. "Go, go."

Sam plucked up a folded sheet of paper nestled on the console between them and shook it out. "Is this Gabe?"

Dark eyes pinned her in their gaze from the thin face of a man with a goatee and wavy hair swept back from a high forehead. "It's Gabe."

"That's what I thought." He dropped the sheet of paper where it floated to her lap. "His real name is Chris Contreras."

"Is that name in the criminal database you use?" She folded the paper to escape those eyes. She hadn't much cared for Gabe in person and didn't like him any better in one dimension.

"No. That was the problem. I entered *Gabe Altamarino* in the system and no criminal record was returned. I then... uh, looked at Melody's autopsy photos." He squeezed her fingers. "Sorry."

Jolene swallowed. "What did they tell you?"

"Melody had a tattoo on her lower back with the name Chris. Did you know that?"

"Haven't hung out at the pool with Melody since we were kids. I'm pretty sure I haven't seen her lower back in years." She pinched the crease on the paper to make sure Gabe stayed in there. "How did you make the connection between Melody's tattoo and Chris Contreras?"

"In the same file that contained the photos, there was a list of fingerprints found in the apartment—ours were listed—so were those of some guy named Christopher Contreras. The name didn't ring a bell when I first saw it. Figured it was some friend of hers, maybe someone in the program. Then I saw the tattoo and had a hunch. When I looked up Contreras, saw his rap sheet, saw his photo, I guessed he might be Altamarino."

Jolene clasped her knees with her hands, her nails digging into her flesh. "That would explain why he's still alive, wouldn't it? He must've noticed the other Pink Lady mules' disappearing act and figured a name change would go a long way toward saving his life."

"Exactly. He resurfaces as Gabe Altamarino, starts going out with Melody and keeps seeing her even when Wade tells him to get lost." Sam rubbed his chin. "I just can't figure out how Wade knew about Gabe's criminal past if he were no longer Chris Contreras."

"I don't think Gabe made a secret of the fact that he was a reformed bad boy. Maybe he got in front of that story so Wade wouldn't do any checking on his own and dig up Gabe's real name."

"Gabe must've put together that list of mules he gave Melody for safekeeping, and he probably knows why those mules disappeared." Sam flexed his fingers on the steering wheel. "And he must have some idea how that land is linked to Pink Lady and the disappearances and the casino."

"He's not going to want to tell us, is he?"

"Maybe we won't give him a choice."

"Are you sure you have the right address for him in Tucson? Why would he give an accurate address if he's trying to hide out?"

"He doesn't have a choice about that, either. He's still on parole. His parole officer has to have a correct address for him, or he goes back in the slammer. And if he goes back inside as Chris Contreras…"

"The drug cartel will find him." Jolene bunched her skirt in her hands. "Why did Melody keep seeing him?"

"You know your cousin liked bad boys, right? That's why she handed me off to you. I was on the wrong side of the law for her."

"While I'm glad she handed you off to me, as you so delicately put it, I wish she would've found a good guy of her own."

"I guess the joke was on Melody because I didn't turn out to be such a good guy, after all."

She flashed him a quick glance. Was he fishing for compliments? That wasn't his style.

His tight jaw and turned down mouth told her otherwise. He was still beating himself up for lying about the last time he'd hooked up with his ex.

Who was she kidding? *She* was still beating him up for that. Could she ever stop?

"At least you're on the right side of the law." Jolene bit her lip. That hadn't come out right.

Sam snorted. "At least that."

As they made the drive to Tucson, the sun set over the desert floor, the scattered clouds creating pink-and-orange streaks across the sky.

Sam talked about San Diego and after some tentative starts, told her more about Jess. She must've given him the impression that she blamed his daughter for their separation. Didn't she? She hadn't wanted to think about Sam with his daughter, but he seemed like a great dad and she liked this side of him. So, she encouraged him this time and learned even more about him as a man and a father.

As the signs began to herald Tucson, Jolene asked, "So, where are we going to find Gabe or Chris?"

"His address is near the university."

"He's not going to want to talk to us."

"Me. I brought you along, but I want you to wait for me someplace public. I'll deal with Contreras."

"That's not gonna work, and you know it, Sam. You're not going to get any information out of him." She held up her hand as he opened his mouth. "I have an idea. Let me finish."

"Go ahead, but I can already tell I'm not going to like this idea of yours."

"Chris knows me, right? Or at least Gabe does. He'll talk to me. I have an excuse to see him. I'll bring him the news about Melody, tell him that she confided in me that they were still a thing. I'll get him talking. Just tell me what you want to know."

Sam had been shaking his head during her entire speech. "Bad idea. We don't know that he didn't kill Melody. His prints were in her place."

"Gabe didn't have a motive to kill Melody. She loved

him and would've done anything for the guy—and he knew it. She defied her brother to be with him on the sly."

Sam flicked on the turn signal to exit the freeway. "Do you think Contreras cares about that? Melody knew too much. She was cousins with you—a woman who wanted to know more."

"You know I'm right, Sam. He's not going to give you the time of day. Let me go in first. You can be close by." She snatched up her purse and unzipped it. She spread it open to show her dad's gun. "I came prepared. I'll be okay."

His eyes widened. "You told me you knew how to use that thing, right?"

"Dad taught me." She zipped up her purse and stashed it at her feet. "If it makes you feel better, I can call you first and leave the line open so you can hear everything that's going on between us."

"That would be dangerous." When Sam ran his knuckles across the stubble on his jaw, she knew she'd hooked him. "I can keep out of sight while you make contact with him. He starts acting aggressive, get out of there. He asks leading questions about the casino project and your interest in it, get out of there. If he's hostile, suspicious—"

"I know." She snapped her fingers. "I'll get out of there. This will work, Sam—better than the law marching in there making accusations."

"We'll see what the setup is first." He hit the steering wheel with the heel of his hand. "Damn, I wish I had a wire or something to listen in—and don't mention leaving the phone line open. Too much could go wrong in that scenario."

A few turns after the freeway exit, and Sam was wheeling through downtown Tucson. A little more wheeling, and they'd be exiting downtown Tucson.

"How close to the campus is he?"

"Close enough to have a thriving street business with the students, if that's his game here. He's in an apartment off Broadway."

Two minutes later, Sam turned onto Broadway itself, the street busy with cars. The GPS informed them they'd be turning right in two blocks.

"Looks like school started or is about to." Sam pulled into a grocery store parking lot and took a spot near the street. "Let's plan this attack. I'll wait here. You take the car, so he's not suspicious. Will he recognize you?"

"Probably." She tossed her hair over one shoulder. "I had shorter hair, but I don't look much different."

His gaze appraised her, and she hoped a blush hadn't accompanied the warmth she felt in her cheeks.

"Then I'll tell him I'm there with news about Melody... or I'll ask him if he heard about Melody because I'm supposed to know they've been seeing each other. I'll explain that I was in town and wanted to make sure he knew what had happened. Will that work?"

"I don't like sending you in there alone."

"I won't be alone." She dragged her purse into her lap and patted it. "I'll have Mr. Smith and Mr. Wesson with me."

Sam rolled his eyes. "Now, I'm really worried. That gun is a Glock."

"Better yet." She hitched the purse over her shoulder. "I'll have Ms. Glock with me."

"Okay, this is where you and Ms. Glock are going." He rattled off the address, and then slipped out of the car.

She followed suit and skirted the rear of the car to get into the driver's seat. Before she got behind the wheel, Sam pinched her shoulders with his fingers. "Be careful."

She stood on her tiptoes and kissed his chin. "I will."

She drove the two blocks to Gabe's house and pulled right in front, as if she had nothing to fear. Her hand had a slight tremble when she removed the keys from the ignition.

She marched past a typical Tucson front yard—a few scrubby cactus, gravel and a tangle of weeds spilling to the curb. She knocked on the door and held her breath, repeating in her head, *This is just Gabe Altamarino, Melody's boyfriend.*

Blowing out a breath, she knocked again. They hadn't discussed a plan B if Gabe wasn't home, or worse, didn't live here anymore.

The door creaked open, and a man stood framed by the doorway, yawning and scratching his bushy hair. Not Gabe.

"Hi, is Gabe around?"

The man poked his head outside practically over her shoulder, and she got a whiff of sweat and weed. "If you're a student looking to buy, you don't come to the house."

She looked like a college student? She liked this guy—despite the sweat and the weed.

"I'm not a student. Gabe is, was, dating my cousin, Melody. I was in Tucson and wanted to touch base with Gabe."

"Oh, yeah, man. Bad news about Melody. Gabe was destroyed."

Jolene blinked. "I-is he home?"

"Naw, he went to University Ave. to hit up some bars and maybe do a little business."

"Oh." Jolene sawed at her bottom lip. "Do you know which bar?"

"There aren't that many down there. He's in one of them, or you could try coming back tomorrow. What's your name?"

"Jolene. I'll find him on University."

As she drove back to the grocery store parking lot, she decided not to tell Sam that she gave Gabe's roommate her name—just in case that was a stupid thing to do. She pulled into a space in front of the store where she saw Sam leaning against a pillar, drinking a coffee. He had another cup in his hand.

She put the car in Park, and it idled as he placed a cup on the roof of the car and opened the door. "I got you a latte. How'd it go? Not there?"

"I talked to his roommate. Gabe's barhopping on University. I can catch up to him there."

Sam retrieved the cup from the top of the car and ducked inside, placing both cups in the cup holder. "What kind of guy is his roommate?"

"Stoned."

"That makes sense." Sam moved the seat back. "This will make things easier. You look for Contreras in the bars, and I'll tag along after you. Text me when you locate him, and I'll saunter into the bar like a stranger—a stranger who can keep an eye on you. I like the idea of you meeting Contreras in a public place better than holing up with him in his house."

"Oh…" she reversed and pulled out of the lot "…he knows about Melody's death."

"Because he heard or because he killed her?"

She parked the car a block away from University, as they didn't want to chance Gabe spotting them getting out of the same car. Sam waited while she slipped out of the car and strode toward the lights and sounds of the main drag outside the gates of the university.

She didn't have to turn around once. She knew Sam had her back and wouldn't let her out of his sight. She could trust him—for that.

Most of the bars gathered on one side of the street with

one big restaurant-bar on the other side, which catered more to the parents of the college students, especially at this time of year. Gabe wouldn't want to show his face there and freak out Mom and Dad.

She tripped into the first bar, had a quick look around and slipped out. A bigger crowd in the next place had her squeezing between groups of students and poking her head into the patio area.

As she left that place, she spotted Sam sitting on a bench sipping his coffee. She looked away and ducked into the next bar where live music blared and frat boys shouted their beer orders to the bartender.

She squeezed her way up the stairs to the balcony that hung out over University. When she reached the top step, she scanned the students starting their school year off with a bang, the boys all male bravado, the girls flexing the power of pouting lips and bared midriffs. A few shell-shocked parents cropped up here and there, and the older hangers-on who flitted around the edges of university life to take advantage of naive girls and profit from misguided boys.

Her gaze skittered to a stop when she located Gabe, one of those hangers-on. She turned from the balcony and sent Sam a quick text that she'd found Gabe.

She smoothed her hands down the front of her denim skirt and launched herself into the fray. She wended her way to the table by the balcony edge, zeroing in on Gabe.

He must've felt her attention, as his head jerked up from his beer and his eyes widened. He half rose from his chair, plopped back down and sent the two boys he was probably scamming on their way.

Approaching his small table, crowded with empty beer bottles, she waved. "Gabe, do you remember me?"

"Yeah, yeah." He coughed a smoker's cough. "You're Mel's cousin."

She indicated the chair. "Can I sit for a minute?"

He shrugged. "Yeah, sure. What the hell are you doing here? H-how's Mel?"

"You don't have to pretend with me, Gabe." She flattened her hands on the sticky table. "I know you two were still seeing each other, and I know you know she's dead. I just talked to your roommate."

His eyes darted to the side and back to her face. He licked his lips. "How'd you know where I lived?"

"Melody." She flicked her fingers, eager to move on. She had no clue if Melody knew Gabe's address here in Tucson or had it in her phone—her missing phone. "I was in town visiting a friend and thought I'd drop by and tell you what happened."

"I heard some homeless guy killed her." He gripped the edge of the table with stubby fingers sporting tattoos on every space before the first knuckle. "That guy who was squatting in the apartment next to hers. I told Mel to rat him out, but she felt sorry for him."

"That was Mel." She shredded the edge of a napkin. "When was the last time you saw her?"

His jaw hardened, and his dark eyes narrowed. "Not sure. You tell the cops about me?"

"No." Now she proceeded to fold the tattered napkin, unable to keep her fingers still. "No reason to tell them. They got their man."

"You tell her brother Wade?" As he finished pronouncing her cousin's name, his lips stretched into a grimace.

"I didn't tell anyone—not then, not now. Just thought you should know in case you hadn't heard about her death."

"I heard." He gulped down some beer from his bottle and slammed it down on the table.

Jolene flinched. Is that what he wanted? To scare her off? Not so fast.

"Was Melody doing drugs? I know she'd started drinking again."

He wiped the back of his hand across his mouth. "You blaming me for that?"

"No." She rubbed her sweaty palms on her skirt. Now it was time for *her* gaze to dart, and she did a double take when she noticed a cute coed sidling up to Sam, a bottle of beer clutched in his hand.

When her eyes made it back to Gabe's face, his nostrils flared and his eye twitched. He hunched forward and grabbed her wrist, his tattooed fingers biting into her skin. "What the hell are you doing here, and what do you want from me?"

As Jolene wrenched her arm from his grasp, a couple of girls squealed behind her and a chair banged to the floor.

Gabe looked up and swore. As Sam swooped down on their table, Gabe launched himself over the ledge of the balcony.

Jolene shot up in her chair and leaned over in time to see Gabe land on top of a canvas umbrella on the restaurant's patio and roll off to the sidewalk.

Sam flew past her and shouted over his shoulder. "Stay here."

He took the same path as Gabe, landing on the same umbrella, now with a little less bounce, and scrambled to his feet to give chase.

The students took the chaos in stride, and a couple were already moving in to claim the prime table. "You leaving?"

"Damn right I am." Jolene snatched up her purse and took the safe route down to the street.

She looked both ways when she hit the sidewalk. Would Gabe run back to his house? Probably wouldn't want to lead Sam back there, but he wouldn't want to be running through campus, either, with the campus police on watch.

She hustled down the street and veered around the next corner. She'd guessed right. Sam was running ahead of her with a weird, halting gait. As she opened her mouth to call out to him, the sound of gunshots cracked through the night.

Sam dropped to the ground and Jolene screamed, her whole world collapsing in front of her. The adrenaline fueled her system, and her legs pumped harder and faster.

When she reached Sam, she crouched beside him. With a sob in her voice, she asked, "Are you hurt? Did he shoot you?"

"I'm fine." Lifting his head, he aimed his gaze down the street. "They got Contreras."

Jolene jerked up her head, noticing Gabe in a heap in the middle of the road. A few neighbors had poked their heads out their front doors, too scared to come outside. She didn't blame them.

"Where'd the shot come from?"

"I saw a car slow down on the block ahead, and I'm pretty sure that's where the shots came from. I don't know why the shooter didn't turn the gun on me or, God forbid, you, but he could circle around."

Jolene rose to her haunches. "Gabe might still be alive. We have to talk to him. These neighbors probably already called the police. I'm not done with him."

As she launched forward, Sam made a grab for her leg and missed. "Jolene, stop."

Her sneakers slapped on the pavement as she ran crouched over toward Gabe's fallen form. As she reached his side, she glanced up to see Sam hobbling after her. Had he lied about getting hit?

Gabe's chest rose and fell with each tortured breath he took, blood spurting from the wound in his chest.

Jolene grabbed his hand and put her face close to his. "What do you know about Pink Lady?"

Gabe gasped, but his lips began moving through the blood.

Sam had reached them, his body coiled and tensed, standing over her, his head swiveling from side to side. He had her back.

She hissed in Gabe's ear as the sirens started bearing down on them. "Pink Lady. The casino property. What do you know?"

"The thumb drive." Gabe choked. "I have a video on the thumb drive. Couldn't touch me. EGV couldn't touch me. Video from the drone."

Gabe's body slumped, and the blood stopped pumping from his chest.

As the red-and-blue lights bathed the scene and the sirens wound down to an echo, Jolene cranked her head around to stare into Sam's face. "The thumb drive? What does he mean?"

Sam raised his dark eyebrows. "Thumb, drum, crumb. Tucker had incriminating video of the casino property—and I'd bet my life it's in the vacant apartment next to Melody's."

Chapter Seventeen

With the police on the scene, a few neighbors had gathered in their driveways. A patrol car squealed to a stop, feet from Sam and Jolene.

When the officer exited the vehicle, hand hovering over his weapon, he shouted, "What happened here?"

Sam tipped his head toward Contreras laid out in the street. Jolene still crouched beside him. "Gunshot victim."

"Did you shoot him?"

Sam raised his hands. "No, we just stumbled onto the scene. When we heard the shots, we hit the deck."

"Is she with you?" The officer pointed his finger at Jolene.

"Yes. It looks like he was hit in the chest and stomach. He was gushing blood, but now it's just pooling around him. He's dead."

The cop's chin jutted out. "You law enforcement?"

"Border Patrol." Sam reached for his back pocket and flipped out his badge to show the officer.

The EMTs had joined Jolene next to Contreras, easing her out of the way. She sat on the street, knees drawn to her chest and a pair of bloodstained hands wedged on the asphalt behind her.

Sam kneeled beside her. "Are you okay? My heart

stopped when you took off for Contreras, but you done good, kid."

Her glassy eyes tracked from the EMTs working fruitlessly on Contreras to Sam's face. "We have to get that video."

"Shh. We will."

She sat forward, bringing her hands in front of her face. "There was so much blood. What did you tell the police?"

"Not much." Sam glanced over his shoulder at the approaching officer. "We heard the shot and saw him fall. You tell the EMTs anything?"

"Nothing…but, I mean nothing." She placed a hand on the ground and struggled to her feet, as the officer hovered over her.

Sam took her arm and helped her up.

"Ma'am, are you all right?" The officer's gaze dropped to her hands, streaked with Contreras's blood.

"I'm fine."

"Are you a nurse?"

"A nurse?" She shook her head. "I just thought I'd see if I could help."

"Did you?"

"No. He was already dead or fast on his way. There was no way to staunch that blood."

The officer had a few more questions for them, and by the time he was finished, Contreras had been pronounced dead. The cop held his card out to Sam. "We have your information, Agent Cross. Now you have mine. If you remember anything about the incident or the car, let us know. The deceased is a known drug dealer in Tucson, so his manner of death is not all that surprising. Ma'am, the EMTs can see to your hands. Are they injured?"

"No." Jolene spread her fingers in front of her, as if just noticing the blood. "Thanks, I'll walk over."

Sam pressed his hand against the small of Jolene's back and steered her to the ambulance, calling out to the EMT. "Do you have some solution to clean off her hands? Murder victim's blood."

"Of course." One of the EMTs ducked into the back of the ambulance and emerged with a clear liquid in a bottle and gauze pads. As Jolene held out her hands, the EMT squirted the solution over her hands and wiped them with the gauze. He did it one more time, removing all traces of Contreras's blood.

The EMT handed her a pristine dry towel. "Are you all right, otherwise?"

"I'm fine." Jolene hopped off the back of the ambulance. "Sam?"

"All good. Let's get back to the car." He took her hand, and they walked down the middle of the street, the residents still gathered in small clusters in driveways and curbside.

Sam tipped his head toward Jolene's. "It came from the car. Did you see it roll by right before the shot was fired? Two shots, one kill."

"I didn't see anything but you running in front of me… limping, like you are now. What happened to your leg?"

Sam squeezed his left quad. "Jammed it up when I jumped from that balcony. Did I overreact? When I saw him grab your wrist…"

"He was gonna run one way or the other." She untangled her hand from his, and wrapped her arm around his waist. "Lean on me if you have to. When you saw Gabe grab my wrist, you couldn't have felt any worse than I did when I watched you crumple in front of me."

"You thought Contreras had turned and shot me?"

"Yes." She covered her eyes with her hand for a second. "Filled me with panic."

"So much so, that you didn't hear me yelling at you to keep down. That car could've made a U-turn and come back at us."

"But it didn't. Much better for a lone drug dealer to get gunned down than three people tied together by one person—Melody Nighthawk."

His shoulder bumped hers as he stumbled. "You figured out that was no random killing or drug deal gone wrong."

"Someone's been watching Gabe…or us. Wanted to keep him quiet…about that video."

"It almost worked."

Jolene glanced over her shoulder before they turned the corner. "What do you think is on the video? It was enough to keep Gabe alive for two years."

"We'll find out. Do you remember when Tucker was babbling about his thumb?"

"Vaguely. He said so much nonsense."

"He said Pinky gave him the thumb drive and that it was in the floor."

Jolene stumbled. "You think it's in the floor of Melody's apartment or the one next door?"

"I think Melody gave it to Tucker to hide in the place next to hers. I just hope it's there and not in some hidey-hole of Tucker's. Maybe she gave the thumb drive to Tucker, maybe not. Maybe he saw her hiding it in her place, in the floor."

"And Gabe… Contreras must've given the thumb drive to Melody for safekeeping—putting her life in danger."

When they reached the car, Sam pulled out his phone, tapped it and crouched next to the rental.

"What are you doing?" Jolene hovered over him.

"The person who shot Contreras knew we were here to meet him. That means they were keeping tabs on him, or someone is tracking us. I'm going to check the car chassis for a GPS device. We have the capability on our phones now—mandatory after several of our agents were personally targeted by the cartels."

His ears primed for the telltale beep that would signal a device, he continued his sweep, crawling on the ground, waving his phone beneath the car as Jolene followed him, functioning as his lookout just as he'd kept watch when she was talking to Contreras. They made a good team.

Satisfied, he rose to his feet, brushing off the knees of his jeans. "Nothing, which means Contreras was being followed, whether he knew it or not. His name change didn't fool them. They must've been watching him for a while, knew he'd been in contact with Melody. Even though he had that video over their heads, they watched him."

He opened the passenger door and nudged her inside. Then he limped around to the driver's side. As he repositioned the seat, she ran her hand along his thigh.

"Is your leg okay?"

"Just sore. I'll be fine." He laced his fingers with hers and brought her hand to his lips. "We're falling apart piece by piece, aren't we?"

"Nobody else I'd rather fall apart with." She caressed his chin. "I'm glad to have you on my side, Sam—now let's find that thumb drive."

By THE TIME they got back to Paradiso, it was almost midnight. Once again, Sam pulled into the parking lot of Melody's apartment building. With the car idling, he said, "Maybe we should leave this for the morning."

"Are you crazy?" Jolene released her seat belt. "Melody and Contreras were killed for that video. It's the proof you've been waiting for."

He cut the engine. "Maybe *you* should leave this for the morning. I'll go inside and you can take the car home."

"I'm in this, Sam, just as much as you are." She patted his forearm, tense and corded as he gripped the steering wheel. "I'll be fine. Nobody's going to be here. Nobody followed us, nobody is tracking this car."

He opened his mouth, and she pushed open her door before he could raise any more objections. She knew he'd been spooked when someone shot at them, but this wasn't the same. Was it?

She skipped across the parking lot before Sam even got out of the car, taking advantage of his bum leg. She did wait for him at the base of the stairs, palming Melody's key. She had every right to be here.

When he caught up with her, he panted. "You don't play fair."

"Can you make it up the stairs okay?"

"Yeah, yeah, let's get going. We don't want anyone seeing us hanging around here."

She jerked her thumb over her shoulder. "Too late. There's a couple standing outside a car in the parking lot."

Sam said, "Then let's do a search of Melody's place first, as you have the key. When they're gone, we'll get into the vacant unit."

They reached Melody's front door, and Jolene unlocked it and stepped over the threshold. Sam crowded in behind her, whispering in her ear, "Don't turn the lights on. We don't want to signal anyone. I've got my flashlight."

Sam snapped the door closed, secured the curtains at the front window and flicked on his flashlight. "We've already searched all the conventional places and didn't see any thumb drive. The cops would've scooped up anything like that. It's time to search the unconventional."

"What did you remember Tucker saying about the thumb drive?" Biting her bottom lip, Jolene peered into the dim, disheveled room. Had someone besides the police tossed the place?

"Besides thumb, drum, crumb?" Sam aimed his light at the tiled floor. "He said the thumb drive was in the floor."

Jolene stamped her sneaker against the tiles. "How can something be hidden under tile?"

"That's what worries me about any information from Tucker. He wasn't exactly rooted in reality." He skimmed the light across the room. "Let's check the closets."

They combed the floors of Melody's apartment, which were tiled throughout. Jolene skimmed her toe across two squares. "This is new stuff, too. No chips or cracks or loose tiles. In fact, I remember Melody talking about how she'd had a water leak that ruined the wood floors and the management company was replacing everything with tile."

"Wood floors?" Sam cocked his head. "Some of these units have wood floors?"

"I know. You could actually hide something beneath wood flooring. Maybe the place where Tucker was hiding has the wood."

Jolene strolled to the wall Melody's place shared with the vacant unit next door. "That would explain why Melody gave Tucker the flash drive—so he could hide it in the floor."

"Then, that's where we need to be." Sam snapped off the flashlight and made a move for the front door. "Is that couple gone now?"

Jolene stepped outside and peered over the railing into the parking lot. "They're gone. How are we going to get in there?"

"Give me some credit. If Tucker Bishop can break into an abandoned apartment, so can I."

Five minutes later, Sam made good on his promise as

he picked the lock on the empty unit and pushed open the door.

Jolene held her breath against the musty smell, as she stepped inside the unfurnished unit. "If the cops came in here, they didn't have much to search."

Sam's flashlight lit up a dirty blanket in the corner. "Tucker's bed."

Tapping her toe against the tile floor, Jolene said, "Looks like they replaced this floor, too."

Sam crept to the back of the apartment and called over his shoulder. "Not in the bedroom."

Jolene followed the light and joined Sam in the bedroom, the hardwood floor stretched out before them like a treasure map. Now they just had to find the treasure.

Sam slid open the mirrored closet door and lifted a wooden clothes rod from its brackets. "You use this to tap the floor, and I'll crawl around and use the end of my flashlight. You're listening for a hollow sound or looking for any irregularities in the seams of the floor."

They started in opposite corners of the room, tapping away like a couple of deathwatch beetles. Jolene hit each panel of wood with the end of the rod, cocking her head, listening for different sounds.

She approached the lone window in the room and rapped the end of her stick against the piece closest to the wall. Instead of the light, tinny sound she'd grown accustomed to, she heard a deeper sound. She tapped again and tapped the panel next to the first one.

The dark hollow sound had her heart racing and she dropped to her knees. "I think I found something, Sam."

He was at her side in an instant, the light from his flashlight playing over the floor.

"These two." She ran her fingers along the two panels

of wood next to the wall. As she pressed on one side, the wood wiggled. "This is it."

Sam withdrew a knife from his pocket and flipped it open. The blade gleamed in the low light as he inserted it along the edge of the wood. He jiggled it a few times, loosening the piece. He then jammed it into the crease and eased it back, using it as a lever.

The other edge of the wood lifted from the floor. He worked the sides until it popped up, and Jolene grabbed it.

Sam aimed the flashlight into the small cavity, as Jolene bent over the space. "See anything?"

With trembling fingers, Jolene reached into the dark area and pulled out a thumb drive attached to a long ribbon printed with the pecan-processing plant logo where Melody had worked.

She released a long breath. "It's here."

SAM DROVE TO Jolene's place with her squirming in her seat beside him and his gaze pinned to his rearview mirror. That thumb drive she had squeezed in her fist felt like a ticking bomb to him and the longer they had it in their possession, the greater danger they were in… *Jolene* was in.

When they got to her house, Jolene grabbed her laptop and booted it up at the kitchen table as Sam hovered above her and Chip circled around their legs, sensing their agitation.

She double-clicked to open the thumb drive, and a list of videos popped up, organized by date.

Sam squinted at the dates, which went back about a year. Then he took a deep breath and said, "Let's dive in."

Jolene brought up the first video, which showed drone footage of the Yaqui land slated for the casino. "Why did they have a drone out there?"

"To monitor the area. Make sure nobody was snooping around—like us."

"Or my father."

Sam squeezed her shoulder. "Keep going. I don't see anything incriminating yet."

They studied each video, and Sam noted that most of the coverage was for the border area, along those ridges. Would he have found a tunnel across the border if the shooters hadn't stopped him? What would he have found in that tunnel?

When the next video started, Jolene gasped and jabbed her finger at the screen. "People."

Sam leaned in close but couldn't make out any faces. "They don't seem to be too worried, do they? They're not sneaking around."

The next few videos were more of the same, and then things got interesting.

Sam whistled. "Hello—there's evidence of digging."

"Sam, look at the edge of the display. Two people are carrying a tarp—an old, dirty tarp—and it looks like they're disappearing into the ridge."

"It's a tunnel, just like I thought. They're moving…bodies into that tunnel. They're digging up the mules who were murdered after transporting Pink Lady across the border and stashing them in that tunnel." He tapped the screen. "This is all prior to the studies done on the land. They knew the casino was coming and had their own preparations to do."

Jolene displayed the next video, and the drone zoomed in close to the people this time.

Sam's pulse jumped. "Stop!"

Jolene paused the video. "You know that man?"

"That's Ted Jessup, El Gringo Viejo. We need to put

these videos in the hands of the DEA, the FBI, the Pima County sheriffs."

Jolene started up the video again. "I hope the bones are still in the tunnel, but you don't know where Ted Jessup is, do you?"

"No. Wait!" Sam's heart slammed against his chest. "Go back a few seconds."

Jolene dragged back the video that showed Ted Jessup talking with a few other people. A woman. He had his arm draped around the shoulders of a woman.

"Freeze there. Can we zoom in on those faces? That woman?"

After a few false starts, Jolene was able to zoom in on the youthful face of a woman with a long braid over her shoulder, a braid streaked with gray.

"I know that woman. She's Karen Fisher, the representative of the consortium of financers backing the casino. She's here in town, and she's behind everything."

Jolene blew out a long breath. "We have her, Sam. La Gringa Vieja."

Chapter Eighteen

Sam straightened his bowtie in the mirror, and Jolene came up behind him and wrapped her arms around his waist, careful not to smudge the collar of his white shirt with her red lipstick. "Are you sure we're doing the right thing?"

Sam patted the flash drive in his pocket. "We don't know who we can trust right now. I don't want this getting lost or deleted or corrupted. You saw what happened to Tucker in custody where he was supposed to be safe."

"I'm glad we didn't see my cousin Wade in any of that drone footage, but do you think he could be involved?" Jolene dropped her arms from Sam and rubbed the goose bumps that had risen on them.

"Do I think he knew that land was a dumping ground for dead drug couriers? No, but he knew those people wanted access to the land prior to the casino going up—and he gave it to them in exchange for money and support."

"Sounds like something Wade would do." She smoothed the skirt of her glittery white dress over her thighs. "When Rob Valdez's girlfriend, Libby, ID'd Ted Jessup in Rocky Point as El Gringo Viejo, did she mention a wife or a girl-friend? Where did this Karen Fisher come from?"

Sam shrugged, the tuxedo jacket tightening across his broad shoulders. "I don't know, but she and Jessup sure seemed cozy in the videos, didn't they? She's obviously the face of the financial empire EGV has built up with drug money. Jessup made sure to stay away from the public eye."

"We could just turn this information over to the cartels, and they'd handle it in their own way. They don't look too kindly on double-crossers."

"There's been enough bloodshed over Pink Lady, and if we can get Karen in custody, she'll most likely sing like a bird and the DEA and FBI can shut down the production of Pink Lady for good." Sam spun around from the mirror. "Does this look okay? The rental shop didn't have time to do any tailoring."

She trailed her fingers down his lapels. "A little tight across the shoulders, but that just makes you look even more buff."

"Okay, because that's the look I'm going for." He rolled his eyes. "You, on the other hand, look like a shimmery white cloud of perfection. Actually, you look like one of those princesses Jess always wants me to read about. Wait until I tell her I know a real princess."

"When she meets *this* princess, she's going to be extremely disappointed." Jolene caught her breath as Sam grabbed her hand.

"Does this mean you want to meet her?"

Jolene nodded, afraid to speak around the lump in her throat, afraid to ruin her carefully applied makeup with tears.

"Let's get through this, first." Sam pulled her close and kissed the side of her head. "Let's go."

As they drove to Tucson for the casino gala, Sam drummed his thumbs on the steering wheel, running through their plan. "Are you sure the AV guy you know at the hotel is working this gig?"

"He said he was, and if not, he'll give his replacement a heads-up."

"He's not worried about losing his job?"

She jabbed Sam in the side. "If everything unfolds as planned, he's going to be the hero of the evening. He won't have to worry about his job."

"I've put all the other agents who are going to be there on notice." Sam ran the tips of his fingers across his clean-shaven jaw. "Even Nash."

"How'd he react?"

"Nothing surprises Nash. He'll do his job."

When they got to Tucson, they had to drive several more miles into the foothills to the Hacienda del Sol. Sam left the car with a valet.

As they walked into the resort, Jolene pressed her hand against her stomach where the butterflies were flapping their wings furiously. They followed the signs to the ball-room, and when they entered, Sam slipped his hand into his pocket, withdrew the thumb drive and pressed it into her hand.

They'd edited together the most pertinent pieces of the videos—the digging, the relocating of tarps into the side of the ridge along the border and the people behind it all. Thank God, she'd never seen her father on the videos—too recent for him—but she was almost sure now that Dad had discovered that tunnel or those bodies and had paid the price for his knowledge—just like Melody, Tucker, Contreras.

Did Wade know the people he'd been dealing with had murdered his uncle, the man he revered and emulated? He must have guessed.

Jolene spotted the AV setup at the back of the room. Lucky for her and Sam, the gala tonight was supposed to feature a presentation on the Yaqui tribe and their land in the desert, straddling the US and Mexico. The video would still feature that land—just not in the way the backers imagined.

She squeezed Sam's bicep through his jacket. "My guy's here."

As she started across the room with purpose, Wade touched her shoulder. "Looking beautiful, cuz. I'm surprised to see you here."

"Oh, I've come around. I see the light now." She nestled her hand with the thumb drive in the folds of her dress.

Wade's dark eyes glowed. "Glad to hear it because I just got word on those bones that mysteriously appeared at the construction site."

Jolene blinked. "Oh?"

"Just some dried out bones from an archaeology site, not even from Arizona. Funny, huh? But that means, I'll be announcing tonight that the project is proceeding as planned."

"That's great." She spread her red lips into a smile. "It just may not be proceeding with everyone on board."

She twirled away from him and snatched a champagne flute from a passing tray. Gran wouldn't be here tonight, not her thing, but other tribe members stood in clusters around the room and Jolene headed for one of those groups.

She could feel Wade's eyes drilling into her back and didn't want him to see her talking to the AV guy. As she chatted with family members, she glanced at Wade from the corner of her eye hobnobbing with the mayor and his cronies.

Making her move, she swept up her skirt with one hand and sauntered toward the back of the room. "Derek?"

The man behind several computers looked up. "You're Jolene?"

"Yeah, just like we discussed." She slipped him the flash drive and five hundred bucks.

"Is anyone going to come for me once they realize the approved programming is going to be replaced by this?" He held up the flash drive.

"They'll be occupied with other things."

As she turned, Derek stopped her. "Hang on. I'm going to put this video on my hard drive and give the flash drive back to you. That way, if someone does come back here and tries to stop the video by removing it, you'll have your original."

"You're worth every last penny. I do have another copy at home, but that's a great idea."

"I'm doing it for our mutual friend, not really the money. I owe her." He clicked and dragged and clicked again, and then handed the flash drive back to her. "Done deal."

Jolene slipped the drive into her white beaded evening bag and downed her champagne. No turning back now.

She found Sam just as the lights began to dim, and soft music started to play. Slipping her arm through his, she whispered, "It's all set."

Sam nodded toward Nash, spiffy in a custom-tailored tux, sticking close to Karen Fisher's side.

Karen sported a silver sheath, her salt-and-pepper hair braided over one shoulder. She didn't look the part of a murderous drug dealer.

As the hors d'oeuvres circulated and the champagne flowed, the speeches began. Wade announced to a delighted crowd that the bones found at the ground-breaking ceremony were planted and not native to the land.

Sam bumped her shoulder and she replied, "Oh, yeah. Forgot to tell you that."

Wade continued, "The Desert Sun Casino is going to provide jobs and boost the economy, just like the pecan-processing plant did. As proud Yaqui, we will be good stewards of the land and property. Now, to thank the tribe, we put together a video of our heritage and culture to share with you tonight."

Sam put his lips close to her ear. "That's our cue."

They split up, Sam ducking out of the ballroom to re-enter near the stage—and near Karen Fisher. Jolene crept along the back wall, returning to the AV center. As Derek handed her a mic, she slipped behind a green curtain.

She watched through a slit in the curtain as Derek clicked on the drone video. She licked her lips and flicked on the mic as the video displayed on screens around the ballroom.

The crowd oohed and aahed at the majestic aerial shot of the desert landscape in all its glory. As the pink-and-orange streaks of a desert sunset faded from the screen, replaced by footage of the ridge along the border, Jolene began to speak.

"The Desert Sun Casino may come to fruition one day, but that land was used for something else before this project—something sinister. Buried in the sand are secrets, evidence of Yaqui land being used to move drugs and murder the mules in the know."

Shouts went up. Demands to hit the lights and stop the video echoed over the hushed silence of the ballroom. Jolene continued her narrative. When the video displayed Ted Jessup with Karen Fisher directing the relocation of people's remains to the border area, the room erupted.

Jolene took a deep breath, ready to identify the people on the screen, but before she could, shots rang out. People screamed and there was a stampede for the doors.

Jolene dropped behind the curtain, reaching out and tugging on Derek's pant leg. "Get down."

She squeezed her eyes closed and silently prayed that Sam hadn't been hit by any of those bullets. Seconds later, bright lights flooded the ballroom, and Jolene blinked as strong arms lifted her from the floor.

Sam folded her against his chest. "You're all right?"

She peered around his large frame at the stage. One man was down, and Karen Fisher, blood on her sleek dress, had her hands behind her back and Nash was cuffing her.

Jolene swayed as she grabbed on to Sam's arm. "We did it. Who's the guy on the ground?"

"Karen's security. When she saw her face on that video, her guy tried to hustle her out of the room. Nash stopped him, and the man pulled a gun. The three of us were on him before he even had a chance to aim, so his bullets went into the ceiling and Clay shot him. He's not dead, but Karen Fisher and Ted Jessup are finished."

Jolene rested her forehead against his shoulder. "How'd I do?"

"You killed it."

"And Wade?"

He stroked her hair. "He looked shocked. He may have to answer for some questionable business practices, but I don't think he knew how they'd been using that land and why they were so anxious to have a hand in its development."

"I'm glad. I am." She disentangled herself from his arms and tipped back her head to look into his face. "And I got justice for my father and all the others. That casino, if it goes up, won't be built on lies and secrets."

Sam cupped her face with one hand. "Nothing worth having should be built on lies and secrets."

Epilogue

"How much longer until you move back to Arizona, Sam?" Nash looked up from flipping burgers on the grill.

Sam dragged his attention away from Jolene sitting on the steps of Nash's pool with Jess on her lap. "Rob's gotta be processed out first. Hey, Rob, when are you leaving Paradiso, already?"

Rob Valdez, the youngest agent who'd barely been on the job two years answered without looking up from rubbing suntan lotion on his girlfriend Libby's back. "My transfer to LA should have final approval in a few months. Anxious to get rid of me?"

"Anxious to get back to Paradiso. You're going to be a different kind of busy out there in LA, but that's probably what your career needs right now."

"Yeah, most of my family is in LA, and I'd like to be closer to them."

Libby rolled over and sat up. "Thanks to you and Jolene, I don't have to worry about Ted Jessup coming after me for IDing him anymore, so we're free to go wherever."

Nash's fiancée, Emily, sauntered onto the patio from the house, balancing their son, Wyatt, on her hip. "I wish I'd been at that gala. The look on Karen's face must've been priceless when she saw her mug on that screen. I never liked her, anyway."

Emily took a seat next to Jolene in the pool, and Jess started pinching the baby's toes and squealing.

Clay and his wife, April, jogged across the lawn with their dog, Denali, and Chip at their heels.

April pushed a lock of blond hair from her face. "Are we talking about EGV again? I'd rather forget him. He killed my father and was responsible for the deaths of Libby's mother and Jolene's father. He was a one-man wrecking crew."

Clay told the dogs to Stay and grabbed a beer from Nash's outdoor mini-fridge. "His gal pal Karen sure turned on him fast once the FBI had her in custody."

"I wish I'd been there when they busted down his door." April huffed out a breath and reached for a bottle of water. "Hey, Sam, you want some water?"

He held up a hand and she tossed him a bottle.

Libby sat on the edge of the pool, dangling her feet in the water. "The casino project is going forward, isn't it, Jolene?"

"It is. My cousin was able to provide some evidence about the financials that helped the DEA, so they're going easy on him. I think he lost the confidence of the tribe, though. They're looking for some new leadership."

"How about you, Jolene?" Nash raised a plate of burgers. "Food's on."

"Yeah, how about you?" Dropping his bottle by the side of the pool, Sam slipped into the water and paddled over to Jess. "The tribe trusted your father, and they'll trust you, especially after you took care of business at the gala."

She made a face. "Not for me."

The others vacated the pool to swarm the food Nash and Emily had set out.

Sam ducked his head under the water and popped up in

front of Jess, who squealed and giggled. Sam blew bubbles in the water. "She likes you."

"The feeling is mutual." She tucked a wet lock of Jess's hair behind her ear. "Her mom is okay with your move and the custody arrangement?"

"She's thrilled, Grandma not so much."

"Gamma. Gamma."

Emily traipsed back to the pool, holding out her arms. "Do you want me to get this little one some food?"

"Thanks." Sam scooped up Jess and handed her over to Emily.

As Denali trotted behind them to the table, Jess kicked her legs and yelled, "Chip, Chip."

Jolene laughed. "We're going to have to teach her that not all dogs are named Chip."

"We." Sam pulled up next to her on the step and curled an arm around her waist. "I like the sound of that."

She hung her arms around his neck. "You're sure you want to return to Paradiso? Never mind Rob, California could be better for *your* career."

"I love Paradiso. I love the shifting moods of the desert. I love the pulsating heat and the violent monsoons. But most of all, I love the woman who took me back, the woman who taught me to love this mysterious land like I hope she'll teach my daughter."

She grabbed his face with both of her hands and planted a hard kiss on his mouth. "Lessons start tomorrow."

* * * * *

COMING SOON!

We really hope you enjoyed reading this book. If you're looking for more romance, be sure to head to the shops when new books are available on

Thursday 3rd September

LET'S TALK
Romance

For exclusive extracts, competitions
and special offers, find us online:

 facebook.com/millsandboon

 @MillsandBoon

@MillsandBoonUK

Get in touch on 01413 063232

For all the latest titles coming soon, visit
millsandboon.co.uk/nextmonth

MILLS & BOON

THE HEART OF ROMANCE

A ROMANCE FOR EVERY KIND OF READER

MODERN

Prepare to be swept off your feet by sophisticated, sexy and seductive heroes, in some of the world's most glamourous and romantic locations, where power and passion collide.
8 stories per month.

HISTORICAL

Escape with historical heroes from time gone by. Whether your passion is for wicked Regency Rakes, muscled Vikings or rugged Highlanders, awaken the romance of the past.
6 stories per month.

MEDICAL

Set your pulse racing with dedicated, delectable doctors in the high-pressure world of medicine, where emotions run high and passion, comfort and love are the best medicine.
6 stories per month.

True Love

Celebrate true love with tender stories of heartfelt romance, from the rush of falling in love to the joy a new baby can bring, and a focus on the emotional heart of a relationship.
8 stories per month.

Desire

Indulge in secrets and scandal, intense drama and plenty of sizzling hot action with powerful and passionate heroes who have it all: wealth, status, good looks…everything but the right woman.
6 stories per month.

HEROES

Experience all the excitement of a gripping thriller, with an intense romance at its heart. Resourceful, true-to-life women and strong, fearless men face danger and desire - a killer combination!
8 stories per month.

DARE

Sensual love stories featuring smart, sassy heroines you'd want as a best friend, and compelling intense heroes who are worthy of them.
4 stories per month.

To see which titles are coming soon, please visit

millsandboon.co.uk/nextmonth

JOIN US ON SOCIAL MEDIA!

Stay up to date with our latest releases, author news and gossip, special offers and discounts, and all the behind-the-scenes action from Mills & Boon...

 millsandboon

 millsandboonuk

 millsandboon

It might just be true love...

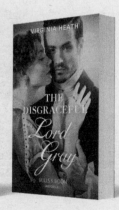

MILLS & BOON
MODERN
Power and Passion

Prepare to be swept off your feet by sophisticated, sexy and seductive heroes, in some of the world's most glamourous and romantic locations, where power and passion collide.

Julia James

Heiress's
PREGNANCY SCANDAL

MILLS & BOON

Jennie Lucas

Chosen as the
SHEIKH'S ROYAL BRIDE

MILLS & BOON

Kim Lawrence

A WEDDING
at the
ITALIAN'S DEMAND

Sharon Kendrick

The
SHEIKH'S SECRET BABY

MILLS & BOON